JUNIOR

ST JOHN'S

KAÏ-RO

KAÏ-RO

GRAHAM MARKS

USBORNE

To Megan, who has been a true inspiration

First published in the UK in 2007 by Usborne Publishing Ltd.,
Usborne House, 83-85 Saffron Hill, London EC1N 8RT, England.
www.usborne.com

A CIP catalogue record for this book is available from the
British Library.

JFMAMJJA OND/07 ISBN 9780746078884 Printed in Great Britain.

REMEMBER THIS...
...GODS ARE LIKE TINKERBELL,
IF YOU DON'T BELIEVE IN THEM,
IF YOU DON'T *NEED* THEM, THEY FADE AWAY.
BUT, BECAUSE THEY'RE GODS, THEY DON'T DIE.
AND IF THE NEED RETURNS, SO, TOO,
DO THE OBJECTS OF BELIEF.

REMEMBER THIS, BECAUSE IT IS TRUE.

1 A BAD THING HAPPENS

Dusk fell, the light fading like a lamp running out of oil, and the temperature began to plummet. On the southern edge of the Vix territory, where it met the banks of the wide, tidal river, a boy, thin and wiry, small for his age, nervously waited for his father to return – hopefully with something to eat – to the outskirts of the shanty area where they lived.

The boy's job, ever since his mother had died five years ago, just before his sixth birthday, was to light a fire and keep it going so they could skin and cook whatever his dad might've caught. But today his dad was late. And the night was no time to be out hunting because, as Stretch Wilson's father never tired of telling him, it was all too easy to end up as prey yourself.

What was keeping him Stretch didn't know, but in the near distance, over towards the dark, slime-covered tunnel that went under the river, he thought he heard something. • He stood up from where he'd been crouched, tending the fire, and caught the sound again: raised voices and the soft thunder of hoofs. And he knew this could only mean one thing...a raiding party from the other side, from the place people called Kaï-ro.

Kaï-ro...

The name, more than the cold night air blowing in from the north, gave Stretch gooseflesh. It was an evil place, if you believed all the stories that were told about it, and because of all the stories he'd listened to, it was somewhere that he'd grown up fearing more than anything. *"Be good,"* every child was told, *"or you'll get taken to Kaï-ro..."* This threat was the seed of many a nightmare because no one ever went south by choice. And nobody who'd been taken over ever, ever came back.

Nobody.

Then, out of the gathering darkness Stretch saw a figure running towards the confusion of discarded rubbish, sun-bleached wood, mud bricks and weathered tarps that only a close inspection would reveal as homes, places people had built to live in. Behind the man, whose arms and legs were a blur, dust exploding round his feet as he ran, he could now see the riders; one of these men, he knew from experience, would soon be whirling a weighted net above his head. Was it his father they were chasing? He couldn't yet see clearly enough, but he didn't think so. Surely not.

It couldn't be, he was always so careful...always.

Stretch was torn between wanting to break cover and run to help the man who might be, could be, his dad and obeying what he'd had drummed into him since almost before he could walk. Which was that survival came first. Above all else. Everyone knew this, it was like a religious belief, and as Stretch glanced around the neighbouring lean-tos he realized that he couldn't see another person anywhere. They'd all got out of sight, so *they* didn't end up being caught themselves. His legs appeared to make the decision for him, backing him into the shadows.

Folded into a tiny, cramped space, he watched as the leading hunter trapped his quarry, bringing him down with the net as if he was nothing more than an animal. Stretch could feel the dread and fear of capture spread its cold, cold fingers through his gut and he wanted his father there with him, now, to protect him.

Where was he? Maybe he'd heard the riders coming out of the tunnel – they didn't seem to care who knew about their arrival as people rarely, if ever, fought back. Maybe he'd hidden so they wouldn't get him. That had to be it. He was waiting until they'd gone before he came back. Maybe...

Then, as the last of the blood-red daylight seeped into the darkness of the horizon, Stretch had a thought that made him bite his lip so hard it bled. What if it really was his father he was watching being hauled off the ground by his hair and shackled like a beast?

Watching, and doing nothing.

Stretch saw the hunter get back up onto his horse and ride away, the man he'd caught and roped stumbling into the night after him; just before the gloom swallowed them up, Stretch saw the man glance backwards over his shoulder, and then he was gone. For a moment Stretch was quite positive the man was looking straight at him. Did he shout something? Stretch couldn't tell as it had all happened too quickly and too far away. But all he did know for sure was that he had just witnessed a disappearance and, as a single, hot tear ran down his cheek, he felt alone in a way he never had before...

2 SEEK, AND YE SHALL FIND

Stretch Wilson pulled off the thick leather gloves that used to belong to his father, sat back on his heels, resting for a moment as he took a sip of warm, slightly cloudy water from the battered plastic bottle he always carried with him. The bottle, which was vintage, a real antique, had been given to him by his mother; it had a proper screw top, and was probably his most valued possession. He took another sip; it was still early, the best time to be out working the heaps, before the sun got too high up and you could fry an egg on a stone. If you had an egg. Stretch hadn't seen one for he didn't know how long...since at least a month or so after the night his father didn't come home. And that was five, maybe six months ago.

He screwed the faded blue cap back on tight and put the bottle in the bag slung over his shoulder. Every scav had a sack to hide anything of value they might find. It didn't do to advertise that you had something someone else – someone bigger or hungrier or just plain nastier – might decide to take for themselves. And now that he was completely on his own, with no one in the world to look after him, he needed to keep everything he found that he might be able to sell.

His father had told him no one knew exactly how old Bloom's Mount was, or who had started building what was by far the biggest and oldest of Dinium's many heaps. His dad had said it truly was the most massive man-made construction in the entire world, although his dad had never been outside of Dinium's walls.

What amazed Stretch was that there'd ever been enough things people hadn't wanted any more to make something the size of Bloom's Mount, not to mention all the other heaps as well. People still threw things away, so the heaps grew even as the scavs took material off them. There were times when Stretch thought of the heaps almost as living things, crawling with scavs, like his bed sometimes crawled with bugs.

Since dawn, when he'd arrived at Bloom's Mount, Stretch had unearthed nothing that would remotely interest Cheapside Mo, the broker he was sort of allied to. But if he didn't find something, and then get himself over to the sprawling complex of cellars under the vast covered market of Vieille-Dam where she did her business, he wasn't going to eat today.

"Two days without food's not good, is it, Bone?"

Sitting next to him a dusty, off-white mutt, with a reddish-brown face and long, pointed ears, wagged his tail in a silent reply. He'd found Stretch some eight or nine weeks ago, not letting him out of his sight since, and it really wasn't very clear who was looking after whom; Bone, so named because that's what he'd got in his mouth when Stretch first saw him, was not only very protective of his new companion, he'd also turned out to be a hunter of some talent.

The way it worked now, Stretch searched while Bone kept watch, warning him if anyone approached. They made a great team, as Bone also seemed acutely aware of changes in conditions on the various heaps they visited, getting very nervous and wanting to move if something bad was about to happen. Bloom's Mount was an especially dangerous place to work; the unpredictable and often violent methane explosions could be lethal, and getting burned was a bad way to die. Not that Stretch, as he picked his way through a thick vein of what looked like compacted plastic bags, could think of a good one.

"Always got to look underneath, Bone..." At his name, the dog turned to watch the work progressing... "Like my dad said."

There was no one else anywhere near where Stretch was working as the area had become particularly unstable after a recent series of spectacular gas blasts. But Stretch knew that the blasts might well have revealed strata of debris and rubbish – layer upon layer of possibly very valuable rubbish that hadn't seen the light of day for hundreds and hundreds of years. But there was no way of telling unless you took a risk and had a look.

Pulling at the hard plastic – it looked as if heat had welded all the bags together – he saw the glint of sunlight reflecting off something metallic, and his heart raced.

Any metal was good metal, from dull, soft lead to the hardest, rarest ones; he took a deep breath and hoped that this wasn't the old type of plastic they somehow made to look like metal. Stretch, who couldn't read or write but knew the worth of everything, animal, vegetable or mineral, began to pull harder, because metal which didn't go rusty...well, that could mean more than just food for today.

"Might've got something, Bone..."

Stretch put the gloves back on; you had to be careful working the heaps or you'd end up with your hands cut to shreds, infected and useless. He began pulling away at the material surrounding the gleaming object, hardly daring to believe that he might have found something really valuable; by prising away a thick layer of brittle, yellowed cardboard, he created enough room to get his arm into the dark, narrow space and reached down, his leather-clad hand closing around the edge of whatever it was he'd seen.

He pulled, pulled again and still the object wouldn't move. Stretch sat back; this was when you needed to work in a team. He glanced at Bone, who cocked his head and looked straight back at him. Okay, Stretch nodded, so they were a team, but what he *really* needed was another pair of hands, and there was no way he was going to ask anyone here on Bloom's Mount to come and help him. Some of the younger scavs worked in gangs, for protection, and shared what they found, but generally people worked alone. That was just the way it was.

From his position, not very far up the heap, Stretch couldn't see a lot; nearer the summit, though, you got much better views across the city, down towards the river. And over it. On clear days, when he could see the other side, he'd sat and watched and wondered about his father and what had happened to him. They were building something over there – huge skeletal structures which looked like black scars on the horizon. It was said that was why Mr. Nero, the man who ruled Kaï-ro and the whole of the southern territory, sent the riders to take people. Slave workers had a short, hard life and more were always needed.

Sometimes Stretch would creep down to the river's banks, hiding in the thick reed beds that grew there, and he'd stare across the water. And sometimes, when he was angry – angry with his father for being caught, angrier with himself for not trying to help the man he'd seen being dragged away – he'd imagine getting across the river and fighting his way to wherever his father was. In his mind's eye he would see himself rescuing his dad and getting him back home, where he belonged.

This morning he wasn't angry, just hungry, with no time to waste thinking of what might have been. To his left the morning sun was rising, a huge beaten-copper disc moving slowly upwards to its zenith, where it would hover like a white-hot hole in the sky. He looked south where he could see the light shining off the river that was the dividing line between the very loose alliance of northern territories and the city of Kaï-ro. Although he was sure his father was over there, somewhere, in his heart of hearts he knew there was no chance he'd ever see him again, none at all. He was as good as dead.

Stretch felt the knot of his outrage tighten in his stomach and tried to concentrate his feelings somewhere they could make a difference; kneeling down, pushing his arm back into the crevice again, he took hold of what he'd found and yanked with all his might. Which was when everything seemed to happen at once.

Whatever it was he'd discovered came loose without any kind of warning; Stretch fell backwards, grinning like a maniac, and, as the rubbish beneath his feet gave way, he tumbled downwards into the dark.

Until Bone stuck his head over the lip of the hole in the side of the heap, Stretch had no idea how far he'd fallen. Lying on his back, winded from the fall, he stared at the silhouette of Bone's head; the dog's ears pricked as he tried to work out what was going on. It looked to Stretch as if he was about twelve, maybe fifteen feet down. Not *so* far. Although he might not be saying that when he tried to climb back out.

As his eyes got used to the lack of light, Stretch elbowed himself up into a sitting position and took a look at where he'd landed. It was quite a big space, big enough to stand in if you hadn't just had all the breath knocked out of you, with the edges of the hole curving above him in a rough dome shape. And there was a smell, sour and sharp at the same time, that he'd smelled before. Gas had probably built up here...he knew it did that. It could have burned rather than exploded, pushing the rubbish outwards as it expanded.

Looking round he saw the thing he'd been trying to get, leaned over and picked it up; it was a thin, rigid piece of green plastic, about the size of his hand, covered with an intricate pattern of what appeared to be tiny gold wires that connected up various small objects stuck all over one side of the board. Some of these objects had minute, gold-coloured legs and looked like strange oblong insects.

Old-tek.

He smiled. Stretch had no idea what it was or what it was supposed to do, but he thought it could be the kind of thing that Cheapside Mo might like and might therefore pay well for. Standing up, Stretch put the board in his bag and looked back up at Bone.

"I'm coming, boy!"

Above him the dog whimpered, gave a small, nervous bark and started trying to make his way down towards him.

"No, boy! Go back, go back!" Stretch frantically waved the dog away. The last thing he wanted was both of them trapped in the heap. What he wanted, needed, was a pole or a stick, something he could use to help push himself up the side of this cave. "Stay there, Bone. Don't move, I'm just looking for something, okay?"

He didn't care that Bone had no idea what he was saying, because he was sure having someone else to talk to over the last few weeks – even someone who couldn't answer – had kept him from becoming so sad he didn't want to live any longer. And he'd been feeling more and more like that, until the day Bone had turned up.

As Stretch was feeling around in the darkness, his gloved hands touched stone. Flat and wide, with an edge, like a step. He stopped. What was that...had he heard something? Tiny feet scrabbling, maybe? Rats, cockroaches, some of those white, blind things which lived deep underground in the heaps and sometimes got flung to the surface? This was no time to be scared of what you couldn't see when what you could was bad enough and Stretch tried to ignore the noises, which, if they weren't some creature out to bite him, might well be the sound of this bit of the heap about to collapse on him.

Taking a moment to clear his thoughts, he reached forward, his hand following the shape of the stone, and felt another step and below that another. Knowing he should be trying to go up, not making his way further down, but for some reason unable to stop himself, Stretch sat on the top step and inched his way into the unknown. Four, five, six, seven steps, and then, in the complete and total darkness, he stopped and took a small candle stub out of one pocket, a lucifer out of another. He knew it was risky, lighting a match actually *inside* a heap, but so was going any further without light...

He held his breath and flicked the sulfur head of the match with a thumbnail. The black vanished in a blaze of yellow-white light. No explosion. Stretch breathed out and wiped the sweat off his forehead. He put the match to the candle's wick and in the faltering, oily light he found he was in a long, narrow stairwell at the very bottom of which was a door.

It was slightly open.

3 WHO TO TRUST?

Behind him, Stretch could hear Bone whining. In front of him, down the steps, was a door that he knew he *had* to go through. It was an opportunity he'd be mad to ignore, but one he'd also be crazy to do anything about with only half a dozen lucifers and a rapidly diminishing stub of candle. He knew he had to prepare properly for this, and he couldn't do that stuck down where he was.

But he still had to check there was *something* worth coming back for. Which meant going all the way down. Further into the heap. On his own. He'd just have to be brave, like his dad had told him to be, after his mother had died. He knew how to do that; he'd been doing it ever since she'd gone.

Taking a deep breath, Stretch started down the staircase, one hand guarding the flame. With each step it seemed like the air got colder, harder to breathe; down he went, until he finally got to the door. He reached out and pushed it, but the door wouldn't move. Stretch stood for a moment and listened: no sounds. He looked at the candle flame and saw it was leaning towards the gap in the doorway...air going in, not coming out.

The space looked just big enough for him to get his head and shoulders through to take a look, so he did.

He could make out what appeared to be a debris-strewn passageway; dank corridors which went in three directions. In the flickering globe of yellow light he held in front of him he could see objects, reflecting back at him. Metal? His heart felt like it had skipped a beat. Could it possibly be *gold*? Stretch knew he didn't have enough time left to find out, but this was definitely worth making a return journey. Always supposing he could get out.

He began to retrace his steps, having to blow out the candle before he burned his fingers. Making his way over to where he'd fallen in, Stretch stared up at Bone, glad to see the little dog was still there waiting for him. He looked at the ragged hole his descent had created. If he was careful – really, really careful – he might be able to wedge himself against the sides and slowly inch his way up, bit by bit. "Slowly does it," his dad had often said when he was out hunting big-rat, "that's the way to get the job done." And, right now, it looked like the only chance Stretch had.

* * *

Stretch's progress was unbelievably slow and, by the time he'd got almost three quarters of the way to the surface, he'd fallen back down a couple of times and had to start all over again. Now, with only a few feet to go, he was tired, bruised and even hungrier; he *had* to do it this time, or he'd be too exhausted to try again and would end up dying inside Bloom's Mount, just a pile of remains waiting to be discovered by some other scav.

His whole body ached with the tension of keeping himself wedged in the gap, trying not to push too hard – which might dislodge something – but using just enough pressure to keep from slipping and tumbling down again. With the utmost care, Stretch readied himself for the next few small nudges upwards.

There were some ominous creaks, but it felt like he was safe...for the moment. And then, to his right, and looking tantalizingly *just* within reach, were a whole load more of the green boards. Dozens of them, and *way* too valuable to leave.

Stretch twisted himself sideways, so that he was facing the treasure trove he'd found; his breathing fell to a measured slowness, completely the opposite of the panic he felt coursing though him. He reached out, taking hold of a fistful of the green boards. He pulled, very, very slowly...

They didn't budge.

And then they moved a little bit...then a bit more...and finally, finally he had them and they were shoved in his bag. Even though his plan had worked better than he could possibly have hoped for Stretch didn't feel like a genius, still jammed in this hole in the side of Bloom's Mount. He felt wiped out, and he had some way to go before he was safe.

But the thought of all the money Cheapside Mo was surely going to give him in exchange for what he'd found spurred him on.

He was *so* nearly there... All he had to do – *the only thing* – was get himself up the last foot or so. A survival instinct took over, an ancient, automatic process that didn't need to be thought about. It just had to be obeyed. Later, when he thought back, Stretch imagined he must have walked up and out of the fissure, because one moment he was trapped, hanging, waiting for disaster to happen, and the next he was lying on his back in the sunshine, in the open air, with Bone licking his face all over. And he had no idea how he'd done it, except that his arms and legs were scratched in quite a few places and every muscle in his body was shrieking.

Stretch had let himself rest for a few minutes, drunk some more of his water and shared the very last piece of stale bread with Bone; the piece he'd been saving for an emergency, but felt he could now eat in celebration. In his bag were fifteen – *fifteen!* – of the green boards, which he had the highest hopes Mo would pay handsomely for. And at the bottom of those mysterious steps, through the half-open door, there could be things so valuable he didn't dare think about it. So he didn't and decided to make a move instead.

"C'mon, Bone...let's go."

As the two of them started down the side of the heap, he checked again to see who else was about that morning; there were a few individuals working the Mount, a couple he recognized, one or two he didn't, but it didn't look like the side he'd chosen to search was very popular. Probably the gas explosions had put them off, which was good he thought, as it made it a lot less likely that anyone would discover the hole he'd made. He'd covered it as best as he could, using a few bits of wood and plastic to disguise the fact that it was there at all.

"You!"

The harsh croaky voice made Bone freeze, his ears back, tail low; it stopped Stretch in his tracks. He looked round to find a ragged boy, not a lot older than himself, a couple of yards behind him. How he'd got there without being heard, Stretch had no idea.

"What d'you want?" Stretch moved closer to Bone, who he could feel was quivering.

"Gimme your bag."

"What?"

"You 'eard." As the boy waved his left hand towards Stretch, his right seemed to acquire a thin-bladed knife from nowhere. "Give it me, right...or I'll cut you."

Stretch looked at the boy, saw the raw patches on his arms and the patches on his head where clumps of hair had fallen out, evidence he'd not been too careful where he'd scavved from. I give the bag to you, Stretch thought, you'll cut me anyway. He cursed himself for being so careless, for allowing this chancer to creep up on him. His own knife was at the bottom of his bag, and he knew he'd have no way of getting it out before the boy was on him. "Why should I?"

The boy, who Stretch now saw had lost two fingers on his left hand and one on his right, moved a bit closer. "Got no time for this..." He waved the blade from side to side, his arm like a snake waiting to pounce. "Drop it!"

Stretch kept looking straight at the boy, staring right into his mean little eyes because he knew that it was part of the unwritten laws of a fight – the one who breaks the stare first loses. Then Stretch saw his opponent's eyes shift slightly for the merest fraction of a second, later wondering whether Bone had been watching, too, because he suddenly went into action. The dog leaped forward and with a low, menacing growl, he flew through the air, his jaws clamping round the boy's right wrist.

Stretch watched, open-mouthed, at the freaked boy and the small, frenzied dog. His dog...Bone, who'd never given the impression that he'd ever had a bad thought in his dog head. Stretch saw the knife arc out of his attacker's grip and fall to the ground, he watched Bone hang on like grim death while the boy swore, shouted and finally collapsed with a hoarse scream.

"*GeddimOFFme!*"

"Bone?" Stretch glanced left and right as he picked up the knife; this boy might well be up here on the heap with more of his scabby friends. "*Leave him, Bone!*"

The dog's ears twitched as he heard his name, but he still held on, his teeth red, his jowls dripping with saliva and blood.

"Bone!" Stretch deepened his voice and almost grunted the dog's name, then turned and walked away. Behind him he heard the boy let out a groan and start sobbing, and then Bone was there, padding along right next to him, just as if nothing had happened.

"Coulda *kilt* me!"

Stretch stopped and turned round. "Next time, I might let him..."

The rest of the way down the heap, Stretch was extra careful, keeping a hawklike watch as he came off Bloom's Mount and began threading his way through the narrow, crowded streets that would take him and his precious find the mile or so east to the Vieille-Dam souk. He could rest just as soon as he'd done his business with Mo, but not until then.

He was tired, hungry, thirsty – still jumpy from what had happened up on the side of the heap – and as he walked quickly – with Bone, his shadow and guardian, glued to his heels – Stretch began to think about who he should get to help him. Who should he tell about the stairs leading down to the open door...the entrance into the very heart of Bloom's Mount? He could feel his own heart beating faster as he imagined what could be down there. Monsters and devils, far worse than anything there was supposed to be over the river in Kaï-ro? Riches beyond his imagination? The moment of his death – the time everyone had waiting for them and no one could escape from?

Who would go with him to a place like that?

4 THE DEAL

You couldn't simply walk through any of the doors that led into Cheapside Mo's subterranean domain, and traipse through the passages and past the rooms crammed with merchandise of every kind until you came to her inner sanctum. It didn't work like that.

There were guards, everywhere. At every entrance you'd find someone waiting, someone who needed a bribe to let you in. And then, at various points on your journey through the lamplit shadows, there would be other people, watching and waiting to see if you might be up to no good. And in case you were, they all had guns. Big ones that fired shells which could, so Stretch had been told, go through brick walls – proper *old* bricks, ones that had been fired in a kiln, and not just the mud-and-straw ones they made down by the river and baked in the sun.

Stretch had given his own knife as payment to the man at the entrance he'd chosen; a small price, as the knife he'd taken from the boy up on the heap was a bit of a find. On closer examination he'd found it had a better than decent blade, and a sturdy leather-bound handle as well. It was an old piece, with history, which the scav who'd threatened him had no doubt stolen.

The guard had wanted him to leave Bone outside, as no dogs were allowed loose in the tunnels, but Stretch had put a choke rope around Bone's neck and they'd both been let in. Bone was staying right with him, not pulling; he didn't like it down here, but it was the lesser of two evils as he liked being left alone even less. Coming to the end of a passage, Stretch had no idea which way to go and chose left at random.

A couple of minutes later he rounded a corner and came to a thick, moth-eaten curtain. The man standing in front of it looked them both up and down, then pulled it to one side, gave him a glazed, terracotta tile with a mark on it and allowed Stretch and Bone to go into a big, low-ceilinged room. It was full of people squatting on the rough concrete floor, waiting. Waiting for their turn to be called to the front to see Mo.

You waited and you watched – watched very, very carefully, because there was no rhyme or reason to how people got called up to the front. Mo sat in the middle of a huge pile of cushions, surrounded by a half-circle of glowing, flickering glass bulbs. To her right two boys pedalled furiously on a pair of rusty old machines that were attached in some way to a strange box of wires; somehow – Stretch had never worked out quite how – this provided the light for Mo to see what she was being offered.

A sallow-skinned, barrel-shaped woman ("with a face", his dad used to say, "like a drunk potato"), Mo's red hair matched her nose, as well as the complex henna tattoos which covered her surprisingly delicate hands and went up her arms as far as anyone was ever likely to see. She had small, kohl-rimmed eyes that never missed a trick, a thin-lipped mouth, not much given to smiling, and a lot of gold on view when she did.

To Mo's left sat Deaf Jericho, an old, old man in a grubby turban, with skin like dried, cracked earth, eyes that looked in different directions and fewer teeth in his mouth than he had fingers on one hand. His only job appeared to be to reach into the large bowl in front of him and take out a random tile; this he gave to a boy standing behind him, who then shouted out what colour it was, and what letter, number or symbol was stamped on it.

If the tile matched the one you held in your hand, you had to get to the front quick, before Mo ordered it tossed back into the bowl; if that happened, Deaf Jericho picked another tile and you missed your turn. People frequently fell asleep while waiting and if you noticed that your dozing neighbour's tile had come up, it was possible – though risky – to make a switch and steal a turn. If it wasn't your tile that had been called, you simply carried on waiting. Such was the lack of any system or logic a person could be seen within minutes of arriving, or they might have to wait what seemed like the best part of a day, and sometimes actually was.

Predicting what might happen was not possible. "Just like life itself," as Mo always said to anyone who questioned her methods.

Stretch found a space, big enough for him and Bone to settle down in, and looked around the wide, brick-built room to see who else was in today. He saw maybe one or two others from the Vix – just a couple of telltale crimson bandanas, like his, that he could spot, though no one he knew very well – plus a mixture of types from all over the city: some Cuventers, the odd Wyte, a handful of Saynts, a pair of Hydes, a Guilder or two and the majority were Luds and Spits, which was no surprise as they were the ones who actually lived closest to Vieille-Dam.

There were other sharks, dealers in absolutely anything of worth, that you could go to – a couple of them a lot nearer to where Stretch lived than Cheapside Mo – but his dad had said she'd got a blood connection with the Vix and was the only one to be trusted. Although, that being said, he'd added, in reality this still didn't mean an awful lot. But, since his father's disappearance, Mo had always been fair with Stretch and it was the money he'd earned from dealing with her which had kept him and Bone alive.

Looking down the room towards the circle of light at the end, he watched a man leave, frowning as he examined some coins in his hand. Then the next tile was being called; Stretch saw a couple of people get up and trot awkwardly to the front, holding a heavy sack between them; he saw Mo lean forward as they opened the sack to show her what they'd brought, and saw her raise her eyebrows, sit back and shake her head. He heard one of the men say something, his voice whining and wheedling and he knew that was just not the thing to do. When Mo said no, that was it. No arguments. Mo's rules.

"Next!" Mo barked, waving the two men away.

Stretch, watching the men stagger out of the room, to much catcalling and heckling, almost missed the boy calling the next tile.

"Blue snake – we have *blue snake*!"

Blue snake? Stretch glanced at the tile in his hand and leaped to his feet, almost hurdling over the people in front of him as he ran towards Mo. "I'm here!" he yelled, aware than Bone was now in front of him, determined to win this unexpected race.

He skidded to a halt in front of the massive pile of cushions, pulling Bone back before he could get anywhere near Mo.

"Stretch...been a long time." Mo's dumpy face broke into a golden smile. "And what have you got for me today?"

"Old-tek, Mo...I think it's old-tek."

"Show me." Mo snapped her fingers.

Stretch pulled the green plastic boards out of his bag and handed them up to Mo, the light glinting off all the gold wires and little silver blobs as if they were alive. Behind him he could hear someone whistle.

"Lovely..." Mo squinted at one of the boards, holding it so the light played on it properly; then she turned and looked over her shoulder. "Harder! Make them pedal *harder*!"

Behind her Stretch heard the thwack-thwack of a cane on skin, the pained grunts of the two boys and then faster pedalling; as if by magic, there was more light. But his eyes never left Mo's face, not for a second.

"Lovely..." Mo repeated, looking down at Stretch. "And these would be *all* you've got, wouldn't they?"

Stretch nodded. "Everything, Mo."

"Good."

Stretch was desperate to ask how much she was going to give him, but knew better than to say even one word unless he was spoken to. Mo's rules.

"Co'stanza!" Mo shouted, putting the boards on the cushion next to her and rummaging in the many pockets of her voluminous overdress. "What d'you want, cash or credits?"

Before Stretch had a chance to answer, a girl, as pale and thin as Mo was big and dark, appeared at Mo's side. "Mother?"

"Take these to Benedict, girl."

"Yes, mother."

Stretch followed Co'stanza's exit for a second, wondering, as did most other people in the room, how on earth Mo got a daughter like her.

"Well?"

Stretch looked straight back at Mo: cash or credits...he didn't know which to choose. It sort of depended on how much she was going to pay him.

"I'd recommend credits..." Mo's black eyes bored into him, her face expressionless as she wrote something on a piece of paper.

Stretch nodded; that could only mean he'd hit pay dirt.

Because carrying too much cash around was asking for trouble, and finding somewhere safe to keep it almost impossible, credits were the only alternative if you wanted to keep your money safe. And you trusted Mo.

Mo's credits operated on a tally stick system, using a scored piece of wood (four notches per dollar, five dollars per stick), which was split in two. You could keep your tally sticks at Mo's and then cash as much or as little as you wanted. The territories and parishes being the kind of places they were, people often didn't live long enough to cash out all their sticks, which were absolutely non-transferable – Mo's rules. And so she often never had to pay out. "Win-win," as she said.

"I'll take credits, Mo."

"Sensible choice, Stretch." Mo showed him her gold teeth again as she handed him the piece of paper she'd been writing on. "Go and see Wallet..."

Stretch took the folded note, turned and almost sprinted off to where he'd find Nehemiah Brown – Wallet's real name – sitting in the heavily guarded strongroom where all Mo's money was kept.

Back outside, Stretch felt light-headed, hungry, elated and confused. In various of his pockets he had, in pennies, schillings and quarters, a whole $1.50's worth of change. *A dollar-fifty!* He couldn't believe it – that was ten, twelve very good days' money! And he also had his half of one stick with $3.50 still left on it. But what was even *more* unbelievable was the fact that, back underground, behind a row of thick iron bars and under Nehemiah's locks and keys, he had two more untouched tally sticks in his account. Mo had paid him $15! More money than he'd *ever* dreamed of! His head was spinning. He *had* to get back to Bloom's Mount and see if he could get more of the boards before anyone else found them.

And then there was the door.

Stretch stopped walking. The door...he had to find out what was beyond that door, but what should he do first? He felt something nudge him and looked down to see Bone looking back up at him expectantly.

"Okay, boy," Stretch patted the dog's head. "The first thing we'll do is eat."

A butcher had provided Bone with a bone, a big, meaty knuckle with plenty of marrow; Stretch had bought three or four apples from a street seller, a couple of pies and some bread, and the two of them had found a piece of shade to relax in.

As he was finishing the last of the apples, Bone polishing off the cores, Stretch tried to think through his problems. He wasn't used to doing more than try and work out where his next meal was going to come from, which, as problems went in his world, was usually big enough. But now he had a real job on his hands, with no idea of what was the right thing to do.

He kept on wanting to talk to Bone, to put into words some of the things that were going around and around his head, but what was the point? What he *really* needed was a *real* person to discuss things with because all this thinking was making his head hurt, and if he didn't make a decision soon, someone else would stumble on what he'd discovered and that would be it.

So who did he know who would know what to do?

And who, in all the territories and parishes, could he trust?

Once Bone had realized there were no more apple cores, he'd gone back to his gnawing activities, leaving Stretch to sit and ponder...who, who, who? He knew people who were good at certain things, things like stealing and climbing and fighting and making you laugh, but none of them were the kind of people who were good at thinking. And as for trust...

Now he thought about it, there was someone who might fit the bill. Reeba. Reeba Moore, the girl he'd met one day at Cheapside Mo's. Reeba was a Cuventer, a few years older than him, fair-skinned, with henna-patterned arms; she was quiet and slightly built with dreadlocked blonde hair, random hanks of which had also been brightly hennaed, and tied with a green Cuven flash. And she had piercing blue eyes you wouldn't lie to. She'd been at Mo's looking for books to add to her collection.

For someone who could read and write she was nobody's fool and, as Stretch had discovered, would hit out first, asking questions later, if she thought trouble was brewing. He'd been astonished the first time he'd seen Reeba in a fight, her fists flying like a pair of angry wasps. But he wasn't nearly as astonished as her opponent.

She wasn't at all what he'd imagined a person with learning would be like, but then she was the first one he'd ever met. Both her parents were still alive, but had thrown her out onto the street when she'd refused to work in the family's small factory making buttons from re-syk plastic, saying she wanted to learn more. "Well then let the idiot who filled your head with all these stupid ideas look after you!" she said her father had yelled as he slammed the door in her face.

So Reeba now worked for the old man who had taught her to read and write. He was, she'd told Stretch, extremely clever – the cleverest man alive, she claimed – but not very organized. He needed a housekeeper as much as she needed a roof over her head, and it was an arrangement that worked very well. Stretch had no idea what the old man was called, or where he lived, but he was sure it wouldn't take him long to find out. Surely everyone in the Cuven parish would know who he was.

Stretch got up. He didn't feel like walking all the way over to the Cuven; with the food sitting heavy in his stomach, what he felt like was lying down and having a sleep. But there was work to do, and no one else to do it.

"C'mon, Bone," Stretch whistled through his teeth. "Places to go..."

Across the street, slouched against a wall and looking as though he was fast alseep, Samson Towd watched the thin, wiry boy get up and yawn. He followed the boy's movements through slitted eyes, watched as he clicked his fingers at his dog, who picked up the remains of the bone it had been eating and followed the boy off down a narrow street that led west.

Samson Towd had been waiting his turn in Mo's cellar, hoping to sell her some snippet of gossip that would buy him a drink, when he'd seen the boy's transaction. His scheming brain whirred into play, quickly working out that his time would be better spent doing something other than hanging about on the off-chance of a few of Mo's cents and pennies. Because where some old-tek had been found, maybe there was more – which, if he followed the boy, he might be able to get his hands on...

5 ACROSS THE RIVER

Nero Thompson – Mr. Nero to the people of the desert land south of the river that he ruled absolutely and totally – sat alone in the cool courtyard, under the shade of a massive palm. He felt...*itchy*, that was the only word he could find to describe it. Everything was going according to plan, the plan that had been his life for almost ten years now – ever since he'd found the statue – but his brain was in complete, utter turmoil.

Instructions and demands and orders, complaints and specifications and directives. It was never-ending. The voice in his head hadn't stopped for hours, hadn't let him rest, hardly allowed him to eat, but oddly, he didn't care about that. He wanted to do what was being asked of him by his master, Setekh. He wanted the Completion to take place on time...he *wanted* to make everything perfect. And as far as he could see, everything was. Until early this morning.

As Mr. Nero stood up, cracking his knuckles, the two night-black canix silently watching him – strange, dangerous, hybrid creatures that were part canine, part feline – leaped to his side; accompanied by them, he marched quickly across the courtyard, his black robes flying behind him. The two canix never, ever left him and were all the bodyguard he needed; every sense they possessed was astonishingly highly tuned, making them the fastest and deadliest creatures to walk the earth.

Mr. Nero went through into the marble-floored house, shuttered against the heat of the day, and gestured to the guards that he wanted to go outside.

As the massive, iron-studded doors swung back, the guards bowed, arms crossed on their chests, and Mr. Nero, the UnderMaster, strode out onto the wide, colonnaded terrace and down the steps, stopping about halfway. He stood, a canix on either side, and looked out across the flatland, heat haze making the vista shimmer. Growing up out of the parched earth were the three giant constructions Setekh had told him to build. Why, he did not know, though he suspected that he'd find out once they were finished. The Completion was everything...

"**There is...no time...no time to waste!**" said the voice – a voice, the first time he'd heard it, that he thought sounded more ancient than he'd ever imagined possible. "*NO TIME TO WASTE!*"

Mr. Nero pressed the palms of both hands hard against

his forehead, closed his kohl-rimmed eyes and ran his fingers through his black, oiled hair. *Can't you see? I-AM-DOING-MY-BEST...* he thought, his teeth gritted, thin, mean lips stretched in a rictus. Shaking off the wave of panic that hit him in the stomach – *what would happen if he failed?* – he straightened up and pushed his shoulders back. The rest of the Board were going to share his pain...

As he went to find Messrs. Carne, Cleave and Webb, Mr. Nero recalled the fateful day, ten years before, when his life had changed – and he had set in motion the events, which, when they eventually came to their final conclusion, would change his life for eternity.

"**Time everlasting,**" that is what Setekh said.

Time everlasting.

Ten years ago, time had hung heavy on Nero Thompson's hands. His father, Caleb Thompson, was a powerful man, head of the Hyde clan, one of the biggest and most powerful tribal groups in the territories; he was respected and feared in just about equal measure. The last thing he wanted or needed was a *clever* son, a son who could actually read and knew things. You didn't hold onto what was yours – and take what was other people's – by *knowing* things! You did it by being more brutal, more vicious and more belligerent than anyone else. Like Nero's four older brothers – older, bigger, stronger...and so much less intelligent.

Caleb Thompson cut his youngest son no slack, and his brothers paid him scant attention, making it clear they thought he was a dreary, dull, puny, waste of space. Even his own mother had little time for him. And so, by the age of fifteen he was spending most of his days on his own, attempting to learn about the world he lived in, about what it had been like in the Before Times. While his father and brothers tried to gain wealth, he tried to gain knowledge, and if that meant he had to be on his own, so be it. At least that way no one could get at him; on his own he didn't need friends and rarely encountered enemies.

He had read that knowledge was power, and he would have liked to believe that this was true, even though all around him the opposite seemed to hold true. The more he learned, the less anyone seemed to care about him.

In his rooms in the heavily fortified maze of houses that, apart from being where he lived, also acted as the headquarters for the entire clan, he kept his collection of artefacts and books he'd found, as well as the notebooks he'd written himself. Although they were his most precious things, they were about as valuable to the rest of his family as kindling. But from the books he'd learned about many of the events that had happened in the Before Times. The people who'd lived then, the machines they'd made, their wars, which were cataclysmic and had made things the way they were today. He'd read about the accidents which were responsible for the creation of some of the more extreme creatures roaming the land, as well as the death of much of that land itself.

South of the river was now a virtual desert, but he'd got pictures that showed it had once been a place of rolling hills covered with grass and trees, hundreds, thousands of trees. Proper ones, too, not the thorny scrubs and squirrel-infested palms that were just about all that grew there now.

The day he discovered the statue was a day Nero would never forget.

The dawn had brought a big storm: torrential bullets of rain, ear-splitting thunder and jagged lightning strikes that had kept the people off the streets and alleys. Then black clouds had rolled away and some colour soaked back into the morning sky, steam rising from the heaps and drying earth. Once the storm had receded Nero – this was long before anyone would dare refer to him as anything other than *Mr.* Nero – got ready to go on one of his expeditions.

He left the family compound on his horse and went south-east, over towards the Nites' parish; he wore the red and white tribal flash ("Blood and purity!" was the Hyde's battle cry) and the family's eagle feather headband, riding safe in the knowledge that no one would dare touch him. His brothers might have little respect for him, but they would kill – or at least seriously maim – anyone else who they found out had been disrespectful to him. He didn't begin to understand their logic, but was glad of the invisible armour his name and their reputation gave him.

Nero was going to an area that he'd heard was good for digging – excavating, as one book he'd read had called it. When he got there, if things looked promising, he'd hire some local grunt labour to do the hard work for him. He might even stay somewhere nearby for a couple of days, instead of returning home each evening. Travelling at night was always a risk, as the rats, some as big as dogs and even more vicious than the crocodiles in the river, couldn't care less which family you came from.

To find anything worthwhile you had to dig down a long

way, and the ragged urchins you saw picking at the surfaces of the heaps were never, ever going to find much of value. That was always going to be covered by the discard of more generations than you could count, and he did often wonder about the people who had thrown away enough things to create mountains.

Mr. Nero remembered everything in crystal-clear detail; it was sometime before the middle of the third day, before it got too hot even to think, let alone watch other people sweat for pennies and cents, that it had happened. He'd chosen an extremely good area to work, his calculation that it had once been a place with a number of massive storehouses looking like it might well be accurate; he'd found a lot of interesting material, much of it far more ancient than he'd ever seen, from a time even before plastic and metal.

He was some fifteen or more feet down, examining a compacted layer of ancient pottery shards, when he found the edge of what appeared to be a substantial block of basalt. As he carefully exposed more of the cold, black stone he came across a series of pictures carved in the black rock. He had no idea what they meant, but was drawn to find out more, the notion occurring to him that he might have found the base of a statue.

Two exhausting days later, in a special tent Nero had had constructed over the dig, the twenty-foot figure of a strange, unearthly creature was finally uncovered and raised to stand vertically on its five-foot high plinth. He had driven the labourers like animals to get the statue upright, and now there it was towering above him, its head well above the level of the ground. Carved from solid rock, inset with coloured stone, it looked like a man from the neck down, with strong, broad shoulders, muscular, athletic and imposing. A man grasping the remains of a metal staff in his right hand, while holding his left arm horizontally, palm out.

From the neck up the being stared back at the world through dark, hooded eyes rimmed with gold, one each side of a long, almost dog-like muzzle. The man-creature had a shock of thick black hair carved away from his temples and down his back, but, oddest of all was the pair of rectangles, too straight-edged to be ears, jutting upwards from his forehead.

That night, after Nero had sent his workers away, he stayed down in the trench, just staring up at the thing he'd found and wondering what or who it was. Could this be a representation of a *real* person? Could people like this actually have existed in the Before Times? Or was it someone the makers had conjured from their own imaginations?

And whatever the answer, what was the statue's purpose?

Nero could feel himself being drawn to the figure, wanting to know more about it and what it meant. If, indeed, it meant anything at all. People – musicians, artists, craftsmen – often made things just for the sake of it, in the same way that his father was always accusing him of learning things simply because he could. But this find was more than that, Nero could feel it.

In the uneven orange light cast by a handful of pitch-tar torches, Nero examined the statue, marvelling at the quality of workmanship, the fineness of detail and the sheer perfection of what had been made. This was an object which had been intended to instil submission, demand respect and reverence. Be worshipped.

He could feel it.

Nero put out his hand and for the first time let his fingertips touch the statue, tracing the delicate outline of the foot, so smooth it seemed like real flesh that had somehow been turned to stone. Once the rays of the sun bathed it again, would it warm up and come to life?

He climbed up one of the ladders out of the trench and stood opposite the head, staring.

This creature, this man-beast was everything he wasn't; it made him feel light-headed just looking at it, wondering what it must be like to be worthy of adoration, devotion and obeisance. What must that kind of power be like? Oh, there were gods aplenty all over the territories, each with their own images and priests and shamans, but Nero had never found any kind of faith within himself for any of them. But here, now, with the light from the torches casting competing shadows, this was somehow different. Very different.

Without really knowing why, he leaned forward, reaching out and putting his right hand flat on the creature's narrow forehead.

"You are magnificent...beautiful," he said out loud.

"Chaos *is* magnificent. And beautiful..."

Nero's hand shot off the statue's head, like he'd touched something hot. The voice, sounding older than the stars, had been *inside* his head. Inside! Gingerly he put his palm back down on the smooth, cold stone.

"Who are you?"

"Setekh, God of Chaos, ruler of all things dark..."

6 WORDS DO NOT BUILD THINGS

Mr. Nero sat in the Board Room, waiting for Messrs. Carne, Cleave and Webb to arrive. Mr. Darcus Cleave, the UnderTaker, would be on his way from the Ministry, a subterranean complex where science and Setekh's ancient knowledge came together in an unholy, but incredibly powerful way; Mr. Everil Carne, the OverSeer General of the Dark Soul Army, would be riding in from the cantonment in the east where the army was stationed. And Ms. Phaedra Webb, the Oracle, would just know in that mysterious, inexplicable way she did, that her presence was required. No need to send a messenger for her, ever.

"Delays, delays, delays..." Mr. Nero could almost feel

Setekh's rasping breath in his head. **"Time is finite – IT RUNS OUT!"**

Standing up, ramrod straight, Mr. Nero sent his chair crashing backwards as he clasped his hands to his ears. The canix, unfazed by their master's sudden actions, surveyed the room suspiciously.

"I...am...doing...my...best!"

"Not. Good. Enough!"

From the moment that Nero Thompson had submitted to Setekh – mesmerized by his strange magnificence and awed by the astonishing power he radiated – his life had acquired something it'd never had before: a direction. It was a course which took him away from everything he'd ever known, and he never again went back to the fortified place which had been his home. That moment had changed him from a boy, lost and unwanted, lonely and without purpose, into a man with a quest, a goal. A *function*.

And he knew he was different, as did everyone else with whom he subsequently came into contact. Some of the statue's power – Setekh's power – now flowed through him and gave him the unassailable authority of the messenger of a god. And not just any minor deity or faded idol such as you might find worshipped in the parishes and territories. This was an immortal, a divinity, a supreme power...

"I am the God of Chaos, ruler of all things dark..."

Setekh's words had echoed in Nero's head, so loud he was surprised the men who'd trudged back the next morning to begin the back-breaking work of getting the statue out of the trench, hadn't heard them. But they had realized that something had happened, that there'd been a transformation; the night before they'd left the site joking amongst themselves about the bookish strip of a boy they were working for, returning the next day to find a wolf where there had been a puppy.

Everil Carne had been one of them, but instead of being cowed by the fierce energy that seemed to make the boy's eyes glow, he'd been instantly drawn to his intensity. Everil immediately understood that there was a connection with the statue, although he didn't know what it was, and he didn't care. He could feel that this was a person who had, overnight, somehow found the road he *had* to take, the journey nobody in the world was going to stop him from completing. That morning Everil Carne had become Nero's first acolyte and he hadn't left his side since.

Things had moved very fast from then on, with Nero taking Setekh's instructions, devising the strategies and plans that would make the Ruler of Darkness's urgent, insistent demands a reality. Step by step, Everil had set about putting the plans and strategies into action, making the words and wishes of a god into a reality. And it didn't matter what was wanted, how difficult or even impossible it seemed, Nero accepted that it had to be done and Everil found a way to do it.

As the operation to transport the statue to its new home got under way, word had spread across the nearby parishes that this was no ordinary madness. At first no one really cared very much what Nero was up to, the feeling being that if he wanted to waste his family's money hauling some piece of old masonry round, that was his business. But by the time he'd attracted a sizeable number of people to him, it was too late to argue. As the days passed into weeks, the Thompson boy, like his father and his brothers, just took what he needed – people, provisions, land and material – as if it was his given right. And no one dared to stop him.

Everil Carne's militia, the genesis of what would become the Dark Soul Army, guarded the area surrounding the excavation site like packs of feral dogs, keeping prying eyes away. Even when his brothers appeared one day to see what "Little Nero" was up to, they'd gone home scarred by the experience, tails between their legs, pride dented and more than a few ribs cracked.

Rumours spread, like a virulent disease, about who Mr. Nero was and what he was doing...that he was worshipping fiends and evil spirits...that the people closest to him were risen from the dead...that he himself was a devil, with cloven-hoofed feet, forked tongue and a tail. Like all rumours there was the tiniest kernel of truth, surrounded and obscured by a huge, ever-changing mass of lies and speculation.

Everyone who was drawn into the thrall of Mr. Nero and the hallowed statue he had discovered knew, instinctively, that this was a powerful god, though not a kind one. But power attracts, in the same way a magnet creates an aura of iron filings around it, and Setekh's was a seductive and alluring power. The kind of people who yearned to control the destiny of others – the sort who wanted to be told what to do and then be given the means to do it – started finding their way to the feet of Mr. Nero.

There was no roadway down to the river's edge; one was built.

There was no way to move the towering statue; a means was found.

There weren't enough hands to make it happen; slaves were gathered.

Setekh wanted to be taken south, over the wide, croc-infested river, to the desert wasteland. Over the river which had no bridges left, to the wasteland even the vermin had abandoned.

It was done.

So Setekh went over the river on a huge, tar-coated barge constructed out of great bundles of reeds, built to a design Nero had woken to find himself drawing one night. The growing team of slaves and craftsmen Everil had gathered round him, along with the people needed to feed and look after them, followed Nero and the statue across the water, without a glance backwards.

And once on the other side they had built a city. A city Setekh had declared should be called Kaï-ro...

Mr. Nero's trance-like reverie was interrupted as the sharp aroma of a complex blend of rare, aromatic oils caught him unawares. He turned, frowning, eyes searching the room, taking some moments to find the figure in the shadows, standing so still she could have been carved.

"Ms. Webb..." Mr. Nero's thin lips twitched, annoyed that even the canix could be caught out by the woman's uncanny ability to simply *be* somewhere, seemingly without the need to use doors, like normal people. "How long, Phaedra?"

"Minutes, UnderMaster; I didn't want to disturb you."

"How thoughtful..." Mr. Nero watched as his Oracle

appeared to float out of the gloom and glide over to the table. She was an oddly beautiful, if strangely disturbing sight, wrapped in swathes of dark silk, shot with silver, which hid everything except her head. A head that was completely shaved, the pale, luminous scalp covered in a delicate silver filigree, a fine web of precious metal. Candlelight made her wide, crimson lips shimmer, glinting off the emerald she had in one ear and the sapphire in the other, an echo of her one green and one blue eye. The woman's strange eyes, with their gold-painted lashes, watched him like an exotic snake.

"The others?" Ms. Webb smiled as she sat down.

"On their way..." Mr. Nero took a deep breath, his Oracle's perfume, as it always did, calming his jangled nerves. "They don't have your abilities."

"Few do." From beneath the flowing folds of cloth first her left then her right hand appeared, each covered in an array of jewel-encrusted rings which sparkled with an internal fire. "Why have you gathered the Board together – do we have a problem?"

"Speed is of the *very* *essence*!"

The voice hissed inside him, making Mr. Nero shiver as if someone had walked across his grave. "Yes, I think we do."

Ms. Webb's eyes narrowed, her nostrils flaring as she watched the UnderMaster and he stared back at her. "Lord Setekh has felt something, hasn't he...a disturbance somewhere?"

Before Mr. Nero could say any more there was a rap on the door and his major-domo came in. "Messrs. Carne and Cleave have arrived, UnderMaster."

"Bring them straight here."

The senior household steward bowed low, his arms crossed over his chest. "At once, UnderMaster."

Mr. Nero looked back at his Oracle and nodded. "Yes, there is something. But why is he so...so..." He wanted to say "worried", but the sheer idiotic notion of a god – the God of Chaos, ruler of all that is dark – being worried, stopped the word from crossing his lips. "Why is he so... insistent?"

Ms. Webb closed her eyes, and in the awkward stillness Mr. Nero saw a vein running down the left side of her head pulsing so sharply that her filigree skullcap shivered.

"It's across the water, the other side of the Isis...in Dinium."

"What is?"

"I don't know...he feels something there, like the flutter of a heart about to beat."

"What's going on – what is she saying?"

Mr. Nero tore his gaze away from his Oracle and saw Mr. Cleave standing in the doorway, a puzzled expression on his face. "Nothing, Darcus..." He saw Mr. Carne, the Overseer General, standing behind him. "Everyone is here, we have our quorum and can begin." Mr. Nero beckoned the men into the room. He waited until they had taken their assigned places and then sat down himself.

Ms. Webb's eyes snapped open and she glanced at the new arrivals. "We must be on our guard, all of us!"

Mr. Carne, a large bull of a man dressed in dusty khaki, removed a sweat-stained pair of riding gloves, dropping them on the table, and undid his tunic. "We," the head of the Dark Soul Army pointed to himself, "are on guard *all* the time; it's what *we* do, Phaedra."

The rather owl-like Mr. Cleave took off his rimless glasses, blinked and polished the lenses on a small piece of cloth, which he then carefully folded and put away. "If there is something we don't know, if there is something *I* do not know," he paused, raising one eyebrow and peering over the top of his spectacles at Ms. Webb, "well, now would be a very good time to explain what it is, as I am extremely busy and had to leave in the middle of an operation to get here."

"There is, how can I put it...an *unhappiness*..." Mr. Nero looked away. "Since this morning I have been aware...the Master has, to put it mildly, made it extremely clear that something isn't right. And Ms. Webb," Mr. Nero glanced at his Oracle, the silver gossamer on her skull gleaming as if it had just been spun by the most exotic of spiders, "Ms. Webb feels quite strongly that what is troubling Lord Setekh is over on the other side. Somewhere."

"Do we know where?" Mr. Carne asked.

Mr. Nero looked enquiringly at Ms. Webb, who shook her head. "No, Everil, we don't."

"I'll get word to The Peeler," Mr. Carne stood up, "tell him we want to know if anything unusual has happened anywhere in the territories recently."

Mr. Cleave made a face like he'd just encountered a really unpleasant smell. "I don't know why you deal with that man. I wouldn't trust him as far I could spit."

"You must've heard the Before Times saying, Darcus: *'He must needs go,'*" Mr. Carne smiled and looked straight at Mr. Nero, "*'that the devil drives'*."

Mr. Nero frowned, holding his breath; he could feel the very spirit of his Master move within him and he knew what it meant. He sat back and stared in front of him, right through Mr. Cleave, as if his solid, rather portly figure wasn't there at all. Then he closed his eyes.

"WORDS DO NOT BUILD THINGS!"

The Master's voice erupted out of Mr. Nero's gaping mouth, sounding as if it came from the depths of a deep black pit, scratching and clawing its way up his throat. Even the canix were spooked, their ears lying flat, both snarling nervously.

"IF THE LOWLIEST *ANT* KNOWS THIS TRUTH... YOU CREATURES OF MY DOMAIN MUST *SURELY* UNDERSTAND!"

The unearthly howl left each razor-cut word hanging in the air. Mr. Nero's chest heaved as his wheezing lungs sucked air into his rigid body, hands gripping the arms of the chair as if his life depended on him not letting go.

"THE *HAND* CREATES, THE TONGUE MERELY *WAGS*... YOU *WILL* BUILD ME MY SHRINE, MY SANCTUARY, MY ENGINE OF ETERNITY – I *WILL* HAVE MY COMPLETION!"

Messrs. Carne, Cleave and Webb stared at Mr. Nero as the final word spilled from his lips and he slumped in his chair, as if he were a puppet and someone had cut his strings. Only Everil Carne had witnessed Setekh speaking through the UnderMaster before, and, he had to admit, it was not something he was ever going to get used to.

"We are making an engine of eternity?" Mr. Cleave frowned. "Is that what he...what the Master said?"

Mr. Carne nodded. "That is what he said."

"I wonder what he means." Mr. Cleave pushed his chair back and stood up, ignoring the limp figure of Mr. Nero.

"We will no doubt find out," Ms. Webb's ring-covered hands disappeared inside her dark, lustrous silks, "when the job is completed..."

7 FINDING REEBA

Stretch made his way through the chaos, weaving in and out of the teeming mass of humanity clogging the narrow streets and alleys, with Bone sticking as close to him as he could. Everyone had something to sell, from the crone sitting cross-legged in the doorway hawking cheap, shoddy trinkets, to the merchant who did his business from a warehouse bursting with goods.

But Stretch wasn't looking to buy anything. He was going in search of a needle in a haystack. As he walked his mind was in turmoil because – for almost the first time since his father had been taken across the river – he found himself in the position of not knowing what to do next. Even though he was young, he was sharp enough to know how to survive – his dad had taught him well enough for that – but this wasn't about survival, about the next meal or how to stay out of trouble. This was bigger.

Behind that door he'd seen in Bloom's Mount there could be anything, or nothing; a fortune that might change his life, or possibly some vile creature which would end it. He could, of course, always go back alone to find out which it was, but even though it was his custom not to work with other people, he knew that this was the moment when he should break his rule. And Reeba was the only person he could think of to ask what he should do; clever people knew the answers to big questions, and even if *she* didn't know, then her teacher – the cleverest man alive, after all – would be able to help him. All Stretch had to do was find them.

From Vieille-Dam, the turf of the moneylenders, the brokers and the exchangers, Stretch went past the dilapidated remains of what they said had once been a huge, domed temple, but was now home to a brewer and stillsman. The cloying smell of hops and yeast filled the air as he left the Luds' territory and made his way into the Cuven.

Approaching a quite substantial two-storey shanty building, its scaffolding framework clad in everything from plastic sheeting to old floorboards, Stretch stopped. It was a Lozzi Shrine and now he had some money, he thought maybe this would be a good time to put a little of it to work. He and Bone went through the open doors. The interior was stiflingly hot and lit by the hundreds of long, thin candles planted in the sand-filled boxes which ran down each side of the shrine.

The whole interior of the place was soot-blackened from decades of worship. At the back, roped off and guarded by armed Lozzi Brothers, the barefoot iron totem stood on a crude brick plinth; a battered, rusty statue of Lozzi himself – half man, half machine – stared blankly ahead, holding some strange instrument in his hands.

Stretch wasn't specifically a Lozzite himself, and hadn't been brought up in any particular cult; he would light a candle to anyone's god if he thought it'd be of some help. Standing in the smoky gloom he wondered if the Fates had sent him past this place. Whatever the reasons for him being there, it would be as good a place as any to make a plea for a god's assistance and intervention on his behalf. He went over to where one of the Brothers was selling candles.

"How much?"

"Two cents apiece." The man proffered a handful of tallow candles.

"Two *cents*?" Stretch's jaw dropped.

"Salvation don't come cheap, brother; a *true* believer would know that...you wann'em or not?"

"I'll take five." Stretch handed over two five cent coins and waited while the Brother, tutting as he did it, separated out the required number.

"Anything less than ten won't change much," the Brother sneered, handing the candles over.

"It's only a small favour I'm asking," Stretch muttered, walking off to find a propitious site for his offering to Lozzi; he finally chose an area where most of the surrounding candles had burned right down, so his would be more noticeable.

"Help me find Reeba!" he whispered fiercely under his

breath as he lit the wicks, glancing over his shoulder at the Lozzi statue. *"Please..."*

Stretch was making for the massive, sprawling marketplace, a central distribution point for all kinds of provisions and a place that never closed. It was at the centre of the maze of streets he was threading his way through, and somewhere here he hoped he'd come across someone who knew where he could find Reeba and the old man she worked for.

His short stop and small investment at the Lozzi Shrine had obviously paid dividends because finding them ended up being an awful lot easier than he'd imagined it would be. Reeba's boss was really quite famous and turned out to be a man called Dexter Tannicus, or, as Stretch discovered, more commonly known as Bible Pete. He had no idea what a bible was, but assumed it must have something to do with being clever.

Bible Pete lived in an area called The Dile, a short walk north-east of the main market, and it was in the early afternoon that Stretch found himself, with Bone right next to him, standing outside a nondescript mud-brick building, rapping on a weather-beaten door with his knuckles. What he could see of the face of the large, bearded man who eventually answered his knock was as lined and ancient as the sun-bleached door itself.

"Yes? Hello?" The man peered down at him over the top of a pair of dusty, flyblown spectacles; he had another pair propped on his forehead, its arms lodged in a shock of receding white hair, and just the lenses of a third pair hanging round his neck on a piece of knotted string. "Do I know you?"

"No..."

"Ah..." The old man, a slightly confused expression on his face, glanced up and down the narrow street.

Stretch turned to see what he was looking for. "Are you Bible Pete?"

"Me? How did you know that?" A huge smile broke through the man's beard, the creases round his eyes deepening even further. "Why, yes, I am!"

"My name's Stretch, Stretch Wilson..." He stuck his hand out.

"I, er...I didn't know that." Bible Pete raised his eyebrows; this was by no means the cleanest example of a hand he'd ever seen and he seemed in no hurry to do as expected and shake it. Instead, he absent-mindedly wiped his hands on his trousers. "People think I know *everything*, you know...which is just not possible, of course. Especially if you're missing some rather important volumes, like me. Is that your dog?"

Stretch grabbed the scruff of Bone's neck. "Yes," he said, "he's very friendly, really...when he gets to know you."

"I had a dog once, when I was young, like you. Called him, what was it now...that's right, his monicker was Aurelius, which was the name of a man I read about in a book. Eons ago he was something called a Caesar, a position of power later referred to as a Kaiser, which was a story I liked. He's dead, of course, Aurelius. Well, they both are...he doesn't last very long, your dog; if you're after something that lasts you have to go for a parrot, or maybe a tortoise. What's your dog's name?"

"Bone."

"Ha!" Bible Pete's eyes lit up. "I like it, a dog called Bone

– one of which he has clamped in his chops! How very appropriate."

"Who are you talking to, Pete? Who's that at the door?"

"It's a dog, with a lad! He's called Bone, the dog, that is." Bible Pete roared the information over his shoulder, then frowned back down at Stretch. "What was it you wanted? I've completely forgotten what you said."

"I didn't."

"Oh, well goodbye then, been nice meeting you both..."

"Wait!" Stretch put his hand out to stop the door closing completely. "It's Reeba, I came to see Reeba."

"Stretch?" The door opened again to reveal that a smaller figure had pushed her way in front of Bible Pete; her blonde and hennaed dreads gleamed in the sun and her eyes looked even bluer than Stretch remembered. "What are you doing here, is something the matter?"

"I, um...I found something, and..." Stretch felt a shiver run down his back as his scalp tightened, the way it sometimes did when you were being watched. He scanned the crowded street, looking up at a couple of nearby balconies, but there was no way of telling who, if anyone, was observing him. "Can I come inside, please?"

"Pete?" Reeba looked up at her teacher.

"As long as he brings the dog." Bible Pete nodded to himself. "And if he washes his hands. They're quite a different colour to his face, which I think is never a good thing."

Some way down the street, hidden in the deep shadows cast by a brightly coloured awning, Samson Towd watched as the boy and his dog were ushered into a house. He'd seen the girl before, down at Mo's, and had at one time thought he might try and palm some rubbish off on her, until he'd seen her loosen the teeth of someone else who'd attempted the selfsame ploy. So what was the boy doing with Bible Pete and that vicious little vixen of his?

Samson spotted an old lady with a hole-in-the-wall shop from which she sold sweet coffee and bitter tea. She had a couple of saggy old bamboo chairs, one of which would afford him an excellent view of the house. He'd make his coffee last as long as he could...

Stretch stood in the middle of the room, staring open-mouthed at what he saw. Every wall, from floor to ceiling, was lined with books, hundreds and hundreds of them, books beyond counting. They were heaped up on the carpeted floor and smaller stacks had been created to serve as the "legs" for a tabletop that had once been a mirror, on which were more books. He could see through into another, similarly cluttered room.

"The whole place is like this, in case you were wondering."

Stretch looked round at Reeba. "Why?"

"'Cos he likes them. Says you can never have too many of them."

"It looks like, if you moved one, the whole house would come down...it wouldn't, would it?"

"Hasn't so far, boy...it has not done so far." Bible Pete shambled into the room, carrying a tray with three glass cups and an ornate teapot, which Stretch thought could well be made of silver; he set everything down in a space Reeba had made on the makeshift table. "But you never know, do you, Reeba?"

"Never know what, Pete?"

"Anything. Unless you've seen it with your own eyes."

"Or read it in a book."

Stretch, a freshly washed hand stroking Bone's head, sat where he'd been told to, on a pile of books, listening to Reeba and the old man banter with each other, aware that this was a conversation they must have had many, many times before.

Bible Pete moved some books off the only chair in the room and sat down; leaning forward, he picked up the teapot and poured hot, resin-coloured liquid into each of the glasses. "So, Stretch Wilson, what have you found?"

"A door."

"A door?" The old man handed a glass to Reeba, then one to Stretch; he picked his own up and sat back. "Is it locked?"

Stretch shook his head. "No."

Reeba blew on her steaming cup of honey-sweet cinnamon tea. "What's the problem, then?"

"It's inside Bloom's Mount..."

8 FINDING LOVE...

Bible Pete's glass stopped halfway to his mouth. "*Inside Bloom's Mount?*" He put the tea back on the tray. "*Inside?*"

"Yes..." Stretch took a sip from his glass. "I fell into a big space I think the gas must've made...the door was there, at the bottom of some stairs."

"Did you go through it?"

Stretch nodded. "Sort of..."

"What does that mean?"

"I looked in to see if there was anything worth coming back for."

"Sensible." Pete smoothed his beard. "But why are you

here, what's Reeba got to do with doors?"

Stretch shrugged. Now he'd found the people he'd been looking for he didn't know what to say...what *had* made him think Reeba, or this Bible Pete, would be able to tell him what he ought to do next?

"Did you want her to come with you?"

"Dunno..." Stretch looked from Pete to Reeba and back again.

"Just as dim as he is dirty." Pete raised his eyebrows and shook his head, peering over his glasses at Reeba. "Why's the boy called Stretch anyway, is that a *real* name?"

"No idea." She smiled across at Stretch. "Is it?"

"Only name I have." Stretch felt like he was being ganged up on, that these two were making fun of him. "My dad gave it me...from when I was little and I was always trying to get things that were out of my reach."

"You see!" Pete beamed and slapped his knee. "A reason! I *like* things that have a reason, a meaning...unlike *your* name, dear girl," he grinned furiously as he pointed at Reeba, "which means not a jot – ha-ha!"

"What's the reason for your name, then?"

The old man stopped laughing and looked at Stretch. "Mine? Oh, that's easy..." He pulled out a battered leather-bound book that Stretch hadn't noticed was tucked under his arm. "...it's this!"

"A book?" Stretch looked confused.

"Yes, a Bible, a name which comes from a word in some ancient language or other, I've forgotten the actual one, that in fact means 'book'..." The old man shivered like a jelly as he laughed quietly to himself. "...which always tickles me. In fact it's *The* Bible, see, it says on the cover..."

"He can't read, Pete." Reeba shook her head as Pete thrust the worn and dog-eared book at Stretch.

"No? Right-o..." Pete tucked the book back under his arm and nodded at Stretch. "It's a book of books and it's my favourite of all the ones I've got – full of the most *fantastic* stories, isn't it, Reeba? Like when one of the way-back-then gods gets angry, and the people get visited by plagues of blood and frogs – *frogs*, imagine! And then there's flies and boils and locusts, as well. They must've had some gods in those days, eh?"

Reeba nodded, smiling as she poured herself another glass of tea. "He carries that book with him all the time. Even sleeps with it."

"Well you never know when you're going to want to read something, do you, girl?" Pete sank back in his chair, pulled his book back out and buried his nose in it.

"So..." Reeba got up and brought the teapot over to fill Stretch's glass. "Why *did* you come to find me?"

Stretch shrugged again. "Just didn't know what to do...and you're the cleverest person I've ever met..."

"Until," said Pete from behind his Bible, "you met my good self, that is."

Reeba raised her eyebrows at Stretch and ignored the comment. "You were saying?"

"I thought you'd...maybe you could help me work out what to do." He picked a flea off Bone and cracked it between his fingernails. "I mean, if I *do* find stuff, I might not know what to take and what to leave behind. I'm a pretty good finder, but I don't have *real* knowledge. I could miss something; I need someone with me – but who? And..."

"And what?"

"It's dark down there, and you can, y'know, *hear* things... moving and stuff..."

"He should talk to Tyson." Pete peered over the top of his book for a moment, then disappeared back behind it. "That boy's fearless...completely fearless."

"Tyson *Love*? That muscle monkey?" Reeba's face screwed up in disgust. "He's not fearless, he's just too stupid to be scared."

"A *handsome* dunce, though," said Pete, who you could just tell was smiling to himself as he continued reading.

Reeba looked like she was about to boil. "Are you suggesting...?"

Pete closed his Bible. "I'm suggesting that, if young Mr. Stretch here is looking for someone to go with him, into the depths of a heap, then Tyson might be the lad for the job. *If* you could persuade him it was a good idea to go with you. Which, if he's as stupid as you say, Reeba, shouldn't be beyond you."

"Why should *I* want to have anything to do with that Tyson Love, *or* going inside Bloom's Mount, for that matter?"

"Because..." Pete stood up and tucked his book back under his arm. "...for one thing, you have the curiosity of ten cats. If not more."

"I do *not*!"

"We shall see." Pete wandered off towards the stairs, stopping a few steps down and looking back into the room. "You'll probably find the rascal up in the Yards, Stretch; ask around, someone'll point him out to you."

Stretch watched Pete disappear downstairs. "He's a

Saynt then, is he?" The Yards were a manufacturing area up in the Northside, bordering Fin territory, which Stretch didn't know at all well; he couldn't remember the last time he'd been that far from his home turf.

"Yes." Reeba swatted at a fly as it buzzed past her. "He is."

Stretch observed the girl, puzzled by her behaviour. "And you don't like him?"

"Did I say that?"

"You said he was stupid."

"I could call *you* stupid..."

"Why would you do that!"

"'Cos you can't read."

Silence.

Quite a long one.

Just the sound of Bone's panting. Then Stretch got up, a thoughtful look on his face.

"Gotta go...want to find this Tyson bloke before it gets dark."

"Right. Bye, then."

"Yeah, c'mon, Bone..."

"If we cut across the lower Fitz parish, we'll get to the Yards quicker, *and* we can go by the heap on the way and see if it looks like anyone's found the hole you made."

Stretch wasn't quite trotting to keep up with Reeba, but she was a bit taller than him, with longer legs, and he really had to stride out not to fall behind. Which he would not allow himself to do. Stretch had seen the I-told-you-so look on Pete's face when they'd left the house, Reeba ignoring it as she told him that she was just going to show Stretch the best way to the Yards, that was all.

But Stretch had a feeling that wasn't true. She was going to come inside Bloom's Mount with him. "What's Tyson do, Reeba?"

"Whatever anyone pays him to do."

"How come you know him?"

"Pete pays him to do things."

"What kind of things?"

"Stuff."

"Stuff?"

"Yeah..." Reeba glanced at Stretch. "Like if a person owes Pete and won't pay up, Ty is one of the people he uses to persuade them. For a fee."

"Pete's a lender?"

"How else d'you think he can afford to have all those books?" Reeba grinned, shifting the satchel she had slung over one shoulder. "He's not just clever, he's cunning and he's crafty and he's sharp...he only lends to those who need *big* dollar, doesn't do cents and pennies."

"But there was no sign outside."

"The kind of people who need Pete know where to find him."

Some way behind, and wishing he hadn't had so many cups of coffee, not to mention glasses of lemon water, Samson Towd cursed the two urchins he was following and the speed at which they were travelling. There was no way, right now, that he was going to find the time or the place to relieve himself; if he stopped, he'd lose them and have wasted too much of a day for nothing. And he was not going to do that. The girl and her grubby little friend were up to something, and he was going to find out what it was...

As they skirted round the Mount, Stretch had used Reeba's small but quite powerful spyglass – a beautiful piece of brass old-tek she said Pete had given her – to quickly scan the area around where he'd fallen inside the heap. From what he could see it didn't seem like there was any activity there at all, and they'd carried on walking, still at Reeba's demanding pace. As they walked, Stretch did wonder why Reeba wasn't asking exactly what he had seen beyond the door, and ended up putting it down to her not asking just to annoy him.

A couple of times on their journey north, Stretch again got the same odd feeling he was being watched, but when he mentioned it to Reeba she said that wherever you went *someone* was going to be looking at you. So they made their way up towards the Yards, the temperature beginning to fall.

It was a fact of life in these times that where you came from could affect where you were allowed to go. Everyone always had their colours on show, or at least the colours they thought would get them into the least trouble. Stretch's crimson Vix bandana was the only thing he washed with any regularity and Reeba always wore her green Cuven flash in her hair.

Depending on how relationships were between the different territories, crossing borderlines was either as simple as walking across a street...or somewhat more difficult. And relationships could change like the weather. The family who ran the Fitz parish – which meant they ran Bloom's Mount, or tried to – were on reasonable terms with all their neighbours. And they tried to keep it that way so no one – like the powerful and belligerent Hyde – was tempted to forcibly take them over. Keeping on friendly terms with the Saynts, who would be very unhappy if the Hyde annexed the Fitz parish, kept the situation reasonable and the borders relaxed.

Reeba, Stretch and Bone crossed over at the Woeburn Point with no trouble at all, making their way through the crowded market that had grown up along the Yards' walls like a fungus; this was where you went to buy what was manufactured on the other side, things made out of re-syked metal and glass and plastic. The Yards, criss-crossed with the remains of ancient iron trackways which all ran northwards, out of the territories and up-country, was a vast tract of land covered in innumerable single-storey shacks and larger ramshackle buildings, each with a ragged plume of pungent black smoke billowing from one or more chimney stacks. The smell was acrid and the air, if the wind was in the wrong direction, eye-watering; on a bad day the smoke hung, a dirty blanket in the sky, almost low enough to touch, almost solid enough to cut.

Walking through the Stephenson Gates, Stretch stopped to take in the vista spreading out in front of him; for as far as he could see, the Yards were alive with movement and industry. A sadness made his shoulders fall: his father, if he was still alive, was somewhere across the water being made to work on whatever it was they were building in Kaï-ro. From up on Bloom's Mount you could see the huge black structures rising out of the desert flats, crawling agonizingly slowly up from the skyline, and every day he wondered why they'd had to take *his* father...

"Stretch – are you all right?"

"What?" Stretch snapped back from his dark thoughts.

"You went all dismal and somewhere else for a minute, what happened?"

"Just thinking about my dad, that's all..."

"Oh...right, I'm sorry."

"S'okay..." Sniffing, Stretch rubbed what might have been a tear away from his eye. "So, how're we gonna find Tyson, then?"

"Think I may have spotted him already."

"You have?" Stretch stood on his toes and peered out across the Yards, thinking to himself that, even if he knew what Tyson Love looked like, he'd have no chance of finding him in this chaotic place. "Where?"

Reeba nudged Stretch. "Closer to home." She pointed down the wide, dusty roadway that ran to her right at the edge of the wall; some kind of disturbance appeared to have broken out and, somewhere in the middle of a growing crowd it was obvious there was a fight.

"He's in there?"

"Taking bets on the winner right now..."

9 A PROPOSITION

With the judicious use of her elbows, dug hard into ribs, and heels stamped on feet, Reeba carved a way through the crowd until she got to the front; as Bone wove through the forest of legs, behind him Stretch pushed and shoved until he managed to join them both at the edge of a makeshift ring where two youths were fighting. Their faces were painted to look like savage creatures and they fought with a kind of wild, primitive fury.

"There he is." Reeba pointed towards one of the corners where a grinning, sallow-skinned Nikkei boy, with pale blue dragon tattoos twisting down both arms from his shoulders, was taking bets off the audience. His long dark hair – with sky-blue Saynts ribbons plaited into it – swung as he worked, his black, almond-shaped eyes glinting in the low sun.

Stretch watched as one fighter, blood streaming down his face from a savage cut above his left eye, landed a high kick on his opponent's head, sending him flying backwards into the crowd, who roared their approval as they flung the boy back into the ring.

"What's the rules?"

"Ty runs ay-gee fights – anything goes, right?" Reeba's eyes were fixed on the action. "No need for rules."

Then Stretch saw the second fighter's face, which looked like he'd been mauled by one of the clawed beasts he'd heard you could come across up-country, and he spotted that the kicker's shoes had been specially adapted for ay-gee and had razor-sharp nails poking through the soles.

"There's one pot, five rounds and no time limit," Reeba leaned over and yelled in Stretch's ear, above the noise of the baying crowd. "You fight till you fall, and as soon as a round's finished, a new fighter comes in to take on the winner, and the pot gets smaller each time that happens... unless one person carries on winning. Fighters *can* win all five bouts and take all the money, but only if they fight short rounds and get a fight over as fast as possible, in any way they can. Otherwise, if you let rounds go on too long, you end up dead meat."

As if to prove her point, the fighter with the slashed face took a swift double kick to his head, slumped to the ground and didn't get up. Stretch watched as he was dragged out of the ring, feet first, while the winner sat on the ground and a flurry of women and girls appeared out of the crowd, fussing over him and cleaning him up.

"I've never seen anything like this down where I come from," Stretch yelled back at Reeba. "It's mad."

"It's Ty's idea, he invented it," Reeba explained. "If there's no one left standing at the end of the fifth round, he gets to keep the prize money, as well as all the lost bets."

Stretch watched Tyson Love as he paced up and down on the other side of the ring. He was probably about the same age as Reeba, if you looked past the tattoos and bravado. Why would someone like him want to go into Bloom's Mount? Just because Bible Pete and, grudgingly, Reeba said he was the kind of person he needed, should he believe them? And could he trust them?

For a long moment Stretch felt like he should just fade into the crowd and disappear; maybe he should just bite the bullet and do this thing by himself. Then he remembered how it had felt down there, inside the heap. Stretch squared his shoulders. He supposed it couldn't hurt to at least talk to the Nikkei boy.

Coming out from behind a scraggy, dust-covered bush, after a much needed visit, Samson Towd breathed a huge sigh of relief; he'd thought he was going to expire from the pain that had begun to bring tears to his eyes. With a spring in his step, he moved slightly nearer the mêlée surrounding what looked to be some kind of semi-organized street fight and stood leaning up against the wall, trying to see where his quarry had gone.

But the girl and her ratty little companion were too short for him to be able to see them. A niggling worry, one that made his right eye twitch uncontrollably, was that they'd realized they were being followed and were using the crowd to lose him; but Samson was pretty sure this wasn't the case...not certain, but pretty sure. Moving quietly and quickly round the periphery of the rabble, checking his targets hadn't made their way through and out the other side, Samson eventually found a place where he could make himself as unobtrusive as possible – something he was extremely good at – and settled down to wait for this impromptu event to finish...

The fighter with the spiked shoes made it all the way into the fifth round, and it looked to Stretch like his vicious, dirty style and awesome speed might take him right through and make him the outright winner. But his success had made him cocky and he started to act as if he was invincible. He knocked his new opponent down almost immediately the last round began, but all turned out not to be quite as it seemed.

The moment the new fighter hit the ground, the kid Stretch had started to think of as Spike had begun bowing and accepting the applause of the mob. What no one had realized was that the other fighter's fall had been a fake. One moment there was a body lying in the blood-soaked dust, the next the spring-heeled New Boy had leaped up; in a move he must have practised for hour after hour, the boy jumped, spun in the air and came down on Spike like a hammer, nailing him flat on the ground. Fight over.

A feeling of anticlimax rippled through the crush of people as a lot of money had been riding on Spike to win. The majority of the crowd faded away into the late afternoon, leaving just a small group milling around and waiting for their winnings. Stretch followed Reeba over as she joined them, waiting to catch Ty's attention. As soon as he spotted her he pushed a few coins into someone's hands and strode over to them, grinning.

"Reeba! Long time no see!"

"Good fight, Ty..." Reeba remained straight-faced, nodding at Stretch. "Friend of mine I want you to meet; he's got a proposition you might like, wanna hear it?"

"So, Stretch, why has Reeba brought you all the way up here to see me?" Ty put down a tray loaded with a battered coffee pot, three cups and a plate of sweet pastries.

They were sitting up on the flat roof of a makeshift, three-storey tavern and darkness was falling fast.

"I've, um...I've found something." Stretch glanced at Reeba, who gave him an almost imperceptible nod of encouragement. "Thing is, I'm gonna need some help, and Reeba said you'd be the person to ask."

Ty didn't say anything, just sat staring at Reeba as he traced the outline of one of his tattoos with a finger.

"If you're waiting for me to pour the coffee 'cos I'm a *girl*," Reeba shook her head, "Hell will freeze over first, my friend."

"I bought it, I gotta *pour* it too?"

"Whoever told you life was fair was lying, Ty." A smile twitched Reeba's lips. "Anyway, we're your guests."

"Yeah, yeah, yeah..." Ty grinned as he poured out three cups of the bitter-sweet coffee and gave one to Stretch. "What've you found?" He picked up his own cup and took a small honey-coated pastry.

"I don't know what's there, exactly, but I found a door inside Bloom's Mount, and I need help to find out what's behind it."

Ty frowned. "You've not looked?"

"Not properly, my candle was running out."

"You mean there could be, oh I don't know, *nothing* there?"

"No, there's something, I saw it shining..." Stretch looked round to check if, for whatever reason, anyone was trying to eavesdrop. *"I think there could be gold down there,"* he whispered.

"Gold!" Ty spat the word out as he choked on bits of paper-thin pastry.

"Ty!" Reeba shot him a killer look. "Jeeziz, you trying to let *every*one know?"

"Are you *sure*, kid?"

"No, I'm not sure, but I think it's worth the risk to go back and find out...and don't call me a kid, right? I'm not one of your ay-gee boys."

"Okay, okay...are you Vix always so touchy?"

"Are you Saynts always so big-headed?"

"Will you two stop it?" Reeba looked at them like they were children. "We have some planning to do if we want to get in there, and get out again."

"We?" Ty frowned. "You coming too?"

"I was going before you were..." Reeba flicked a glance at Stretch. "We need *some* brains on this expedition."

Ty got up and dropped a few coins on the table as he turned to walk away. "I don't need this..."

Me neither, Stretch thought to himself...except that going into the heap with someone else, even someone like Tyson

Love, would definitely be better than doing the job on his own. It really would. It was dark down there, it was...

"Ty, come here a minute." Reeba's command broke into Stretch's thoughts and he looked up to see her beckoning the Nikkei boy over.

Ty stopped and you could tell he was about to ignore her, then changed his mind and came back. "What?"

Reeba leaned towards him and Ty bent down to meet her. "*Gold*...remember?"

Stretch almost didn't hear what she'd said, her voice was so low, but the effect on Ty was instantaneous. He sat back down and poured more coffee. "Yeah, right...there is that."

Reeba smiled a cat-who'd-caught-a-mouse smile. "But we need somewhere to stay tonight, any ideas?"

"We can stay at my place tonight; my old lady won't mind."

Stretch felt a pang of jealousy. This boy had a place he could call home, a place with a mother, just like he'd once had; even if they did find gold inside Bloom's Mount, no matter how much it was worth he'd knew it'd never be able to change the fact that *his* mother was dead.

Samson Towd had thought about following the trio up onto the tavern's roof terrace, but knew it would be hard not to find himself getting too close. Watching needed distance, otherwise there was a grave danger you'd get caught and have nowhere to run. And Samson Towd always liked to have a way out.

The place he'd found wasn't perfect – he was perched on the narrow walkway that ran along the top of a wall on the southern edge of the Yards. Crouched behind a large shrub that had somehow found a way to root itself between the bricks, he was uncomfortable but hidden. It would have to do. Towd's vantage point was slightly higher than the tavern's terrace and he could see the silhouetted shapes of his targets, sitting and eating and drinking. He was hungry too, but he wasn't going to get anything to eat until he found where these three were staying the night.

From where he sat, with the small oil lamp on the table lighting up their faces and accentuating their expressions, he could tell they were deep in discussion about something. Towd was too far away to be able to hear what it was they were actually saying, but he was pretty sure he'd heard one word. The Nikkei boy had almost yelled it, Bible Pete's girl reacting angrily at what he'd done.

Gold!

He'd said gold, Towd was sure of it...

10 INTO THE HEART

Ty had woken them before dawn, rousing Stretch – who was curled up with Bone – with a poke in the ribs; taking some fruit with them, as well as two bags of things they thought they'd need where they were going, they'd left Ty's sleeping mother behind and gone into the grey, end-of-night streets.

It was cold, and there were a surprising number of people up and about. As they approached the border road at Woeburn Point the last of one of the massive caravanserai which made the hazardous journeys up north and back was crossing over. The three of them sat at the road's edge and wasted a few minutes of the new day just watching the sight, the end of the great road train rolling past them, loaded with goods from all over the up-country.

The procession of horse-drawn wagons and carts, driven by tired, dusty men, lines of camels, donkeys and packhorses was on its way to the Cuven's market. They'd been travelling for weeks to bring food stuffs – cheeses and dried fruit and meat – cloth, metalware, pottery and more to sell and trade. It was a hard, hard journey, only worth taking when well-armed and in the safety of large numbers, because up-country was a dangerous place, full of wild animals, even wilder people and, depending on who you listened to, much, much worse.

That's what you heard, anyway, everywhere stories were told. Harrowing tales of the fierceness and savagery that was played out on the barren, windswept plains and inhospitable terrain outside the parishes...blood-soaked legends of barbaric tribes and their frenzied battles. The Sorrow Roads, they were sometimes called, and with good reason; but still the caravans came and went, which Stretch thought must mean that the risks, no matter how grievous, were obviously worth taking. He had never been out of Dinium, and if the stories were true he never wanted to go.

"Time to move!" Reeba yelled as she leaped up and started running, Ty, Bone and Stretch in hot pursuit.

Weary and irritable after a bone-cold night spent catnapping in a cramped doorway, Samson Towd was quite unprepared for their sudden dash across the road and into the warren of narrow streets on the other side. One moment they were sitting, with the dog, watching the ragged column pass by, the next they were gone like a breeze!

Samson was flung into such a panic that he almost ran out from behind the palm where he'd been watching and called out to them to come back. Just managing to stop himself, he hotfooted it across the road, hoping that they wouldn't disappear like the rats they were into some Dinium hole-in-the-wall. He *couldn't* lose them, not after all the time and effort he'd put in!

He was sworn at by a shopkeeper he bumped into and kicked by a mule whose rear end he got too close to, but as he pelted into a small square he was just in time to see the smaller of the two boys haring round a nearby corner. Giving all the thanks in Heaven and on Earth to Big Yelo, Samson made the holy sign – east, west, arc of the sun – cursed the ancestors and unborn children of whoever owned the mule, and continued his pursuit.

It wasn't that far to Bloom's Mount but when they got there Reeba appeared to be the only one who wasn't out of breath and massaging a stitch. The heap was shrouded in a veil of dirty grey mist, tendrils of steam rising up in lazy swirls from its towering flanks, the vast accumulation of centuries of debris. It was a cold and ominous sight.

"In there?" said Ty, still getting his breath back.

"S'right..." Stretch nodded. "Right inside."

Ty looked distinctly unimpressed. "This better be good, Reeba."

"Only one way to find out." Reeba took a bite of an apple. "Come on, let's get up there before it gets too light."

Ty looked up at the heap. "Gonna be *really* dark in there... you think candles and oil lamps are going to be okay?"

Reeba shook her head and patted the satchel she had slung over her shoulder. "Pete gave me something."

"What?"

Reeba opened the satchel and brought out a palm-sized piece of blue plastic old-tek; it was sort of cone shaped, with the wide end covered in clear plastic. "I've got two of them."

Stretch moved in for a closer look; he'd never seen anything like the object Reeba was holding. "What does it do?"

"It lights up." Reeba flipped out a small handle that was hidden in the side of the thing, and the two boys watched, puzzled, as she turned it very fast for a few seconds; then, pointing the clear plastic at Stretch, she pressed something on its side. A bright white light appeared in her hand. "Like *that*!"

Stretch jumped backwards, almost as if he'd been physically hit; spooked by his master's reaction, Bone's hackles went up and he growled.

Ty laughed nervously. "How the...how did you...?"

"Lectricity." Reeba shone the light at Ty and then switched it off. "That's what Pete says it's called. They had a lot of it in the Before Times, he says it was everywhere. With this, every time the light fades, you just wind it up to get some more, so we'll be fine in there."

"Why didn't you say before that you'd got them?" Stretch frowned as he looked at the magical old-tek. Light with no fire, no heat? How was that possible?

Reeba smiled as she put the tek away in her satchel. "You didn't need to know."

* * *

By the time they'd climbed up to the area where Stretch thought he'd fallen into the heap – it was hard on the mostly featureless landscape to be *absolutely* sure exactly where you were – the sun was finally crawling above the horizon. In the distance a few tiny silhouettes could be made out crawling up the sides of Bloom's Mount. They were no longer alone.

Ty, crouched down like the others so they wouldn't stand out, looked at Stretch as he cast about. "So, where is it?"

"Give him time..." Reeba waved a hand at Ty, her eyes restlessly sweeping the vicinity as she watched for anyone coming their way.

"S'around here somewhere." Stretch squinted as he searched for the pieces of junk he'd used to cover the hole.

"We have to be *quick*, man." Ty gestured nervously. "People could be here any time!"

"I think I see it..." Stretch scrambled across the side of the heap, his crimson bandana bright in the early morning light, keeping as low as he could to the heap's uneven, treacherous surface; Bone followed, stuck to him like his shadow.

Reeba and Ty watched and waited as the boy and his dog zigzagged about like a couple of flies, no obvious pattern to what they were doing. Then Stretch stopped. Reeba saw him lean forward and lift something up, turn and wave at them to join him.

By the time they reached him, Stretch had shifted the junk away to reveal a small, ragged hole in the side of the heap, a black scar in its grey flesh. Standing by the edge, Bone shivered and let out a plaintive whine.

"He knows I'm going to leave him again." Stretch patted the dog's coarse fur. "I'll be back soon as I can, boy...soon as I can. Can't take you in there."

Reeba peered into the darkness. "How do we get down?"

"*I* wanna know how you think we're gonna get back *up* again!" hissed Ty. "All we got's ropes and hooks, man... ropes and hooks for Lozzi's sake! How's *that* gonna work?"

Stretch took the rope out of the bag he'd been carrying and undid it, dropping one end into the hole. "A lot easier than when I did it all on my own, okay? Take the end, I'm going down first..."

Ty grabbed Stretch's arm. "Why you first?"

"Okay, *you* go." Stretch stood to one side, wrapped the rope around his arm and sat back from the edge of the hole. "It's not far down; Reeba'll come next and the two of you kind of catch me when I come down. Easy."

Ty stayed where he was. "And coming back?"

Stretch sighed and shook his head. "Look...there's three of us, we got hooks, I reckon you and me can boost Reeba up first, and then...look, we'll work it out, okay!"

"We'll work it *out*?" Ty glowered angrily at Stretch, fit to spit.

"You worry too much, Ty."

"Yeah? Look, there's one thing I've learned the hard way and that's if you're going to start something it's a good idea to know how to finish it, before it finishes you."

"Normally I'd agree, but we don't have time." Reeba grabbed the rope Stretch had thrown into the hole. "Hold tight, Stretch – see you both down there!"

Momentarily shocked, Stretch immediately braced himself to take Reeba's weight as she rappelled out of sight and into the blackness; this was the second time in a day that she'd taken command of the situation, and while part of him was very glad someone had broken the stand-off with Ty, another part wished it'd been him. Seconds later, feeling the rope slacken, he relaxed slightly and then he saw a torch beam sweep across the dark gap. "You all right?" he called.

Before Reeba had a chance to answer, Ty grabbed the rope. "Don't let go..."

Stretch cursed him under his breath, leaning almost horizontal, his heels dug right into the heap's dew-damp surface, as Ty followed Reeba down. Then he heard a grunt as Ty landed and let go of the rope. His turn now, with no one to help him. He turned to Bone, stroked him and gave him a hug. "Just wait here, boy...we'll be back as soon as we can, honest. Soon as we can..."

He looked at the dog, who stared right back at him. Bone's head was to one side, ears down and he was softly whining. Like he was pleading. He looked so sad, but there was nothing Stretch could do about it...he had to go and there was no way he could take Bone with him. He dragged his eyes away. "I'm coming down!"

"Take it slow," Reeba yelled back up. "We'll try and catch you!"

Stretch put his gloves on, inched forward and slid slowly, feet first, into the hole; the day before he'd just fallen through and hadn't had to think about it, now he knew he had to make sure he didn't tense up or he might hurt himself when he landed. So much easier said than done. He let himself go some more, bracing himself with his arms against the sides of the hole...thinking stuff like, there was no way he was going to be able to cover the hole up before he went down...thinking about anything but what he was just about to do.

And then Stretch realized his feet were dangling in mid-air and he was going to have to let go. He took a deep breath, closed his eyes even though he was going into the dark, and slid forward. He felt hands grab him as he hit the ground, then a hail of rubbish landed on him. He'd made it!

As Stretch stood up, about to brush himself down, there was a yelping and a strangled howl as more junk rained down – along with Bone. The dog plummeted through the hole, all legs and fur, and fell on top of Stretch, knocking him over. Lying on his back he was greeted by a delirious Bone, licking his face and wagging his tail.

"Well-trained dog you got there, Stretch." Reeba kneeled down and patted Bone. "Although I suppose it can't do any harm having an extra pair of eyes and ears down here, can it? I mean, who knows what we're going to find..."

11 THE OTHER SIDE OF THE DOOR

With both hand lights fully wound up Reeba and Stretch were ready to set off down the stairs, but Ty had insisted they could only go after a quick prayer to Lozzi and a couple of the other gods he felt it would be good to have watching over them. Considering where they were going.

Before either Reeba or Ty could take the lead, Stretch, acting a lot braver than he felt, grabbed it; shining the light in front of him he began the long journey to the half-open door, way down at the bottom of the stairs. With each step all he could think was that this could either be a day which would change his life for ever, or there would be no riches on the other side and the two people following him were going to be very unhappy. Especially Ty. Reeba had chosen to come on this journey – had insisted, really – but Ty had needed a bit of convincing. And Reeba had sort of *promised* him that there was definitely gold to be found.

And gold really would change everything.

There were other, rarer metals, like titanium, but clan leaders and tribal chiefs didn't want something which looked like it might be some cheap base metal. They wanted *yellow* metal, the kind of metal bees would make, if that's what they did, as his dad had used to say. Maybe, if they found a lot of gold he could somehow use his share to get his dad back from over the river in Kaï-ro. Cheapside Mo always said that everything in this world had its price, you just had to find out what it was. How much could one man, among the thousands they'd taken, be worth to the people working for Mr. Nero? Even though he meant the world to Stretch...

Then he was at the door, with Bone by his side and Ty and Reeba right behind him. He inspected it in the light, took a deep breath and reached out to push it further open, but as before it wouldn't budge. Stretch knew he had to get it open more or all this would've been for nothing. He put his shoulder to the door and pushed hard, the wood and hinges shrieking in pain as they shifted ever so slightly. Right then it occurred to him that maybe he should be careful what he tried to move, because it might be holding something else up; Stretch suddenly became very aware of what was above him, the thousands and thousands of tons of compacted rubbish just waiting to fall...

"Come on, let me do it." Ty shoved his way past Reeba and, pushing Stretch out of the way, heaved himself at the door. It hardly moved.

"Maybe if all three of us do it, together..." said Reeba. "You know, teamwork?"

Ty grunted, but moved so the others could join him and get their hands on the door for a joint effort. "On the count of three," he said. "One...two...three – *PUSH!*"

With Bone a couple of steps behind them, barking along in encouragement, the three of them pushed and heaved, grunted and sweated; Stretch felt like he'd never, ever made this much effort, and he could see the dragon-covered muscles on Ty's arms straining; finally the door squeaked and squealed in protest, then juddered forward and stopped again. It had opened just enough to let them get through.

"This..." Ty was breathing heavily, "...had better be worth it."

Stepping in front of the two boys, Reeba went through the gap, glancing back as she went. "Let's find out, shall we?"

Stretch and Ty looked at each other, knowing they were both thinking the same thing: how come she always managed to get the jump on them? And then Stretch made a dive for the gap and just managed to beat Ty to the other side.

Back up above ground Samson Towd, who was lying on his stomach, as flat as he could possibly get, slowly pushed himself out of whatever mouldering refuse formed this particular part of Bloom's Mount and peered up the slope towards where he'd last seen the girl, her two friends and their dog.

His eyes were not deceiving him...they were definitely nowhere to be seen.

One minute they'd all been there, clear as day; then, because he'd thought the flea-bitten mutt had spotted him, Towd had had to bury himself under the filth he was sprawled in. When he'd looked up again, they were gone! He glanced around, checking to see if there was anyone else in the vicinity, and not until he was completely sure he was alone did he begin to scurry, crablike, up the gently steaming side of the heap.

In his panic he almost missed the hole, thinking it was just another of the thousands of shallow depressions scattered all over the pitted surface of the heap. But something made him stop and take a proper look at this one. It was a hole. An actual hole, like a small tunnel, going *inside* the heap; this had to be where they'd gone. All of them – he worriedly glanced about – including the dog. Towd crouched down by the edge, giving thanks to Big Yelo that he hadn't blundered across the thing and fallen in. A cold hand clutched his thudding heart at the thought.

He peered down into the darkness, straining to see or hear anything. Were those voices? Or was it just the heap moving, like he'd heard it did? Towd had no idea. At that very moment he had no idea about anything. Why had they gone *inside* the heap – what could they be looking for? What was he going to do – follow them? Wait for them to come out? Wait where, though, and for how long? Questions, questions, questions!

Towd felt like crying. He was tired, thirsty, very, *very* hungry and on top of everything, he now smelled like a midden. But whining to himself was going to get him nowhere, and what he had to do was make a plan. Think. Concentrate. Work something out. Except his brain was slurry, all he could think about was what on earth could they be doing *inside* Bloom's Mount? It just wasn't natural!

Just the *idea* of what they'd done, let alone actually doing it himself, made Towd's knees feel weak, and he was now more sure than ever that they knew what they were doing, that they were after something of real, serious value. And he was going to get his share of it if it was the last thing he did. He must *not* give up. Not now, not after all the time he'd already invested in following these three. Samson's eye began to twitch; he'd find a way of doing this, he would. He had to...

No one said anything as the seconds ticked by. The three of them just stared at the three different directions they could go in, listening to all the small, sharp, chittering noises that came from above them, beside them, around them. It was like they were inside a living thing that, at any moment, might move. Might attack. Bone's low growl was at once comforting and disconcerting; the dog was ready to set upon anything that moved, totally spooked as they all were.

"Okay, we're here..." Ty nudged Stretch, "...where's the gold?"

Stretch nervously shone his light up the buckled, uneven corridor to his left, the beam shaking slightly as he swept it from side to side, searching for the object that the weak flame from his candle had picked out in the damp, chill gloom. If he'd been wrong, if what he'd seen wasn't gold, would Ty not want to go on?

And then his light caught something...a flash of yellow reflecting back at them!

Reeba turned her light on as well and shone it at the same place. There, on the floor, ten, maybe fifteen feet away, there was something in the dust. Ty was the first to break the spell that seemed to be holding them fixed to the spot and he ran up the corridor, skidding to a halt by the object and crouching to pick it up.

"Well?" said Reeba. "Is it?"

"More light..." Ty beckoned them closer.

Reeba glanced at Stretch and smiled. "Fingers crossed..."

They ran up the corridor keeping the torch beams on what Ty had in his hands; as they got nearer they saw him wipe dust and grime off what now looked like some kind of brooch with blue enamel set into the smooth, yellow metal. That had to be gold, absolutely definitely had to be. And now he was closer, an arm's length away, Stretch could see that it was shaped like an insect. Like a dung beetle in fact. But why would anyone want to make something so valuable look like that?

"Weird, huh?" Ty stood up, huffing on the metal and rubbing it on his trousers; he tested its weight, hefting it in his hand. "It's gold all right. And just lying in the dirt like that." He looked up the corridor. "There's got to be more, a *lot* more..."

Reeba reached out and touched the surface, brushing it with her fingertips, touching the sides. "It's from a necklace, I think...see where it was attached to something?"

"But why a dung beetle?" Stretch plucked the ornament out of Ty's hand and shone his light close at it, so he could see all the detail.

"Hey!" Ty tried to grab it as Stretch jerked his hand back. "That's mine, I found it!"

"All right, hold on." Reeba stood between the two boys. "Nothing's anybody's until we get out of here, and then we split three ways, by weight. Okay?" She shone her light into Ty's face, then Stretch's. "Okay?"

They both nodded.

Stretch looked at the golden dung beetle; it was the strangest, most beautiful thing he'd ever seen. He held it out to Reeba. "You keep it, for now."

"That all right with you, Ty?" she asked, taking the object from Stretch.

"S'pose so..."

"Well, this way looks as good as any." Reeba wound her fading light back up to full strength and pointed it down the corridor. "Let's see what else there is to find."

"Where d'you think we are?" Stretch asked no one in particular as they walked.

"Yeah," Ty joined in. "What's a place like this doing here, how'd all these corridors get under the heap?"

Reeba stopped and looked at the two boys, shaking her head. "Whatever it is, this building we're in was here *way* before the heap!"

"Okay..." Stretch nodded as he thought about what Reeba had said, that they were now in a place that had been built long, long ago in the Before Times, and then stopped as they came to another staircase, leading further into the heart of Bloom's Mount.

"It must've been abandoned at some time, I suppose, and more and more stuff just got dumped here..." Reeba played her light downwards and they saw the stairs end. "And still does get dumped here."

"But what was it?"

"Who knows..."

"Are we just going to stand here, or are we going to look some more?" Ty made a half-hearted grab at Stretch's light, but missed.

For some reason no one moved and they stood for a moment, listening. They stood together in this place which no one had been to for more time than any of them could imagine, in this corridor no one had walked down since the Before Times. Each of them had had to build a wall around their own personal fears, hiding them away somewhere just so they could set foot in this place. But here, at the top of these stairs, their fears were slipping out, like snakes' tongues, licking the air and hissing *We're back!*"

"It's...it's going to fall in on us..." Ty's voice was very quiet. "We're gonna be buried alive..."

"There's things in here...alive..." Stretch backed up a step. "I heard them before..."

"Can either of you smell gas?" whispered Reeba, as both the hand-wound torches faded to nothing within seconds of each other. In the blanketing darkness all the tiny sounds seemed to grow louder, come nearer, almost reach out and touch them.

"Oh, Lozzi..." Ty croaked in the pitch-black.

12 NO WAY OUT

Fear is a strange and often uncontrollable thing. Fear is where man and animal meet and are equals, each terrified beyond rational thought and only able to rely on instinct, forced to obey ancient compulsions. It was Bone's feral howling and high-pitched barking that jolted Stretch into action, making him grab the handle on the light and wind the thing as if his life depended on it. The darkness instantly shrank back, the infinite black replaced by the secret, dilapidated architecture they'd found hidden inside Bloom's Mount.

"For Lozzi's sake..." Ty took a deep breath and started down the stairs, "...do *not* do that again, you two."

Reeba and Stretch looked at each other, nodding in silent agreement, both sure they would never, ever let the lights go out. Too scary by half. As Reeba recharged her machine, they followed Ty and found him at the bottom of the stairs, looking down a short corridor which ended with a pair of doors. Doors secured by a large, rusty iron padlock.

"Great..." Ty cracked his knuckles. "Anyone got a key?"

Reeba turned to go back up the stairs. "Maybe we can find another way in, Ty."

Ty stayed where he was. "Know what? I *hate* locked doors."

"So we'll find one that *isn't*, then, okay? Come on."

Stretch was about to join her when Ty leaped down the corridor like he'd been shot out of a catapult. Yelling "Stupid door!" he launched himself in a flying kick, one of his heavy leather boot heels landing right on the padlock. Which shattered, shards of brittle metal flying everywhere.

"How did you do that?" Stretch ran down to where Ty was now standing.

"Dunno..."

Stretch bent down to examine what was left of the lock. "There's almost nothing left...it's turned to dust."

"Must've been really old to do that," Reeba said, joining them. "I mean really *ancient*...Pete says they used to be able to make steel that wouldn't ever rust in the Before Times."

"Bible Pete reads too much." Ty unlatched the door and shoved it open; grabbing the light out of Stretch's hand, he dashed through.

"Just 'cos hitting something worked this time," Reeba called out after him, "doesn't mean it's *always* the answer, you know!"

"Bet he forgets to keep the light wound up," Stretch muttered to himself as he held Bone and let Reeba go through the door first. "Just you see...wha?"

Stretch's voice echoed weirdly as he bumped into Reeba, who for some reason had stopped a couple of steps in; when he saw where she was shining her light – up and up and up the side of the huge room they now found themselves in – he realized why. This place was far bigger than the main Lozzi shrine, the huge one up near the Yards that his dad had taken him to once; with its massive iron statue of the seated god leaning forward as he planned the world, it was supposed to be the biggest building anywhere.

This place was *so* much bigger. It was circular, and it had a domed ceiling so high Stretch could only just make it out, held up by a huge building in the middle. Their lights weren't powerful enough to see very far but this place appeared to be piled high with wooden boxes and awesomely large statues; there were glass cabinets crowded with glittering things and shadowy objects stacked along the walls. And as Reeba and Ty shone their lights here and there, not knowing where to stop and look first, Stretch thought he could make out other rooms leading off the curved sides of this extraordinary place they'd found.

They were in a storehouse the like of which even Cheapside Mo could only dream about! It was packed with so much old-tek and Before Times material that there were only the smallest gaps between the piles. Stretch felt light-headed at the thought of what he was looking at, the riches, the wealth, the treasure there must be here right in front of him; maybe his dreams of getting his father back were actually more of a reality than he could ever have hoped.

He knew that was how the world worked, that those with nothing got nothing, while those with more always, *always* got what they wanted.

Stretch's head felt like it was going to burst as he tried to work out what they were going to do...because there was no way the three of them were going to be able to handle all this on their own, that much was obvious even before they started looking at exactly what they'd discovered. Truth was, they were going to need help and protection, but from whom would they get it? His own allegiances lay with the Vix, which meant that he would have to deal with The Peeler and his Twelve Angry Men – people definitely not known for their reasonable behaviour. But Reeba was Cuven and Ty was a Saynt, and would they be prepared to let a man like The Peeler take over and run things? He did not think so. *He* didn't trust The Peeler, so why on earth should they?

"D'you think it's safe to split up in here?"

"Split up?" Reeba's question brought Stretch back from musing about all the difficulties the future might have in store for them. "But there's only two lights."

"Actually..." Reeba dug into her satchel, rummaged round and brought out a third torch. "I've got another one. Just in case." She threw it over to Stretch who caught it and immediately began to power up.

"Why didn't you say before?"

"Always good to have a spare, you never know when you might need it. So, what d'you two think about splitting up? We can cover more ground that way, and just keep shouting out to each other, so we know where we are."

"If we find stuff, good stuff, we should bring it back here, right?" Ty pointed his light over to the door they'd come in by. He looked back at the room, shining a beam over their awesome discovery. "This is going to take a *lot* more than just one trip..."

"A lot more." Reeba walked over to a large darkwood box on the floor, kneeling down to examine it more closely; from where he was standing, Stretch could see that it had an elongated doglike creature carved on the side, like it was guarding whatever was inside. He could also see that the box was covered in colourful, highly stylized images and drawings. With her fingers Reeba traced an image of a man in a strange, tall headdress sitting on a throne. "I've seen pictures like this before, I'm sure of it..."

Stretch walked over and stroked the head of the dog. "Where?"

"In a book, part of a set that Pete's got...I think it was called *Edwa to Extract,* but I've no idea why."

"What was it about?"

"Wasn't really *about* anything, just a book full of different facts."

Ty stopped fiddling with the door of a nearby cabinet. "Can you two stop wasting time, we've work to do!" There was a sharp crack, followed by the almost musical sound of glass shattering as Ty's attempts to get into one of the cabinets finally paid off, although not quite as he'd planned. "I'll, um...I'll start going through this then..."

Reeba stood up. "I'll see if I can find out what's in this." She patted the box. "Without breaking it."

"I meant to do that."

"Oh sure..."

"C'mon, Bone..." Stretch left the two of them to carry on

provoking each other and went to have a look at what was in the smaller rooms off to the side. He hadn't gone very far when he found himself looking up at a large, imposing statue, beautifully carved out of a light-coloured stone; it looked like a bird. It's sleek body rose up six, seven feet from the plinth it was standing on, its majestic face staring down the vast room. Stretch followed the bird's gaze with the torch beam and found himself looking at another statue ten or so feet away; this one was of a bare-chested man, taller than the bird and sculpted from a highly polished black stone. The man was standing with both arms outstretched, palms upwards, and he had the head of a bird. A hawk? No, Stretch thought, it was more like a falcon.

He moved the light from one statue to the other, then noticed the huge slab of stone between them. It was as tall as he was and almost filled the space between the two statues; the flat surface was covered in more images like the ones on Reeba's box, only these weren't painted, but carved into the stone in columns. One image, roughly in the centre, was much larger than the rest. It showed the falcon-headed man in a similar pose to the black stone statue, but this time wearing some kind of ornate headdress.

This strange being was surrounded by a lot of much smaller figures of men and women, all reaching out to touch him, all looking up at him in awe and wonder. Exactly the same way people prayed and muttered and *begged* the statues of Lozzi, the ones of the sun god, Big Yelo, and all the many other idols and talismans you could choose from, to make dreams come true.

Which was when it slowly dawned on Stretch that *this* must be a god.

He had found a god!

His father always said that sometimes, not often, the right thing happened at the right time. And when it did, he'd said, you had to grab the opportunity because you had no idea when it was going to happen again. Or if it ever was.

Gods were all-powerful. They were creators and destroyers; they knew everything there was to know because they had made everything. Gods could watch over you or turn a blind eye to your pain and suffering; they could ignore your pleading or they could grant any wish they wanted. And all Stretch wanted was to know how to get his father back. He'd give everything, his whole share of whatever they managed to get out of this place to do it. *Everything.*

He looked up at the statue of the falcon-god and knew that like the people in the picture on the stone, he wanted to touch him, too. He knew he had nothing of great value to offer, no candle to light, no food to leave...although he realized he did have the money he'd got from Mo. He could give that, it was all he had and the best he could do.

Stretch hoisted himself up onto the plinth the statue was standing on, crouching as he emptied his pockets of all the coins he had, piling them in front of the falcon-god. Leaving the light by his feet he stood on tiptoes and reached up to touch his palms on the statue's cold, bare chest. "It's everything I've got, strike me down if it isn't..." He closed his eyes. "Help me...please?"

Below him he could hear Bone whining, and then a weird, charged shiver seemed to jump from the statue into Stretch's hands; in a split second it ran down his arms and across his shoulders, making his hair stand on end. And then he was aware of his head clearing of everything in it, the way it could feel if you ever took a breath of camphor oil. In his head a deep sigh echoed around his consciousness and a sense of relief flooded though him. In the eerie vacuum of silence a voice spoke a single word. It said, *"Brother..."*

Stretch jumped back, his eyes snapping open. A voice... he'd heard a *voice*! But it wasn't Ty's and it certainly wasn't Reeba's. He shone the torch around, aware that Bone had stopped whimpering, but there was no one there. And that voice had come from so near that it seemed to have been spoken *in* his head. Which was impossible. Only mad people heard things, and he wasn't mad...at least he didn't think so, although maybe this was the first sign.

He looked up at the great hooked beak and the glittering eyes. If there was no one else here, could it be the statue, the falcon-god who had spoken to him? But why would a *god* call him brother?

"Was that you?" he whispered, reaching out and touching the black stone again. "Who are you?"

"I am Horus, the distant one; god of the sky..."

13 OLD WOUNDS

Fear is a strange and often uncontrollable thing.

Mr. Nero had felt its ice-cold needles puncture his fragile ego before, more times than he cared to remember throughout a childhood spent living with vandal hooligans for brothers. But this black terror and ancient dread that – from one minute to the next – seemed to have replaced the very blood in his veins was like nothing he'd ever experienced.

The small, almost insignificant part of him that remained aware but not in control as he was consumed by the Lord Setekh's abject panic, understood that whatever his Master had been terrified might happen, had actually occurred.

It had, according to Ms. Webb, happened somewhere across the Isis in the fetid rat-runs of the parishes and territories. But, as he fell to the floor, shaking as his muscles jerked and twitched uncontrollably, Mr. Nero still had no idea what the event was.

Eyes wide open, head flicking from left to right, left to right like a crazed metronome, he could see that the two canix, assuming he'd somehow been attacked, had adopted an attack/guard position and were warily circling him. Mr. Nero knew he was screaming, although for some reason, he couldn't hear the noise. He knew he was screaming one word, louder and louder, again and again: *"No-no-no-NO-OOOOOOOO!"* He also knew that any moment now his major-domo would come bursting through the doors of the antechamber, but whether the canix would let the man get anywhere near him was another matter altogether.

And then as suddenly as he'd been invaded by Lord Setekh's fear, he felt his Master's seething anger flood through him, swamping the panic and regaining control. By the time the four guards wrenched open the doors and ran in, swords drawn, followed by the major-domo, Mr. Nero was standing behind a wide slate-topped desk, one canix seated to his left, the other to his right. As if nothing had occurred.

"UnderMaster?" The major-domo looked both worried and perplexed. "There was...that is, we thought we heard..."

"It was...nothing." Mr. Nero was only just managing to appear calm. "Send word that I would like to see the Board. Now."

The House of Nero's senior steward crossed his arms over his chest and bowed. "At once, UnderMaster."

"I will be in the temple's sanctum."

The major-domo left the room and Mr. Nero stood for a moment, feeling his heartbeat slowly fall back to something approaching normality. He'd been woken before dawn by his Master's turmoil, the growing anxiety and the manic demands fighting for space in his head. Unable to sleep and not knowing what else to do, he'd made his way over to the temple buildings, to this room where the Lord Setekh's iron will had so completely crumbled. Whatever had happened over the river it wasn't good, and he had to find out what it was.

Mr. Nero came out from behind the desk and, closely followed by the now spooked and very wary canix, he parted the heavy curtains and went down the passage which led to his own private entrance to the temple. This was the first building that Lord Setekh had ordered constructed when they'd crossed the Isis all those years ago, and it was, he supposed, the heart of Kaï-ro. Built on a hill, it was the place they'd made for the statue, symbolically placing the stone embodiment of the Master to give him the best possible view of the progress of the three great structures he had demanded.

The Master had been uncharacteristically quiet for some minutes now and Mr. Nero thought that maybe this was the moment when he might be allowed to ask a question, instead of simply receiving demands. And he knew he'd feel happier doing that looking Lord Setekh in the face, rather than talking to himself.

He entered the vast interior of the open-roofed temple; it was a magnificent and at the same time humbling sight, the serried ranks of brightly coloured stone columns leading the eye out of the building to the view of the flatlands where, even at this early hour, he knew whips were cracking and men sweated, strained and died at their tasks.

Mr. Nero walked over to stand in front of the statue he'd found buried so deep beneath the ground, waiting for the light of a new day. Waiting for a believer. Every time he looked at it he thought about how different his life would have been had he not made the discovery. He would still be the nondescript, ignored, unloved Nero Thompson. A Nero Thompson who was completely unlike the powerful, feared – yet still unloved – man he'd become.

Hands clasped in front of him, he let his gaze travel slowly up the statue until he was looking straight at the Master's alien face. "You have to tell me," he said, almost in a whisper. "I can do *nothing* unless you tell me what has happened."

A dry, throaty intake of breath reverberated in his head, but Setekh didn't speak straight away. Mr. Nero waited, unsure of what to do next; could you ask a god to hurry up and say something? He thought probably not. So he waited some more. All in good time. He would be told – *if* he was to be told anything – all in good time...

"He breathes again."

Mr. Nero, who'd almost given up hope of getting a reply, took a surprised step back. "Who, Master? Who breathes again?" This time Mr. Nero could feel the palpable anger in the Master's slow exhalation; not a sigh, but a barely contained roar of hate.

"My brother!"

"Your bro—"

"Horus is alive again – here! Now! He will *know* what I

am doing...he will try to *destroy* what I am doing, as he has always destroyed what I have tried to do! All those many eons ago..."

"But how—"

"He should not be here! How did he *get* here? This is *my* place, *my* time – *MINE!*"

"Where—"

"He must be stopped, he must *not* be allowed to do this again!"

"Master! Master, I cannot help you if you don't tell me what you know...tell me what has happened and where I can find your brother so I can kill him."

"*Kill* him? Gods do not *die!* EVER!"

"But—"

"You must wipe out the *belief,* tear out the roots before they have time to become strong and spread. *That* is what you must do...now, *immediately!*"

The Board had gathered and were sitting in their allotted places around the table, all except Mr. Nero, who paced the room continually, watched by Messrs. Carne, Cleave and Webb, but ignored by the two canix. Unblinking, they watched everyone and everything else.

"His *brother*?" Everil Carne sat bolt upright, his eyes following Mr. Nero.

Darcus Cleave stopped pushing back the quick from his nails.

"That is what he said, Mr. Carne."

"The distant one has come closer than we'd like..." Phaedra Webb's right hand appeared, an almost luminous white against the folds of the night-black silk in which she was wrapped; in it was a large sphere of translucent crystal which she placed in front of her.

"There are enough riddles to deal with already." Mr. Cleave looked tellingly over his glasses at Mr. Nero. "Speak in the language of actions and reality, if you would, Ms. Webb, rather than that of dreams and imagination."

Mr. Nero stopped in mid-stride, glaring at the UnderTaker. "This is no *dream*, no flight of imagination on the part of Ms. Webb! Over there," Mr. Nero pointed dramatically behind him, "someone has – by chance or by design, we have no way of knowing – resurrected Horus, the god of the sky! Horus, the brother of the divinity whom we know and revere as Setekh. Horus, who is our Master's eternal and immortal *enemy*."

Mr. Carne glanced at Mr. Cleave, whose attention was focused on the crystal ball in front of Ms. Webb, around which her long, white fingers wove an elaborate pattern of blue light. The ball was glowing. The soft, pulsing light made the Oracle's pale, mask-like face look even more ashen.

Mr. Nero walked over to stand beside her. "What do you see?"

"The wings of hope."

No one spoke, all three men wondering what she could possibly mean. Across the Isis all anyone could hope for was a life less terrible than it might be, a death more kindly than experience promised. Mr. Nero was jolted out of his silence by the flash of an image in his mind's eye...a bird of prey, swooping out of the sky and then disappearing.

"Horus..." he whispered. "The god of the sunrise and the sky."

"You see him?" asked Ms. Webb, her hands fluttering over the ball.

Mr. Nero nodded. "I think I did...what else is there?"

"It's faint...I feel there are three human entities and a beast; four spirits, but only one believer. So far."

"Where are they?"

"Nearby..."

Mr. Carne looked up from the crystal ball. "How near? If we are to find them in that rat-infested maze I need more."

"Under a mountain..." Ms. Webb's voice had a slightly dreamy quality to it. "They are under a mountain."

Mr. Cleave snorted. "Ridiculous! There are no mountains across the water, just the hills to the north...I don't know why you're wasting time listening to this when we should be sending Dark Souldiers over there to find these four malcontents before they can start anything."

"You live in a world of certainties, Darcus." Mr. Nero continued staring at the pulsating crystal ball as he spoke. "You are a scientist for whom reality is only what you can see, and who believes only in what you can touch. You believe in the flame and the sword, in pain, fear and enslavement, and they are *all* a part of Setekh's creed and faith – extremely important parts – but there is more, Darcus, so very much more. To be able to *crush* a spirit there first has to *be* a spirit. And that is Ms. Webb's business. Mock it at your peril."

Mr. Cleave blushed at the dressing-down. "UnderMaster...I..."

"This is as a spark to tinder." Ms. Webb peered closer at whatever it was she could see in the swirling shapes, then sat bolt upright. "And if the fire catches, it could well become the light to our darkness."

Mr. Nero threw his head back. Mouth open as if he'd been stabbed with a knife, all you could see of his eyes were the bloodshot whites.

"THAT *CANNOT* BE ALLOWED TO HAPPEN!"

The canix's hackles rose and they both started snarling, daring anyone in the room to move even an inch. They watched as the tension slowly bled out of Mr. Nero and he staggered round the table, slumping into his chair, shaking his head. He took a deep breath. "If, as Ms. Webb has said, the fire catches and word were to get over here into Kaï-ro who knows how that could affect the Completion."

Mr. Cleave got up, the thought occurring to him that all this might be a slight overreaction to the possibility of a god with a solitary believer. As he turned to go, he saw Mr. Nero stand up, teeth bared, eyes slitted.

"It only takes a *single* match to start an inferno, Darcus Cleave." A deep, unearthly breath rattled in Mr. Nero's throat. **"Never forget that..."**

Mr. Cleave felt as if someone had just looked inside his head. He left the room, trying to empty his mind and think of nothing, absolutely nothing at all.

Sitting down again, Mr. Nero turned to his OverSeer General, the oldest and most trusted of his associates, as if nothing had happened. "Mr. Carne, the Dark Soul Army must be on the very highest alert, but for now the main priority is information and I don't care how you get it; send spies out with orders not to return empty-handed."

14 FANNING THE FLAMES

Something had changed, Stretch could feel it, but didn't know what it meant or how to express it. The atmosphere in the room was charged, the same way it was when the huge black thunderhead clouds filled the summer sky and dropped crazed bolts of lightning at the ground.

Maybe, he thought, that's what happened when a god spoke to you.

Horus, he'd called himself; Horus, god of the sky. And if he'd spoken once, did that mean he'd do it again? Stretch put his hands back on the statue. "My name's Stretch, Stretch Wilson..." No reply. "Are you a powerful god, more powerful than Lozzi...do you *know* everything?"

"My brother *must* be stopped!"

Stretch blinked. The voice...the god, he reminded himself...wasn't calling *him* his brother, but talking about his own. Stretch blinked again; he didn't know gods could have brothers.

"His evil walks this place again, I can feel it!"

The voice in his head sounded angry and worried at the same time and Stretch wished there was something he could do to help, then thought how unlikely that was, him being just a boy. What could he do about an evil brother?

"It is not the years that matter, but the will to *do*...the desire to bring about change can be as strong in a child as it is in a man, believe me."

Believe him.

At that moment, standing in front of the most imposing sight he'd ever seen, if there was one thing Stretch realized he wanted and needed it was something to believe in. It could be anything, really, but it would be especially good to believe that someone could help him get his father back. His skin itched, his scalp crawled and every muscle in his body shivered; below him he could hear Bone whimpering as he hid in the dark. Stretch stared up at the face of this granite deity and as the light from his torch finally gave out he was astonished to see a weird, unearthly glow arcing like a miniature firework display around his hands where they touched the statue.

"I believe, I do believe..." he said. Then a jolt hit him and he fell backwards into the darkness.

* * *

It had taken Reeba an inordinate amount of time, and no little effort, but she'd eventually been able to prise the lid off the highly decorated wooden box without breaking anything. Inside, her light revealed that it was divided up into sections, each one packed full of objects wrapped in ancient, yellowed cloth that was so brittle it fell apart when she started to unwrap it. The first thing she took from the box turned out to be a solid gold knife, inlaid with other metals and many different coloured stones. It was breathtakingly beautiful, by far the most exquisite thing she had ever seen, and Reeba was sure it was worth more than she could possibly imagine.

Not much later she had a dozen or more artefacts laid out on the ground – mirrors, jewellery, and some objects that defied description. All, from their weight, were solid gold and many were studded with gemstones. She stood up and pinched herself, hard. She didn't wake up and she was still in the depths of Bloom's Mount, looking at what she knew Bible Pete would call a king's ransom. A stray thought flitted past that she really *must* ask him what that was.

Reeba wound the light up some more and played the beam around the room. Arrayed on the floor by her feet there had to be enough gold and precious stones to buy the whole city of Dinium and still have wealth to spare, and she'd only opened one box. She picked up a small gold and lapis brooch in the shape of a falcon's head; everywhere she looked there were boxes, chests and cabinets beyond counting...it was going to take *years* to get everything out of this place. Years and years.

She was just about to go over and discuss this fact with an unusually quiet Tyson Love when something weird happened. The air seemed to crackle, sending tiny pinpricks racing all over her skin; then, beyond the reach of her torch, there was a glow over to her right like she'd heard you could sometimes see out in the marches. The crones said it was the ghosts of those still waiting to cross over, the spirits of dead people who were trapped on the border between life and death. "Ty?" she called out, her voice very small. "Ty, did...did you see that?"

"See what?"

"Something happened – where's Stretch?"

"He went off down the side." Ty shone his light over to the right of the room. "What did you see?"

Before Reeba could answer the whole place filled with a silent explosion of blue-white light and they heard the thud of something falling to the ground.

"Lozzi preserve us..." Ty whispered. "What was that?"

All around the room Reeba became aware of a quiet cacophony of tiny sounds – creaks, hisses, mutterings and groans – like something had been disturbed, woken up from a long, long sleep by what had happened.

Whatever it was that had happened.

There was no doubt in her mind that the "whatever it was" had something to do with Stretch. "Are you all right?" she yelled out, her voice shaky with fear and worry. "Stretch?"

There was no reply, just muffled mumblings as Ty prayed like he'd never, ever prayed before.

"Lozzi above, Lozzi below,
Spare me the pain,
The grief and the sorrow.
Lozzi above, Lozzi below,

Give me strength,
Let me know
That you are looking after me..."

"Will you stop that, Ty?" Reeba could feel the trickles of cold sweat running down her back and knew that what she wanted, what she *needed*, wasn't prayers to some roadside god but the company and assistance of someone bigger and stronger than she was to go with her and find out what had happened to Stretch. She put the brooch in her pocket and wound up her light.

"Lozzi above..."

Reeba strode over towards Ty, aware of the anger rising in her chest. "You can pray later." She grabbed his jacket with her free hand and shook him. *"After* we've found Stretch. Okay?"

Ty looked at her blankly, frowning like he was seeing her for the first time, and then his face cleared. "Yeah...okay... what was that noise?"

"I dunno, that's what we've got to find out." Reeba shone her light in the direction of where she'd seen the weird blue glow.

Feeling like she was walking towards the fabled boundary line between Life and Death that the crones talked about, Reeba's courage and anger evaporated as the darkness pressed in all around her. One foot moved slowly, begrudgingly, in front of the other as she held the light with both hands, ready to wind it up the moment the beam appeared to fade; she was not going to let it go out, even with Ty behind her.

The narrow corridor of space between the wall to her right and the unopened crates, statues and chests on her left was covered in the dust of centuries, and in the dust she could see Stretch's footprints and Bone's tracks. Then the beam of her light found a hand. Reeba stopped, Ty almost bumping into her, and she jerkily played the light over Stretch, lying on his front, one arm flung back above his head, one leg folded under the other.

"Take my light." She thrust the torch behind her, not caring if Ty grabbed it or not, and ran to the prone figure lying in the dust. As she moved she was aware of a low, plaintive whimpering, but she didn't even bother to look for Bone. Kneeling, Reeba turned Stretch onto his back and brushed dust and hair off his face. "Stretch?"

"Is he breathing?"

"I, um..."

Ty handed both lights to Reeba. "Let me take a look."

"What d'you know?"

Ty leaned over Stretch, checking his eyes, his chest. "My fighters..." He searched for a pulse. "Gotta know which one's gonna make it and who's not worth a doctor's dollar 'cos he's never getting up again, right?"

"Is he...?"

"He's worth the money...must've knocked himself out somehow." Ty stood up, gesturing for Reeba to give him back his light, which he then shone round, searching for clues as to what could've happened to Stretch. He stopped when he found Bone, still wedged in his hiding place between the legs of a black stone jackal. "Hey boy, lookit you...what's up?"

Reeba glanced away from Stretch. "You found the dog?"

"Yeah, and take a look, he's pretty freaked."

As Reeba stood she heard a slow intake of breath, as if

something powerful and formidable had just woken up. She looked back at Stretch and saw his eyelids fluttering and his scrawny body twitch; she bent down and helped him sit up as he hacked and wiped his face. "What happened to you?"

Stretch's head dropped as if he hadn't the strength to keep it upright, and he coughed again. "I saw...no...no I didn't...I *talked* to..." He half raised his head and pointed past Reeba. "I talked to a god, Reeba..."

"Yeah, okay." She looked over her shoulder, just in case there was a god standing behind her that she hadn't noticed; all she could make out was a looming statue which looked like it might have a bird's head. Maybe that's what had scared Stretch. "But how'd you end up looking like you'd been thrown on the ground?"

Before Stretch had a chance to answer there was a yelp, a scrabble of clawed feet on stone and a flash of fur as Bone leaped past Ty and onto his master's lap, licking his face.

"What happened?" Ty asked.

Stretch, still being fussed over by Bone, picked himself up and pointed behind Ty and Reeba. "I found a god. He spoke to me."

Ty shone his light at Stretch's face. "I could've been wrong about him being okay..."

"We have to help him." Stretch pointed at the statue on the plinth. "We must."

"Who?" Reeba asked, watching as Stretch straightened his back and opened his arms wide, thinking that he seemed to have *grown* somehow. "Who must we help?"

Stretch remained standing, arms extended, staring ahead, not at either of his friends but almost *through* them; his eyelids drooped and then snapped back open, his pupils blazing in the light of the two beams shining on him. Except now Ty and Reeba were very aware that somehow it wasn't Stretch staring back at them any more; someone else was looking out of his eyes, appraising them and possibly deciding on their future. And beside Stretch's statue-like figure sat Bone, equally still, ears pricked, eyes coal-black but shining.

Even the orchestra of strange little noises had stopped playing in the background as the air became heavy with suspense. It occurred to Reeba that *this* was exactly when you wanted someone to pray for you, but wasn't surprised that Ty couldn't open his mouth to do it.

"I am Horus, god of the sky, and believe me when I tell you that the eons have not dimmed my powers one iota. As I slept, human empires may have risen and fallen, like weeds in the heat of the sun, but I have remained untouchable and divine. Believe me when I tell you this, because it is true."

The voice was commanding. Not unkind, but the sort of voice which you knew expected to be obeyed. Not Stretch's voice at all. Reeba wanted to answer, except she could think of nothing to say, and fear gripped her so tight she couldn't even scream.

"There is a battle that is still to be finished...there is an evil here that must be defeated... I have a brother whom I must deal with...HE MUST BE STOPPED!"

15 THE FIRE SPREADS...

The lights kept on going out. Both Ty and Reeba, sitting and listening to Stretch, had other things on their minds than winding up their torches. Big things, like did they *really* believe that Stretch had found a god and that this god was talking through him? Ty, who was a fervent disciple of Lozzi, had never seen his local street priests – and not even the Grand High Padre – speak with another voice as they'd witnessed Stretch do.

And there was no doubt about the fact that their friend was now a very different person. He *looked* exactly the same, but there was something about him that had changed.

Somehow being with Stretch made even the dark feel less

scary, as if whatever might be out there waiting would be scared of him. Pacing up and down the narrow corridor, every so often reaching out to touch the falcon-headed statue to reassure himself it was still there, still within reach, he kept talking about how they had to help this god who said he was called Horus.

"But what can *we* do?" Reeba asked, finally managing to jump in with a question. "There's just three of us and from what you...he, whoever it is you're talking to...from what *that person* says, his brother is the god they say Mr. Nero built Kaï-ro for."

"That's what Horus said." Stretch nodded, a distracted look on his face. "I'm *really* hungry, is there any food?"

Reeba got up. "I still have some dates left – but look, what can the three of us actually do? *They* have the Dark Soul Army, *they* have weapons, they have *everything* we don't have!"

"They have magic, too." Ty stood up, shaking his head. "The ones that come here, the ones that took your father? They call them souldiers, and you can't kill them, Stretch."

"Yeah, they have *souldiers*, Stretch...what do *we* have?"

Stretch stood in the soft glow of the fading light, once again just a boy lost in thought, a boy on his own who for a moment imagined he could do something. Then he changed. In the blink of an eye the boy became...different, more than he had been.

He lifted his head, his keen, penetrating gaze piercing the blackness; his head moved left, then right as he appeared to be listening, searching the room for an answer. Focused on something only he could see, he strode off past Ty and, with Bone at his heels, went down the corridor. "**You have something enduring and undying...**" he said in a voice that wasn't his own. "**You have hope...**"

Reeba moved closer to Ty. "What's that mean?"

Ty shrugged. "How should *I* know?"

The two of them followed Stretch with their lights, saw him stop in his tracks, turn and disappear into one of the rooms off the great circular hall. It seemed like an age later that he reappeared, cradling something apparently quite heavy in his arms.

"What's he got?"

"How should I know, Reeba?"

"We have to take this with us." Stretch grunted at the effort it took to hold up a two-foot-high stone effigy, inlaid with basalt and gold; it was an almost exact copy of the massive falcon-headed statue he was standing next to. "Whatever happens, I *need* this...it has to come with me."

There was no arguing with Stretch. Even though it was going to mean leaving behind a lot of priceless things, with no way of knowing when or if they'd ever be able to come back to find them, his main priority – his *only* priority – was getting the statue back to the surface. Without it, he absolutely insisted, nothing could be achieved. With it, he promised, they could change everything.

Ty, who'd only come along because of the promise of gold, was appalled at the thought of not taking everything they could carry that could then be melted down and sold on. And a great lump of stone, even though he had to admit it was a very beautiful thing, definitely did not count.

"We'll come back and get it, on my word, Stretch – Lozzi's honour!"

"*No!*"

Reeba looked round, almost shocked by the severe, icy tone of Stretch's voice; she and Ty were packing up as much loot and booty as they thought they could drag up with them and she'd been ignoring Ty's insistent wheedling about the statue. Within herself she knew Stretch was right, that it was a powerful object and he had to take it; she could feel, for the first time in her life, a kind of excitement building inside her about what the future could hold, and she knew this feeling of hope had everything to do with whoever was talking through Stretch. Yesterday the future had been something she'd never thought was worth thinking about; today she was beginning to believe it might be. Quite why she really had no idea.

"Don't you understand, Ty?" Stretch asked.

"Understand what?"

"*We* need this connection," he pointed at the statue on the floor next to him.

"And *we*," Ty slammed a fist against his chest, "*we* need gold...this is our chance to leave the dust and the flies behind, eat good food, drink sweet water, have the best! No more fighting rats for food, no more fighting for anything... there's places, Stretch, you hear the traders with the caravanserai talking about places where you don't *have* to watch your back every minute of the day – that's what *I* believe in! Some carving's not gonna get you a life like that."

Stretch didn't reply, just rolled his shoulders, almost as if he was getting ready for a fight. Sitting next to him, Bone growled softly.

"Gold is merely metal, nothing more – *nothing more*! It has no spirit, no soul...all that it has is the value you give to it – *nothing more*! It is empty without your belief in its value; it cannot change *anything* without you. Together, we can make changes. Believe *me* when I tell you this, because it is true."

It was a shock whenever Stretch was taken over, although Reeba couldn't help thinking used was a better way of describing it. In the silence that followed this latest utterance she went over to Ty and touched his arm. "We have to take it," she said. "That voice, when he talks, doesn't it make you believe what it says?"

Ty didn't reply, but it was obvious from the tension in his body and the set of his face that he was battling with himself, one side wanting all the gold he could get his hands on, the other part knowing that Reeba and Stretch were right. Deep down Ty knew the voice, the god, was telling the truth and that he should listen. It was just that Ty had always hated being made to do what he was told...

Once the decision had been made it was as if the means to achieve the aim had always been there. While Ty and Reeba were finishing the job of packing as much as they could into the bags they'd brought with them, Stretch and Bone poked around a bit more. And found a ladder.

Pulling the door to the massive storeroom closed behind them, the three of them staggered back the way they'd come. Weighed down by gold, the statue of a god, and a ladder, the journey was a slow one with more than a few stops along the way.

It was during the rest they were taking before they attempted to drag their weary bodies up the final staircase that Bone began to act very agitated. Ears pricked, sniffing the air and whining, he ran to the top of the stairs and stood barking at them.

"What is it, boy?" Stretch called after him, frowning. "Can you hear something?"

"Probably just wants to be back outside again," Reeba said picking up her bag again. "Right boy?"

"Don't think so..."

Stretch looked up. "What is it, Ty?"

"Gas..." Ty's nostrils wrinkled. "Bone can smell *gas* – we've got to get out!"

"He's right." Reeba nodded, sniffing hard. "Come on..."

The thought that they might at any moment be suffocated in a noxious cloud, or blown sky-high by a flare-up, put steel back into their tired, exhausted muscles. Panic and fear made them strain even harder to get their individual loads up the stairs, at the same time pulling the ladder with them. As they drove themselves on, Bone ran up and down the steps, yipping small, worried barks of encouragement.

Ty reached the top first; dropping his bag he reached out to pull Reeba up the last few steps, then turned to take the weight of the ladder off Stretch. As he did, his sweaty hands momentarily lost their grip and he dropped it, the steel-shod end hitting one of the steps, dislodging an already broken piece of stone and sending it clattering down the stairwell.

Stone hit stone.

The noise echoed, eerily.

Sparks flashed and flew.

Ancient gas caught them.

Making a new flame.

It all happened so fast that there was nothing any of them could do. Like butterflies in a storm, they were each thrown away by the careless strength of the explosion. The staircase contained the heat and the power of the blast, sending a roiling column of fire surging upwards, the blast flinging everything out of its way. Including a boy carrying a heavy stone statue.

Stretch, punched almost senseless by the explosion, closed his eyes and clung onto his precious cargo. He didn't see Ty leaping out of the way, grabbing Bone as he fell. He didn't know that he missed Reeba by mere inches as he shot past her. He had no idea it was the stone image of Horus that saved his life, making him drop like a lead weight, out of the way of the ferocious column of flame that shot out of the stairwell and blew a massive hole in the side of Bloom's Mount.

Stretch didn't know any of this because it all happened so fast.

The roar of the explosion was deafening, the heat of the flame like a dozen blacksmiths' fires. And the silence that followed so complete it was as if the world had come to an end. Or that they'd all died. Maybe, Stretch thought as he half opened one eye, death was the most likely explanation. Except that he thought it was very unlikely that the afterlife would smell of rotten vegetables, burned hair and badly singed cloth. And would it feel like every bone in your body still hurt when you died?

"Oh...my...god..." Stretch groaned as he rolled slowly

onto his back, still clutching the carved stone statue of the man with the head of a falcon.

"**Whatever tries to kill you, yet fails, only serves to make you stronger...**"

16 ...AND THE WORD GETS OUT

Samson Towd was fast asleep and dead to the world, curled up like a large, bedraggled dormouse in the scant shade cast by what had, possibly, once been the side of a plywood packing case. He was able to do this, and not worry about missing the three urchins and their dog, because he had paid another urchin an entire dollar to be his eyes and ears. Or rather, he'd torn a dollar in two and told the child she'd get the other half when the job was finished. Never trust anyone, especially a hungry child, further than you could throw them. It was a motto well worth sticking to in this city.

And so, clutching her torn piece of greasy, ragged paper, the girl sat and watched and waited and spent her time thinking about what she'd do with her money. She had thought about trying to steal the half the man had kept, but came to the conclusion the risk wasn't worth taking; better to do the job, which was just sitting around staring into the middle distance, something she'd probably have been doing anyway.

Towd was shaken from his deep, dreamless sleep by the ear-splitting, ground-shaking roar of an explosion so big and so loud that he awoke convinced the underworld must have opened its gates. Towd sat bolt upright, cracking his head on the splintery sheet of buckled plywood above him, to see his wide-eyed lookout staring up at a massive ball of flame as it rolled across the sky through a blizzard of debris. He followed the smoke trail back to where the fireball must have come from, and saw a gigantic blackened hole on the side of the heap. It was right where he'd seen the girl and her two friends disappear into Bloom's Mount.

His finger automatically moving in the sacred half-circle across his chest – *east-west-arc-of-the-sun* – Towd muttered a swift prayer of thanks to the Big Yelo up above as he waited for the rain of burned chaff to stop falling, and then he scrambled to his feet. Followed by the girl, who was far more worried about the man not paying her than she was about the possibility that the heap might erupt again, he made his way very cautiously up towards the smoking crater.

"You think them people might be dead, mister?"

Towd glanced at the girl, wondering for a moment why she was still there. "Crispy...definitely crispy..." he muttered, moving slightly closer to the hole, testing the ground with every step, trying to work out whether you'd be able to hear if another explosion was going to happen.

"I did me job, mister." The girl poked Towd's arm.

"What?"

The girl held out a grubby hand. "I said, I did me job."

Towd looked at her, then at the smoking maw the ball of flame had created. "What's your name?"

"Jazmin."

Towd nodded to himself, scratching his stubbled chin. Anything less like a beautifully perfumed little white flower he'd yet to see. "All right, Jazmin...you go and take a look inside," he jerked a thumb at the hole, "*then* I'll pay you."

Jazmin scowled. This wasn't fair as it wasn't a part of the deal they'd made, but she knew he wanted her to go because he was scared there might be another big bang. And she also knew, because she'd practically grown up on these slopes, that this was extremely unlikely to happen after such a massive blast. She turned the scowl into a very doubtful face, shrugged and shook her head. "Dollar fifty for that, mister. In me hand."

Towd looked at Jazmin's outstretched palm. The thought that the girl might be scamming him crossed his mind, but his survival instinct was stronger and he ignored the probability. Dropping the other half of the dollar bill, plus a few coins, into her hand he waved at her to go up the slope and do as she'd been asked.

Quite how long he'd been lying on his back, still clutching the statue to him, Stretch had no idea. He now knew he wasn't dead, but whether the others had survived was another matter; he couldn't hear them – but that might well be because of the almighty ringing in his ears – and all he could see was what was straight in front of him as it hurt every time he moved his head. Even a little.

But he also knew that he couldn't stay where he was for ever. He had to shift. He had to get up so he could find out what had happened to Reeba and Ty, and then get out of the heap. He had a purpose now, a god whose bidding he had to obey, and although he – the voice in his head – had said that what didn't kill him would make him stronger, it didn't feel like any kind of truth as he rolled sideways and onto his knees.

Laying the statue down very carefully, amazed to see that it seemed to have survived the mad, fire-driven flight up and out of the stairwell completely unscathed, Stretch stood up a little shakily and looked round to find that a chunk of the heap had been blown away and he was now standing in a large crater. No need for the ladder, even if he could still find it in one piece.

"Ree..." Stretch coughed and tried to swallow, his tongue feeling like a piece of old leather, his throat dry and dusty. "Reeba? Ty?"

There was an answering cough and a small, pathetic whimper, but he couldn't work out where from. And then he saw a movement and Bone appeared out of the soot-blackened trash. Soot-blackened trash that carried on moving and turned into Ty. Bone shook himself, grey dust billowing out into the air, and made his way over to where Stretch was standing.

Kneeling down, Stretch smoothed Bone's fur down and patted his head. "Hey, boy, you made it!" He glanced around, eyes searching for any sign of Reeba, a small black knot of fear growing in his stomach. "Where's Reeba, Ty?"

Ty coughed as he brushed dust and assorted rubbish off himself. "No idea..."

"Bone...where's Reeba?" The dog pricked his ears, listening. "Can you find her, boy?"

"Gods talk to you..." Ty hacked, spat and wiped his mouth, "...and you, *you* talk to dogs."

"Find her, boy...find her!" Stretch ignored Ty and watched as Bone padded away, searched here, sniffed there and then stopped still for a long moment. With an excited yip, he then began digging at the junk on the ground with his front paws. Stretch leaped up and ran over to join him, frantically pulling at stuff and throwing it behind him. "Quick, Ty, help me!"

And then there was a hand. Reeba's hand, it couldn't be anyone else's, pale and lifeless under the dirt.

The two boys and the dog all redoubled their efforts, Stretch wondering whether there was any point in asking, pleading with Horus, the god of the sunrise and the sky, for the life of his friend, because he did not want Reeba to be dead. She had only come to this place because of him. It would all be his fault, something he'd have to live with for the rest of his life.

He was muttering *"don't-die-don't-die-don't-die"* under his breath when Ty uncovered Reeba's face and only then, because he couldn't see her clearly, did he realize there were tears streaming down his face.

"She's alive!" Ty yelled, grabbing her shoulders and pulling her up. "Lozzi be praised! He was certainly looking after *us* today...first thing I'm gonna do is get to a shrine and give 'em a piece of gold...*big* piece...light some candles and stuff."

"Reeba? You okay?" Stretch wiped his face with the back of his hand, waiting to hear the voice that would tell him an upstart street god like Lozzi didn't have anything to do with their survival, but the god of the sunrise and the sky remained silent.

Reeba looked blankly at the two boys, completely dazed, absent-mindedly patting Bone as he licked her cheek. "Feel like I've been kicked by a donkey." She accepted the outstretched hands and let Ty and Stretch pull her up. "Actually, a couple of donkeys...what happened?"

"We were incredibly lucky." Stretch gave Reeba a hug. "Even the statue didn't break."

"But what about the...?" Reeba's face fell.

"*Gold!*" Ty spun round and dashed back to the place that he'd crawled out of and began digging into the rubbish.

"Come on, Stretch," Reeba kneeled down and started searching where she'd fallen, "gimme a hand, we've got to find it!"

Without waiting to be asked, Bone started digging as well. But as Stretch was hurriedly clearing away unrecognizable pieces of burned and melted plastic and metal, in the corner of his eye he saw a shadow move. He looked up and saw the silhouette of a small child, the sun now higher and right behind her. She was standing at the ripped and jagged edge of the new hole, arms crossed, head on one side, observing them.

"You int crispy then, like he said you'd be." She sounded almost disappointed.

Stretch got up. "Like who said?"

The girl glanced over her shoulder. "The man what was waiting for you. I'll tell him."

"What man?" Stretch asked, but the girl had disappeared.

Reeba stopped what she was doing. "Who was that?"

"Dunno..." Stretch shrugged. "But she said there was someone out there, waiting for us..."

"Got it!"

Ignoring Ty's excited cries, Reeba stood up next to Stretch. "If he was waiting..."

"...he must've followed us here." Stretch bit his lip. "Get Ty to help you find your bag, I'm gonna have a look, see if I know who it is."

Ducking low, Stretch crept up to the lip of the gaping hole and lay down flat; inching forward he finally raised his head up, scanning left then right to see what was happening. Apart from the little girl, who was thirty or so yards away now, there was no one to be seen; the scavs had yet to arrive from other parts of the heap to see what the eruption might have uncovered and the man the girl had said had been waiting was nowhere to be seen.

"Anything?" Reeba called out.

Stretch slid back down, and saw that Reeba's bag had been found. "No, but I think we should get moving right now...pretty soon there's gonna be more scavs here than flies round a camel."

"Where're we gonna go with this stuff?" Reeba tapped her bag with her foot. "D'you think we should stash it at Bible Pete's?"

Stretch picked up his statue and shook his head. "I think we should go to Cheapside Mo's, it's the safest place there is."

"It'll be safe, once we get there." Ty shouldered his bag. "But it's a long way from here."

"Got any better suggestions?"

"Not really."

"Let's go then..."

It was hard to act normally, as if the staggeringly heavy bag you were carrying wasn't actually filled to the brim with jewel-encrusted gold things, but Ty and Reeba tried their best. Stretch had found a piece of tattered and faded tarpaulin to wrap the statue in, and looked like he was cradling a very badly swaddled baby. The three of them made a very odd sight.

"How come you never died in there?" Jazmin asked as they made their way past her.

"We had Lozzi looking over us," replied Ty.

Stretch stopped for a moment, Bone sitting down next to him. "The man who was waiting, where's he gone?"

Jazmin held out her hand, rubbing her thumb and forefinger together. Stretch put his precious cargo down and dug around in one of the pockets he'd stuffed with as many small trinkets as he could before they'd left the buried storeroom, coming out with a tiny, gold earring. He dangled it in front of him and Jazmin's eyes lit up.

She grabbed the bait, speedily moving back out of reach. "He's down there, watching."

They all looked to where Jazmin was pointing.

"Why don't you come with us, see if you can spot if he's still watching us? I'll give you the other one of these if you do..."

There was always a catch, Jazmin thought as she nodded and put the earring somewhere safe. Always a catch...

17 A STORM BREWS

At one point Everil Carne had thought they might have to tie Mr. Nero down. His convulsions had been so violent, his rage and anger – the rage and anger of the Master *inside* him, he had to keep reminding himself – was so powerful it looked as if he might physically tear himself apart. That hadn't happened but the man was a mess, covered in bruises and cuts. In the end Phaedra Webb had used all her arcane skills and somehow managed to calm him down enough so that they'd got him into a room where at least there were carpets on the floor, should he begin throwing himself around again.

It was clear something had happened across the river,

but Ms. Webb had been unable to pinpoint what or where, and as he left the temple Mr. Carne made a mental note of who he was going to send over the water to find out what was going on. It had to be something major, something cataclysmic for it to have this extraordinary effect on the Master; the wrath and fury were so intense, so close to utter panic and dread that it was hard to tell if Setekh was terrified or completely outraged.

Mr. Carne called for his horse and as he rode away he thought about what had been said, about there being a brother – what was his name? Horus? In the pantheon of gods he'd grown up with there were none with brothers; gods were gods, they had their powers and their functions in the minds and lives of those who believed in them. You always knew where you were with a god: how much to pay for what kind of service. And if the service was no good, you could always switch gods. There were an awful lot to choose from, something out there for everyone.

Or at least that was how it had always been, until the fateful day Nero Thompson had dug up the statue of Setekh. There and then everything had changed. This was a real god. You could feel the power, and while he himself had not actually heard him speak he knew and truly believed with all his heart and soul that Setekh spoke through Mr. Nero. He had seen the difference in him, turning overnight from the boy who paid labourers to dig holes for him into the man for whom an army of slaves was building the three structures commanded by the Master. Surely only a true god could bring about that profound a change.

Mr. Carne knew there was important information he was missing. He knew that Setekh was an ancient god, from somewhere far, far back in the Before Times, and if he knew more about him – where he'd come from, what were his origins and his place in the heavenly order of things – maybe if he knew that he'd be able to help. Maybe he could end the chaos that was enveloping Mr. Nero and could destroy all they'd worked so hard to create.

He slowed his horse to a fast canter to allow himself the time to think things through before he arrived at the Dark Soul Army barracks. There was someone he remembered hearing about, before he had crossed the river with Mr. Nero, who might be able to help him. But that would mean returning himself. Could he do that? Leave his command and go back across the Isis and into the streets of Dinium? If he wanted the information that could help stop the madness that was affecting the Master, and might even kill Mr. Nero, he had little choice but to go. He would have to go alone and incognito like the other men he was planning on sending over, and it would be dangerous, but he could see no alternative.

By the time he'd arrived at the barracks his mind was made up. He went straight to his command post and gave the orders to have certain individuals brought to him. They would be leaving as soon as possible to infiltrate the other side. He knew Darcus Cleave favoured a rather more direct approach and thought they should be sending a number of snatch squads to bring back people who could then have the information tortured out of them. Except how would he know where to send them and who to take? It would be like firing shots in the dark, and about as useful.

As it was, Mr. Carne didn't really know what he was going to tell his men. What *were* they looking for? All he had were tiny shards of information, none of which joined up to form a picture that made any kind of sense. What had Ms. Webb said? Wings of hope; a mountain; three people and "a beast". And one of these people believed in Horus, the god of sunrise and the sky, if he'd heard correctly what Mr. Nero had whispered. It wasn't much to go on. Truthfully it wasn't anything to go on, but it was all he had.

His men were going to have a hard time bringing back anything of value; he, on the other hand, might have slightly more chance...

Mr. Carne pulled hard on the paddle of the small trade boat that was making its way as fast as possible to the Dinium side of the Isis. The owner had been only too happy to use an extra oarsman, especially one prepared to pay to make the journey. Mr. Carne's story about missing his own boat had rung completely true as no one stayed in Kaï-ro for any longer than they had to: the stories about people delivering goods being kidnapped to work in the city and never seen again were absolutely true.

Stripped of his Dark Soul Army uniform and dressed in typical labourer's clothes, with a crimson Vix scarf wound round his neck, Mr. Carne knew he was indistinguishable from any of the hundreds of men scratching a living along the river's edge. Since the recent collapse of the one remaining tunnel under the Isis, boats were the only way across a river that was supposed to have once boasted a dozen or more bridges and as many if not more tunnels. Time, earth tremors and war had destroyed them all.

Upriver, as they approached the trader's small docking

stage, Mr. Carne saw the dark shapes of a handful of crocodiles slide off the banks and into the water. Anything up to twenty feet long, with a vicious temper and a bite that could snap a man in half, they were the reason no one ever tried to escape from Kaï-ro by swimming back to where they'd been taken from.

Six of his best men were already scouring the maze-like confusion of alleys and streets, markets, coffee shops and ramshackle houses that made up the extraordinary chaos that was life in Dinium, casting their nets as wide as possible for the smallest fragment of information; he at least had a target. Stepping out of the boat onto the sun-bleached wood of the jetty, Mr. Carne stopped and let a thought sink in as the realization hit him: it had been almost a decade since he'd set foot on this side. Ten years that had seen his world change out of all recognition.

Here, though, were the familiar sights and raucous sounds from the days before he'd met Nero Thompson. But when he looked closer he found the far more subtle echoes and shadows, the hidden features he only half remembered, clues and signs that this must have once been a magnificent city. Growing up he'd never really noticed or paid them much attention, but as he walked he saw, under the centuries of weathered paint, neglect and deterioration, memories of a long-gone grandeur and power.

Across the river, Kaï-ro had risen out of the desert like a phoenix, fresh and pristine and truly magnificent. All the things he could now imagine Dinium had once been, so far in the past. The new city across the river was the complete opposite of Dinium: ordered not chaotic, a clean place where everyone knew their place and everything worked. Looking around he found it hard to remember that he'd ever lived in this city.

Mr. Carne pushed the thoughts of the past away. They were distracting him from why he was there and what he had to do, which was find a man he'd never met and knew only by reputation. And he had to find him quickly, as he wanted to be back across the water before nightfall; if he wasn't down by the quays and wharfs, where all the feluccas and barges docked, well before the sun even began to set he wouldn't find anyone to take him over. No one sailed at night, too superstitious and terrified: scared both of the possibility of ghosts and the reality of being taken by the Dark Soul Army, especially The Risen.

Mr. Carne was a battle-hardened warrior, but even he had taken some time to get used to The Risen; they were Darcus Cleave's greatest achievement, more incredible and awe-inspiring by far than the canix. How Mr. Cleave did it Everil Carne did not want to know, but the Dark Soul Army was certainly very well named. Rumoured to use a combination of the most hellish, ancient sorcery and rediscovered alchemical skills – secret mysteries passed down from the Master – the UnderTaker and his acolytes in the Ministry were able to bring the dead back to a kind of life. These men were called The Risen, and creating them was one of the blackest of arts.

But blacker still was the knowledge that allowed the UnderTaker and his people to make new souldiers. They could somehow reanimate bodies, each one put back together from the limbs, organs and muscles of a dozen or more battlefield cadavers and victims of the torture cells. These butchered creations – men with piebald skin, mismatched faces and covered in a lunatic network of terrible scars – were the most deranged and unstable things to come out of the cold, white rooms deep under the Ministry. Mr. Cleave, in his self-satisfied way, referred to them as his collages; everyone else called them Mongrels.

The Risen, even the Mongrels, were certainly alive and sentient in their own strange way, but there was an impenetrable blankness about them, a vacant hatred in their cloudy eyes that made them far less than human. Strangers to fear, pain or compassion, they made cruel, merciless fighters and the Dark Soul Army had an increasing number of souldiers in its ranks who had been taken into the bowels of the Ministry as dead bodies, later walking out ready to fight again.

And if The Risen made Mr. Carne feel just a little uneasy, the ordinary fighting men disliked them so much that they had to be billeted in their own quarters. What the rank and file really hated was the knowledge that they themselves, should they die in battle, could be brought back as one of The Risen, or much worse as part of a Mongrel. But their reputation for mindless savagery was by now so widespread that their effect on opponents was extreme: even the bravest would rather run than fight a man brought back from the dead by evil magic.

Walking through streets crowded with humanity, for a moment Mr. Carne forgot about The Risen as he passed by a street trader selling bitter-sweet tea from a battered old metal urn that was kept hot by glowing coals, and saw a boy hawking freshly baked salty bread. He wanted to stop, like the old days, and have some. But he couldn't. He'd put himself on the shortest of leashes and he would not allow himself to deviate from the course he'd set.

Somewhere out there, in the teeming anthill of Dinium's run-down streets and alleys, he needed to find a man called Dexter Tannicus. If he was still alive and hadn't died or been killed in the last ten years, he was the only person Mr. Carne could think of who might be able to tell him who this god called Horus was. And why his discovery was having such a profound effect on the Master.

18 A GOLDEN OPPORTUNITY

If there was something that Samson Towd was particularly good at it was not being found. In his line of work there were plenty of times when having the ability to disappear was what made the difference between dying and seeing another sunrise.

Right now, he wasn't afraid someone was going to kill him. In fact, right now *he* was the person who actually wanted to kill someone. That Jazmin, that dirty little ill-bred guttersnipe...no sooner had the dog, the girl and her two friends finally come back out of the heap, bringing what looked like a *lot* of stuff with them, than there she was, pointing out where he was hiding! Kids these days – was there no such thing as loyalty and trust? Hadn't he *paid* her? Even when you treated them reasonably fairly, this generation just turned right round and sold you down the river...

He watched as the Cuven girl and the Vix boy, the one who'd stopped to talk to Jazmin, followed where she was pointing; it seemed to Samson that they were looking straight at him. From his hiding place Samson muttered a prayer asking Big Yelo to curse all small, weaselly children, especially those named after flowers. And then he cursed himself for leaving the feckless brat behind and not dragging her away with him.

He was now facing a real dilemma, and he hated making choices. On the one hand, his cover had been blown and his targets now knew they'd been followed...which meant keeping on their tail was going to be much more difficult. But so be it, because he wasn't going to give up now. Then, on the other hand, maybe he could just forget the kids and take a look inside the heap himself; if he was prepared to gamble there might well be an awful lot more of whatever they'd brought out with them still left inside Bloom's Mount. Always assuming what they'd found was valuable, and that the rest of it hadn't been blown sky high.

Or...*or*, he could sell the information about what he'd seen and let someone else take all the risks. And all the loot. It was an idea. But, with his reputation, no one was going to put money in his hand *before* they'd checked out if what he was saying was true. And was there anyone he'd trust to pay him *after* they'd found valuables? He thought not. What to do, what to do, *what...to...do*? Why did this always happen to him?

Torn between the rising number of alternative courses of action, Towd's eye started twitching again and he felt as if he was about to burst with frustration; he could see the Nikkei boy and the girl staggering down the side of the heap, followed by the Vix boy and that little rat Jazmin. He had to make his mind up...

"What is it you're carrying, then?"

Stretch glanced down at the girl, opened his mouth, then shut it again. What was he carrying? After a moment, when the only sounds seemed to be the distant, plaintive calls of seagulls, he heard an answer, a voice...*the* voice. "**Faith...**" it said inside his head. "**Nothing more, nothing less.**"

"Worth a lot, is it?"

Stretch shifted the statue's weight from left to right, wondering just exactly what faith was worth. "**Everything,**" said the voice, and Stretch felt an odd calmness flood through him. "**And more...**"

"What's your name?" he asked.

"It's Jazmin."

"Nice name...look, Jazmin, y'know Lozzi and Big Yelo and stuff?" Jazmin nodded. "Well...this is Horus, the god of the sunrise and the sky."

"What's he made of?"

"Made of?" The question took Stretch by surprise. "Stone, why?"

Jazmin ignored the answer, instead pointing at Reeba and Ty, who were some way down the heap in front of them. "What've they got, more gods?"

"No..."

"You wanna donkey?"

Stretch stopped, frowning; he was finding the girl's butterfly thoughts hard to keep up with. "A what?"

"A donkey."

"What for?"

"Carrying. That's what donkeys is for, int it?"

"You got a donkey?"

"Not *here*!" Jazmin shook her head at the stupid comment. "Know where I can get one, though."

Stretch smiled at her. "How much?"

Jazmin grinned back at Stretch; she liked this boy, he wasn't as silly as he looked and he knew how things worked. "The other earring."

Taking the weight of statue in one arm, Stretch held out his right hand. "Deal."

Once they'd all got off the heap Jazmin had sort of taken over, telling them to wait where they were as she had to go somewhere, and then disappearing; it was odd being ordered around by someone who looked to be no more than eight years old, but Stretch, Reeba and Ty were so exhausted by everything that they'd just been through that none of them had the energy to argue. Jazmin told them she had an uncle – at least she claimed the man, who might soon have one less donkey than he'd started the day with, was her uncle – and that she'd be back soon.

Ty squatted on his heels, one arm draped protectively over the bag on the ground next to him. "*Who* is she?"

Stretch sat down cross-legged, with the statue on his lap and Bone next to him. "The man she says was following us paid her to keep watch...told her to wake him when we came back out, she said."

Reeba leaned back against the wall, eyes closed and rolling her aching shoulders. "Wish I could go to sleep."

"First of all I thought she could keep an eye out for us... y'know, see if she could spot the man who's been following us. So we'd know who he was." Stretch yawned. "Then she said she could get a donkey. Which seemed like a good idea."

"It's a *great* idea." Ty waved a squadron of flies out of his face. "But why's she doing it?"

Stretch held up a small gold earring, cupped in his hand so only Ty could see it. "I'm paying her," he said, spiriting the piece of ancient jewellery away again.

"So was the other bloke."

"Yeah, but I bet I'm paying her better..."

From his cramped hiding place, hunched in a filthy doorway, almost entirely covered by the loose hood of his grimy djellaba, Samson Towd peered through the slit he'd left to see out of and observe his targets. Having finally made his mind up to follow the kids, once again he was plagued by indecision. Where had the little gutter rat gone? Should he have gone after her and forced her to tell him what was going on? And then why were the others sitting around waiting? Should *he* wait and see what they were going to do? Or, or, or...he thought those two letters must make up the most annoying word in the whole, entire language. And then he caught sight of the little girl, Jazmin, coming back down the narrow street; it looked like she was leading a donkey...

* * *

Neither Stretch, Ty nor Reeba asked Jazmin anything about how she'd managed to persuade her uncle to part with one of his donkeys, complete with halter and panniers; they were too tired to care and just loaded the beast up and set off south through the teeming Fitz streets, into the Cuven, where they'd turn eastwards towards the Lud territory and Cheapside Mo's.

No one, apart from the ever-present shadow that was Samson Towd, gave them a second glance as they made their way across the city. They were nothing special, just a group of working kids in transit, going from somewhere to another place; there was hardly a time of day when every street and square in Dinium, every alleyway and ruined boulevard wasn't full of human and animal traffic that was on its way to collect, or coming back from delivering.

And ever since the raiding squads had started kidnapping able-bodied men, for the construction teams building the new city on the other side of the Isis, children had had to take on the responsibilities of their absent fathers, brothers, uncles and cousins. This was a place full of the young, the old, the halt and the weak; a place missing so many people, but too frightened to do anything about trying to get them back.

They'd not long crossed the König's Way, the road running south to the river which acted as the boundary line into the Cuven, when Reeba hung back and called out for a stop.

"What's the matter?" Stretch asked. "Are you okay?"

"I'm fine, I just have to do something...you go on, I'll catch you up."

"Do what?"

"Go and tell Pete that we're all right...I know him, he'll worry."

Ty shrugged. "He didn't seem too worried you were going."

"It's been two days, he might be by now." Reeba jerked a thumb to her right. "It's not far; I'll run, catch you up in no time."

"Say hello to Pete from me," Ty called after her as she ran off; grinning, he slapped the donkey's hindquarters. "We aren't going anywhere faster than this old bag of bones." The donkey's left leg jerked like a piston and narrowly missed Ty.

"Stupid to stand by an ass's arse and slap it," Jazmin said to no one in particular. "Else it might kick you. Thought everyone knew that."

"Your mouth could get you into trouble, kid." Ty aimed a swipe at her, which she easily evaded.

"Not from you, by the look of it," Jazmin muttered to herself.

"What about your mum, Ty?"

Ty frowned at Stretch. "What about her?"

"D'you think she's gonna be worried?"

"'Cos I've not been home for two days? I doubt it..." Ty wiped sweat off his forehead with a sleeve. "Dunno why Reeba's so worried about Pete either."

Stretch watched as Jazmin thwacked the donkey with her switch to get it moving again; she was a street child who belonged to nobody and probably never had. He thought about Reeba, whose parents might not care about her, but who had Bible Pete who did; and Ty, who didn't seem bothered either way whether he had a mother or not. And then there was him. He felt the sudden, empty pain of loss spread out from the pit of his stomach, its sour taste stinging the back of his throat.

His mother was dead, and his father was lost to him. He looked at the loaded panniers the donkey was carrying and wondered what good any of it would really do them, or whether the gold and the god would simply bring with them more pain and misery. "**Have faith,**" said the voice in his head. "**There is always a dawn at the end of even the darkest night.**"

Samson Towd could almost have cried in frustration. Here was yet *another* choice! Another one! He looked pleadingly up at the sky where Big Yelo hung like a pearl, and silently muttered a prayer that he might be spared any more of these tests of his sanity. And then, shaking his head, he realized there was no choice. Why should he care where the girl was going? The donkey was carrying everything the toerags had brought with them out of the heap, and that was all he cared about.

You see, you see, he thought to himself, smiling, an added spring in his step, *a bit of praying to the right god really does do the trick!*

19 FEET OF CLAY

Everil Carne had forgotten what it was like to walk the streets of Dinium and the sights and sounds, not to mention the smells, brought it all back in a rush. This was where he'd grown from boy to man, in this loud, dirty city where – like everyone else – he'd been reared on a diet of myth and magic, served up by his mother and his aunts. As he made his way through the bustling crowds, ignoring the street sellers and the beggars – the poor and the poorer still – he thought about all the stories he'd been told as a child, particularly stories about The Peeler that had been used to scare the wits out of rebellious and wayward children. Much as he imagined The Risen and the Mongrels were used today.

The tall tales about The Peeler had said that he only ate raw flesh – animal or human, he wasn't supposed to care – and that the shrunken heads of some of his victims hung from his belt, swinging from side to side like a silent chorus as he walked. And he wasn't called The Peeler for nothing. His belt was rumoured to be made of leather tanned from the skin of his victims.

Everil Carne now knew the truth was somewhat less vivid and not quite as gruesome but The Peeler, and what he called his Twelve Angry Men, were without doubt very bad people to get on the wrong side of. He lived in the dilapidated remains of some palace, surrounded by walls topped with vicious spikes, some with actual heads on them. Left there to feed the rooks and crows, they were also a reminder of what happened to anyone who transgressed. Which, as The Peeler was known to make up the rules as he went along, was very easy to do.

The old man in the old palace had lost a lot of his power since the rise of Mr. Nero. Before that he had been the only person who demanded, and received, respect and honour in Dinium, and Everil Carne found himself wondering about reputations. What about this man Dexter Tannicus's reputation as someone who knew everything? If The Peeler was no longer the man he used to be, what of Tannicus? Would he still have his wits about him? A lot of memories and learnings could be lost in ten years and this journey he was making could well be nothing more than a dangerous waste of time.

Dangerous because although there was an uneasy truce between The Peeler and Kaï-ro, Mr. Carne didn't give himself much of a chance if the old man ever discovered that he was here on his own in the city.

Everil turned a corner and saw, at the end of the street, what was left of an old stone pillar; he recognized it as the one which was the central axis of where seven roads met and knew he was now in The Dile, the area where Tannicus lived. Five minutes later, having invested a few coins in a boy selling watermelons, he'd got the information he needed and had found the place he wanted. He crossed the street, knocked on a wooden door, grey and weathered with age, and waited.

Somewhere in the house he heard footsteps; then after what seemed an awful long time, there was the sound of a latch being lifted. Finally the door opened to reveal an old – very old – bearded man who appeared to be wearing three pairs of glasses, two of which were on his nose at the same time.

"Dexter Tannicus?" Everil enquired, smiling.

Bible Pete frowned momentarily; he hadn't been called by his given name for, well, he wasn't sure how long it was, just that it had to be a very long time. "Well I was when I woke up, hopefully I will be when I go to sleep...how can I help you?" He looked Everil Carne up and down, then stared at him over both pairs of glasses. "Do I know you?"

"I don't think so...might I come in?"

"You might well, *if* I gave you permission, but why should I?"

"I think you could possibly help me, with some information...information of an ancient, *historical* nature."

"Historical?" Bible Pete's eyebrows raised and the corners of his mouth turned down as a look of interested surprise spread across his lined face. "Well, yes...hmmm, yes, historical did you say?"

"Yes. And ancient."

"I thought so...why don't you, um, do come in...what did you say your name was?"

"I didn't."

"Ah..."

Reeba ran towards Bible Pete's house at a pelt, dodging from alley to street to lane, and taking the occasional short cut through a house, if the opportunity arose. Her route, which had more in common with the way a fly flies than a crow, might have looked totally random but it was extremely fast and quickly brought her, via a narrow, litter-strewn passageway, to the door that let into the house's high-walled backyard.

It was shut, with no handle to twist and seemingly no other way to open it; Reeba patted a couple of pockets and pulled out what looked like a short stick, about finger thick, which she poked through an oval-shaped hole in the door and pushed down. A latch the other side of the door lifted and she slipped through, closing it behind her and putting away her wooden "key". It wasn't much in the way of security, but any stranger who did decide to try and get into the house the back way would have to contend with the six rather vicious geese that lived there. Fortunately they now knew Reeba, and while they didn't especially like her, they didn't think it necessary to attack her either.

To make sure the birds stayed sweet, Reeba reached up and took a handful of corn out of the basket that hung near the door and chucked the yellow niblets onto the dust a way over to her left. As the geese hurried in search of food, she trotted down the yard to the house; all she had to do now was get past the goat and she could pour herself a cool cup of water...

There was something about the person he'd let into the house that made Bible Pete uneasy. He was dressed like a simple working man but the way he spoke, the way he held himself, something about his eyes, all told a different story. Who was he...and why had he turned up, unannounced, outside his door? As Pete led the way into the room at the top of the stairs he surreptitiously swapped the Bible that he had tucked under his arm with another book; it was called *Gunfight at the OK Corral* and it weighed a lot more than it ought to because a space had been cut out of its pages, just big enough to fit his oiled and loaded revolver. Just in case. Speak softly and carry a big stick, as the old saying went.

"So," Pete smiled. "How can I help?"

The man looked round at the room. "You have a lot of books..."

"True..."

"Would any of them happen to say anything about a god by the name of, ah, Setekh? Or one called, what was it," the man frowned, pursing his lips as if he was thinking *very* hard. "I remember now – Horus?"

Pete started to walk slowly round the room, taking his own turn to make a big show of pondering, cogitating and turning things over in his mind as he examined the row upon row, stack upon stack of books. "I'm sure...somewhere

here...quite *positive* I saw it, really not *that* long ago..." Shaking his head, he turned to look at the man. "What did you say your name was?"

"I didn't."

"That's right, you didn't. Might you now?"

"Why?"

"You have me at a disadvantage." Pete shrugged. "I don't like that. And no one's called me Dexter Tannicus in twenty years or more, which is odd to the point of being strange. Wouldn't you say?"

The man ignored the question and, without being asked, sat down on the one and only chair. "My name's Carne, Everil Carne."

"I recall a Guild family of that name."

"You have a good memory."

"That I do..." Pete scouted round the room some more, watched by Everil Carne; finally he bent down and, from a dusty shelf low to the floor, pulled out a large book that had once been bound in red leather, with gold embossed lettering. Now its cover was wrapped in scuffed and stained Manila paper and written on the spine in black ink was the number 8, below which were scrawled the words *Edwa to Extract*. Pete stood opposite his guest, putting *Gunfight at the OK Corral* on a table close by his right hand. "Why, exactly, have you come from Kaï-ro, in disguise, to ask me about ancient gods from the very beginnings of the Before Times?"

"How do..."

"Like you said, I have a good memory." Pete opened the book and began leafing carefully through its fragile pages until he eventually found what he wanted. "You went across the water with Nero Thompson, and that statue he found, didn't you?"

Everil Carne, his face a mask, nodded. "Have you found something?" He pointed at the book Pete was holding.

"Setekh and Horus, you say?"

"Yes."

"Setekh, or Seth, Set, Setesh...that is what, or who, you found, you and Nero and the rest, isn't it? I heard about the discovery and, curiosity being my middle name, I went down and had a look...not much to see as you hadn't raised the statue upright yet, but I do remember the head." Pete turned the book round and indicated a small line drawing of a man with the strangest beaked head, with what looked like very upright "ears".

"What does it say, the book?" Everil shook his head as Pete made to hand the volume over. "I can't read."

"Few can..." Pete tutted to himself, turning the book back. "It says that he, Set, or whatever name you use, is the god of chaos...he's associated with, let me see, violence and savagery, anarchy, bedlam and tumult..." Pete's finger ran down the page some more. "His day of birth was 'an ominous and unlucky day'; he would speak 'as thunder from the sky' and had 'a brutal and murderous temper'. There's a lot more, but all much in the same vein, although I'm sure it's nothing that you who worship him are not fully aware of."

"And the other one?" Everil leaned forward. "What does it say about the other one?"

"Horus?"

"Yes, yes, Horus!"

Pete walked up and down as he carefully examined a

couple more pages. "Horus..." He looked up at his guest. "The falcon god, the distant one, the god of the sky, the uniter, the symbol of divine kingship...quite the opposite of his brother, wouldn't you say?"

"He *does* have a brother..." Everil Carne looked away; so it was true and not just some insane flight of fancy.

"The story is, I must say, somewhat confused...because, whilst Setekh is sometimes referred to as Horus's brother, he's also accused of killing Horus's father, who is also his own brother, Osiris." Pete shook his head. "This book claims he cut Osiris up into many pieces and threw them away; according to the texts, these two *hated* each other, that much is clear, but it was all a very, very long time ago. Even for gods."

"Who won?"

"Who won?" Pete looked surprised, almost shocked by the question. "Why Horus, of course! He became the ultimate ruler of everything...in all the best stories, good always beats evil."

"This isn't a story, old man." Everil Carne stood up and took a pouch out of a pocket hidden in the folds of his burnous and threw it across to Pete, who caught it easily. "These brothers are with us again, and I have a feeling their war will soon be ours. Only this time, with the help of Mr. Nero, Setekh will win."

Pete looked at the small, heavy leather bag in his hand. "What's this?"

"My thanks to you, for your help."

Putting the book down, Pete undid the string that held the pouch closed, opened it and looked inside. "Kaï-ro gold, very pretty..."

* * *

Reeba had been so thirsty when she came into the house she'd poured herself some water before calling out that she'd arrived. And then she'd heard voices from upstairs; realizing Pete had someone with him, she decided it would be more polite not to yell but go up and introduce herself. At the bottom of the stairs she'd heard the other person say *"And the other one?"*, and Pete's reply of *"Horus?"*

In the shadows at the bottom of the stairs, Reeba slowly sat down, stunned. She could not believe what she'd just heard – how did Pete know the name? It was impossible, she thought, as Stretch had only just found the statue! And as she tried to make sense of what she'd overheard – part of her believing she *must* have got it all wrong, part of her feeling guilty for eavesdropping – she heard the exchange of money. Kaï-ro gold.

Bible Pete, the man she trusted and loved like a father, was in cahoots with a man from over the river. Reeba got up; stunned and shocked by her discovery, she slipped out of the house...

20 THE LONG ROAD

"How're we gonna get all this stuff in?" Ty nodded at the panniers. "The donkey's not going down into Mo's, is it."

"Have to carry the bags then, won't we." Stretch frowned; he did not feel like hauling everything they'd got all the way through the maze of tunnels to show it to Mo, and, truth to tell, hadn't really thought through this bit of the plan.

"Would she come out here to look at it?"

"Mo?" Stretch looked at Ty as if he was mad. "You've gotta be joking...if you don't take it to Mo, Mo won't buy it."

"She got a flunky'll come out?"

Stretch shook his head, a drop of sweat running down his cheek and onto his lips, wet and salty. "We want to sell it, we've got to get it in there."

"Better start shifting the stuff, then, eh?"

"Shouldn't we wait for Reeba?"

Ty grinned. "You need a girl to help you?"

"No!"

"Well pick up a bag then." Ty went to lift the cloth covering one of the panniers. "We'll leave the kid to watch the donkey and the statue thing."

"You will, will you?"

Ty and Stretch stopped, aware that Jazmin, squatting a few feet away, was observing them, a rather scornful expression on her face.

"What?" asked Ty.

The sun was beating down, the meagre bit of shade offered by a solitary palm tree was taken by a man selling salted nuts and sugared fruits, and for one moment, there were a few seconds of quiet in which all there was to be heard was Bone's panting and the buzzing drone of the flies orbiting the donkey's head.

"Well, what?" Ty asked again when Jazmin didn't respond.

"You int leaving me anywhere." Jazmin waved a fly away and spat.

"No?" said Stretch.

"No." Jazmin got up. "'Cos if this Mo's like you say, people won't just be bringing things they can carry to sell her, will they? I reckon there's got to be a way in for bigger stuff as well."

Stretch and Ty watched as the apparently fearless little girl walked off towards the shop entrance Stretch normally used to get down into Mo's, her bare feet padding in the dust.

Ty shook his head. "Who went and put *her* in charge?"

"Looks like she did."

Samson Towd couldn't tell if the two boys and the little guttersnipe knew they were being trailed; if they did, they didn't seem to care. And now here they were, back where this had all begun, outside the entrance to Cheapside Mo's where he'd had the idea to start following the boy and his dog in the first place.

Towd slipped back around the corner and leaned against the rough mud-brick wall, hard bits of straw digging into his back. In his mind's eye he looked at the pieces of this particular puzzle. Up till now every move he'd made had been beset with the problems that came with having too many choices; now, it seemed to Towd, there was only one choice open to him. Mo certainly wasn't going to cut him in on anything as he hadn't brought anything to her. And he knew for a fact there was no way she was going to sub him any cash so he could go back into Bloom's Mount with a team, to find out what else was there.

Towd's eye began twitching again as the cogs in his brain clicked together and a solution occurred to him; almost as soon as it had he tried to push it back where it had come from. But the idea just sat there and wouldn't go away. Finally he had to admit to himself that it was his only way out – Towd knew better than most that beggars could not be choosers – and that the only option left to him was to go and see The Peeler...

Samson's stomach knotted and he could feel bile rising in his throat.

There was no other way. Because if The Peeler ever discovered that he'd held back on this kind of information his death would be long, slow and certain. And Samson Towd wanted, if at all possible, to die an old man in his own bed. This lack of choice didn't make Towd any happier as the last thing he really wanted to do was to have to deal with the likes of Turpin Jakes, the man who decided whether you were going to be ushered into the presence of The Peeler or not. Jakes was known as the Necessary Evil, and also known as a man who always lived up to his name.

With one last glance round the corner he saw that the girl, his erstwhile lookout, was walking off somewhere, but what did he care? Towd straightened his shoulders, took a deep breath and started making his way back down the crowded street. It was going to take him about an hour, maybe less if he walked fast, to get from Vieille-Dam to The Peeler's fortified grounds, but even Big Yelo would have no idea how long it might take to actually get inside. Or if he'd ever get out again.

Another hour's slog through Dinium's raucous streets, at the end of which he knew he'd be treated like camel dirt by Turpin Jakes and his associates.

A small voice in his head wondered if he shouldn't just forget the whole thing, but he knew better than to listen to it; The Peeler had ears and eyes everywhere and it just was not worth the risk. If there turned out to be a valuable hoard inside the heap, and The Peeler found out Samson Towd had known and kept it to himself, his head would end up on a spike. Of course if there turned out to be nothing there he would, probably, be equally dead. Or in very, very bad trouble. Which with The Peeler probably amounted to the same thing.

"Told you, dint I." Jazmin, followed by Stretch and Ty, was leading the donkey down a wide street, following the instructions she'd been given at the other entrance. "Had to be another way, dint there."

"Why don't you just give her the other earring so she'll go away, Stretch?"

"Because it's her donkey...here, boy!" Stretch whistled for Bone to leave whatever it was he'd found some way back down the street and catch up with them. "And I don't want to break my back carrying all that stuff."

"What about Reeba?"

"She'll find us."

They came to a break in the wall, a wide open double doorway that gave onto a vast loading area, a huge, chaotic room full of people and beasts and boxes and noise. Just inside the door, sitting high up in an old, weathered stone pulpit, was a small, wizened man with a megaphone who seemed to think he was in charge; for such an insignificant figure he had the voice of a bull, his amplified rantings echoing above the racket, people occasionally taking notice of what he was saying. Jazmin handed the tether to Stretch and went straight up the steps into the pulpit.

He watched as she tugged at the man's sleeve and asked him a question. Once he'd got over the surprise of finding a child at his side demanding answers, the man listened, nodded, glanced down at the donkey and then nodded again; pointing over to the rear of the room he shooed

Jazmin away as if she were a bad smell and then lifted up his megaphone. "Goods coming through, you lazy, goodfernuthin wastrels back there!" he yelled. "Get the hoist moving, double quick!"

Jazmin came back down, took the rope out of Stretch's hand and started off through the bedlam in the direction the old man had pointed.

"You sure all you promised her was an earring?" Ty asked as they pushed their way through the mayhem after her, Bone at their heels.

Ten minutes later, after a juddering ride down in one of a pair of creaking, noxious wooden cages, they were in the big room. The place, as usual, was full and Deaf Jericho's haphazard tile-picking lottery was in full flow. Stretch had the green tile with a dragon motif that they'd been given.

Mo was wrapped in dark blue silk that was shot through with gold and silver thread, and could only have looked more regal if she'd been wearing a crown; she was sitting on her huge pile of velvet cushions eating grapes. To her right, a couple of boys were pedalling as hard as they could to keep her bathed in the pallid, anaemic light that struggled to make her dress sparkle and shine.

Ty nudged Stretch. "So, when do we get to see her?"

"Who knows...not until our tile's called, that's Mo's rules."

It was hard to tell how long they spent waiting as there was no way of charting the passing of time down in the hot, airless underground room. It certainly wasn't minutes, and it definitely felt like hours – almost days – when the boy standing behind Deaf Jericho finally yelled, "Green dragon!"

Stretch jumped up and weaved his way through the crowds towards Mo, tile held high up so people could see it really was his turn; behind him Ty and Jazmin were attempting to get a by now extremely uncooperative beast of burden to move.

"You again." Mo spat a couple of pips out. "Got more of that old-tek for me, have you? That was good that was."

"Something else, Mo..." Stretch glanced over his shoulder, beckoning for Ty and Jazmin to hurry up; Mo did not like to be kept waiting. "Much older, gold and stuff..."

Mo frowned as she shifted on her mountain of velvet, peering past Stretch at the donkey. "You got a lot of it then?"

"Yeah."

Mo impatiently clicked her fingers. "Show me..."

Stretch ran back to the donkey, uncovered one of the panniers and took out the first thing that came to hand. "She wants to see something..." he said to Ty as he ran back.

Mo had her henna-tattooed hand held out as Stretch got back and she snatched the cloth-wrapped object he was holding. "What've we got here?"

She tore the flimsy material apart to reveal a startlingly beautiful gold bird, its outstretched wings, some eight inches wide, inlaid with glistening, multicoloured enamels and precious stones, all as bright and lustrous as the day it had been made; her kohl-blacked eyes widened and her jaw dropped, a whisper running through the people sitting nearest, who'd caught a glimpse of what she was holding.

"There's a lot more of this?"

"Yeah." Stretch nodded.

"Where'd you get it?"

"You think we're stupid or something?" Stretch looked

round and saw Ty was standing next to him, head on one side, smiling at Mo. "We tell you that and there's no more business to do."

"Who's this, Stretch?"

"A, um...a friend, Mo."

"Doesn't he trust me?" Mo ate a grape and spat the pips in Ty's direction.

"I..."

"Course he trusts you, Mo!" Stretch butted in, nodding backwards. "It's, you know, everyone else..."

Mo raised an eyebrow as she slowly looked Ty up and down; she knew Stretch was right, that the place was full of thieves, pickpockets, bandits and villains who would rob anyone, given half a chance, which was why she had so many heavily armed men guarding the premises. But she also knew that the boy, whoever he was, did not trust her, either. And he was no innocent child whose sweets she'd be able to take as easily as blinking.

But even though the boy was undoubtedly right to be cautious – about the disreputable clientele *and* the mistress of the house – Mo was in no mood to be trifled with. If these urchins had found a source of Before Times gold and jewellery, she wanted first dibs. And she was going to get it.

"Guards!" Mo bellowed, pushing herself up off the cushions. "*GUARDS!*"

From the shadows all around the room, and from within the crowd itself, men appeared; large, armed men. Some had short, stubby pistols or crudely modified shotguns, others oiled and polished blades of various shapes and sizes, and all of them were moving forward to surround the small group of three children, a dog and a donkey. Usually, whenever it looked like there was going to be a fight, someone would always be there to take bets on the outcome. Gambling – like breathing and eating – was second nature to the residents of Dinium. But this was such an unequal challenge everyone knew there really was no point in putting any money down. The outcome was obvious.

"Get them and take them to the back!" Mo shouted angrily, pointing over her shoulder with her thumb.

Stretch became aware that the crowd was quietly inching away, creating a clear space around them; a killing floor, if they were stupid enough not to do what they were told. He felt Bone move closer, could just make out Jazmin, half-hidden by the donkey, and see Ty...Ty, who unlike him wasn't standing still without a clue what to do but moving like a fox, almost too fast to see! One moment he was to Stretch's left, then in a heartbeat the Nikkei boy was up behind Mo and pressing the thin, shiny blade of a razor-sharp stiletto knife against her fat throat, with another poised over her heart, waiting to strike.

They were going to die...

The realization that this would surely be his last day alive made Stretch feel scared and indignant at the same time, fear and fury mixing like oil and water as his ears sang. He did not want to die, didn't *deserve* to die! He had a mission! What did Ty think he was doing?

"Keep back!" Ty moved the blade in his right hand. "I will cut her!"

Stretch watched, fascinated, wanting to tell him to give it up and let Mo go, that there was no point in what he was doing; right now he was absolutely positive they were dead whatever he did. Bone began to growl, and a flurry of movement to his left made Stretch turn round; when he did he saw a couple of the guards moving towards Jazmin, coming up behind the donkey.

"Watch it!" he heard her shrill, and then he saw the donkey buck and kick, not once but twice, like he'd seen when fighters did a lightning-fast double punch. As the two guards were flung backwards, one of them dropped his gun, which skittered over the floor and came to a stop by Stretch's foot; quickly, he bent down and picked up the old six-shot revolver. A gun, a dog, two knives and a donkey, against what amounted to a small army. Some hope.

"What did I tell you?" Ty yelled, watching as the crowd moved even further away; a low murmur spread around the room, stopping immediately Ty touched the blade to Mo's throat and a tiny ruby jewel of blood welled out of the cut and ran slowly, erratically, down her neck.

Oh my...there was no way on this earth they were going to live now...

Then, with the circle of sharpened steel and firepower moving closer and closer, tightening its grip, he heard the voice, calm, but loud, so loud he was surprised no one else could hear it. Horus.

"Believe in yourself...speak, and they will listen," he said. **"You have the power..."**

Stretch was conscious of his panic and dread being replaced by a rage so fierce and hot that it was as if his skin was on fire. It felt like he was growing, that inside of him was such untapped strength and energy he might burst if he didn't do something with it. It was only then he realized that against all the odds there was a chance he might not die. Beside him he heard Bone growl again...

"You have the power!"

The power. Stretch gripped the pistol with both hands and tightened his finger round the trigger. He *did* have power, and he was going to make them listen. Unseen by anyone, because every pair of eyes was fixed on Mo's throat, he raised his arms. And fired.

The pistol kicked and leaped in his hands, but he didn't let go. The explosion roared and echoed in the confined space, acrid smoke filling the air as the whining bullet ricocheted wildly off the low ceiling, making everyone duck for cover. And then all eyes were on Stretch, this small, wiry boy with a barbaric, strangely adult set to his face; this child who held himself somehow like he was a warrior. It should have been a faintly ridiculous sight, but no one was laughing.

"They are listening..."

And Stretch could see that they were, but for the life of him he had no notion what he should say or do next. It was Bone's raw, feral growl, warning him that someone in the crowd had made a move, that brought his mind back into sharp focus. They might be listening, but unless he said something it wouldn't be much use. But before he could open his mouth Bone barked and his hackles rose; Stretch looked to his left and saw a shadowy figure coming at him, knife in hand; bringing the pistol up and round Stretch loosed off a shot without even thinking. The bullet tore through the man's right ear and buried itself in the wall behind him.

Silence.

Shock.

Blood pouring from the man's wound.

It was now or never. Stretch knew that if he didn't make his move in the next few seconds the illusion of dominance and authority he'd somehow managed to create would fade like a mirage and everything would be lost.

"**We are *leaving*!**" He was aware that this wasn't his voice, that he sounded far older than his years. It was Horus speaking. Stretch looked at Ty and nodded towards the way they'd come in to the room. "**No one move...**" Stretch, arms steady and straight out in front of him, swung the pistol back and forth like the beam from a lighthouse.

It was as if he was asleep. Everything was happening with a dreamlike slowness that made it appear as if nothing was real, that nothing bad could happen. And for a handful of long, long minutes nothing did: Ty leaped off the mountainous pile of cushions, pushing Mo forward in a heap as he did so, Jazmin scuttled past him with the donkey in full flight behind her as Stretch began moving out of the space the crowd had cleared. And then the awed silence was broken.

"*DON'T JUST STAND THERE!*" Mo, red-faced with fury, rolled onto her side and tried to get up. "*STOP THEM, YOU BRAINLESS, CRETINOUS SPAWN OF GOATS AND CAMELS!*"

"**We will *not* be stopped!**" Horus's voice boomed out as Stretch stepped backwards, moving swiftly out of the room and in the direction Ty and Jazmin had gone. His eyes flicked from left to right, waiting to see who moved first. Who would get the next bullet.

"THEY'RE JUST *CHILDREN*, YOU ADDLED, YELLOW-BELLIED CHICKEN-HEARTS." Mo reared up and stood unsteadily in the cushions. "*CHILDREN!*" she screamed, arms windmilling as she lost her balance and fell sideways. She looked ridiculous but the spell was broken and Stretch saw gun barrels rising, men moving forwards.

He fired once. Twice. The pistol bucked and reared in his hands, the bullets screaming out into the room on their lethal flight. Both found targets, flinging large, burly men out of their way as if they were filled with feathers. And then as he retreated Stretch pulled the trigger again.

KLIK...

And again. With the same result. The pistol hadn't had a full load; the dream was over and the nightmare was about to start.

21 WHILE THE WORLD TURNS...

Gripping its hot barrel, Stretch heaved the now-empty pistol at the guard coming towards him brandishing a vicious, double-edged sword. The solid lump of blued steel cartwheeled through the air and struck the man right between his eyes; poleaxed, he fell backwards, skittling the two people close behind him.

With Bone at his heels Stretch turned and ran after Ty and Jazmin, hurtling down the short passage and through the door at the end. As he slammed it behind him Ty shoved a hefty length of timber down into the waiting slots, jamming it shut. Stretch stopped and caught his breath, looking up and down the maze of corridors, one of which might, if they were lucky, get them back up to street level.

"What now?" Ty asked.

"Um...dunno..."

"You don't know?"

"Gimme a chance...I'm trying to work out which way to go." Stretch stood for a moment, paralysed by indecision – which direction *should* they take? Back down the passage they'd come in by – but which one was that? He'd not really been paying attention.

"This way."

Stretch and Ty looked over to where Jazmin was standing, jerking her thumb down one of the passages. "Why that way, for Heaven's sake?" grouched Ty. "Why not *that* way?" He indicated the opposite direction.

"'Cos *I* remember, that's why...'cos it's the way we come in, int it." Jazmin pulled on the donkey's reins and started walking. "Let's go."

Behind him Stretch could hear the sounds of people, angry people, trying to get the door open. And he certainly did not want to be there when they eventually made it – which if the axe head splintering through the wood was anything to go by, wasn't going to be very long.

Moving as fast as their slowest member – the heavily loaded donkey – the motley group hustled down the ill-lit passage that Jazmin said would take them back to the lifts. With Ty up front, and Stretch taking the rear, they turned a corner and came out into the loading bay and face-to-face with a man. A man with his long, greased black hair pulled back and a gold front tooth glinting in the flickering lamplight; he had a big revolver stuck in his belt.

"What's the big hurry?" The man smiled, revealing two

more gold teeth. "You're going the wrong way to see Nehemiah and pick up your money, or did Mo not give you the deal you wanted?"

"We did fine business with Mo." Ty straightened his shoulders, trying to make himself look bigger. "We just wanna get out, that's all."

"That so?" The man slipped the revolver out of his belt and pulled back the hammer. "Maybe we should check on that..."

A long, strained silence followed, which the donkey eventually broke by dumping a steaming pile of dung on the floor by Stretch's feet.

Quite why he did it he didn't know, but Stretch found himself ducking down and grabbing a warm handful of prime manure; popping back up he lobbed it at the gold-toothed man's smiling face. His aim, as with the pistol before, was true, and the stinking load landed right on target.

"Gettim!" Jazmin screeched, as the man tried to wipe the muck out of his eyes, and then Stretch saw Ty run, leap high into the air and power into the man's solar plexus with both feet. He went down like a split log.

Ty jumped up and pulled open the door to the lift cage that was down at their level. "Load ready to come up!" he yelled as he waved at the others to get a move on.

Running past the groaning figure curled on the ground, Stretch bent down and picked up the revolver he'd dropped.

"You have the power," said the voice in his head. "Now we must find out what you can do with it..."

* * *

Dexter Tannicus. How very odd it had been to be called that name again after so many years. Bible Pete shambled over and stood at the window, adjusting the wooden slats so that he had a better view of the street below without himself being seen. Peering through the narrow gap he frowned as he tried, unsuccessfully, to work out why this man, Everil Carne, should come to Dinium and seek him out. Why him? Why now? And why pay a not inconsiderable amount of gold for a very small amount of information?

Pete hefted the pouch in his hand; it weighed a lot more than you'd expect such a small bag to do. And the fact that this man had paid quite so much could only mean one thing: what he, Pete, considered worthless must have altogether more value to this man – and therefore, probably, the man he worked for.

So why did Mr. Nero want to know if an ancient god from an unimaginably long time ago had a brother? And what could possibly make finding out so necessary, so urgent?

Before he could focus his mind on that particular thought, Pete heard the front door close and a couple of seconds later he saw Everil Carne, who had insisted on showing himself out, setting off down the crowded street. No matter how hard he tried to blend in, once you'd spotted him it was clear that he was a man on a mission, eager to get somewhere as fast as possible. Pete was just starting to ponder on what a strange name Everil was, and had worked out that it was actually an anagram of "revile", when he saw something that made his heart sink.

Reeba.

There was no mistaking the girl's beribboned dreadlocks.

But what was she doing weaving through the crowds, darting looks here, there and over her shoulder as she made a rather obvious job of following his recent visitor?

It wasn't often that Pete was at a loss for what to say or what to do but he now stood rooted to the spot at the window, watching first Everil Carne, then Reeba, disappear out of sight as he tried to make sense of what he'd just witnessed. True, he had been beginning to wonder where Reeba was but had assumed she was still with the boy – whose name he'd completely forgotten – and his dog, Bone. She was off doing something or other on Bloom's Mount, possibly with that rascal Tyson Love, not hanging round outside the house. Spying. Which she must've been doing, else why would she be stalking the man from Kaï-ro?

Pete blinked as he tried to create a picture of what might have happened. It was a game he often played with himself, like a reverse chess match, working his way backwards from an event to see what had caused it in the first place. And as he searched for a reason why Reeba should be following the mysterious visitor Pete imagined he could see the girl coming back to the house – knowing her, through the back alley – and saw her in the kitchen. Why hadn't she called out that she was there? Why had she gone back outside?

Pete scratched his head. Maybe he was wrong. He smoothed his beard. No, if Reeba had returned, she would have come into the house. He knew in his bones that Reeba had come to tell him she was all right, worried he might be worrying.

Ergo, she had come into the house; he just hadn't heard her.

And if that was true her present behaviour would lead

you to the only logical conclusion: she'd overheard his conversation with Everil Carne, or at least enough of it to make her do something as idiotic as follow the man. An action that could very well get both of them into uncomfortably hot water – if she got caught he could get the blame for her spying.

Kicking off his threadbare slippers, Pete pulled on the pair of old leather boots that were sitting by his chair. From right at the back of a very untidy cupboard he hauled out a shabby but serviceable shoulder holster that hadn't seen the light of day for many a year and put it on; he then opened the copy of *Gunfight at the OK Corral*, took out the pistol, checked its load and stuck it into his holster. From a number of different drawers around the house he collected extra shells, squirrelling them away in various pockets, and then he shrugged on a loose waistcoat which hid the fact he was carrying a weapon.

Putting on a wide-brimmed hat, Pete tucked his Bible under his arm and left the house. If Everil Carne touched a hair on that girl's head he was surely going to live to regret it, because like the god in the book he carried with him, Bible Pete would want retribution – *lex talionis*, the law of retaliation, as he'd read in another of his volumes.

Samson Towd twitched, itched, scratched and wrinkled his nose; even he was beginning to find his own odour distinctly unsavoury. He was tired and hot and he'd been standing outside the rusted iron gates for a very long time, waiting for someone to get back to him. But that was just the way it was, the way The Peeler ran things. And now he was here he had to stay; he'd said who he was and if he left now they would only come looking for him. That was what they were like.

"Oi!"

Samson was jolted out of his dissatisfied musings, turning to find Turpin Jakes, the Necessary Evil himself, standing on the other side of the gates smiling. When Turpin Jakes smiled, his acne-scarred, stubble-covered face split apart to reveal a gruesome cemetery of cracked, yellowing teeth; it was, he knew, neither a pretty nor an amusing sight and he often did it just to rattle people. He found it made them feel extremely uneasy. Right now he was giving the look to Samson Towd, who, as expected, appeared distinctly apprehensive.

"Wat'choo want, Towd?"

Samson licked his dry lips and tried to stop his eye twitching; people rarely asked to see The Peeler, they were usually dragged into his presence kicking and screaming. But here he was, about to ask for an audience with a man who was rumoured to regard skinning a person alive as an acceptable form of entertainment.

"If you don't *need* your tongue, you witless half-breed, I'll cut it out."

"I, er...I want to see, um..." Samson tried to swallow and failed. "I want to see The Peeler," he croaked. " Please."

"Are you sure?"

Samson nodded, although he'd never felt less sure of anything in the whole of his worthless life.

* * *

Reeba had been confused and angry; she'd also been scared, disappointed and puzzled. What was Pete mixed up in, and how could he *possibly* be in league with anyone from across the river?

Her mind had been a jumble of confusion. The only thing she'd been sure of was that she *had* to find out the truth, and so she'd waited outside Pete's house, mooching around and trying hard not to look like she was up to anything. She'd wanted to see who it was that Pete had been talking to, exactly who had been offering him Kaï-ro gold. It hadn't really been part of her plan to follow the man, mainly because she hadn't actually got anything you could call a plan, but when the mystery person had come out of the house going after him had seemed like a good idea.

He'd looked quite ordinary, really. Just a man, nothing special, certainly not someone you would imagine was walking around with a pocket full of Kaï-ro gold. Knowing that's what he was, Reeba had watched the man as closely as she could, and as she'd followed him it had gradually dawned on her that even though he was dressed pretty much like everyone else he wasn't the same. His clothes weren't quite frayed and work-worn enough, his face and hands, his feet in their sandals, weren't quite as dirty as they should have been.

Who on earth was he?

Why was someone from across the Isis walking the streets of Dinium in disguise? The more she'd thought about it the more Reeba had been sure that following the man was the right move, and at first it had seemed easy; all she'd had to do was hang back and keep him in view as he made his way through the crowded streets. But she'd kept on losing him and had had to push and shove her way through the throng to find the man again, a couple of times almost running into him because he'd stopped to pick something up from a stall. Once he'd even looked her directly in the eye, or at least it'd seemed like he might have.

Now, as she lay tied up and gagged on the damp slatted decking of a small boat, she realized she'd ignored every warning sign and carried on tailing the man, regardless. With the sun sinking on its timeless flight towards the western horizon, Reeba knew, without one iota of a doubt, that there could be only one place the felucca was going.

Kaï-ro.

22 ...EVERYTHING CHANGES

The lift cage creaked to a halt and the doors were hauled back by a couple of ragged boys to reveal the crowded loading area, light streaming into the huge room from the entrance. The outside, the freedom of the warren of streets and tiny alleys that could swallow them up and let them disappear, was a matter of a few yards away!

"Don't run," Stretch said, looking straight ahead. "Act like nothing at all's the matter..."

Considering the noises they could all just about make out – the raised, angry voices coming from below them – this was going to be easier said than done. But if they were going to get out of this alive they all knew Stretch was right.

Panic now and everything would be lost.

Stretch led the way, carving a path through the swarm of people, who seemed to sense that they should let this small, determined boy pass. The others trooped behind him in a line, passing by the wizened old man high up in his stone eyrie, who didn't even give them a second glance, and out into the street.

"*Now* we can run!" Stretch said, hurrying Jazmin and the donkey past him, and grinning at Ty. "We did it!"

"Don't speak too soon." Ty glanced over his shoulder as a ruckus broke out down by the lift cages, and he shook his head. "Only thing we've got going for us is that it'll be dark soon." A couple of shots rang out behind them. "But maybe not soon enough..."

As the two boys ran after the little girl, Stretch blinked and rubbed some grit from his eyes; up ahead the sky was the palest of greys, with an almost honey-coloured hint of yellow spreading up from the horizon and growing more amber by the second. He noticed the air tasted gritty, and felt what had been a light breeze becoming more of a wind as it created small twisters of rubbish.

"Sandstorm..." he said.

"What?"

"Straight ahead, Ty, look." Stretch spat some grit out of his mouth. "There's going to be a sandstorm!"

With every moment the sky above them turned a deeper brown and breathing became increasingly difficult as the air filled with hurtling particles, tiny missiles that heralded so much worse was yet to come. *So* much worse. Because a storm like this could last for hours, or go on for days. There was no way of telling which it was going to be and all you could do was find somewhere you could hide and then wait for it to end. These things came out of the desert regions with no warning, stopping life in its tracks, and then faded away, leaving behind huge drifts across the scarred and ravaged city. A bad sandstorm could destroy mud-brick buildings and kill anyone unlucky enough to be caught where there was no shelter.

"We have to find somewhere!" Stretch peered at Ty through slitted eyes, his words muffled by the sleeve he was using to cover his nose and mouth; up ahead in the rapidly worsening visibility he could just about make out Jazmin and the donkey turning into a side street.

"Where's she going?"

"Just getting out of sight, probably." Stretch checked that Bone was still with them and speeded up his pace.

"Any ideas where we could go?"

Stretch shook his head as he and Ty followed Jazmin and the donkey, slowing as they caught them up. It was getting harder and harder to see, let alone breathe, and Stretch knew they had to get off the streets even if it was just into a doorway, somewhere they could stop and hunker down. Then, out of the corner of his eye, he saw Jazmin stumble and nearly fall; grabbing her, Stretch picked the girl up as if she were a feather – for all her spirit and pluck, she was still so small – and put her on the donkey.

All thoughts of who might be following them, and what would probably happen to them if they were caught, were pushed to the back of Stretch's mind. He had to concentrate on leading the donkey at the same time as trying to keep track of where Ty was, worrying if Bone was still with them and whether Jazmin was all right. He felt totally responsible for everyone. Except Reeba, he reminded himself. At least she was going to be safe with Bible Pete. The others were out here in danger of their lives, because if the storm didn't get them Mo's people surely would. Eventually.

By now, after taking a twist here and a turn there, Stretch was so disoriented he had no idea where they were or what direction they might be going in. It was like nightfall except there were no stars and no moon, just a sick, dull orange glow that he realized had to be the sun on its way to setting. Soon it would be night and then the darkness and chaos would be total, the howling, painful wind all he would be able to feel or hear.

Just then, appearing out of the swirling, choking murk, he saw the silhouetted shape of a figure. A man, tall and wide as a door, walking purposefully towards them and blocking their path.

Stretch's first instinct told him that this surely had to be one of Mo's guards and therefore the only thing to do was shoot the man with the revolver. But the white stick stopped Stretch pulling the gun out. This *huge* man was using a white stick to tap his way along the narrow street! And, now he was closer, Stretch could just make out that he was also wearing a pair of dark glasses.

What on earth was a blind man doing out in this madness on his own?

"Ty, stay with Jazmin." Stretch thrust the reins into Ty's hands and went over to the man and pulled his sleeve. "Mister? You okay...you lost?"

The man stopped, his free hand patting Stretch's arm, moving up to his shoulder and then feeling the shape of his head.

"Can we help you find where you're going?" Stretch shouted, his words whipped away by a gust of biting wind. Above the storm he heard the man reply, heard words but not what they said.

"Where are you trying to get to?" he shouted back.

The great looming figure bent down until his head was level with Stretch's. "I know exactly where I am, boy," he said, his voice a loud rumble, "but I would guess that it's you and your companions who are, unlike myself, the lost ones."

Stretch frowned, wondering how a blind person could work so much out, and then saw the man was smiling at him.

"Don't need eyes to know where *I* am in this city, boy. Never have," the man continued, a big hand grasping Stretch's shoulder as he waved his cane in the general direction of Ty and the donkey. "Now I think *you* had all better follow *me*."

The blind man turned out to be a trader, a man by the name of Marley Sheppard. Like a homing pigeon he'd taken them straight to some old warehouses where, once inside and the doors securely closed, they found themselves surrounded by chaos and hubbub. Marley Sheppard ran a business he said was called The Great Northern, a caravanserai named after a company an ancestor of his was supposed to have owned way back in the mists of the Before Times.

Everyone belonging to the caravan was holed up in the warehouses, crammed together until the storm passed. As he'd closed the door Marley had thanked Lozzi and Big Yelo that they hadn't left Dinium that afternoon, as had been the plan. If they'd set out then they'd have been caught on the open road and that, he'd said, would have been a disaster. Once inside he'd taken them to meet his right-hand man, who was in fact a woman called Sara Decima.

"She's my eyes," Marley had said.

"He might not be able to see," Sara Decima had replied, "but he can smell a good deal, feel a bad one and hear when people are lying, because there's absolutely *nothing* wrong with any of his other senses."

Together this unlikely pair ran the caravanserai, paid the guerra soldiers who acted as guards, decided where they would go and who should come with them. Services for which they took ten per cent of all profits.

"Sara looks after that side of the business," Marley had told them with a deep chuckle. "It's where she gets her name from."

Neither Stretch not Ty had the slightest idea what he meant.

Stretch sat on the ground next to Ty, Bone slumped at his feet; he watched as Sara Decima fussed over Jazmin, gently wiping sand out of her eyes with a damp cloth and helping the girl sip water from a battered tin mug. She looked about half the size of Marley, but he seemed to treat this dark-haired woman as if she was his equal in every respect.

Stretch looked down at his own tin mug, now almost empty, then at Ty's face; deep lines were etched around his red-raw eyes and wind-chapped lips and his skin and hair were the colour of stone. Stretch realized he must look exactly the same: half dead and so lucky to be alive.

They were at the back of a long, narrow, arch-roofed warehouse which, if the earthy aroma was anything to go by, was normally used to store vegetables. Now, though, it was packed with any number of people from all kinds of places and tribes, together with all their animals; horses, donkeys and camels were everywhere and the noise was awesome, echoing off the brickwork and almost drowning out the sound of the storm still raging on the other side of the battened-down doors.

"What d'you think we should do, you know, when the storm's died down?" Ty's eyes were still watering and a couple of silver drops escaped down his cheeks as he blinked, creating rivulets in the dirt caked on his face.

Stretch remained silent for some time, thoughts, emotions and fears whirling round his head. Since he'd fallen into the hole in Bloom's Mount his life had been a series of extraordinary incidents, the most incredible of which was finding Horus. Had the god been responsible for saving their lives in the explosion? Had he got them out of Mo's clutches, and rescued them from the sandstorm? Was it all, Stretch wondered, because Horus needed to keep him alive so he could do battle with this brother of his?

The god remained silent.

It was all way too big and far too complicated for Stretch to comprehend. He was, after all, just a boy who didn't know anything. Except that to have a voice in your head telling you that you had the power to do things was not normal, to say the least. All he *really* knew was that staying in Dinium was a bad thing to be thinking of doing; they were going to have to go, even if that meant leaving Reeba behind. Stretch looked over at Ty, who was still waiting for an answer to his question. "I heard the blind man... whatsisname, Marley...I heard him say they were going north again, as soon as they could." Stretch glanced over at where their donkey was tethered. "Maybe we should go with them."

"Go with them?" Ty looked at Stretch like he'd just suggested they should tie feathers to their arms and leap off a roof. "You mean leave Dinium?"

"You think it's safe to stay?"

"No, but..." Ty scratched his head and thought for a moment. "Not safe where they might think of looking for us, but there's other places...'cos Dinium's big, it's a huge place."

"And Mo's gonna be spitting bricks, Ty. We made her look stupid, I mean *you* cut her throat, right? And I shot the place up – she's not going to stop till she finds us."

"But there's dragons out there." Ty pointed vaguely northwards. "And cannibals and monsters too – we can't go there!"

"And we can't stay here."

Ty beckoned. "C'mere..." he whispered, lowering his voice so much Stretch had to lean towards him to hear what he was saying. "Why should we trust *them* any more than Cheapside Mo?"

"What choices have we got?" Stretch stood up.

"Where you going?"

"To talk to them, Marley and Sara." Stretch crouched back down in front of Ty. "They'll take us, 'cos we can pay."

"Yeah," Ty shook his head. "And, if they find out *how* much we've got to pay with, they'll feed us straight to the dragons..."

Stretch stood up again, quickly, and his head swam; he was tired, hungry and nervous, but he wouldn't be able to relax until he knew they had a least a chance of being safe.

"Be strong, people respect strength and purpose. You have both."

Yeah, Stretch thought as he walked over to talk to Sara Decima, easy for you to say...

23 A STRANGE ALLIANCE

Pete stood on the street, fretfully switching glasses until
he found the right pair for looking in the distance. Reeba
and Everil Carne could be anywhere by now, but he had to
try and find the girl as soon as possible; the nasty feeling in
his gut that she'd overheard some of his talk with the man
from Kaï-ro just would not go away. It worried him what the
headstrong creature might do. And what might happen to
her if she got caught by a man he wouldn't trust as far as he,
or anyone he knew, could throw him.

"What's the matter, Pete?"

Pete spun round to find Missy Jana where she seemed
to spend all hours: sitting in a chair in her doorway,

watching the world go by and smoking her pipe. "Nothing, Missy, nothing's the matter...just looking for Reeba, that's all."

"Went off up the way." The old lady pointed in the direction he'd seen Reeba following Mr. Carne. "Same way that bloke you had visiting went."

"Ah, did she...thanks, Missy." Pete smiled. There were no secrets in these streets and someone was always watching. That being the case it occurred to him that what he needed was assistance, and, therefore, assistants. Half a dozen should do the trick, and he knew just where to get them.

Sitting in the shade of a wide bamboo awning outside one of the Cuven's least salubrious cafés, Pete signalled to the waiter, a man so slow and bored that buzzing round his lugubrious face he had his own collection of flies he was too lazy to swat away.

"Another coffee, and try to get it here while it's still lukewarm, eh!" Pete shouted to him. "Although *hot* would be nice..." he muttered to himself.

Pete changed glasses, choosing the pair with no arms and lodging them on his nose. Pushing up his sleeve he then peered at his battered old wristwatch, a wind-up model that for all its antiquity generally kept decent enough time, given that no one really cared that much for punctuality. Pete checked the sky; the watch appeared to be approximately right, which was he felt all you really needed from a timepiece.

The assistants – he'd eventually been persuaded he should hire eight ragamuffins, rather than the six he'd originally intended – had now been out doing his looking for about an hour and a half. Pete knew that they wouldn't come back as soon as they'd found something worth telling him, but only after they'd spent enough time away to make it *look* like they'd been working really hard.

Fifteen minutes or so later the ragged crew assembled in front of him with, Pete assumed, the oldest standing in front, hands on hips and ready to do the talking – as well as any extra price negotiations he thought they might be able to get away with. Every extra cent was worth asking for when all you had was nothing.

"Well?" said Pete, swapping glasses again so he could see the boy better. "What's the news?"

The boy set as serious a look as he could muster on his face, sighed and shrugged. "Ain't *good* news, Bible."

"Only no news is good news, lad. If you've got beans, spill 'em."

"Like I said, it ain't good, but...also it ain't *all* bad..."

"Will you please save me the frills and decorations?" Pete took his glasses off, huffed and made them only marginally cleaner by wiping the lenses on his shirt. "Just get on with it, lad."

The boy moved back, out of what he reckoned was swiping range. "She's been taken across, Bible. To Kaï-ro," he said, flinching slightly.

The expected blow never arrived and for the longest moment Pete simply stared at the boy, aware that he and his seven comrades were staring back at him wondering what might happen next. Pete blinked hard and sat back. "And exactly why isn't that news *all* bad?"

"She weren't dead, Bible."

"That so?" Pete nodded. "Well some say that life over there's a fate a lot worse than death, lad. A *lot* worse..."

After he'd paid the kids off, giving them considerably more than they'd expected, Pete stayed sitting at his table and tried to marshal his thoughts. He couldn't work out *why* Everil Carne had seen fit to kidnap little Reeba Moore and take her back with him to Kaï-ro, because it didn't make any kind of sense. Not to Pete anyway. What use could she possibly be to the man?

And then reality bit him like a dog. He would probably never see Reeba again. It was an absolute fact that no one ever came back from a trip across the Isis to Kaï-ro.

Trying for a moment to banish this distressing thought from his head, Pete attempted to make some sense of what the boys had told him. It wasn't much more than a collection of gossip, hearsay and speculation and the details were sketchy at best. From what he could gather someone answering Carne's description had been observed in an altercation with a girl who sounded just like Reeba; people had assumed he was angry because she'd tried to steal from him and had left them to it. A number of other people said they'd seen a man, his hand on a girl's neck, pushing her roughly through the crowds – but if *that* was true, why hadn't she called for help, why had she just gone meekly with him?

There were a few other stories of a man with a girl, the trail ending up with somebody apparently seeing two people answering their description down by the river's edge; here, depending on who was telling the story, the man met up with maybe three, or quite possibly ten other people.

So, Mr. Carne hadn't made the trip to Dinium on his own.

It was from this point on that everyone agreed how the story ended. The men, under the orders of the one with the child, had forced an old trader to cast off from one of the docks and steer a course across the river. Once under way the old man had been thrown off his own felucca – an incident unfortunately also witnessed by the crocodiles – and he'd gone under screaming for help that never came.

Pete felt totally deflated and helpless, incapable of coming up with any kind of plan that had a rat's chance in Hell of getting Reeba back home again. There was, he had to admit, no way he was going to achieve anything constructive on his own. Which meant, logically, that he was going to need help of the really serious kind. The assistants had, for the moment at least, outlived their usefulness. Pete swore angrily under his breath and pounded the flimsy table with his fist, sending his empty coffee cup flying. The waiter, taking this to mean his solitary customer wanted more, heaved himself up onto his feet and, with his flies, went off to get another cup.

What made Pete's blood boil was that if it was serious help he was after there was only one person he could turn to: the last person he really wanted to see.

Someone he hadn't clapped eyes on for almost thirty years, since he'd last lent him money and not been repaid, and had sworn he'd never see again.

His brother.

He got up and straightened the kinks out of his neck. Throwing a greasy dollar bill on the table Pete took a deep breath, readying himself for the disagreeable task of having to eat his words. It wasn't, he thought to himself, just ancient gods who had brothers they didn't get on with...

Samson Towd felt a mess. His bowels were turning to water, his knees to jelly and as he stood in front of this door he was also cross-eyed with panic. Next to him, Turpin Jakes was raising his fist to knock and ask for permission to enter; even the Necessary Evil appeared to be nervous, which just about said it all. Samson was beginning to wish he'd never been born, or failing that, that he'd never seen the boy at Cheapside Mo's and followed him to Bloom's Mount. How much simpler, and possibly longer, his life would have been.

Jakes's fist rapped on the scarred wood.

Samson could hear the hysterical rush of blood thumping in his head.

A voice in the room yelled something; its owner, Samson thought, sounded at best extremely tetchy.

Seconds ticked by, then he saw the handle turn and the door creaked open. There was soft violin music, lilting but quivery, like an old lady singing and then a Porto Novo dwarf appeared, skin like polished wood and dressed in a shabby blue uniform. Silently he beckoned them in.

Jakes pushed Samson through the door which, like a sentence of death, he heard close with an ominous thud behind him. He stumbled into the room, its windows shrouded by vast swathes of moth-eaten curtains, only then realizing that Jakes hadn't come in with him.

Samson desperately wanted to make the sacred half-circle and pray as hard as he could to Big Yelo to let him live, but he was unable to move his lips or his hands.

The room was huge, its high ceilings disappearing into the deep shadows cast by hundreds of candles. The Peeler didn't appear to have the trick lamps that Mo had. Instead Samson could see a retinue of servants constantly on the move and tending to the needs of the candles; small children stood on the shoulders of adults so they could reach the elaborate candelabra which hung down out of the dark in the centre of the stuffy, airless room. In a corner stood a short, old man, wisps of white hair clinging to the sides of his head, a violin tucked under his stubbled chin. The source of the eerily beautiful music, he swayed gently from side to side, his eyes half-closed, his hand moving slowly up and down, lost in the sounds cascading from his strings.

Samson had never actually met The Peeler before, but if it wasn't the dangerously elegant, bearded man who was lounging in an ornate gilt chair at the head of the long table at the other end of the room, it was no one else he could see. The man watched him, his eyes flicking up and down as if he was appraising an animal at market, and Samson had no idea what he was supposed to do next.

Then the music stopped, the final note fading away like smoke in the night air.

"Jakes tells me you have information, but he didn't tell me your name."

Samson blinked and stared, slack-jawed. The Peeler's lips hadn't moved!

"Well, what is it?"

Samson's mouth opened and closed, but no sound came out. What was this magic? The tom-tom beating of his heart increased and he realized he'd forgotten to breathe. "T-T-T-T-Towd..." he stammered, still staring ahead but aware that a figure was moving into his field of vision. "Sam-Sam-Samson Towd."

"Samson?" said the old man, smiling and shaking his head as he walked in front of Samson and gave his violin and bow to the dwarf. "Appalling sense of humour your mother must've had, naming a runt like you after a fabled giant."

Samson frowned, no idea what the old man was talking about. As far as he was aware he'd been called after his father, Sam. "Who...who...?"

The old violinist snapped his fingers at the man in the chair, jerking an authoritative thumb for him to move, which he did immediately. "I..." he brushed crumbs off the chair and sat down, "...I am The Peeler. But you can call me liege or master, or maybe...maybe *lord*."

"You?"

The old man nodded. "Yes, me."

"But..."

"Age may shrink a man, on the outside, but it doesn't stop him having big ideas and dreaming grand dreams." The Peeler's small, hooded eyes almost disappeared as he smiled and smoothed a liver-spotted hand over his shiny, bald head. "A talent for striking fear into the hearts of men doesn't fade with the years, it gets honed to perfection, wouldn't you say, Solomon?"

The bearded man, now sitting a few seats to The Peeler's right, raised a half smile. "Practice makes perfect, liege...or master, or maybe *lord*."

The Peeler nodded at Solomon and looked over at Samson. "He can get away with a joke or two today, Samson Towd, because *today* he's my very favourite. But that won't last for ever because I change my mind *all* the time, and they never know when it'll be someone else's turn. It keeps Jakes and my Twelve Angry Men on their toes, not knowing." Laughing to himself, The Peeler danced his fingers on the table then picked up a knife and stabbed an apple from the bowl in front of him; with surgical care he proceeded to remove the skin from it. "Now, Towd, tell me what you have to tell me, or I'll stop practising on fruit."

"I think they've found something big, *very* big," Towd blurted out, his eyes clamped on the knife as The Peeler quartered the apple and gave a piece to the dwarf. "Something *valuable* from inside of Bloom's Mount. Gold, I heard them say gold!"

Before he had a chance to say any more about who "they" might be, there was a sharp rap on the door behind him and it was pushed open. Rooted to the spot, Towd saw Solomon leap out of his chair, a large pistol in each hand, and he watched as The Peeler motioned for his sideman to relax.

"Very little *ever* surprises me nowadays." The Peeler stabbed his knife into the table, where it stood vibrating slightly. "But, after all these many years, brother, I must say that this is *completely* unexpected. What brings you here, Dexter?"

Samson, turning to see who had come into the room, got the shock of his life when he saw Bible Pete standing a few yards behind him...

24 ACROSS THE ISIS

Reeba sat hugging her knees, on the floor of a small, dark, dank cell. The only light came in through a narrow grille up higher than she could reach; since she'd been thrown in and the door locked the only sounds she'd heard were the furtive scurryings of rats and mice.

Was this to be it?

She was still in a state of shock about what had happened. Her whole world had spun completely out of control from the moment the man she'd been following had grabbed her in the street, threatening to kill her if she uttered a single word – and if she so much as whimpered, he'd added, he'd go right back and do the same to Pete after he'd finished her off.

What was going to become of her?

These were people who thought life was cheap, at least the lives of those from Dinium. She could still hear the fading screams of the poor man whose felucca the men had stolen, after they'd thrown him in the Isis and left him to the crocs. If they could do that they could do anything...and wouldn't think twice about it. What could they be planning on doing to her? Especially the really sinister and terrifying guards she'd seen. The ones whose faces looked like her mother – a sloppy seamstress at the best of times – had hastily sewn them together from oddments.

And *why* had the man taken her?

The question kept returning like a moth to flame.

She realized now he must've known she was following him right from the start but that didn't explain why, if she'd been so bad at it, he hadn't simply shaken her off or just told her to stop. No one had attempted to help when the man had finally caught her and she'd yelled out, but then people were always squabbling in the street and whoever had seen her probably thought it was a family quarrel. And why get involved with that, especially if it wasn't your family?

A tear welled up in one of Reeba's eyes and ran, hot and salty, down to her lips. She sat up straight. This was no time to cry like a baby, no time at all. They hadn't hurt her, yet. She was still alive, so far. It could be so much worse. And it still, the thought occurred to her, might be.

Another tear fell down her cheek...

Mr. Nero's face, deathly pale and shadowed with fatigue, was a mask of anger. He stood up, paced the vast room with a frenzied energy, then stopped again, turning to stare intensely at Everil Carne.

"You went *where*?"

"Dinium, UnderMaster."

"Why? *Why*? WHY?" Mr. Nero pointed a shaking finger at his OverSeer, the master of the Dark Soul Army, curling it back into his fist as he tried to calm himself down. "Why did *you* go there?"

"Because that is where the problem is."

"And what did you find?"

"Nothing. There is no sign of any unrest, no sign of anything but a city on its last legs. They still live on the edge of poverty and in fear of what's across the river."

"*Some*thing is happening over there..." Mr. Nero sat down again, leaning his elbows on the table, only to be convulsed by a spasm and thrown backwards so hard the chair almost toppled over. "*NEARER!* **I feel him, I feel his *effect* nearer!**"

A soft knock on the door was followed by the arrival of the obsequious major-domo. He bowed and stayed looking down. "Master...my apologies..."

Mr. Nero shook his head, trying to clear it, and turned to look over his shoulder. "What?"

"There is a sandstorm approaching, a bad one; we have to..." the major-domo waved in the direction of the open windows.

"Do what is necessary." Mr. Nero ignored the influx of servants and turned back to find Ms. Webb was now standing next to Mr. Carne, the silver filigree on her head glittering. "Phaedra?"

"There is a presence, so much *closer* than before...

someone is on this side." She lowered her gold-coated eyelashes, tipping her head back as she looked directly at Mr. Carne. "Who is she?"

Footsteps.

Two, three people? Hard to tell...

A key going into the door and the lock's mechanism squealing as it turned.

Reeba pushed herself as far back into the corner of the cell as it was possible to go and saw a wedge of light break through the blackness and grow as the door was pushed open. Was this it? Were these her last moments?

A guard, half in shadow, came into the cell. It was one of the men with the badly patchworked skin, and as he bent down to grab her Reeba saw the raw scars on his wrist and the mismatched hand. It was white, with crude stitching attaching it to his dark brown arm. What was this person?

The guard hauled her upright and dragged her out into the corridor, where another guard was waiting. Reeba couldn't stop herself from staring at these men who looked like something you might imagine in your worst nightmares. Except they were real, right there in front of her. She could smell them, had been touched by one of them, his skin cold and dry; but it was the eyes that were somehow the oddest of all. Their pupils, instead of being an impenetrable black, glowed a strange, silvery white. These men were alive, but everything about them told each one of her senses that the opposite was true.

"Go." A guard, whose voice had a sharp metallic rasp to it, pushed her forward. "Follow," he said, pointing at the second man, and Reeba knew there was no point in arguing.

They took her down corridors lined with cells just like hers, behind some of which she could hear sobbing; they went along a series of brightly lit passageways, past a number of half-open doors to rooms that had the same pungent odour as the street of butchers' shops in Dinium, finally stopping her at a door that was wide open.

The room was floored with white tiles, as were the walls and the ceiling; glowing balls of incandescent light hung down, eliminating every shadow and making the highly polished metal tables, chairs and cabinets gleam. There was a body on one of the tables, almost as white as the tiles, and on the wall behind it a wide, delicate slash of brilliant red spread upwards like a bird's outstretched wing; Reeba couldn't help noticing that the blood was still dripping.

A man was standing bent over the table, his back to her. He was dressed in shirtsleeves and was wearing a white, floor length apron over his black trousers. The man's dark hair was combed backwards and a curl flicked up above each ear, like a horn.

"Here," rasped one of the guards, pushing her forward again.

The man turned round and peered quizzically at Reeba over his rimless glasses, head slightly on one side; he looked at her the way a bird of prey might. His apron was spattered with blood, both fresh and dried, a few drops of which had landed on his face; he had a small, metal-handled blade in his right hand and a heart – a heart that Reeba could've *sworn* was still beating – in the other.

"Close the door, child. We don't want to be disturbed, do

we?" The man turned back, busying himself with whatever he was doing to the body. "I won't be a moment...Ostinelli!" the man snapped. "Come here and finish this up!"

As Reeba pushed the door to, shivering and feeling as if she was going to be sick, a thin, stork-like man appeared from out of another doorway, ignoring her as he made his way across the room.

"I've got the other one ready, Mr. Cleave, sir."

"Good." Mr. Cleave took his apron off and handed it to his assistant, then went to sit behind his desk; the flat expanse of polished metal in front of him was almost empty, except for an extremely neat arrangement of glinting knives, probes, pliers and a saw on the right-hand side. He picked up one of the knives, took a white handkerchief out of his pocket and proceeded to polish it. "So..."

Reeba watched the man, waiting for what was to come next. It could not be anything good. Nothing good had ever happened in this room...you could feel it. The pain and anguish had been absorbed into every part of it.

"...what has Mr. Carne brought back from that *fleapit* of a city across the water, then? Why you, my dear?"

Reeba frowned. That was exactly the question she'd been asking herself: why her? She shrugged.

"Come now, child, speak up!" Mr. Cleave smiled, showing a mouthful of very tiny, widely-spaced teeth, and his whole face lit up. "If you won't tell me, then I'll have to *remove* it from you..."

At that point the assistant, Ostinelli, walked back across the room carrying a white enamel tray full of vaguely recognizable blood-soaked objects. Organs.

"As you can see," Mr. Cleave waved the knife at

Ostinelli's back as he disappeared into the other room, "I am quite good at removing things."

"I...I dunno why...he just took me..."

"Of all the people swarming the streets of that place, of *all* the people he had to choose from, Mr. Carne took you?" Reeba nodded her head; Mr. Cleave shook his. "I really do think there is more to it than that, child." He put down the knife he was holding and took a moment to pick out another one, carefully inspecting its sting-like blade. "This should do the trick..."

"I was, um, I was *following* him!"

"Ah!" Mr. Cleave looked extraordinarily pleased with himself. "You see? You *do* know why! And what possible reason could you have had for following a man like Mr. Everil Carne? Eh, tell me that?"

Reeba looked away, biting her lip. What could she tell this man that wouldn't get her, and Bible Pete, into more trouble? Nothing. But keeping her mouth shut wasn't going to do her much good either.

"Speak up."

She didn't know what to do; her first instinct was to make some story up, but what story? And then it occurred to her that there was no reason for her to try and protect Pete, if he was actually in league with these people anyway. Except...except what if he wasn't?

Mr. Cleave stood up, came round the table and grabbed Reeba's arm. "I really don't have any more time to waste... Ostinelli, bring me the chair!"

"I don't think that will be necessary, Darcus."

Mr. Cleave swung round and did a double take. Standing behind his desk was Ms. Webb, the swathe of black silk she was wrapped in so dark it was like a hole, a blank space in the wall. Which, Darcus Cleave's mind insisted, *just was not possible!* The logical, analytical, meticulously rational side of him would never, ever get used to the witch-queen and her weird, eldritch ways.

Mr. Cleave pulled Reeba round so she was between him and Ms. Webb. "She knows something."

"She knows a lot of things, some of which I'm sure she doesn't even realize, Darcus." Ms. Webb smiled. "And *I* won't have to cut her open to find out what they are."

Reeba watched the woman, her head capped in delicate, snaking rivulets of silver mesh, move across the white tiled floor as if she was floating. It seemed as if she'd appeared in the room out of nowhere, or maybe she'd come straight through the wall because Reeba couldn't see how else the woman had got in. In the strangest way she scared Reeba far more than the man, even with all his knives and threats.

The woman stood in front of Reeba, who saw a hand slowly appear from between the folds of night-black silk and reach out towards her. She shrunk back, but stopped immediately she bumped into the man behind her.

"Don't be frightened, too much." Ms. Webb tilted Reeba's chin up and stared down at her. "What have you brought with you, Reeba Moore?"

"Nothing..." Reeba felt as if her soul was being looked into; she tried to close her eyes and couldn't, mesmerized by the woman's eyes. One green and one blue.

"It's in your pocket."

"My pocket?" whispered Reeba, unable to even blink. She hadn't brought anything with her, but almost unbidden her hand delved into her pocket and came out again.

"Open your hand." Ms. Webb held her own out, as if to show Reeba how.

Reeba looked down as her fingers slowly uncurled to reveal the falcon brooch she'd had in her hand when Stretch had found Horus. The falcon god.

"She has seen him." Ms. Webb took the brooch from Reeba, who was powerless to stop her, and held it up in front of her. "And she has heard him..."

25 OPEN MINDS

The atmosphere was pleasantly warm, the air smoky and aromatic; it was a combination of smells that Reeba found impossible to untangle and translate. Sweet cinnamon? Fragrant sandalwood? Fresh pine? The individual scents melded together in a complex, exotic pattern in her head, at once stimulating and yet relaxing.

Sitting cross-legged, Reeba looked slowly around at her new surroundings. This room, lit like a summer dusk with petal-covered cushions covering the floor, had dark, lustrous silks flowing down from the centre of the ceiling. It was the most beautiful place she'd ever seen. And she had absolutely no memory of how she'd got there. The last thing she remembered was looking up into the woman's gold-rimmed eyes and wondering how on earth she knew her name.

"I reached inside, that's how."

Reeba whirled round to find this woman was now sitting opposite her, when moments before the room had been empty. This was magic or sorcery, possibly both; it was dark and enchanted and it scared Reeba witless.

"My name is Phaedra, Phaedra Webb, and I mean you no harm, I just need you to go back again, but much deeper this time. I need to know where you have been and what you've seen." Ms. Webb reached forward with both hands and Reeba flinched. "You can help me, or you can go back to Mr. Cleave and his rather more *direct* approach to these things. Your choice entirely."

"Who are you?"

"I told you my name."

"*What* are you, then?"

"I am the Oracle. I see things, things that have been and those which have yet to be. I am a sibyl, a foreteller, an enchanter...I know, I understand, I *decipher*." Ms. Webb smiled and it reminded Reeba of a cat. "I know you are frightened but determined to fight it, and I understand that...I understand it means you have spirit, child. True spirit."

"But what's going to happen to me?" Reeba could only imagine that, once this Phaedra Webb had got what she wanted, she would have no use for her any more. She would be discarded.

"That depends."

As hard as she tried, Reeba couldn't stop her lip from quivering. "On what?"

"The future..." Ms. Webb leaned forward, hands reaching upwards; as her fingers neared Reeba, blue sparks twisted from their tips, zigzagging to Reeba's temple. The air filled with the sharp zest of ozone and Reeba froze, her eyes closed.

"She is not the one who – like you, Mr. Nero – has the godhead within her. But she was there when it happened to the boy." Ms. Webb remained a part of the shadows, watching Mr. Carne and Mr. Cleave as they in turn watched over the UnderMaster. He was, for a rare moment, calm and lucid. The two Dark Souldiers who were now constantly by his side, there to stop him flailing around when Setekh took hold of him, had relaxed slightly. As had the canix, who had stopped their obsessive pacing and were now sitting either side of their master.

"Where is he, Phaedra?"

"The girl has no idea, no idea at all."

Mr. Nero's eyes narrowed. "How can you be so sure she's not lying?"

"The truth can't hide from me." Ms. Webb came out into the light. "They split up; she went to see the man Mr. Carne visited, Dexter Tannicus, and the other two went to the Vieille-Dam souk to trade the things they'd found with a dealer. That is what happened."

"Where did they find the statue?" Mr. Carne asked.

"You said something about, what was it...a mountain? If I remember correctly, that is." Mr. Cleave didn't look at Ms. Webb as he spoke; he was still angry at the way she'd undermined his authority and taken the girl from him.

"It was inside Bloom's Mount." Ms. Webb raised an immaculately plucked eyebrow in Mr. Cleave's direction. "You recall that huge accumulation, one could almost say *mountain* of rubbish in the Fitz territory – the one which is so big you can, on a clear day, see it from over here?"

Mr. Carne shot a look at each of his colleagues. A look that said, in no uncertain terms, that they should step away from any personal disputes they might have and keep their attention on the matter in hand. "Inside the heap?" he said, frowning with puzzlement.

Ms. Webb nodded. "A chance discovery. The boy had found a staircase which led almost to the centre of the heap; it went into one of the buildings which must've stood there in the Before Times, a museum perhaps. I went into the girl's memories...they found a room, a large room, full of precious things from the time when the Lord Setekh was last here as the power to be reckoned with."

"*A* power. Not *the* power..."

They all looked at Mr. Nero, the two Dark Souldiers readying themselves for trouble, but nothing happened and he remained staring straight ahead, eyes focused on something far, far away.

"I always shared power...it was never *all* mine. I had thought now, this time, it would be different, but the Fates seem to have other plans. Reasons of their own – inexplicable, secret, *confusing* reasons – which mean that I will, once again, have to fight my brother."

"The Dark Soul Army is ready to do your bidding, Master." Mr. Carne bowed his head.

Mr. Cleave bowed even lower. "I have almost completed a new squad of Risen, Master."

Mr. Nero shuddered and blinked; he took a deep breath...and he was in control again. "And Ms. Webb, what have *you* done?"

"Kept my mind open, UnderMaster."

"What have you seen?"

"That we must..." Ms. Webb's eyelids fluttered so fast they were a gold-tinted blur, "...that we must move fast because events are moving faster. And I see elephants..."

"Elephants?" Mr. Cleave, to his own annoyance, couldn't quite keep the profound disbelief out of his voice.

Mr. Nero drummed the marble tabletop with his fingertips. "Mr. Cleave...did you say that you had *almost* finished a new squad of Risen?"

In the second it took the UnderTaker to realize he would do himself a huge service by leaving and going back to his white-tiled domain, he saw a satisfied smile pass across Ms. Webb's face. As he left he promised himself he would, very soon, try to find a way of making sure she had a lot less to be happy about.

"As you say, Phaedra," Mr. Nero watched the door close, "we must move. And as soon as the sandstorm has subsided, we will. Be ready, Everil, to take the Dark Soul Army across the Isis."

26 CLOSED RANKS

The atmosphere wasn't what you could call pleasant. Not much of what Samson Towd would call a feeling of brotherhood in the air. But the present situation did have the very great advantage of having directed all of The Peeler's attention away from him and on to Bible Pete. In this unexpected lull in his own personal ordeal Towd moved himself slowly out of the way. Very slowly as he was fully aware that the dwarf and Solomon, the man with the large guns, were both watching him.

From what felt like the relative safety of the side of the room, Samson stood and watched these two men who no one had had any idea were brothers. Neither seemed very happy to see the other, which he completely understood as he felt pretty much the same about his own brothers, who were all no-good, cheapskate, lying cheats. The last time he'd been in the same room as one of his brothers they'd tried to kill each other, and Samson wondered, as he observed the scene, what the outcome of this meeting might be.

"Were you just passing by, Dexter?" The Peeler yanked his knife out of the table and started cleaning his nails. "And did you just think, after all the water that's gone under all those many bridges, that now might be a good time to come in and talk about old times we've never had?"

"No, Asbel, I did not."

"Why then?" The Peeler smiled; he hadn't been called by his given name in so long he'd almost forgotten what it was. "Why come here, what could either of us possibly have to discuss?"

Samson noticed that Bible Pete's face was screwed up, as if his tongue had turned into a greasy rag.

Finally he spoke. "I need your help," he said, eyes everywhere but on his brother.

"*My* help?" The Peeler appeared genuinely surprised, looking over his shoulder. "Hear that, Solomon? After all this time, *now* he wants his little brother's help? Look me in the eye and say it, Dexter. Look me in the eye..."

Samson was transfixed, all thoughts of his own problems pushed to the back of his mind. This was an historic moment he was witnessing and he wanted to absorb every memory of it; if Big Yelo saw fit to let him walk out of here alive and with all his wits about him, *this* would be a tale to tell to anyone who would listen.

Pete squared his shoulders and turned to his brother. "A man came to me today, asking for information...and paid me far too well for it."

"And what has that to do with me?"

"He was from Kaï-ro, Asbel."

A frown came and went on The Peeler's face. "Strangely enough I, too, had a visitor from across the river today, also requesting information. I had none that he wanted, but he still paid me." Behind him the dwarf laughed, a high-pitched, hiccuping giggle. "I wonder if it was the same person?"

"Everil Carne?"

"Ah...so *you* got the organ grinder, whilst *I* got a monkey. Interesting." The Peeler indicated that his brother should join him at the table. "But why d'you need my help? Why should a visit from the OverSeer General, as Mr. Carne likes to call himself, necessitate breaking decades of silence?"

"Firstly, something has happened. I don't know what it is, but it involves that statue Nero Thompson dug up and took across the Isis – may I?" Pete picked up a ripe pear from the fruit bowl; his brother nodded. "The statue was a god, a powerful, evil god from the Before Times," Pete took a bite, juice running down his chin and disappearing into his beard, "and Everil Carne wanted to know about this god's brother. He said that the brother was with us again, and that their war would soon be ours. And then he kidnapped my...what should I call her? My assistant, just a child, really. Kidnapped her and took her back with him across the river..."

"*What?*" Samson was so shocked by what he'd just heard he'd let the question escape, because if the girl had been taken, did that mean the others had too? And now, to his great distress, he once again found himself the centre of attention. Even the candle lighters were staring at him.

"Who's that?" Pete asked.

"That," The Peeler pointed with his knife, "is Samson Towd, who came grovelling to me with a story of gold. Gold he said had been found inside Bloom's Mount. I was about to tell him to take his idiot stories back to the souk where they belong when you arrived, brother. And now I think there's possibly more to Towd than meets the eye."

"If he's telling tales that there might be something *inside* the heap, then you're right."

The Peeler sat back in his chair. "*You* know about it as well? What kind of secret is this?"

"One that's been let loose." Pete looked directly at Samson. "I apologize for interrupting your story, please do continue."

Samson's shoulders sagged. He could see no way he was going to come out of this well, and no way at all of getting out of telling the story. The truth, the whole truth and nothing but the truth, as his father used to demand of his children if he caught any of them in a lie. And if he told anything less, he suspected he'd get more than the kind of thrashing his father used to deal out.

"May Big Yelo strike me down, but I don't know *exactly* what the girl and her two friends brought out of the heap with them, but it looked heavy. And I did hear 'em talking about gold, honest to Lozzi I did..."

"You saw them on the heap?" asked Pete.

Samson nodded. "Followed 'em...been following them so long I'm tired to my bones."

The Peeler stood up, smiling. "So where's this 'gold' now?"

"Cheapside Mo..." Samson shrunk back, glancing at Solomon and wondering if his time was nearly up. "They split up, the girl went off somewhere and the others went to Vieille-Dam with the gold. It's the truth, I swear!"

"Well, we shall have to pay the delightful Mo a visit, won't we?"

"You'll have to wait, brother." Pete reached for another piece of fruit. "There was the mother of all sandstorms coming in as I arrived here..."

27 LEAVING DINIUM

With Bone panting at his side, Stretch stood next to Sara Decima, the little woman only a couple of inches taller than him, if that. Marley Sheppard sat opposite them, knitting; Stretch had never seen a man knit before and it looked...odd. Especially odd when you knew the man was blind.

"It's going to be a scarf, in case you were wondering, boy." Marley smiled at no one in particular, lamplight glinting off his dark glasses. "It gets colder than Hell out there at night."

"He means up north, on the journeys," explained Sara. "In case you were wondering about that as well."

"Oh..." Stretch, who hadn't been wondering about either things, nodded, "...thanks."

"You got a question, boy, you ask it...I can knit and talk at the same time."

"They want to come with us, Marley."

"Allow the boy to speak for himself, Sara. Let a person dig their own hole, I always say." Marley sat, the wooden needles clicking hypnotically as they added stitch after stitch to the multicoloured scarf, and waited.

"We, um...we need to get out of Dinium, me and my friends." Stretch, forgetting for a moment that Marley couldn't see, waved back to where Ty was now standing next to Jazmin watching what was going on.

"Anyone *needs* something, Marley, it probably means trouble," Sara, glancing sideways at Stretch, folded her arms, "and..."

"...we need trouble like I need to go deaf, I know." Marley stopped knitting and checked the tension of the wool. "Tell me, why d'you *need* to leave this benighted city?"

"Well..." Stretch thought about how to put their problem in the best possible light, but realized there was no good way of looking at what they'd done. "We got on the wrong side of Cheapside Mo, and she's not happy with us."

"Mo? Not happy?" Marley's face was split by a huge, wide grin and he roared with laughter so hard he had to take his dark glasses off and wipe his heavily shadowed eyes with a piece of cloth Sara gave him. "Tell me who she *is* happy with!"

"Will you take us?" Stretch asked; he wasn't going to offer to pay, or even admit they had anything of value they could pay with, until he was asked. And then, in the very middle of his head, he had the weirdest sensation of hearing someone taking a breath... **"We need to go somewhere, you and I."** Horus said. **"Somewhere we can gather people. We need an army."**

"D'you have *any* idea where we're going, boy?" Marley put his glasses back on. "Any idea what it's like out to the north and the west?"

Stretch shook his head, Horus's words still echoing in his mind – an *army*? "No," he finally replied, staring at his reflection in the lenses of Marley's glasses. "But Ty says there's dragons and monsters. Is there?"

"Children's stories..." Marley started knitting again. "There's worse, boy; strange creatures and stranger people, and the further away from what's left of civilization you get the more weird and uncanny it all becomes. Not one word of a lie."

"We don't need this, Marley." Sara shrugged. "More trouble than they're worth, this lot, if you ask me."

"You could be right, Sara." Marley smiled and raised his eyebrows questioningly. "What *are* you worth, boy?"

"What?" The question took Stretch completely by surprise.

"That donkey of yours..."

Stretch felt the hairs on his neck rise as a cold shiver ran down his back. "What about him?"

"I'd say he's carrying more than mud bricks and pemmican." Marley's fingers quickly checked the fresh row of stitches. "There's metal in those bags and I'd put good money down that it's not lead. And as Sara will tell you, I'm not a betting man – am I, Sara?"

"No, but only because no one trusts you not to cheat."

"What've you got, boy...something nice?" Marley's voice lowered, acquiring a steely edge. "Something that'll make you worth the trouble?"

"How d'you...?"

"I listen. I listen to everything, all the time." Marley cupped an ear. "I could hear there was something interesting in those panniers, and I knew they were heavy from the effort it took you and the other ones to take them off."

"He doesn't miss a trick." Sara went and sat next to her partner.

"Hand it over, boy, or I'll hand *you* over to Mo, soon as this storm dies down."

Stretch looked from Marley to Sara, cursing himself for being stupid enough to think he'd be able to fool either of them about anything; these two wouldn't still be in business if a kid could pull the wool over their eyes. He was beginning to wonder whether he should simply throw himself on their mercy and plead to be taken out of the city when the same weird feeling he'd had when they'd been trapped underground at Mo's came over him again.

It rose up from the pit of his stomach like a cold fire and the next thing Stretch knew the pistol was in his hands, its trigger fully cocked, and it was pointing unwaveringly at Marley. Beside him, Bone, hackles up, was growling softly and Stretch was aware that he felt absurdly calm.

"**You *will* take heed, because this is not about mere metal...**" Staring down the barrel of the pistol, Stretch listened to Horus's dark, commanding words as they issued from his mouth, expecting at any moment to be attacked from behind by one of the caravanserai's guerra soldiers.

"I need to leave this city, and you *will* take me."

"What?" Sara began to get up. "Who d'you think you..."

"I have work to do...I have a duty and a task to fulfil. I have history to make and destinies to change, and I *must* leave this city so that I might return to finish what I started millennia ago."

"Listen, Sara." Marley put a calming hand on her shoulder and sat her back down again. "Listen – this isn't the *boy* speaking, this is someone else."

Sara dug her elbow in her partner's ribs. "It's a trick, Marley!"

"I am nobody's fool, Sara, and I can hear the shadows and ghosts of centuries past in this voice..." Marley knitted a couple of stitches, as if nothing untoward was happening. "Who are you?"

"I am Horus, the distant one, god of the sky."

Sara sighed loudly. "Just what we need...*another* prophet, another god..."

Marley laid his knitting to one side, leaning forward on his elbows. "I do believe, Horus," he took his dark glasses off and his cloudy, sightless eyes were staring directly into Stretch's, "that you might be..."

The sandstorm had died down sometime during the night and as soon as it had everyone started to get ready. It might still have been dark but, Sara had said, they had a day's time to make up and they were going to move out just as soon as possible.

The mayhem and disruption was astonishing, or so it had looked to Ty and Stretch as they packed everything back on the donkey and then waited to be told what to do. Because they were going. Marley had said so, even shaken hands on the deal.

"I can't believe he knows we're carrying all this gold and he doesn't want even one piece." Ty checked the bindings on the panniers again, just to make sure they were secure. "What did you do, apart from threaten him with the gun?"

"*I* didn't do anything, remember..." Truthfully, what had happened was a bit of a blur and Stretch couldn't recall all that much; all he really knew was it was only when Marley had touched the statue of Horus that Stretch believed they really would be leaving Dinium. The blind man had clasped it with both hands and stood, feeling its unnaturally smooth, cool surface and shaking his head slightly. This was, after all, an object it was hard to imagine an ordinary man having any hand in making. "It was nothing to do with me, Ty."

"It was you with the gun, nobody else but you." Ty looked Stretch up and down, regarding him now with a new-found respect since he'd proved that what had happened with Mo wasn't some freak occurrence. "Gods can ask, but we're the ones have to do the bidding."

"Maybe..." Stretch didn't know what else to say, not really feeling he was due any credit. And now that they really were going to be leaving the city he was wondering about Reeba. There was no way of getting in touch with her, no way of letting her know what they were about to do or when they might be back. If she made any kind of enquiries at Mo's she'd soon find out what they'd done, or some version of it, but that would be as far as she'd get. What would she think – that they'd tried to bilk Mo and were now trying to swindle her? Why should she trust them? Stretch's attention was caught by Jazmin, who had found a kitten and was playing with it on the floor. He nudged Ty. "What're we gonna do with her?"

"What d'you mean?"

"We can't take her with us," Stretch whispered. "Marley said there was worse than monsters where we're going. But what'll happen to her if we leave her behind?"

Ty shrugged. "She'll be fine, she's just a kid, none of Mo's people will remember what she looks like. We'll give her something..."

"I may be just a kid," Jazmin butted in; she didn't look up, just carried on playing with the tiny ginger and white kitten, "but I ain't *deaf* and you're not leaving me behind. 'Sides, it's my donkey, int it. Won't get very far without a donkey, willya?"

The new dawn was still mostly hidden under the blue-black horizon when the Great Northern Caravanserai was finally ready to leave. At its head was an elephant, a real one; this Stretch knew to be true because as soon as he'd heard about it he'd been up there with Jazmin to take a look.

He'd heard stories about elephants, but had never seen one before. Spectacularly huge, magnificently tusked and almost mythical, the awesome creature was made even more extraordinary by the fact that its massive ears, its face, trunk and legs were all painted in rich, vibrantly coloured patterns. On its head it wore a delicately embroidered, ruby-red silk cloth, and on its broad back it carried a carved teak howdah with a tasselled roof, in which sat Marley

Sheppard, with Sara Decima by his side. Regal, like a king with his queen, Stretch thought as he and Jazmin had walked back to find Ty.

And then, with the dark, almost purple orange leaking into the sky, the call went up from the front and they were on the move!

With red and white chequered scarves wrapped round their heads and across their faces, all bundled up against the last of the night's cold, Stretch, Ty and Jazmin became three of the sixty, seventy people who made up the group of traders, travellers and guerras about to leave the city. Indistinguishable, hiding in plain sight and safe. If Mo's people were still out looking for them there was surely no way they'd be recognized.

The pace was frustratingly slow, the caravan acting like one ungainly, gigantic beast that moved on wheels and legs with a lumbering slowness. Dust and voices rose and fell, axles squealed, animals complained and colourful pennants fluttered in the early morning breeze the rising heat created. Walking next to the donkey, Bone keeping pace, the three unlikely companions looked at each other; they all knew this journey was going to be a trek; a long, hard voyage into an unknown world. But they'd all agreed it was better than staying and trying to keep out of Mo's clutches.

It took ages, but they finally came to the Woeburn Point and crossed into Saynts territory, where Ty made doubly sure his scarf wasn't going to come undone; this was his home parish and the last thing he wanted was to be seen by anyone who knew him. Then, with the sun well on its way, they came to the outer edge of the city and the towering DeLancey Gate which was set into the crumbling wall that curved in a lazy, erratic arc all the way from the Wyte parish in the east, to the Bowfort Turret in the west.

As Marley's elephant approached DeLancey a rider was sent forward to pay the toll, and the guards then set about the process of having the two iron-shod doors hauled open. It wasn't long before the fugitives from Mo's rough justice were through the gates, Jazmin waving at the people on the walls watching their progress. Once outside the city the winding column carried on going as due north as the road would allow them, Dinium receding behind them with each step and every turn of a wheel.

"D'you think we'll ever get to come home?" Ty glanced over his shoulder again, suddenly aware of a sense of loss that grew with the distance between him and the city.

"We have to, we *must*..." Stretch, who was determined to stop himself from looking back, felt a small hand take hold of his and squeeze. He squeezed back and looked down at Jazmin. "Thanks..."

"Can I have me other bit of jewellery now?"

28 THE WILD BLUE

The start of the journey had been sluggish – mainly because of the very long, very steep hill that had to be climbed not long after they'd left the city. It was a seemingly endless incline that draught horses with their wagons and heavily loaded pack animals had to be prodded and cajoled to make their way up.

And then they were in the wastelands.

Cutting a meandering path through the ragged trees and low scrub, which stretched off into the distance everywhere you looked, was what was left of the Northern Way. It was wide, much wider than even the biggest streets in Dinium, and it must once have been a well-travelled route; now it was a devastated ribbon of poorly repaired tarmacadam, pitted with collapsed drains, potholes and flash-flood damage. But it was far, far better than no road at all.

At its disintegrating edges there was evidence that people had once lived out here – the faded, ivy-covered ghosts of buildings, the faint markings that might have been roadways but now led off to nowhere. Out into the lawless domain of the feral creatures, human and otherwise, who lived there.

You did not want to stray very far off the Northern Way, it was said, or you might never get back on it again.

There had only been a couple of rests during the day, once when the sun was at its blistering height and carrying on would have been stupid, and again when they'd come to a ford across a shallow tributary to the Isis and had refilled water carriers. It had been a long and tiring day and Dinium was now far out of sight. An exhausted Jazmin was asleep, curled up with Bone in the back of a small cart belonging to an old trader Marley had told them to stay close to. Stretch and Ty, both footsore and weary, were still tramping alongside with the donkey, who appeared to be able to go on for ever. Neither one had wanted to be the first to admit defeat and get up with Jazmin.

As dark began to fall and the first intimations of stars appeared, guerra guards on horseback came down the winding column with word that the caravan was soon going to stop for the night. In a move obviously much practised, the caravan formed itself into a defensive ring, larger wagons facing out, everyone else camped within the circle and the heavily armed guerras on watch at their posts. With the light finally fading and the temperature beginning to drop, lamps were lit and fires kindled. Outside the circle the bleak, forbidding wastelands closed in.

Isaak, the old trader, adjusted a faded, threadbare skullcap on his bald head. "This is the bit I hate," he muttered as he hung a battered tin cooking pot, half full of water, over the small fire he'd just finished making. "The waiting."

"Waiting for what?" Ty asked, watching Stretch cover Jazmin with a rough blanket.

"Wait and see, laddy...won't be long now."

"*What* won't be long?"

As if to answer Ty's question, there was the sharp, brittle crack of rifle fire, three, maybe more shots, from somewhere nearby. Then silence.

"Told you," Isaak smiled, revealing his two remaining teeth. "Didn't take long."

"What're they shooting at?" Stretch joined Ty and Bone by the fire, putting an extra stick on.

"Anything what comes close, laddy. 'Cos you don't want what's out there..." Isaak nodded behind the boys, "...getting in here. You do *not* want that."

"Is it monsters and dragons? And cannibals?" Ty's eyes had popped right open.

"Ain't never seen a dragon, laddy," Isaak added some vegetables and small pieces of meat to the pot and stirred. "Not so far, anyway."

It was a night that dragged its feet. A moonless night that didn't want to end. In the pitch-black the weird screams and howls, the wails, moans and growls from all around the encampment were like a conversation in a guttural, alien language; along with sporadic rifle fire, the constant noise kept Stretch and Ty awake and Bone fretting and nervous. It meant that the boys greeted the morning tired and grumpy, unlike Jazmin and Isaak, who'd slept through everything.

"Is it like that *every* night, Isaak?" Ty asked, stamping his feet to get rid of the pins and needles he'd got when he'd finally fallen asleep in an awkward heap on the ground.

"You think that was bad?" Isaak looked up from coaxing the fire back into life. "You wait till something actually gets past the guerras...that's when you'll have a reason to complain, if you survive."

Stretch crouched down opposite Isaak and watched the old man's gnarled and wrinkled hands feed twigs to the embryonic fire. "How much further is there to go?"

Jazmin plumped herself down next to Stretch. "Don't that depend on where you're going?"

Isaak glanced at Jazmin, eyebrows raised. "How old're you, girly?"

"Dunno." Jazmin shrugged. "Where we going, anyway, Stretch?"

"I did wonder when somebody was going to ask that question."

Stretch looked round to find Marley Sheppard a few feet behind them, smiling; standing tall and straight with the early morning sunrise setting his dark glasses alight, he looked like a devil with fire in his eyes. Sitting beside Stretch, his ears flat, Bone growled softly; he'd taken a distinct disliking to the blind man, and he didn't care who knew it.

Stretch stood up. "I just wanted to get out of Dinium... I didn't think..."

"For street-raised you're very trusting, boy. And despite what your mutt thinks," Marley waved his white stick at Bone, "*I* can be trusted. I'm a devout, reverent mortal and I've always thought any man's god was worthy of respect – why tempt the Fates, after all? And as for yours...well I've been in more shrines and lit more candles than you've had days in this world – all to help keep bad luck at bay – but I've never felt a presence such as his before."

"So where you taking us then?" Jazmin asked, squinting up at Marley.

"Cuts to the chase, the young one." Marley nodded. "I like that."

Everyone except Isaak, who knew exactly where he was going, watched Marley and waited. "Slip End, I'm taking you to Slip End," Marley finally said, then turned and walked away. "It's not far from here," he added, over his shoulder.

Stretch looked puzzled, ignoring Bone's attempt to make him tickle his ears by nuzzling his hand. "What's at Slip End?"

"The Guild." Isaak tutted to himself. "You youngsters today, you don't know nothing, do you?"

"But what...?"

"Enough of your 'whats', we got work to do..."

The next day crawled by; exhausting, slow and mind-numbingly boring, each minute was an hour, every hour like a day. Stretch was sure time had never, ever passed so unbearably slowly; as he trudged alongside the uncomplaining donkey, or took a turn sitting in the back of

Isaak's cart, he found that for the first time in his life he had time on his hands. Time to think. He started recalling everything that had happened to him since the fateful day he'd fallen inside Bloom's Mount.

The day everything had changed.

He thought about his mother and how she'd died, simply fading away as he held her hand. He thought about his father, who was either dead or alive but either way was over the river in Kaï-ro. And he thought about himself and how he'd been just another loner scav, someone who'd be lucky to last another five years before the heaps killed him.

Everything was different now.

From a boy for whom every day had always been pretty much like the last, and who had nothing to look forward to but more of the same, he'd turned into someone with a task, someone with responsibility. Truthfully he didn't understand even a half of what had occurred, or what the voice of Horus was saying. But he knew in his heart that he had no choice but to go where this god of the sky wanted him to. Could he raise an army? He had no idea, but he'd got this far and he would carry on and he would try because with an army he could march into Kaï-ro. Where he would find his father.

"**Faith changes you...**" said the voice in his head.

They would be reaching their destination some time during the next day, just one more cold and fretful night in the wastelands. Stretch and Ty had bedded down under Isaak's cart and Jazmin and Bone were curled up together on the back of it. Stretch had been asleep for what seemed like no time at all when he was woken by a hellish shrieking; sitting bolt upright he whacked his head on the cart's axle. Out in the darkness he could hear voices shouting, hear rifle fire and see flitting shadows in the random muzzle flashes. And then he realized something was different. The guns were being fired *into* the circle of wagons, not out at the wastelands...the caravan's defences had been breached!

"Ty...wake up!" Stretch reached over and shook the boy's shoulder.

"Wha...?"

"Something's got in!" Stretch turned back and had just started rummaging for his pistol in the bundle of rags he was using as a pillow when a hand snaked between the spokes of the wheel and tried to grab his face. He yanked himself away, snatched up the gun and fired, the pistol's recoil flinging his hand back. In the momentary explosion of brightness as the bullet fled the barrel he saw whatever had tried to attack him, the image burning into his eyes. It was a small, almost childlike creature, naked and filthy and covered in wispy, reddish hair; but it had blood running down its chin...it had teeth and it had claws and there was a wildness about it that wasn't at all human.

The creature screamed as Stretch's shot tore through its chest. All around the dark was filled with unearthly, guttural howls, frightened screams and gunshots. It was exactly like the terrible place he'd heard Lozzi priests describe, where evil people and those who hadn't lit enough candles went when they died. Stretch suddenly felt trapped underneath Isaak's cart.

"Come on, Ty!" he yelled, scrambling out but staying crouched down, holding the pistol in front of him with both hands. Another of the small things came rushing at him from out of the moonless dark; Stretch swung the gun round and fired, and its head exploded like a melon hitting the ground. The reality of what he was doing didn't have time to sink in; some part of Stretch's brain, the part which instinctively knew it was kill or be killed, had taken over. There was, anyway, no time to think and barely enough to act.

Behind him Stretch heard a strangled cry, and as he turned the moon slipped out from behind a bank of cloud. In its pale silver light he could see someone writhing on the ground, frantically grappling with the small, wraithlike figure clinging to his neck. "*Ty!*" he yelled, bringing the gun up, aiming and pulling the trigger in one fluid move, no thoughts of what might happen if his aim wasn't true. But there was no explosive roar, just a dull *KLIK* as the hammer fell on an empty chamber.

He'd run out of bullets.

Stretch hesitated, about to throw the now useless lump of steel on the ground. Then, realizing it was still a weapon of sorts, he ran over towards Ty and began hitting the creature hard with the barrel; this sudden attack distracted the chittering beast enough for Ty to wrench himself free of its killer grip and boot it away.

There was a strange moment of calm as the thing remained crouched on the ground, tensed, showing its sharp little teeth and screeching as it looked from Ty to Stretch like it was sizing each boy up, trying to decide which to go for first.

And then, just as Ty was getting to his feet, it leaped back towards him as if it had springs in its heels. But the creature never made it. A blur of snarling brown and white fur, hackles raised and fangs bared, knocked it out of the air. Bone's jaws clamped round the creature's scrawny neck and he took it down, whipping his head left and right like Stretch had seen him do with rats up on the heap. As he dropped the body on the ground there was the sound of excited applause.

"Good boy, Bone!"

Stretch turned to see Jazmin's smiling face poking up over the back of the cart. "Get down, stay out of sight!"

"It's okay, Stretch." Ty stood up.

"What?"

"Listen..."

In the eerie silence a cloud moved like a ghost across the moon.

"It's over," Ty said. "Whatever those things were, they're either dead or they've gone."

Stretch shook his head and was about to reply when he felt something grab his leg. As he looked down he heard Jazmin scream and saw one of the creatures, covered in blood from a massive wound in its chest, sink its needle-sharp teeth into his calf. The shock and excruciating pain of the attack stunned him and before he knew it he'd been dragged to the ground.

Stretch lashed out wildly as Bone and Ty joined the fray, finally managing to drag the thing off him and finish off the job he'd started. Lying on the ground, the wound on his leg throbbing like a drumbeat, Stretch began to feel woozy and distinctly odd...

29 THIS BOY

Sara Decima wiped some stray hair out of her face with the back of her hand as she stood up. "That's all I can do for now." She looked at Ty. "Put him on the cart, keep him covered, keep his forehead as cool as you can with a damp cloth and try and make him drink as much as possible of that tea I've told Isaak to make."

"Is he going to die?" Ty asked, still kneeling down by Stretch.

"No!" Standing next to him, Jazmin jabbed Ty sharply with her elbow. "Course he's not!"

Sara took a deep breath. "I can't say, one way or the other. It's a deep bite, a bad one, and the poison's in him now. He has a fever and there's no way of telling what will happen to him...those creatures, they carry so many diseases and for some of them there's no cure. Not a one."

"But he can't die!" Ty got to his feet. "You've got to stay and help him!"

"He's beyond my help now, boy." Sara started to walk away, then turned back. "If he can last till we get to Slip End, he'll have a good chance. Till then, you'd better hope that god of his can look after him."

Ty stood and watched her walk away in the cool dawn light. The whole caravanserai, which should already have moved off, was still circled, everyone in a state of shock. It had been, according to Isaak, the worst attack in a long, long time and as Ty gently lifted Stretch up onto the back of his cart he gave thanks to every god, spirit and soul-catcher he could think of that he hadn't been bitten as well.

Jazmin had laid out some blankets and as Ty put Stretch down she covered him. "Need you to do something, don't I," she said, sitting down next to Stretch.

"Say what?"

"Get his hawk...bring the god statue here to look after him."

The last half day of travel was, for Ty, agonizingly slow. He felt as if he had lead weights attached to his feet, and he had nothing useful to do as Jazmin had taken over looking after Stretch, coaxing him to drink the foul-smelling tea Isaak had made, keeping the flies off him, cooling his forehead and talking to the god statue. Pleading with it.

"Look after this boy; look after this boy; *please* look after this boy..." she said, over and over again as she held Stretch's hand and stroked the black stone carving. Beside her, almost like a statue himself, Bone sat, watching, waiting and guarding.

It wasn't long before word started to spread, up and down the caravan, that there was a shrine...that there was a new god...that this god would protect you from the demons in the wasteland...that he'd saved a boy's life and brought him back from the dead after being killed in the night's skirmish with the hellish shadow creatures.

The story grew by whispers as the day progressed...this god was powerful...he was more ancient than time itself, he was both man and bird, he spoke through children, he was keeping this boy alive...this boy who had been savaged by a pack of wasteland devils.

As he lead the donkey Ty watched the growing number of people who came to walk along with Isaak's cart so they could see the boy who'd been saved – see that he really was breathing – and see the statue of the god who'd saved him. They could touch the statue, too, but only if they paid a few coins to the little follower who was tending to the boy, watched over by his faithful dog. Ty noticed that it hadn't taken Jazmin long to realize there was money to be made if you had your own god.

It was approaching mid-afternoon when the word came down the dusty line that Slip End was finally in sight. They would be safe inside its fortified walls within the hour.

The change was almost instantaneous. Everyone's mood lightened, even the beasts seemed to pick up their stride and quicken their pace as if, like everyone else, they were anxious to get behind its gates well before night fell again.

Their arrival was signalled by the shouts of drivers as reins were hauled back and brakes applied to bring the caravan to a slow, grinding halt, and then nothing seemed to happen.

"What's up, Isaak?" Ty asked the old trader as he was finishing negotiations with Jazmin for a percentage of the money she'd made from people touching the statue. It was, after all, he explained, his cart she'd been doing business from.

"Going to take time to get inside." Isaak pocketed the coins Jazmin had begrudgingly handed over. "Stabling's got to be found for all the animals, food and water as well."

"We need to get Stretch in there..." Ty looked up towards the head of the caravan where, in the heat haze, he could see the spiked outline of Slip End's walls, flags fluttering lazily in a breeze he couldn't feel.

"Animals first in this line of work, or you ain't got no line of work, boy."

Ty hadn't got the energy to argue with Isaak, who left to go and check the bridles on his horses; instead he walked up the column of wagons and pack animals to get a closer look at their destination. He hadn't gone far when he noticed that a guerra was riding down the line in his direction, but he didn't give it much thought until the man pulled his horse up.

"Izaak near here?" he asked.

"Yeah," Ty nodded behind him, "the old man with the skullcap...why?"

The guerra ignored him, spurring his horse on and stopping next to Isaak. Ty wasn't near enough to hear what he said, but as soon as the guerra left Isaak began frantically waving. Ty ran back.

"What's going on?"

"Mr. Sheppard sent word to come out of line and get ourselves up to the gates sharpish, he wants us to take the boy to the healers as quick as we can..."

Stretch woke slowly, aware first of a rich, smoky incense drifting through his head like a lazy moth and reminding him of something, but he couldn't quite remember what it was. Ah...yes...that was it. All the terrible, red dreams had been wrong – he was alive! Then he realized that he could hear things. Voices? Singing? He couldn't tell. He tried opening his eyes to find out but no matter how hard he tried he couldn't. As he lay, exhausted by the effort, he worked out that he wasn't lying on the ground or in the back of Isaak's cart; much too soft, in fact so dizzyingly comfortable he fell back into a deep, deep sleep.

Some time later, he had no idea how long it was, Stretch woke again and this time his eyes snapped open as if they were spring-loaded. He was lying on his side, warm fur pressed against his face and a light blanket pulled up over his shoulders. Wherever he was, daylight streamed in through a shuttered window, making a crisp geometric pattern of thin white lines on the wall; otherwise the room was cool and dark.

"He's back, Auntie," said a scratchy little voice. "Properly back this time."

Stretch turned onto his back and attempted to sit up. Ranged in front of him were five, no, six old women, silhouetted against the window; they were all staring down at him, heads on one side, this way and that, like crows on a wire. It was weird and unnerving; the kind of thing, it occurred to Stretch, that you might encounter if you woke up dead.

"Am I...am I dead?" Stretch's voice was all croaky, and the old ladies looked at each other and giggled. "Who...?" He coughed, his throat and mouth dry like paper. "Where...?"

"Zelda." One of the women, he didn't see which, snapped her fingers. "Water, dear."

A small girl, part Nikkei, with almond-shaped eyes like Ty's, scurried out of the shadows with a metal cup, and held it out to Stretch.

"Help him, Zelda," the woman said. "I'm fairly sure he won't bite."

The little girl, edging forward as Stretch propped himself up on one elbow, held the cup as he took a couple of gulps from it. He lay back down, the cold water spreading down through his body in a slow wave; the girl bobbed a quick curtsy and hurried away.

Stretch found enough strength to push himself back so he was half sitting. "Who are you?" he asked, looking from one woman to the next. "And where am I?"

"Us?" said the woman, the one with the scratchy voice who was standing on the far right of the group, smiling at Stretch in a way that made him feel slightly uneasy. "Why we are the Guild, dear, this is Slip End and you are lucky to be here. Isn't he, Auntie?"

Stretch watched as five of the women all turned in unison to look at the smallest and most ancient of the group, her head crowned with a halo of fine, wispy white hair and her tiny eyes looking Stretch up and down. Her face was so lined it looked like it had been drawn all over with a fine-nibbed pen dipped in brown ink. She was dressed entirely in black, with a white lace shawl covering her shoulders and in the gloom she slowly shuffled over and put the back of her hand on his forehead, and then gently stroked his cheek. Stretch closed his eyes and for a second, just the tiniest moment, he was five years old again and his mother was alive and well and looking after him.

"This boy," said the old woman, breaking the fragile web of the spell, "is more than lucky, Mags. He is blessed. I can feel it."

The other old ladies all began twittering excitedly amongst themselves.

"Ooh, Auntie Skin! You mean he's..."

"Yes." Auntie Skin nodded. "He's the real thing, I'm sure of it."

"Course he's real. Not a ghost, is he."

Everyone turned in surprise to look at the small person who'd just spoken. Nobody had noticed her coming into the room.

"Jazmin?" For some reason he couldn't work out Stretch felt oddly glad to see the girl. "Where's Ty, what happened?"

"You got bit, dint you. They said you was gonna die, but I asked that statue of yours and you dint, did you." Jazmin pointed to the old ladies. "That Marley, he told 'em you was special."

"He did?"

Jazmin nodded, and fragments of what had happened began to piece themselves together in Stretch's mind...the violent, crazed attack out in the wasteland, the gunfire and the screams still loud inside his head. Stretch lifted the blanket and peered at his aching leg, at the bandage wrapped round where he now clearly remembered the creature biting him; some blood had soaked through to the surface. "How long ago, how many days?"

"Just the one."

"And where's Ty?"

Jazmin nodded towards the door. "Looking after the bags, int he."

Stretch turned to the old lady still standing next to him. "Who are you?" he asked, glancing at the rest of the group. "And why d'you think I'm special?"

"I am Auntie Skin and, like Mags told you, dear, we are the Guild; the Guild of Weavers and Spinners. We are the warp and the weft, gathering all the stories, remembering them and telling the tales; and people come to us because we have ways and we know a thing or two as well, don't we, ladies?" Auntie Skin smiled; she had tiny little teeth, most of which were gold. "And we can tell the truth from lies. The charlatan from the real thing. Marley came to us with you, sick from that bite you got, and told us what he'd heard, told us about your god and what he'd said."

Auntie Skin turned and motioned for the other ladies to move out of the way. Behind where they'd been standing, on a low table surrounded by small flickering oil lamps, was the black statue.

"**It only takes a spark**," said the voice in Stretch's head, "**to start a fire...**"

30 ACTIONS SPEAK LOUDER

The sandstorm had broken at some point during the night and Dinium woke a calmer, fresher place; the wind had blown away the city's noxious stink, while the sand had scoured off some of the ingrained filth, at least temporarily. With dawn the inhabitants began appearing, bleary-eyed, to start the business of attempting to scratch a living. Another day to survive, and maybe even prosper a little, if the gods, Fates and spirits were willing. And merciful.

It was some fishermen, down by the Savoy Crossing in the Cuven territory, who first noticed something odd was happening across the river. A gathering of boats and a build-up of men, rank upon rank of them, on the opposite bank.

Whatever it meant, everyone was in absolute agreement that it wasn't good. Not good at all. With the tide on the run out to sea, a lot of the skippers took the opportunity to go downriver with it, away from any conflict that might be brewing; they could always come back with the next high water when, hopefully, the trouble would be over – because there was no doubt at all that big trouble was in the air.

At the same time as feluccas were slipping from their moorings, sails up and searching for any kind of breeze to help them get away downstream as fast as they could, a large party of horsemen, bristling with enough firepower to start a small war, rode out of The Peeler's walled grounds. Taking up the rear, pulled by two gleaming, jet-black horses and steered by an ebony-skinned mute, was a sinister black carriage with black velvet curtains drawn tight across its windows. No one disagreed with those who said the carriage looked like it belonged to the night spirits and the last thing you'd ever want was to be invited to take a ride.

Behind the dark velvet, observing each other with sidelong glances but not talking, were Asbel and Dexter Tannicus; The Peeler and Bible Pete. They were family, there was nothing either of them could do about that, but they weren't friends. Not in any sense of the word.

Behind them, in the luggage compartment, was Samson Towd. Bound and gagged, he was cold, scared and extremely uncomfortable; but he was still alive, which he considered to be something of a minor miracle and entirely down to the fact that he'd prayed to Big Yelo non-stop the entire night.

They were on their way to Vielle-Dam to see Cheapside Mo, whether she wanted to see them or not. He'd overheard Turpin Jakes talking to someone outside the cramped cell in which he'd been kept, saying that every man on The Peeler's payroll had been called in for this piece of business. Quite why he was being taken along as well Samson hadn't the least idea, but he had the feeling that he might not like the answer and was in no hurry to find out what it was.

"Why are you making me come with you, brother?" Bible Pete pushed the curtain back slightly, letting a shaft of light into the gloom. Leaning forward, he peered outside.

"Because I enjoy your company, Dexter, why else? And leave that window alone."

Pete sat back with a grunt. "I came asking for your help, not to be dragged out at dawn and told what to do."

"You help me, *then* I help you."

"What you say goes?"

Asbel nodded. "Exactly."

"You haven't changed at all." Pete put down the tattered volume which gave him his name, took his pistol out of its holster and concentrated on checking it over; not as a threat, just a reminder. "Still the same selfish, inconsiderate weasel you always were."

"And likewise, brother, *you* are still the same pompous, blowhard know-it-all I had the misfortune to grow up with."

Pete put the gun away and clasped his hands together, interlocking his fingers and concentrating on circling his thumbs, knowing that if he didn't he'd surely put a slug in his brother. Not that his brother didn't deserve to be shot but, apart from making him feel better, it would not help matters. "If you're going over to Mo's with this mob, Asbel, why do you need my help?"

"Firstly, most of these men will soon be leaving us to go north and take Bloom's Mount." The Peeler glanced at his brother, smiling. "The Fitz won't like it, but they'll learn to live with it. The rest of us will carry on to Vielle-Dam, where you will go and see Mo. She'll talk to you. Everyone always talks to you."

"Flattery will get you nowhere," Pete said sourly. "What do you want from her?"

"I want to know where on that reeking heap we should be looking."

"And why is she going to tell me that?"

"Because you will tell her that if she doesn't I will torch that warren she operates from. With her in it."

"Diplomacy was never your strong suit, Asbel."

"If you have power, who needs diplomacy? All that talking wastes so much time."

Pete turned to look his brother straight in the eye and was about to reply when the carriage came to a rocking halt and there was a sharp rap on the door.

The Peeler looked puzzled. He leaned back, parting the curtain very slightly. "What is it, Jakes?"

"Something's up, Peeler..."

Pete watched his brother frown, obviously quite unable to imagine what could possibly have happened to stop his heavily-armed progress across the city. He saw him pick up a wide-brimmed hat and jam it on his head, then he opened the curtain a little wider and let down the window.

"Something's up? What does that mean?"

"We just got word...there's boats landing at the Savoy Crossing quay, boats from Kaï-ro, Peeler. Lots of 'em, with troops."

From his safe vantage point, out of sight at the top of a gentle rise which ran down to the edge of the river, The Peeler drew back the curtains and trained an old pair of binoculars on the activities taking place at the Savoy Crossing quay. It looked like an invasion. Two boats had already docked next to the remains of what must once have been a magnificent bridge, and unloaded the men and horses they'd carried over from the other side. Asbel Tannicus could see more on their way across the Isis...this was an army! Why were they sending an *army* to Dinium? This wasn't the way things were supposed to work, this was *not* the deal he'd worked out some years ago with Everil Carne. The deal that made it look like he was still in control, and worked because perception was nine-tenths of the battle for hearts and minds.

Letting the curtain fall, The Peeler sat back. "I want you to go down there and find out what's going on. Everil Carne went to see you, not me. Talk to him, see what he has to say now."

"I thought talking just wasted time, Asbel."

"Only an idiot wouldn't be aware that the balance of power has shifted, brother. And our sainted mother did not raise idiots." The Peeler rubbed his chin as he pondered. "She did not do that...and I can't help but think that this must have something to do with Carne's visit yesterday, something to do with that god they took over the river with them. And maybe what was taken from the heap. What d'you think, Dexter?"

"I have an idea you may be right."

"I know I'm right, I have a feeling for these things." The Peeler took off his hat and threw it on the seat opposite. "Everything gets so much less *straightforward* when the gods are involved!"

Everil Carne, standing up on the stirrups of his piebald horse, was supervising the mustering of the Dark Souldiers as they came off the boats. Behind him towered the shattered remnants of a bridge, hanging over the water; a road to nowhere.

He'd decided to bring just one squad of Risen and use them as the vanguard of their push up through the Cuven territory towards Bloom's Mount. Scare tactics. Their presence was often enough to make any opposition disappear and, from what he and the other men had seen on their previous day's visit, he didn't think they were going to have too much trouble achieving their aim of securing the festering heap of detritus in the Fitz parish.

Once he was sure they had control, and had established a safe corridor from the heap all the way back down to the Savoy Quay, Ms. Webb and the girl would be brought across and they would find where Setekh's brother had been brought back into this world. Although what good that was going to do he had no idea. Not his job to ask questions.

"Sir!"

Mr. Carne looked down at the souldier who was standing a few feet away, saluting him. "What is it?"

The man pointed away up the slope behind him. "Coming this way, sir."

Seeing the figure walking down the wide track towards the quay, Mr. Carne turned his horse and spurred it lightly into action. He recognized the man and wondered why Dexter Tannicus was here, now; he was not a great believer in coincidence.

The old man was alone and Mr Carne took no one with him as he rode up the slope to meet him, reining in his horse when he was a few yards away. "You are an unexpected sight this morning, Mr. Tannicus."

"The very same could be said of you, Mr. Carne." Pete smiled over his glasses at the military man whom he'd recently seen dressed so differently. "And I think I should tell you that while – like you – I've come to this meeting on my own, I am – also like you – not alone."

Mr. Carne stiffened, his narrowed eyes scanning left and right as he tried to see what the old man was talking about. Pete glanced back up the slope. "Oh, I'm not bluffing, Everil, they're there. Out of sight but not out of mind, as the old saying goes. Rather a lot of them as well I might add, but then my brother never could do anything by halves."

"Your brother?"

"Asbel – but I think you probably know him by his rather cruder monicker." Pete watched a puzzled look cross Mr. Carne's face. "The Peeler...my brother is The Peeler."

"Is he now? Yet another unexpected turn of events."

"The world is full of surprises, isn't it?"

"Far too many, for my liking." Mr. Carne forced himself

to stop searching for any signs of watchers. "What does he want?"

"He wants to know why you're here, and in such force. He's worried."

Mr. Carne had to admit he felt just slightly unnerved himself at the thought that he was in the sights of an unknown number of unseen guns. "Why send you?"

"Asbel doesn't like negotiating. He's no good at it. And I agreed to do this for him because I have a question of my own I want answered."

"You do?"

"Yes. What have you done with Reeba?"

"Who?"

"The girl who followed you. The one you caught and took back across the Isis with you. I want her back, Mr. Carne."

"She's yours, is she? Why did you send her to spy on me?"

"She's not *mine*, I don't own her and I didn't send her to spy on you." Pete shrugged. "She's just a child, a clever one who's learning to value what I value, but I have *no* idea why she decided to follow you. It meant nothing."

"Everything means something, Mr. Tannicus. My life is based on that universal truth."

"There's only one universal truth, which is that there isn't one."

"Much as I might enjoy arguing with you about that, I have a job to do." Mr. Carne turned his horse back towards the river. "And when I've done it, the girl will be coming back across the river. I'll see what I can do about her when we've finished..."

"Wait!" Pete called out after him. Something in his voice made Mr. Carne pull up his horse and look back. He found himself staring down the barrel of the large pistol that had appeared in Bible Pete's hand. "I said I was alone, I didn't say I was unarmed."

"Do you have a death wish?" Mr. Carne indicated behind him. "One word, and you die."

"Ditto, Mr. Carne," Pete said as he cocked the hammer, sounding an awful lot more sure of himself than he felt. Pulling a gun on this man had never been part of the job and he actually had no idea what to do next. Shoot him? Take him hostage? He took a deep breath...

31 FIRST SHOTS

The Peeler took the binoculars away from his eyes, blinked and then looked again. What was his brother up to? He was just supposed to ask a question, get an answer and come back. Simple. He was *not* supposed to threaten a man like Mr. Carne with a gun. Certainly not when the man was so obviously mob-handed. If this was the sort of behaviour reading books made you think was the sensible thing to do then he, for one, was glad he'd never read one.

From the window in the house he'd taken over to use as his observation post, Asbel Tannicus looked down at the events playing out at the bottom of the slope. His brother, looking like a solitary, slightly moth-eaten bear, had made an insane move. Did he think he was playing some kind of childish amusement where you were able to get up after someone shot you? Life was a game that had consequences and for Asbel it was all about winning; right now he felt like he was involved in a game where the pieces had decided what was going to happen next.

He stood back and thought for a moment, wondering what *his* next move should be. It didn't take long for him to work out that were only two options available to him. One was to fade away and let Mr. Carne do whatever it was he'd come over the water to do, which meant leaving Dexter to his fate. But then his brother should've learned by now to live with the effects of his actions.

And the other would be to use the element of surprise.

If he was honest with himself, Asbel Tannicus was fed up to his back teeth with kowtowing to the might and high-handed attitudes of those who ran Kaï-ro. He was worth more. He was not a spent force. And he wouldn't fade away quietly.

"Jakes," he snarled. "Come here!"

Bible Pete was a lethal poker player precisely because he didn't look like one. Any player who thought he was too distracted and bumbling to be much of a problem at the card table found that was a sure way to lose his shirt, and quite possibly a lot more. But as he stared up at Everil Carne, Pete could feel his confidence draining away like water poured onto sand. How much longer he could keep up the pretence that he knew what he was doing he didn't know, but as a betting man himself he would not give his chances very good odds at all.

"Don't make the mistake of dismissing me because I'm an old man, Mr. Carne. Act like that and I warn you, it's very unlikely you'll become one yourself." Years of practice allowed Pete to keep his face expressionless – a completely blank slate. Keeping his hands from shaking was another matter entirely.

"Kill me and someone else will take my place." Everil Carne stared down at the untidy old man, with his three pairs of glasses and his book tucked under one arm. This determined old man, with a gun. Why was he taking this insane risk? "It'll make no difference to the endgame, Mr. Tannicus, no difference at all because the Lord Setekh always gets what he wants."

"And all *I* want is an assurance that the girl, Reeba, will be returned. Your word, Mr. Carne. It's not a lot to ask, and not a lot to give."

Mr. Carne wasn't listening any more. He liked the man well enough, but he'd wasted enough time with this ridiculous situation and there was work to do; one flick of his fingers and this annoyance would be removed and turned into a meal for the vultures. But Everil Carne didn't have time to snap his fingers as a barrage of indiscriminate rifle fire abruptly broke out and some kind of grenade exploded behind him. Taken by surprise even his battle-hardened horse was spooked. It reared, almost throwing its rider, and it took all Mr. Carne's strength to stop the horse from galloping away.

It was precious seconds before Pete realized that Asbel had thought the unthinkable and done the unexpected.

Attack. His brother had a talent for the arbitrary and random act that caught people off their guard. He'd had it since they were children, and while Pete knew he might have been the better card player, Asbel was a fearless strategist, especially when he was able to persuade other people to put his daredevil ideas into action. And this, thought Pete as he looked for something to hide behind, seemed to be about as foolhardy as it was possible to get.

With the Dark Soul Army's return fire sending lumps of hot lead very much in his direction, and the ground shaking as more grenades went off, Pete did something he hadn't done in he couldn't remember how long. He ran. For his life.

The nearest piece of cover was an abandoned cart, one wheel missing and leaning like a drunk against a wall some twenty-odd yards away to his right. Uphill. Dodging ricochets and keeping the tightest of holds on his pistol and his Bible, Pete kept as low as he could as he made his way towards it, bullets whistling past him and thudding into the hard-packed dirt. This, he thought as he made it to relative safety behind the cart, is not what a man of his years and intellect should be doing with his morning.

It took Pete a few moments to get his breath back, during which he tried to ignore the frantic, hysterical sounds of pitched battle and work out what his next move should be. Did he fire back at those shooting at him, or wait calmly for the inevitable moment when Mr. Carne's troops beat back Asbel's rabble and proceeded to take their revenge on those who'd had the temerity to attack them? Because there was no way he could see this working out well, from his point of view anyway.

He let out a world-weary sigh, heartily wished he'd

stayed in bed and checked his pistol's load. He hadn't had a bad life, all things considered, and it was better to go down fighting than wait like a dog for the bloody end the Fates were surely soon going to deliver. Carefully peering round the side of the cart, looking for a target to take a potshot at, Pete was astonished by the scenes of absolute chaos which greeted him.

Far from being about to repel Asbel's men and go about their business as if nothing had happened, it looked like the impossible was occurring and the Dark Soul Army, or at least the part Mr. Carne had brought with him, were being put to rout! Pete could hardly believe his eyes. Down by the water's edge it was havoc and confusion; dead and dying bodies were everywhere as the withering fire Asbel's men were laying down kept the souldiers trapped, unable to move forwards and with only the river at their backs. From vantage points high up on the ruins of the bridge he saw that Asbel's men were also raining explosive charges down on any boats that tried to land, cutting off even that escape route and causing more turmoil.

From where he was, slightly above the action, Pete could see the mare's nest Mr. Carne had unwittingly got himself into. He'd chosen to land at the Savoy Quay because it gave him access to the most direct route to Bloom's Mount, never thinking that it left him open to a devastating attack. After all, when had anyone in Dinium ever retaliated? Never, ever. Those who ran Kaï-ro always acted as if they were free to do what they wanted, wherever they wanted to do it. But they'd reckoned without an opportunist like his brother, for whom exploiting weaknesses was a way of life, if not a religion.

Pete opted not to make himself a target by firing, just yet. Instead he observed, watching carefully as the events unfolded. It was hard to see what Mr. Carne could possibly do – he couldn't land more men at the quay without adding to his growing losses and he couldn't easily get his men away either. But was retreat even an alternative, did he and his troops understand the concept of defeat? Mr. Carne was, Pete thought, best described as a man who was between a large rock and a very hard place. And now, as the possibility that they might have to take to the water to escape became more and more of a reality, maybe Mr. Carne and his men might remember the person they'd so casually thrown to the crocodiles the previous day.

Then, out of the pandemonium, some kind of order appeared to be taking shape as a protective half-circle of souldiers formed themselves behind their fallen colleagues. There was something odd about these men. They had a decidedly inhuman lack of fear in the face of this dire situation. Those souldiers who were standing fired volley after volley at the places where the grenades were being thrown from, while the ones who were kneeling aimed at the sniper positions, and none of them moved as they were literally torn to shreds.

To their rear, in an astonishingly orderly fashion considering the hellish circumstances, the remains of the landing party made their way down the quay to where a couple of boats had now managed to dock. It was an impressive if suicidal manoeuvre, but it was allowing Mr. Carne to get at least some of his men away with their lives; as he watched, Pete marvelled at the discipline of these men, prepared to lay down their lives to save others.

What he couldn't know as he saw one after another fall shattered and bloody to the ground was that these were men who were looking for a way, any way, to be destroyed so completely that they could never come back again. The Risen and Mongrels, men who had already died any number of times, men who'd had no choice but to be reanimated, had only one fear and that was another life.

One moment gunfire and explosions, bullets and bombs were flying, the noise so continuous that you really didn't hear it any more your ears were so bludgeoned. And then the next, quiet.

It was over.

They had won.

It hardly seemed possible, but Pete could see that there was no one left standing down by the quay and that the boats were tacking back across the Isis. Back to Kaï-ro. Pete came out from behind his bullet-scarred refuge, clutching his Bible in one hand and unfired gun in the other and stood in the silence shaking his head. Then he walked down towards the river's edge, stopping where the bodies began to pile up. The water was now red with blood, as if the sun was setting and the Isis was rising with the incoming tide.

This was not the end of anything, Pete thought, not quite able to take in everything he'd witnessed. This was just the beginning. They would be back, of that he had no doubts. No doubts at all.

32 NEWS TRAVELS

Standing up in the lead boat, the OverSeer General shook with a barely contained rage. He was cold from shock, drained and covered in blood. It dripped from his hands, it ran down his face and into his eyes, turning the world red; some of the gore was his own. And everything hurt, from his wounded pride to the raw, jagged bullet wounds he'd picked up in the battle. If you could call it a battle. More like an ignominious rout. A defeat inflicted on him by a worthless rabble.

A defeat...

Everil Carne looked away from the groaning, brutally injured men lying on the deck and stared back across the water at the Savoy Quay where he'd had to leave the bodies of so many of his men. Where he might have died himself, were it not for the suicidal bravery of the Mongrels and The Risen, none of whom had come back. Defeat. It was a bitter, poisonous word that left a sour taste in his mouth even though he hadn't actually said it. It was a word he knew Mr. Nero, the UnderMaster, just would not understand because it wasn't in Setekh's vocabulary, and quite how he was going to explain what had happened Mr. Carne didn't know. But he was most certainly going to be expected to come up with some kind of justification.

He could feel the frustration building up inside him. He wanted to scream that *it wasn't his fault*! How could he possibly have known something quite so extraordinary was going to happen? But he was the OverSeer. There was no one else to point the finger at, no one else to take the blame. Mr. Carne dragged his eyes away from the Dinium shoreline as he heard shouts from the prow of the boat. They were approaching their docking point, swinging round so they could be brought in by the rising tide, and he could see a growing crowd of people was there to meet them.

The word was out.

Mr. Carne stood in the middle of the black marble floor. He'd been there, unmoving, for almost a quarter of an hour, watching Mr. Nero sit and stare off into the middle distance. Watching as the two canix paced up and down, up and down, sniffing the air, smelling the blood and death that hung like a shroud around him; looking at him as if he was meat on a butcher's stall. Which wasn't so far from the truth as he was fully aware that under the law, which it was part of his job to maintain, failure was a capital offence.

"Would hanging be too good for him?"

Mr. Carne, whose concentration had momentarily wandered, snapped back, glancing at Mr. Nero, then quickly searching the room. There was no one else there. Who had he been speaking to? Was he supposed to answer?

"Or is the *shame* and the *pain* enough? For now..." Mr. Nero's gaze flicked here and there, never once landing on Mr. Carne. "He stands there, bleeding, as if the fact that he has suffered should make a difference..."

Everil opened his mouth to speak, but stopped, thinking better of it. Mr. Nero appeared to be listening to someone, frowning and nodding his head and muttering in reply; then, as a look of puzzlement passed across his face, he turned and looked directly at Mr. Carne, his eyes cold, lips pursed.

"We cannot imagine how this happened. It is *beyond* our understanding. It is impossible." Mr. Nero's eyes widened. "Do *you* understand? IMPOSSIBLE!" He leaped to his feet, visibly vibrating with fury and outrage, the muscles in his neck standing out like ropes; his right arm shot out sideways, his index finger jabbing at the air. "They *will* be made to rue this day! And *you* will go back and make them feel our pain, Mr. Carne, every single one of them. I want to see smoke rising from all across that rat-infested dungheap come dawn tomorrow!"

There was nothing Mr. Carne could say in reply. He knew that if he spoke now he'd say something he'd die regretting, like telling Mr. Nero the truth: there was no way he could do what was being asked of him in the time. Instead he bowed as low as he could, knives seeming to stab every muscle he owned, turned and strode out of the room.

As he left Mr. Nero's palatial residence a small seed of worry started to grow in Mr. Carne's mind. The UnderMaster had always been a man in complete control, but his recent behaviour, which Everil had put down to the Lord Setekh's increasing demands, was day by day getting harder to deal with. And at this last meeting Mr. Nero's anger, while justifiable, had not been that of a rational person. The question he couldn't stop himself from asking was: had the UnderMaster gone insane?

By the time Everil Carne had ridden over to the Ministry, the underground necropolis that Darcus Cleave liked to call home, he was exhausted and in dire need of the kind of medical attention only the UnderTaker could provide. But he had at least come up with an idea that would buy him some much needed time.

He went over and over the plan as he limped his way down the wide sandstone slope and into the maze of white tiled corridors, and by the time he got to Darcus's suite of rooms he felt sure that – with the Fates on his side – it should work. Without bothering to knock, Mr. Carne opened the steel door and went in. Mr. Cleave was sitting at his desk, poring over a fist-sized lump of flesh in a metal dish; every time he touched the glistening organ with the electrodes he was holding in each rubber-gloved hand it twitched and throbbed, alive for the moments the sparking metal rods touched it.

"Everil." Mr. Cleave looked up from what he was doing.

"Still alive, then. Just. I had a feeling Nero might finish off what I've heard The Peeler started across the water; so glad I was wrong."

"Stop playing with your food, Darcus." Mr. Carne slumped into a chair and began taking off his blood-soaked clothes, dropping them in a pile on the pristine white floor. "Mend me."

"Say 'please'."

"What?" Mr. Carne looked up, teeth gritted and frowning, as he tried to peel off a cotton vest which had stuck fast to his scabbed wounds.

"Nothing." Mr. Cleave sighed as he put down the electrodes, pushed back his chair and stood up. "Ostinelli! We have work to do!" He looked down at Everil Carne. "Flesh wounds...is that all?"

"It's enough."

"This is hardly going to stretch my talents..."

"Just get me back out there." Mr. Carne glanced over his shoulder. "I have a city to destroy."

"Vengeance will be his?"

The voice made both men look round in surprise to find Ms. Webb at the door. The door neither of them had heard or seen open and close.

"Phaedra...does no one knock any more?" Mr. Cleave shook his head, eyebrows raised. "What brings you here?"

"Everything."

"That is...what can I say? Not very *specific*?" Mr. Cleave motioned to his assistant Ostinelli that he should get the stainless steel operating table ready. "What, particularly, is bothering you?"

"Everything." Ms. Webb saw Darcus take a deep breath,

and held up her hand. "By which I mean the way everything is intricately interconnected and nothing happens in isolation...every action always has an effect on something else. I have cast the stones, looked deep into the cards and consulted the astral charts and it's the same everywhere."

"What is, Phaedra?" Darcus didn't even try to keep the sneer out of his voice.

"The closer we get to the Completion, the more I see turmoil, upheaval and disquiet. Chaos, Darcus, I see chaos." Ms. Webb watched Everil Carne hobble over to the operating table, now covered with a crisp white sheet. "Look what happened today in Dinium – the natural order broken, the dust beneath our feet fighting back. And as for Nero..."

Mr. Carne stopped walking. "What about him, Phaedra?"

"I think you know, Everil."

"And what would this be?" enquired Mr. Cleave testily. "Might *I* be allowed to know as well?"

"I don't *know*, but I'm beginning to believe that the UnderMaster is starting to lose his grip on reality." Mr Carne hoisted himself up onto the operating table. "Would you agree, Phaedra?"

Ms. Webb shook her head. "No. I think his reality is changing and what he's losing is control over himself. I believe he's no longer simply the vessel for the Lord Setekh. I suspect the two are becoming one..."

Reeba Moore lay curled up like a cat on the petal-covered cushions, exactly where the witch-woman, Phaedra, had left her. Warily she opened one eye very, very slightly, and then slowly turned onto her back, fluttering her lids in the way she'd seen people do when they really were dreaming. There was no one else in the room, and she'd heard no movement or voices since Ms. Webb had left.

Slowly Reeba opened both eyes and then sat up. She'd done it. She'd fooled the witch into thinking she'd made her go into that deep, deep sleep again! When the strangely beautiful lady with the bald head had stretched out her hands to take over her mind for a second time Reeba had been ready for her. Within seconds of the woman's fingers coming close to her head she'd collapsed, slumping to the floor as if she truly was dead to the world. And it had worked!

But what did she do now? How long was the Phaedra woman going to leave her? Had she gone away, or was she still somewhere nearby? As Reeba had no idea where she was the questions that tumbled into her head had to stay there, unanswered. What she did know was that there were only two choices. She could either stay in the room and wait to see what would happen to her, or she could take responsibility for her own future and try to get back across the river, where she belonged.

Reeba got up. That was no choice at all. She *had* to try and escape. She'd been taken by the visitor she'd overheard Bible Pete talking to, the man she'd then followed so ineptly. If Pete had been working *with* him, surely the man wouldn't have kidnapped her...would he? She'd been trying to work out the meaning of everything that had happened since Ms. Webb had brought her back to the house, and had just about convinced herself that she'd made a mistake. How could she *ever* have thought anything bad about Pete? She *had* to get back if only to apologize to him.

As she stood alone, listening for any sound that might give her a clue as to whether she was alone or not, she wondered what Stretch and Ty were doing, whether they'd done a good deal with Cheapside Mo and were even now back inside Bloom's Mount. Suddenly realizing that pondering would get her nowhere, Reeba snapped into action and went over and began parting the dark, heavy silk that lined the room until she found an exit. She stopped and listened again. Nothing. She poked her head out and glanced left and right. Nobody. Time to make her move...

The house was as silent and empty as a robbed grave. The windows all had their shutters half closed, and the soft breezes that blew through them were perfumed with delicate, flowery scents. This, Reeba thought to herself as she padded silently along the deserted corridors, was the home of a real lady. A really rich lady, if the beautiful decorations and the marble and the sumptuous furnishings were anything to go by. The only thing that didn't fit was the complete lack of servants. Someone with this much wealth would have staff...wouldn't they?

But as far as Reeba could make out Phaedra the witch-lady lived alone. Alone, except for the animals. Standing at the top of the staircase she could see there were numerous large alcoves, made to look like desert caves, where snakes and lizards – big lizards – draped themselves over weirdly shaped branches and on beautiful rocks. There were birds, everything from oil-black ravens to rainbow-coloured parrots, there were small furry things curled up in corners and there looked to be every type of monkey imaginable. It should have been as raucous as a Cuven market, but instead the house was eerily quiet, and as she walked through it Reeba could feel eyes, hundreds of them, following her progress towards what she hoped was a way out.

"Goodbye, girly!"

Reeba, one hand reaching out for the door handle in front of her, whirled round in a panic. There was no one there.

"Be seeing you!"

A huge green and red parrot cocked its head and looked at her, bobbing up and down on its perch as if it was laughing at her nervousness. Heart thudding and sweat making her hands wet, Reeba turned back and gingerly opened the door. As she slipped out of the house, keeping low and darting from one bit of cover to another, she didn't see the raven appear at an open window behind her. Sunlight glinted off its obsidian eyes as the bird followed her progress...

33 BAD NEWS TRAVELS FASTER

It was sometime in the late afternoon on the day they'd arrived at Slip End. Stretch had no idea what the ladies had given him, but whatever it was it had certainly done the trick as he didn't feel like he was going to die any more.

He was with Ty, Jazmin and Bone, just hanging about doing nothing. Stretch couldn't remember the last time he'd had time on his hands, with nothing to do but spend it the way he wanted. He felt oddly guilty, like he should really be out on the heap looking for scrap instead of shooting the breeze with friends. The thought of friendship made him stop.

"I wonder what Reeba's doing?" Stretch said to no one in particular as he kicked at a stone.

"Probably wondering what we're doing." Ty moved in front of Stretch, walking backwards as he talked. "What *are* we doing? Are we staying here, going on with Marley or what?"

"We've got to go back, int we. Back to Kaï-ro." Jazmin threw a stick for Bone to fetch, but he ignored her attempt at a game. "Int that right Stretch?"

"Yeah...leastways *I've* got to go...I've got to go back with an army." Stretch looked back at the house, searching out the window of the room he'd woken up in, where the hawk statue sat on a table surrounded by candles. He knew he had a job to do, but he was waiting to be told how he was supposed to do it.

Stretch watched as a pigeon wheeled out of the pale blue sky; as it fell in a graceful arc he could hear the feathers, like a pack of cards being shuffled, riffling in the updraught. The bird swooped in low, circling once over the dusty square in front of the ramshackle wooden building that was Auntie Skin's house as well as the headquarters of the Guild of Weavers and Spinners, then it disappeared into the pigeon loft under the eaves.

"Carrier," said Ty.

"What?" queried Stretch.

"Bet you that was a carrier pigeon with a message."

"How'd you reckon that, Ty?"

"'Cos he saw it had something tied on one of its legs, dint he."

"Spoilsport!" Ty made a mock attempt to catch Jazmin, who ran off out of reach.

Stretch was just about to ask Ty where he thought the message might be from when the youngest of the Guild ladies, the one he remembered was called Mags, came running out onto the sagging veranda; she was waving like her life depended on them noticing her.

Auntie Skin sat in a rocking chair, slowly moving back and forth as if, like a metronome, she was personally marking the passage of time. Her hands were clasped together on her lap and in them Stretch could see a folded slip of paper.

"We have some news, dear." Auntie Skin smiled. "But I shall wait until Marley and Sara get here to tell you what it is so I don't have to repeat myself. At my age I do believe you have to make every word count."

Stretch nodded.

"I'd give it to you to read for yourselves, but I don't think any of you *can* read, can you?"

Stretch shook his head.

"We'll wait, then..." As the minutes ticked by Auntie Skin looked like she was falling asleep as she rocked in her chair, and then for no obvious reason she perked up. "Lemonade! Would any of you like a glass of lemonade? Auntie Rosie makes it and it is delicious, very tart...and it's got *bits* in it."

Before anyone could answer the door opened and Mags ushered in Marley Sheppard and Sara Decima.

"We came as quickly as we could, Auntie." Sara tugged on Marley's sleeve and he stopped walking. "Mags said you have some news?"

"I do, it's from one of our Guild members in Dinium – we're *every*where you know..." Auntie Skin unfolded the piece of paper she was holding; the paper was very, very thin and when she'd completely spread it out it was quite large and covered in fine, spidery writing. The old lady peered at the sheet for some time, turned it round and then looked up, smiling. "Silly me...no glasses..."

Auntie Skin held out her hand and one of the other old ladies took off the spectacles she was wearing and gave them to her. "That's better. Now let me see...yes, here we are...*'Dear Skinner'*...that's my name, Miss Skinner...*'Dear Skinner, I thought you'd be interested to know that an extraordinary thing happened today'*...which must, I suppose, mean at least the day before yesterday the way the birds fly... *'There was something of an uprising, led by Bible Pete and The Peeler, whose men attacked a force from across the river which had landed at the quay by the Savoy Crossing!'"*

Auntie Skin stopped reading and peered over the top of her borrowed glasses. "Ooooh! How exciting!" she said, eyebrows raised, then looked back at the letter. "*'Rumour has it that the invaders were making for Bloom's Mount, but The Peeler's men saw off those Dark Souldiers and sent them back where they came from, bloodied, bowed and humiliated! Nothing less than they deserve, in my humble opinion. I didn't actually see all this happen, but I know it's true as I've been down to the river and seen the bodies. My dear, it was like a charnel house.*

"*'Don't expect any more letters from me for a bit as I suspect that Mr. Nero won't like what happened today one little bit. The souldiers will be back. I hope this letter finds you well. Best wishes to all, Thea Leni.'"*

The room was silent for a long, long time, the only sound being the creak of Auntie Skin's rocking chair as everyone took in what the old lady had said.

"Bad news always travels fastest," said Marley, breaking the silence.

"What can have got into their heads? That's like poking a hornets' nest with a stick!"

"It is the spark, and now there will be a flame which must be fanned."

Everyone in the room turned to look at Stretch, who was standing, shoulders back and eyes narrowed, with Bone sitting statue-like at his side.

"Well, Marley," said Auntie Skin, "I must say I did think you were exaggerating, but it seems not..."

Marley nodded to himself as Sara guided him back to join the half-circle the Guild ladies had formed in front of Stretch: an audience, waiting to hear what else they were to be told.

"Now is the time to strike back with the army I shall raise...my brother is going to be angry, and anger clouds judgement. He will make mistakes, and that will be to our advantage."

Marley put his fist up to his mouth and loudly cleared his throat. "A-hrmm...*our* advantage, how does that work?" He spread his hands out. "Where does the 'us' come from?"

When Stretch turned to look at the caravanserai boss every single person in the room knew, in the same way they knew night followed day, that it wasn't the boy who was talking. He was merely the channel through which someone else – someone far more powerful – was communicating. And there was now no doubt in anyone's mind that he was, as Auntie Skin had said, the real thing.

"Look at me..." Marley's head swung round. **"Look, and tell me what you see."**

All eyes turned towards the blind man as he stood tall and proud, light glinting on his dark glasses. Marley's whole manner abruptly changed as he jerked backwards, as you might if a curtain had suddenly been drawn from a window in front of you to reveal an unexpected sight.

"I see...I see Dinium..." Marley's voice was hushed and as his head moved slowly from right to left it wasn't difficult to imagine that he really was seeing something through broken eyes that hadn't worked since he was a small child. "It's...magnificent...like it must have been, once."

"You see Dinium," Horus said, **"not as it was, but as it will be. If we win this battle."**

Moths of every size – some as big as dollar coins, others hardly bigger than motes of dust – flew around an oil lamp that hung above the table on the veranda. The pool of yellow light that it cast wavered as the hordes of confused night insects flitted in and out of its orbit.

The news of what had happened in Dinium had spread like wildfire through Slip End and away beyond the village's protective walls; along with it went the story of the boy-god and how he had made a blind man see the future. It was true, the tale-tellers said, the future! And like the moths, people had come. They wanted to see, to touch and to hear the person at the centre of all the excitement. Eventually Marley had had to bring over some of his guerras to keep order.

Now it was dark and most of the curious had been persuaded to leave. Out on the veranda at the back of Auntie Skin's house, where they couldn't be seen, Stretch sat with Ty and Jazmin; they were picking at plates of fresh figs, warm flatbread and goat's cheese, and sipping mugs of Auntie Rosie's bitter-sweet lemonade. It had been a mad, exhausting day.

"When he speaks..." Ty split open a fig, checked for worms, stuffed the whole thing in his mouth and carried on talking. "Y'know, Horus...when he speaks d'you hear him?"

"Course he hears him, he's *there*, int he." Jazmin looked at Ty like he was the dimmest person she'd ever met.

Stretch nodded. "I hear him, but I can't say anything...it's like I'm at the back of a large room, watching what's happening. It's the strangest thing." Bone trotted over and sat, his head on Stretch's lap, waiting for his ears to be tickled; he didn't have to wait long. "Everything changes when he comes to the front. I feel, I don't know...*bigger*. Like I could do anything, and it's like being the most alive you've ever been...and then, when he goes and it's just me, I feel smaller than ever. What can *I* do? He makes me say all these things, about armies and battles and winning fights, but how can *I* get an army?"

Stretch sat back in his chair. He felt tired and not a little scared; he knew that these were questions which were not going to go away, but to which there were no answers. Certainly not in his head. He looked at Ty, the Nikkei boy for whom action was the answer to most problems he came across, and wished that Reeba was with them. Someone he could really talk to.

"S'easy, int it," Jazmin said, taking some bread and cheese, then looking up to see Ty and Stretch staring at her. "What?"

"Easy?" Ty shook his head, then got up and went to lean back on the balustrade, folding his arms so his dragon tattoos appeared to be facing each other off. "What do *you* know about anything?"

Jazmin didn't even bother looking at Ty, let alone reply to him. She took a bite of her bread and cheese and glanced over at Stretch. "Pay 'em," she said. "You've got enough, int you."

Stretch chewed his lip, frowning at this strange, wise child who seemed to be able to see the world so much more clearly than either him or Ty. Of course...he had his share of what they'd brought out of Bloom's Mount. And if money could buy Marley Sheppard the services of the guerras to help protect the caravan, then surely gold would buy Stretch an army...

34 MAKING PLANS

Reeba skirted the wide garden, keeping close to the dense, high hedges that kept prying eyes away from Phaedra the witch's house. She'd quickly worked out that the most sensible thing to do was try and make good her escape via a rear entrance – if there was one – rather than the front gate. A much less public exit.

The whole place was eerily quiet, as if it had just been abandoned. Either that, or it was the moment right before something dreadful was going to occur. A sense of expectation was in the still air, but there wasn't so much as the softest breeze to move the tall palms that filled the garden; they stood in serried ranks, motionless and silent.

No sign of any life, human or animal; the only sound her own breathing.

As Reeba crept through the garden at the back of the house she glanced over her shoulder at the low building, searching all the windows for any evidence that she was being watched.

Still no sign of life.

It was puzzling, worrying even, but this was no time to try and work out why the house and its grounds were so completely empty. This was her one chance to get away and she had to make the best of it.

Heart thumping, Reeba counted slowly to ten, then quickly scurried from palm to palm away from the house, every second expecting a voice to call out or to hear footsteps running after her. Any moment thinking a hand would come from somewhere to grab her. But none of it happened.

And then there she was, at the thick hedge which marked the furthest extent of the grounds, in the middle of which, set into an arched gap in the foliage, was a squat brick gateway with a wooden door. Big and solid, strengthened with iron studs and with a heavy, metal latch. But no lock that she could see. Reeba ran to the door and cautiously gripped the latch ring with both hands and twisted; it moved easily and she pulled the handle towards her, the door quietly swinging back on its massive, well-oiled hinges.

She stopped when it had opened enough for her to poke her head out. And then she waited. Stood listening for something, anything that would tell her she'd been spotted.

No one tried to stop her. No one called out.

Reeba felt twitchy and apprehensive, and the longer nothing happened the more nervous and agitated she felt. Her stomach tight with anxiety, she finally peered through the open doorway, quickly glancing around. Nobody there. Empty streets. Frowning, she ducked back inside, unable to understand why she was feeling so hesitant, then slowly realizing it was fear. Fear that it was totally inevitable that a run of luck *must* be followed by a spectacular fall from grace; it was the way of the world.

Pete, she knew, would disagree absolutely. He would say thinking like this was being superstitious and that superstitions were the blinkers worn by the small-minded and ill-educated. He would tell her that there was no such thing as good or bad luck. All this from a man who, if he spilled salt, still threw a pinch over his left shoulder to blind the demon sitting there. The thought of Pete spurred Reeba on. She *had* to make a move or any opportunity she might have of getting back across the river would fade away to nothing. With one final look back at the house, Reeba slipped through the door, closed it behind her and pelted for the nearest cover.

From the top of the roof – a shadow perched in a shadow – the raven kept watch, following every step Reeba took with his bright, beady eyes. As she disappeared through the gateway he spread his wings and took to the air...

The lights throughout Darcus Cleave's personal suite of rooms and laboratories dipped, flickered and then slowly came back up to full power. It was usually a sign that what he called "an information extraction session" or a new experiment – or possibly a combination of the two – was in progress. Behind tightly shut doors blue lights sizzled, bellows pumped and sighed, surgical instruments clanged on steel trays and the rooms filled with the sharp odour of sweat and ozone-heavy electrified air.

A figure stood in one of the corners, her shaved, silver-webbed head shining dully, a shimmering cloud of dark silk surrounding her. The Oracle watched silently as Mr. Cleave and his assistant worked on Everil Carne. He lay rigid, arms and legs strapped to the steel table, a folded piece of leather gripped between his jaws. She had offered to cloud his mind and make the pain go away but he'd refused, she was sure because he didn't want to appear weak in front of Darcus – a man for whom the infliction of pain was a way of life.

Ms. Webb saw Mr. Carne's body jolt when Darcus clamped electrodes to his chest again, then watched as Ostinelli carefully applied rare unguents and balms to his many wounds. If the UnderTaker was the cure then you could well be better off dead, she thought. Something she was sure The Risen would confirm.

Darcus was a master craftsman whose combination of modern skills and ancient learnings, of science, engineering and the darkest necromancy was, she had to admit, astonishing. Even if suffering and agony played so big a part in his work, there was no doubt he did get results.

Standing back from the operating table, Mr. Cleave threw the final bullet he'd removed from his associate onto the ground and dropped a short-bladed knife into a dish, wiping his bloody hands on a freshly stained apron. "Finish up, Ostinelli," he said, untying the apron and letting it fall to the floor. "And make sure everything is discreet, I want minimal scarring."

"Bravo." Ms. Webb clapped her hands together. "A virtuoso performance, Darcus. I've never seen you work before."

"I deal in life and death, Phaedra." Mr. Cleave smiled but didn't look at her as he walked out of the room. "Absolute realities, not enchantment and illusion."

Ms. Webb watched her fellow Board member leave the room, then went over to the operating table where Ostinelli was squinting through blood-spattered glasses as he used the finest, thinnest needle and an almost invisible thread to sew up the many wounds. Watching his nimble fingers create the tiniest of stitches she gently laid her palm on Mr. Carne's frown-creased, sweat-covered forehead and carefully took the piece of leather out of his mouth. "No need for pain just for the sake of it, Everil."

"It focuses the mind, Phaedra...and why should I suffer any less than my men?" Mr. Carne grunted. "Get a move on, man – I have work to do!"

"We both do." Ms. Webb moved out of the way to let Ostinelli finish off the job by wrapping each of his impatient patient's injuries with neat strips of cotton bandage. "We should talk, you and I..."

Ms. Webb waited in some shade while Mr. Carne talked to one of the souldiers who'd been outside the Ministry when they'd come back above ground. Best that they were away from any unwanted eyes and ears, he'd said, with a glance back down the slope into Mr. Cleave's white tiled labyrinth.

As she waited she wondered whether actively disliking someone, the way she really *didn't* like Darcus Cleave, meant you shouldn't, couldn't trust them either. It was a conundrum and one she realized would have to be solved sooner rather than later, the way things were going.

With her own plans in motion, Ms. Webb now needed to find out exactly what Everil Carne thought. What were they going to do about Mr. Nero? And whatever they did, were they going to involve the third member of the Board? Would there be repercussions if they left him out in the cold?

For all his undoubted intelligence – what he would probably think of as his genius – Darcus Cleave's viewpoint was a narrow and inflexible one that only accepted the rational, the provable and the logical. Life lived by strict, fixed rules. But this was a time and a place where the irrational, unprovable and the completely illogical were the only things that made any kind of sense. This was a world where powerful gods of extraordinary antiquity had woken from a dreamless sleep; it was a world where, if you listened to the spirits – if you were, like her, sensitive to the mystical – you could be in touch with everything. Life seen as an infinite panorama, not as viewed through a small, half-curtained window.

"Phaedra?"

Ms. Webb looked up to see Mr. Carne standing in front of her, an amused smile on his face. "I was thinking, Everil."

"I could almost hear you."

"What are your plans?"

"I have orders that are impossible to follow, but which are nonetheless orders and cannot be ignored. My plan, such as it is, is the only way I can think of to buy myself some time."

"As I think we now both agree that Lord Setekh has almost completely taken control of Mr. Nero, what has he demanded of you?"

"Tomorrow he wants to see smoke across the water." Mr. Carne looked in the direction of Dinium. "The entire city in flames. And I cannot even get an invasion force ready in the time I have, let alone get them over the river."

"So what are you going to do?"

"Send in men under the cover of darkness, men who'll set fires all across the city just before dawn." Everil Carne shrugged. "If he wants smoke, I'll give him smoke."

"And Darcus? Are you going to tell Mr. Cleave?"

"If I was, he'd know by now..."

35 WHISPERS IN THE REEDS

Once away from the grounds of the witch's house Reeba became very aware of just how exposed she was. Out in the open, all on her own. She didn't believe – no matter how good her luck was – that there was any way she'd be able to wander down to the river in broad daylight and just take a boat, even right now when she didn't think anyone was actually looking for her. And once it was discovered that she'd escaped from the house things would only get worse.

There was a niggling, wheedling voice at the back of her mind saying that she should just take her luck and run with it, that she'd be all right, that she should carry on. Look around, it said, can you see anybody? And it was true, there was no one to be seen; the wide streets and flagged pavements (like nothing she'd ever seen before...so clean and new) were empty. While she knew there *must* be people somewhere, she couldn't see any sign of them.

Reeba pushed the voice away and ignored it. Her instincts told her that she had to find somewhere to hide until it got dark. Only under cover of darkness would she have any chance of escaping.

The house, surrounded by its fortress-like hedges, stood on top of a hill along with a number of other similar places. Low brush covered the lower slopes like ragged clumps of hair on an old man's head and Reeba ran down to the nearest thicket; she had to work out where she was, and until she could see the river she wouldn't be able to do that.

Moving at a crouch, she made her way through the spiky brush. As she moved forward she could hear a noise in the distance but couldn't work out what it was; then the vegetation thinned. Reeba stopped and looked out at the vista, her jaw dropping.

On a vast plain stood the three structures she was used to seeing rising up from the Dinium side of the river; she was now so much closer that their colossal blackness seemed to soak up the light. They were all the same shape, two far bigger than the third, and like mountains they rose up, pointing at the sky. The smallest was the one which was almost finished and she knew what the shape was from books on geometry she'd read in Pete's house. In them they had been described as "four equilateral or isosceles triangles rising from a square-sided base".

Pyramids.

She remembered she'd seen drawings of similar shapes in the treasure room they'd discovered inside the heap, but she'd never imagined they could actually exist. Or that if they did that they would be so immense, so vast. These structures were the biggest things she'd ever seen, even the smallest one bigger than Bloom's Mount itself. And like the mount people were crawling all over the pyramids, except there were thousands of them; from where she was standing they looked like nothing more than ants building three extraordinary anthills. The distant sounds she'd heard were the noises of construction and it struck her as she looked on, open-mouthed, that this was probably where Stretch's dad had been taken. It looked like half the world was down there. All those people who'd been taken from Dinium over the years.

Like great slabs of the darkest night the structures sat on the sandy plain and Reeba wondered what on earth they could be for. Evil, she thought, the most evil things I've ever seen...

A silver-bright sickle moon had cut into the night sky when Reeba finally left the hiding place she'd found, a place that had given her a secure, reasonably good view of the river. She'd spent a lot of time observing all the comings and goings, eventually picking the smallest, most isolated and run-down dock as her target. Making her way from shadow to shadow down the hillside towards the Isis, Reeba felt so nervous she would have been sick if she'd had anything in her stomach.

Every step she took sounded incredibly loud, every noise

she heard sounded imminently dangerous, so that by the time she'd made it to the shack next to the dock she was incredibly twitchy. She was pretty sure the place was empty, as the only two people she'd seen working at the small jetty had left at sunset. And tied up at the weathered landing stage was the solitary felucca she'd spotted. Perfect.

Too perfect...? whispered a little voice in her head. *No!* came the reply.

Sometimes things did just work out, the voice reminded her as she waited for a few more moments, just to be quite sure there was no one about. Everyone knew somebody who had had a day when the dice just fell the right way or the cards always came up trumps. Luck was luck, the voice said, and when it was your turn all you could do was go with it. And this time she believed it.

Reeba tiptoed down the creaking jetty and slipped over the side of the felucca. She'd been on a boat, once, but in truth she had no idea how to navigate one, so quite how she was going to get from one side of the river to the other she didn't know. And she also didn't know how to swim. Which was going to make the voyage even more nerve-racking. But, as she'd had to keep telling herself since she first escaped from the house, she didn't have a choice.

As she was about to cast off and push the boat out into the river, Reeba thought she heard voices. Two people, two men...she was sure she wasn't imagining it!

Precious seconds ticked by as she strained to hear if she was right or not, and then it was too late. The voices were no longer somewhere in the distance, but so much closer – right the other side of the shack! And now there was no chance she could get out of the boat and hide.

Heart thudding, a sweat breaking out, even in the cool night air, Reeba frantically looked for a way out, for one insane moment even considering diving into the water. Then she saw the untidy pile of sailcloth scrunched up in the prow of the boat and dived under that instead.

The smell of rotting fish was disgusting, enough to make her gag. Reeba pinched her nose as hard as she could, breathed slowly through her mouth and waited to see what happened next, praying to every roadside god she'd ever heard of, and pleading to the one Stretch had just found as well, that she wouldn't be discovered. Because if that happened she knew she was as good as dead.

Reeba felt the boat rock as the two men got in, dumping whatever they'd brought with them roughly onto the decking, their conversation turning to grunts as she heard them raise the sail. Moments later she realized the boat had been cast off and was on the move...but where was it going? Where were these men sailing to? They could be going anywhere: upriver, downriver, even – Lozzi help her – out to sea! Her head was so full of panicky thoughts that it was a minute or two before she took in that the men were discussing where on the Dinium side of the Isis they should land the boat.

They were going to Dinium?

They were going to Dinium!

Lying under the weight of the damp, scratchy sailcloth Reeba ached to the core – all she wanted was for her extraordinary luck to hold out for a *little* while longer...the tiniest bit! Just enough for her to get out of the boat and back on dry land without these men finding her. That was all she needed. Was it too much to ask?

"Don't ask much," she heard one of the men say, almost an echo, "does he?"

"Who, Mr. Carne?" came the reply. "Ain't him, is it, he's just taking the UnderMaster's orders."

"And it's us who has to do the dirty work."

"It's only setting a few fires, the smokier the better like he said, right? Not as if we've got to go up against anyone, is it? Not like those poor sods at the Savoy Quay...they said the water was red over there, can you believe that?"

There was no answer and Reeba, imagining the other man was probably shaking his head, wondered what terrible thing had happened at the quay.

"In and out, right?" the man continued. "Start the fires just before dawn, so the place is covered in smoke as the sun rises, that's what Mr. Carne said."

"How many of us're going over?"

"Ten, maybe twelve teams? I think it was twelve."

"Don't see the point, me."

"We don't have to, do we...lower the sail, we're nearly there..."

Ms. Webb sat in the pale light emanating from the flawless crystal globe in front of her, a sphere which seemed to be floating the merest fraction of an inch above the pool of mercury in a wide, shallow bowl. The child, like a perfectly trained pet, seemed to have done everything exactly as she should, believing with every step she took that what she had done was all her own idea.

Believing, exactly as planned, that she had free will, when it really was not so at all.

She had no idea that an ethereal, yet unbreakable thread now connected her to Ms. Webb...who now knew where she was and what she was doing. Phaedra had only just managed to get back to her secluded house, having had to deal with Darcus Cleave – who, because he was beginning to feel that he was being pushed into the margins, was being very, very unreasonable.

She sat down cross-legged in front of the crystal – her soul window – with her palms out flat, the thinnest trail of luminous blue rising from her fingertips. Closing her eyes she heard the muffled voice of a man saying that the sail should be lowered.

And high above, invisible against the night sky, she knew that a raven was keeping pace with the felucca as it tacked across the river. Silent, watchful, cunning – hushed wings spread out searching for lift, tail feathers twitching to correct its flight – her aerial spy followed Reeba's progress.

Exactly as planned.

36 MANY VOICES TALKING

Reeba waited. She was desperate to fling back the fetid sailcloth and take deep, cleansing breaths of fresh night air, but she carried on waiting until she was completely sure the two men had gone.

Crawling out, gagging, she found that the boat, its sail mast now down, had been left tied up in the middle of a dense reed bed. From the riverbank, she realized, it would be all but undetectable. Standing up on tiptoes she still couldn't see exactly where she was, but she didn't really care. The main thing was she wasn't in Kaï-ro any more.

There were two things she had to do, apart from making it onto dry land without getting covered in leeches or bitten by a crocodile: she'd *got* to get rid of the foul, nostril-wrinkling smell that now clung to her like a second skin, and then she *had* to find Pete. Because, from what she'd overheard, right now there were people all over the city getting ready to start fires. People sent from Kaï-ro. She didn't know where they were or why they'd been sent, but she was the only person who had a chance of stopping them.

She was soaked from head to foot, but luckily it was a reasonably warm night and Reeba didn't think she'd catch her death of cold. Although she'd probably ruined an entire barrel of someone's drinking water, the faint smell of very old, very dead fish still hung around her like a ghost, but it was the best she could do.

Having worked out that she appeared to be in an area the locals called Old Lupus, Reeba set off, keeping the river in sight to her right, towards the Cuven. At this time of night, with no lights and just about everyone in their beds, she and the cats had the city's roads and alleys pretty much to themselves; by the time she reached The Dile and was making her way down the narrow street towards Pete's house she'd dried out, but she was exhausted, hungry and thirsty. Ahead of her she saw there were no lights burning in any of the windows, which was odd as Pete was a night owl who stayed up all hours, reading, making notes and cataloguing his beloved books.

She got to the door and felt a numb tiredness sap the last of her strength away. If Pete wasn't here what was she going to do? How was she going to find him? How was she going to stop these men with their terrible plans to set the city on fire?

"He ain't in, dearie."

Reeba looked round, frowning; she knew that hoarse, creaky voice, it was the old lady across the road. Searching the layered shadows she caught the faint red glow of Missy Jana's pipe at the same time as the faint aroma of her spicy tobacco reached her.

"Where is he, Missy?"

"Had everyone out looking for you, dearie. Worried *sick*, he was."

Reeba walked over to where the old lady was sitting on a bamboo chair at the back of the narrow, recessed entrance to her house. "Pete knew I'd gone missing? How?" she asked, not quite able to take in what Missy Jana was telling her.

"Dunno, dearie."

"I need...I need to find him..." Reeba's voice fell away and she stood, shoulders slumped, blinking back sharp, bitter tears of frustration and tiredness.

A lucifer flared in Missy Jana's shaky, wrinkled hand, its sudden brightness startling Reeba, the stark image of the old lady cupping her pipe as she relit it vanishing as quickly as it had appeared when she shook the match out.

"He's with The Peeler, dearie. Leastways that's what I heard."

"The Peeler? Are you sure?"

"No." Reeba could just make out Missy Jana shaking her head. "But like I said, it's what I heard."

Reeba sniffed and rubbed her eyes, feeling like she was being tested beyond her endurance as The Peeler's quarters were back the way she'd just come. She straightened up. "I'd better go. Thanks, Missy."

"Hope I heard right, dearie."

"So do I," Reeba muttered to herself as she traipsed back down the street. "So do I..."

Leaning against the wall, feeling that at any moment she really might keel over, Reeba watched the truly ugly man who'd brought her in from the gates knock on the scarred wooden door in front of them. Behind the high walls The Peeler lived in what must once, long, long ago, have been a substantial building, a palace even. But its grandeur hadn't just faded, she thought as she waited for the door to open, it had been stripped away right back to the brickwork. Then the door swung open and Reeba found herself looking at a grinning dwarf in a shabby powder-blue uniform.

"Something for me?" The dwarf giggled, eyeing Reeba up and down.

"Get out the way, Venus." Turpin Jakes pushed the dwarf back with his foot and nodded that Reeba should go in. "My advice," he said as he led Reeba past the leering dwarf, "don't go near him, you've no idea where he's been."

The room, with its heavy curtains drawn tight, was humid and musty, lit by dense clusters of candles that seemed to be producing as much oily-black smoke as they were illumination. At the back of the room she could see a noisy crowd of people sitting round a long table and all talking at once.

"Pete..." she said, aware her voice sounded like it belonged to a small, nervous mouse. "Pete?"

"Bible!" Turpin Jakes shouted, ushering Reeba forward in an oddly gentle way. "I got her!"

Pete turned slowly in his chair, changing his glasses so that he could see better. "Got who?"

"Yer girl."

"Reeba?" Pete got up. "*Reeba!*"

Chaos broke out. Reeba found herself surrounded by a loud bustle of assistance...Venus, the Porto Novo dwarf, trying to edge his way in, Turpin Jakes elbowing him away... Pete fussing and bothering and asking far too many questions...faces appearing in front of her, one of which she was sure belonged to Cheapside Mo, voices each side of her, hands patting her head, her shoulders...and then the sharp crack of a pistol shot brought with it a sudden, ringing silence.

"Enough!" a voice yelled.

"Thank you, Asbel...now if you would *all* just give the poor girl some air."

The crowd parted, as if pushed aside by an invisible force, to reveal a small but rather grandly dressed woman. She wasn't young – she had silver-white hair with two snake-thin plaits trimmed with black ribbons framing her ivory face – but then the bird-like glint in her eye and the way she held herself showed that neither was she old. Sitting at the table, a smoking gun in his hand, Reeba saw a bald-headed man with tufts of white hair over his ears observing her through hooded eyes.

"Reeba?" The woman beckoned. "Come here, dear."

There was something about the woman that made Reeba feel distinctly uneasy, nothing she could quite put her finger on, just a feeling that made her want to stay where she was.

Pete appeared by her side, putting an arm around her

shoulder and starting to walk forward with her. "No reason to be scared, girl...it's only Thea Leni, from the Guild."

Given a place at the table, with whatever she wanted to eat and drink, Reeba tried to ignore the white-haired woman sitting opposite her, staring; she was so hungry she also forgot for a moment where she'd been and what she'd heard on the boat.

Determined to gain as much kudos as possible, it was Turpin Jakes who reminded Reeba of what she'd overheard while hidden in the felucca. "She said she had news, Bible," he said, nodding, "'*important news*' she told me."

Pete stopped the huddled conversation he was having with the man who'd fired the pistol and glanced at Reeba. "What is it, girl?" he asked, just as she took a massive bite out of the hunk of still-warm bread she'd cut herself and then dipped in olive oil.

Reeba glanced round the table, aware that, as oil slowly dribbled down her chin and she tried desperately to chew and swallow the bread, all eyes were on her. Waiting. Expectant. Curious. She reached for a tumbler of water and took a gulp.

"There were two of them, in the boat..." she finally gasped. "They said there were maybe a dozen like them coming over to start fires. That's what I heard, Pete. They said someone called Mr. Carne had told them he wanted to see the city covered in smoke by sunrise."

There was uproar around the table, which it took another pistol shot to stop, bits of lath and plaster showering down from the ceiling.

"I *will* have order at this meeting...who invited you here? Me, The Peeler, that's who!" The bald-headed man's fist slammed down on the table. "And don't any of you forget that!"

Reeba gaped, open-mouthed, down the table. *That* was The Peeler?

"Retribution, brother..." Pete sighed and shook his head. "Catch a tiger by the tail and you have to expect vengeance."

Brother? The Peeler was Pete's *brother*? Reeba blinked and felt slightly dizzy – could all this be true? Could The Peeler *really* just be an old man...an old man who was Pete's brother? She bit her lip, wondering what other shocks might be revealed by the people sitting around the table.

"Vengeance? A dozen fires is hardly *veng*eance, Dexter." The Peeler turned his attention to Reeba. "Did these people say where they were going to start the fires?"

Reeba shook her head.

"Turpin." The Peeler snapped his fingers.

"Chief?"

"Get out there! Get out there *now*, find those men and bring at least *some* of them back alive! I have questions that need answering." He turned to look at Bible Pete. "Something isn't right, Dexter. I know they're going to come back and try to teach us a lesson, that's why I called this meeting. Every territory headman, every parish leader worth their salt is here because *I* know we can only beat them..." The Peeler pointed dramatically, in the general direction of Kaï-ro, with his gun, "...*together*!"

"Cut to the chase, Asbel." Cheapside Mo, her gold teeth sparkling in the candlelight, picked up a chicken leg and tore into it with gusto. "*What* isn't right?"

"Sneaking in here to set fires just isn't right, Mo. When they come, which they will, mark my words, they'll come like a storm, like Hell's own locusts...that'll be their way. Not skulking across the river under the cover of night to make *smoke*. No, this isn't about an eye for an eye, paying us back for what happened at the Savoy Quay...what reason would Mr. Carne have for telling his men he wanted to see the city covered in smoke, eh?" The Peeler looked round the table, but no one answered. "I'll tell you why, because smoke's a signal...it sends a message. I just don't know who it's for."

"Or what it says, Asbel." Thea Leni turned towards the head of the table. "You also don't know that."

Reaching to her right for a jug of water Reeba's sleeve swept a knife off the table and onto the floor. As she ducked down to pick it up Reeba caught sight of the woman's hands, one on top of the other on her lap; her gaze locked on to the tiny, electric blue sparks which flared and died around her delicate fingers...

Ms. Webb finished petting the raven, who had just returned from across the water, rewarding it with the choicest pieces of a freshly killed rabbit and a lark's egg. Its job, to be her eyes, monitoring the girl's progress while she was away from the house, was done now she was safely back in Dinium. Immediately before the bird's reappearance she'd watched as the girl was taken directly to The Peeler's inner sanctum – a turn of events that hadn't been a part of her plan and really was a stroke of luck. Phaedra smiled as she sat back down in front of the crystal ball to see what was happening now.

The girl was glancing up and down a long table, her eyes flitting from one person to the next, never staying on a face for very long; it was as if she was embarrassed and didn't know where to look. Reaching her hands out, ghostly blue tendrils weaving from her fingers and tracing a gossamer lattice on the globe's surface, Ms. Webb pulled voices out of the event she was witnessing from such a distance. As she strained to make sense of the babble of conversation, one voice boomed out above the others.

"You look like you could sleep for a week, girl," it said, a large bearded face of a man, who appeared to have two pairs of glasses perched on his nose, looming into view.

"I'll take her somewhere quiet, Dexter," a woman's voice said from somewhere nearby, and Phaedra's hands jerked backwards, momentarily breaking contact with the crystal. That voice! She was sure she knew that voice, but when the girl had looked round the table there hadn't been anyone there Phaedra recognized.

"Come on, dear..." It was hard to concentrate on the present and the past at one and the same time, but she was *sure* she knew this person.

Then, as the girl stood up from her chair and turned away from the table, the picture inside the floating translucent globe began to fade, the voices going with it. And no matter what she did, no matter how much energy she sent crackling out of her fingers, there was nothing Phaedra Webb could do to stop it.

Moments later she was staring at dead glass. Her soul window had been shut. From the other side. And she didn't know of anyone who had ever been able to do that...

37 A GOD WALKS IN SLIP END

Stretch awoke from a deep and dreamless night, crawling back up out of the vacuum of sleep to find Jazmin's face inches away from his, staring at him as she shook his shoulder.

"Whassthamatter...?" he mumbled, turning his back on her and pulling the sheet over his head; he'd fallen into bed fully-clothed he had no idea how late the night before, and really was not ready for a new day. "Tired, Jaz..."

"You gotta get up, Stretch...you *got* to come'n see!"

"See what?"

"Your army..."

Stretch sat bolt upright, the cobwebs in his head clearing

in an instant. "Army? Where?" His head jerked left and right as if he expected to find a squad of battle-ready men actually in the room with him, not just Bone and Jazmin.

"Outside."

"Outside. Right. How...where did they *come* from, Jazmin?"

"Dunno, but they're there, and more of 'em all the time." Jazmin shrugged, walked over to the window and pulled the curtains apart slightly. "Take a look if you don't believe me."

Swinging his legs out of the narrow cot, Stretch stuck feet into shoes and got up. Accompanied by Bone, he stumbled over to the window and peered through the gap in the curtains. The whole of the square in front of Auntie Skin's house was thronged with people, hundreds of them, far too many to count. No doubt about it. An army.

Eyes wide, mouth open and a look of complete and utter astonishment plastered on his face, Stretch turned to Jazmin. "But...?"

"Good, innit?"

"Yeah, but..." Stretch glanced back out of the window again. "What do I do now?"

"Go and see 'em, I should. That's what they're waiting for, Stretch."

Before Stretch could ask exactly how Jazmin knew that, the door to his room was flung open and Ty burst in, hair flying behind him, and skidded to a halt, pointing outside. "People keep on coming – have you *seen*? It's...it's..." He stopped, thought for a second and then shrugged, unable to find a word to describe what was going on.

"It's not real...impossible." Stretch shook his head in

disbelief, a shiver of dread running down his back. There was, after all, only one thing you could do with an army.

"Accept the truth of what your eyes are telling you. Accept the path you have been given. Accept the future you will help make, because sometimes that is all you can do. Sometimes what occurs is beyond reason. It is your destiny. Fulfil it."

In his dreamless sleep he had been able to forget about Horus and the voice in his head; even though it was now so much a part of his life hearing it still came as a shock. Stretch had never, ever thought of himself as someone with a destiny, as a person whom the Fates even knew existed. He was, surely, too insignificant. And now here he was, being asked to shape the future...he'd been right, it wasn't real. It couldn't be.

"Can't go out there looking like that."

Jazmin's bald statement brought Stretch back out of his thoughts and he looked up to see Ty, standing next to her, head on one side and frowning as he eyed him up and down. "Like what?"

"She's right," Ty nodded.

"About what?"

"Don't really look like a leader, do you?"

"'Cos I'm *not* a leader, am I?" Stretch sat back down on his low bed, head in his hands and sighed.

"*They* don't know that, do they?" Jazmin came and sat next to him. "Them out there."

Stretch looked down at Jazmin, wondering again where this orphaned street child got such a ferocious common sense; it was a bit scary, in the way that uncanny things could be.

"It's true, you just need to make yourself look different, Stretch, like I do with my ay-gee fighters." Ty walked round, examining Stretch. "You gotta give people what they expect to see, right? Except what *we* want is to make you look more magnificent than vicious. More like a god."

"But I'm *none* of those things...I'm not even very *tall*!"

"So you don't go down there..." Ty pointed a finger at Stretch. "You appear up on the balcony at the front of the house!"

"But..."

"And then what we'll do is ask Marley for the biggest horse he's got." Ty smiled at his own brilliance. "We put you on a horse, Stretch, and you'll be tall then!"

Stretch had no idea how much time it would take before Ty was happy that he was ready to make his appearance in front of the growing, expectant multitude outside the house. It seemed far longer than was absolutely necessary, but the Nikkei boy was insistent that every detail had to be right and he recruited a number of Guild members to help.

Stretch's hair was oiled, combed and then plaited with silver beads and gold thread; his eyes were decorated with kohl, using a design taken off the statue of the hawk; Ty brought up some of the jewellery they'd got from inside Bloom's Mount, choosing a lapis, emerald and ruby chest piece, gold bracelets and rings and a magnificent silver filigree belt; Jazmin managed to persuade Auntie Skin to lend her a large black silk shawl. Stretch had never had so much attention paid to him in his whole life.

Then, finally, Ty declared that the job was done. Stretch was ready.

"What do I look like?"

"A god," Jazmin said, with not a trace of mockery in her voice.

Stretch looked questioningly at Ty, who smiled back. "She's right. Again."

"Can I see?"

"There's a big mirror in Auntie Rosie's room." Jazmin went to the door. "Come on."

Moments later Stretch was standing in front of a full-length looking glass in an ornate frame that had once, long ago, been covered in gold leaf. And what Stretch saw when he walked in front of it took his breath away.

Only the fact that Jazmin, Ty and Bone were standing behind him convinced Stretch that this wasn't some strange fantasy vision. The person staring back out of the dulled glass did not look like him at all. Instead what he saw was the most extraordinary imposter. He turned his head and glanced sideways at his reflection, with one thought in his head: who was this person? This bare-chested man-boy, his hawklike eyes lined with black, his jewelled hair and glistening skin...this person who was wearing what looked like enough gold to buy the world.

"Told you, dint I." Jazmin nodded at the mirror.

"You did," Stretch said as a calm strength descended on him; he felt strong, as if his muscles were turning from flesh to woven strands of tempered steel. Somewhere deep inside him he knew that the true owner of the awesome reflection he saw in the mirror was coming to fulfil his destiny. A destiny now as intertwined with his own as the silver beads and gold threads were with his hair...

It was a moment no one who was there would ever forget. The images, the sounds, the power, all imprinted like scar tissue on their memories. At midday, with the sun hanging directly overhead, the doors giving on to the balcony on the first floor of the Guild house swung open and for two, three, four seconds, nothing happened.

And then, with every face in the assembled crowd looking upwards, from the darkened room a small figure, a child dressed in white, came out onto the balcony carrying a dark, heavy object. From behind her another figure appeared and strode purposefully out into the brilliant light and intense heat. Everything about him shone as if he was made from polished stone and beaten metals; he looked like he had stepped into view from another dimension. Another reality. This, everyone instantly knew, was no ordinary person.

Then, as he reached the balustrade, he unexpectedly raised his face to the sun. His jewelled hair streaming backwards he flung his arms high above his head, hands outstretched, fingers splayed.

With a roar so loud it sent a dark cloud of startled birds up into the cloudless sky, his audience mimicked his pose. It was a salute, a greeting, a statement of loyalty: *We are with you! Where you say, we will go; what you say, we will do. No matter what!*

In the silence that followed, all eyes focused on the girl-child as she bowed slightly and gave the object she was holding to the shining, jewelled person standing next to her. He took what those closest to the house could now see was a statue of a hawk, held it above his head and then out to the crowd, first to the left, then the right and finally the centre. In turn they all bowed, like the child had, and watched as this god-on-earth and his attendant turned and went back into the house, the balcony doors closing behind them.

Although not a word had been spoken everyone later agreed that they were positive – they would swear on the life of someone precious – they'd heard a voice asking them to follow; it wasn't an order, it was a request, but it wasn't one any of them felt capable of turning down.

Feeling slightly uncomfortable, Stretch stood opposite Auntie Skin, watching her as she rocked back and forth. She'd asked to see him – more correctly, he reckoned, she probably wanted to talk to the person who'd walked out onto the balcony. And that most definitely was not him. It was the strangest thing, being aware of what was happening – able to see and hear – but having no control over what was said or done.

He *had* been out there on the balcony (it was not, in any way, a dream), and he'd seen with his own eyes the reaction of the people down below. But they hadn't been looking up at him, Stretch Wilson, the Vix scav who knew all about scratching a living and nothing about leading an army. They'd seen what they wanted to see: a god-on-earth. Someone to believe in. And while he too truly did believe in the power and the authority of Horus, there was a part of him that wished he wasn't quite so personally involved in the battle yet to come. Even if it was the only way he'd ever have a chance of getting his father back...

"Is he with you now, child?"

Stretch looked away, aware that close up he must look like some painted carnevalle figure. He didn't say anything because he hadn't got the words that would allow him to explain what it was like being the living, breathing host for a god. Yes, he was with him all the time, and sometimes it seemed as if he, Stretch, wasn't there at all; it wasn't like this eternal presence was at his beck and call, though. He wouldn't come when he was called, like Bone. How could you possibly explain...

"I am here. I have always been here, but for eternities no one was listening," Horus said out loud, interrupting Stretch's thoughts. **"Now they are."**

"Old as I am – and I have seen more summers than I can, or care, to remember – and steeped in the spirit worlds as I am, I have *never* encountered your like before." Auntie Skin leaned forward in her chair. "The power I have seen you wield is far beyond anything we mere mortals understand as either 'good' or 'evil'. Such simple ideas won't do here, won't do at all. And though I feel that you are a benign force, I don't know if you care what happens to those who follow you and do your bidding."

"This is all about balance; *I* feel *you* are wise enough to see and appreciate that. What has risen in Kaï-ro is dark... what you would call evil. My brother is night to my day. We are both a part of creation: equal, connected and yet separate...and one should not ever overpower the other. But if I do not follow this path – if others do not follow the path with me, whatever the cost may be to them – the equilibrium of life will be changed for ever. There will no longer be a balance..."

"A darkness rising..." Auntie Skin had stopped rocking. "I have dreamed of this, but didn't know what it meant. And you..." she squinted over her borrowed glasses, pointing at the person in front of her, not really sure in her own mind who it was she was talking to, "...this boy – you and he can change the way the future unfolds?"

"We are not on our own."

38 FROM THE DARK INTO THE LIGHT

The soft knock on the door went unanswered for a minute or so. Stretch thought this was because, more than slightly deaf as she was, Auntie Skin probably hadn't heard it. The second rap was much louder, but when the old lady still didn't appear to catch it, and Horus said nothing, Stretch cleared his throat.

"Auntie?" He made a little wave.

"Yes, dear?"

"There's someone at the door."

"Must be for you, dear...I can be a little hard of hearing, you know, and my girls don't bother knocking any more. *Come in!*"

The door opened, Bone scooting through the gap, and then Ty poked his head into the room, a perplexed look on his face. "Got a moment, Stretch?"

"Um...probably, why?" Stretch's hands automatically found Bone's ear and started tickling it.

"Something's happened, kind of still *is* happening...and you ought to come."

"What is it?"

"We have visitors," Horus said, this time just to Stretch. **"We should go and meet them."**

"Visitors?" Auntie Skin sat up straight. "Did someone say 'visitors'? Where?"

Stretch looked at Ty, who he knew couldn't have heard anything because Horus hadn't actually spoken out loud this time, then he glanced at Auntie Skin. She was smiling at him, as innocently as only an old lady could.

"Ask me no questions, and I'll have to tell no lies, dear," she said cryptically. "Of course, generally speaking, there's no point in lying to *me* because...well, because I'll know, won't I?"

"What's she on about?" The puzzled look hadn't left Ty's face.

"Tell you later..." Stretch turned to Auntie Skin, one thought in his head: *Are you coming with us?*

"Where are we going, dear?" she replied to the unasked question.

Stretch looked at Ty, whose frown deepened as he tried to work out what was going on. "Where are we going, Ty?"

"Oh, right..." Ty ran his hand back through his hair and shrugged. "It's at the gates, Marley says you gotta come to the gates."

* * *

Stretch was not used to horses, leastways he wasn't used to actually being up on one; rich men and gods might ride them, but common scavs were lucky to have a mismatched pair of half-decent boots. And here he was, in the saddle of one of Marley's horses, the biggest, blackest mount he could ever remember seeing. The ground looked so far away he thought it was lucky he had a good head for heights otherwise he could well be feeling a bit dizzy.

Led by Ty and Jazmin, Stretch, still in full costume – wrapped in fine black silk and bedecked with all the extraordinary Bloom's Mount jewellery – was followed by all the aunts, with Mags in front, pushing Auntie Skin along in a rickety bamboo wheelchair.

They cut a swathe through the crowds in the square, who fell back to let them pass, slowly making their way towards the massive gates which were the only way in and out of Slip End. Set into the fortified walls, they were so heavy they needed two oxen each to open and twenty men a side to close. As they approached in the failing light Stretch could see that armed men lined the walls and chaotic preparations were being made to bring up powder, shot, bullets, arrows, oil and braziers.

Stretch could feel his pulse quicken as he tried to imagine what on earth could possibly be on the other side of the wall. Who were these visitors, and why did *he* need to be here?

Up ahead he spotted Sara Decima coming down from the ramparts; she was waving at them to hurry up, as if she thought they had any choice as to how fast they were going. And then Stretch found himself being helped off the horse straight onto the open stairway by Sara.

"You took your time." She turned and started back up the steps without waiting for a reply. "I've told Marley, whatever caused this, it ain't natural...mind you, him seeing the future is about as peculiar and unnatural an occurrence as I've ever witnessed in my whole life."

Nervously Stretch followed her up the steps, at the top of which he could see Marley, looking out over the spiked parapet. He shot a glance over his shoulder and saw that Ty and Jazmin were behind him, with the aunts getting into a muddle as they tried to organize how they were going to get Auntie Skin up the steps. Reaching the walkway he took a deep breath, stuck his shoulders back and went to stand next to Marley.

"Take a look, boy...from what everyone tells me, I for one am quite glad I can't see what's out there."

Stretch didn't reply. What could you say to a comment like that? There was nothing else left for him to do now but go and see what was the other side of the walls, so he went over and peered between the spikes.

In the falling dusk it was hard to make out exactly how big the gathering was. As the last of the day's sun glittered eerily in the thousands of pairs of eyes staring back at him, like wild diamonds flashing in the soon-to-be-night, Stretch realized he was looking out on another army. Only this one was made up, not of men from outlying areas, but creatures from the wastelands.

In front of him, in a hideous mirror-image of the sight which had greeted his appearance on the balcony earlier, stood a silent, feral horde.

Stretch stepped back in shock. It seemed to him as if the only possible explanation was that the pits of all the hells that the Lozzi priests constantly preached about must have opened and let loose their occupants. And every one of these disturbingly half-human beasts was looking up. At him. **"Ugliness is not a mark of character,"** said the voice in his head, **"like beauty, it is only skin deep..."**

Memories of the onslaught which had left him teetering on the edge of joining his mother in eternal darkness flooded back. The last time these savage devils had come it had been to kill, and he couldn't imagine why else they were here now, or what – apart from lust for slaughter – could have brought them out of the wastelands. And the worst thing of all was their silence, the fact that they were just standing there waiting for something. Someone. And the possibility that it might be him made his guts churn.

"People attack out of fear, as well as hate."

"He's right, child."

Stretch turned and saw that the Guild ladies had somehow managed to get Auntie Skin, and her wheelchair, up the stairs to the walkway. Having a person in your head talking to you was bad enough, but now it seemed that he also had someone who could read both their thoughts. From being a boy who lived out his days by himself he had turned into one who was never alone.

"They fear us, and we, in our turn, fear them," said Auntie Skin. "But something has changed, and it would be foolish to lose the moment, don't you think?"

"She's right."

He wanted to scream at his tormentors – the god and the old lady – that he didn't care if they were right...that he'd never *asked* to be the person they expected him to be, and *that* wasn't right! None of this was his choice and most of it was a fraud. He was just a boy. An orphaned child, with a dog and a few dollars' credit at Cheapside Mo's, who'd been all tricked out to look like he had some kind of significance and power when in fact he was too small, too insignificant, even to see properly over the parapet in front of him.

"They have heard," Horus said, his voice calm and very near. **"And now they need to see."**

"Heard?" Stretch, who was so spooked by what was happening that he wasn't aware whether he was thinking or talking out loud, felt Bone come and sit next to him.

"I called them."

Stretch looked up at the sky. A darkness was pushing from the horizon, reminding him of the expectant mass of inhumanity the other side of the wall. When he looked back down he saw that someone had put a couple of boxes in front of him...makeshift steps that would give him all the height he'd need to see and be seen.

A cooling breeze blew in from the west, making Stretch shiver. The wind sighed through the eucalyptus trees, rattling leaves and fragrancing the air with a slightly medicinal aroma. He could ignore everyone and everything (it was his life, after all), turn around and walk away. He could, but he'd never given up on anything before; in the world he used to live in he'd had it dinned into him by his father that you couldn't give up and still survive.

So was it any different now?

Stretch knew, deep down, that while so much had changed in so many ways, some things had not changed at all. Of course he couldn't turn away. Finding the strength from somewhere, Stretch marched over to the steps and walked up them, Bone with him.

Stretch stood and looked out over the strangely quiet mob below, illuminated by the flaring arc of yellow cast by the tar brands that were now lit all along the wall. His gaze wandered, zigzagging like the flight of a summer insect, not knowing where to settle and picking up odd, unconnected pieces of detail...teeth, fangs and horns. Patterned skin, striped, spotted and piebald, like a horse. Tails. Scythe-sharp claws and hoofed feet. Glistening pelts and ragged fur. Pride, strength and cunning. Expectations...

As he looked, Stretch realized that these were people, that even if they were in almost every respect monstrous, most of them appeared to have a flimsy connection to the human race. It was as if a thoughtless, foolish child had managed to get into the secret place where all life started and, just to see what might happen, had mixed up the things which made animals and people and nightmare creatures what they were. And right here in front of him was the result.

"They deserve respect, just like any living creature..." Stretch could feel himself being gently shifted aside as Horus moved – he didn't know how else to describe it – right between his eyes. And then, without him doing anything, his arms rose up above his head, hands splayed, and he heard Bone let out the most unearthly howl.

The answering roar started low and guttural, rising swiftly to a crescendo that seemed to hurl itself at the walls and then echoed in the darkness. Under any other circumstances it would surely have been the signal for an outbreak of carnage and massacre, but this, it was immediately obvious, was an expression of commitment and trust. It was an act of recognition and acclaim.

"Welcome," he heard Horus think. "**Tomorrow will be different, this much I promise...**"

39 SEEING IS BELIEVING

Reeba opened her eyes and sat up, that strange, not quite
real sense of having done exactly the same thing before
making her feel spooked and uneasy. But this wasn't quite
the same as the last time...she might have no idea how she'd
got to the place she now found herself in but now, as far as
she could tell, she wasn't in Kaï-ro. This time it had
happened in Dinium and she was alone in a dimly-lit room,
with no sign of the witch woman. Another lady was
responsible...what had Pete called her?

"Thea Leni."

Reeba whirled round, searching the shadows, only to
find that the empty chair next to the bed wasn't empty any

more. Sitting on it was the woman with the silver-white hair and intricately woven plaits framing her fine-boned, aristocratic face. She smiled, which was odd to watch as only one side of her mouth moved upwards, as if she was only half amused. Reeba's eyes dropped to the woman's hands, held neatly together on her lap; the lazy blue flashes were still flickering and glinting around her fingers.

"You're the same as..."

"What did she call herself?" Thea Leni asked.

"Phaedra."

"Ah..." Thea Leni's mouth tightened into a thin, very unamused line. "There is a pathway connecting us, that much is true, but we are planets circling *very* different stars, my dear. Very different indeed. She was once one of us, and one of the *most* talented gazers ever to be found by the Guild...she was destined for such very great things, but she fell from grace. And then her path crossed that of Nero Thompson. A circumstance that none of us foresaw which, considering what we do, is really something of a paradox, don't you think?"

Reeba ignored the question and asked her own instead. "Why am I here, in this room?"

"Because Phaedra was using you...seeing with your eyes, listening with your ears, watching everything that was being said and done. And we couldn't allow that now, could we?"

Reeba almost stopped breathing. She bit her lip, her eyes darting here and there. "How...?"

"Don't worry, dear, it's not happening now." Thea Leni reached out, a tiny indigo blizzard drifting towards Reeba, who immediately felt her panic ebb away. "I have closed the window, so to speak, and this room is shielded; Phaedra cannot use you, at the moment."

"But when I go outside?"

Thea Leni nodded. "When you go outside she will be able to see and hear again."

"What am I going to do – are you going to keep me in here for *ever*?"

"Oh goodness gracious, no! We *need* her to think you simply had a turn, or something," Thea Leni waved her hand and a constellation of minuscule sapphires burst in the air, "and the whole point is that she must think that everything is completely as it was."

"You *want* her to see through me and know what's going on?"

"We want her to *think* she knows what we're doing," Thea Leni said. "We want her to see and hear *our* story, the way we want it told."

"So what do I do?"

"Pay attention and remember *everything* I tell you." Thea Leni stood up, the stiff material of her black dress rustling as she moved about the room. "When we aren't in here you must *never* look at me, *never* – Phaedra mustn't see me..."

"But what about before? I know I was staring at you, I couldn't help it; surely she's already seen you?"

"It's possible she may have, but I've changed so much since we last met I think it's unlikely she would have recognized me. In any battle, knowing your adversary – and if you can, knowing them better than they know themselves – while it won't guarantee victory is a very good foundation for it. And we certainly have a battle to fight..."

"Would knowing who you are help her?"

Thea Leni nodded. "It's not just how I look that's changed...I have become, though I say it myself, a woman of some power. More than she could know, and *if* she knew I would lose what little advantage I have, and we cannot afford any losses."

"But if I'm not supposed to look at you, what *am* I supposed to do?"

"I will always tell you. It must seem to Phaedra that you are overhearing snatches of conversation, that you happen to be passing a room with a door open and your curiosity gets the better of you. That kind of thing. It will be like a play, with an audience of one." A soft knock on the door made Thea Leni stop and look over her shoulder. "Yes?"

Reeba heard a voice hiss: "*It's me!*"

"Come in, Pete," Thea Leni replied.

The door opened and Reeba watched Pete squeeze himself through the smallest gap he could manage, as if this would somehow stop something from getting out. Or in.

"Everything all right, Leni?"

"Everything..." Thea Leni opened her hands and an incandescent blueness flowered in the air, "...is fine. Please close the door, dear."

Reeba watched as Pete pushed the door to, peering over the top of the pair of glasses perched on the end of his nose, apparently dumbfounded by Thea Leni's performance. "Didn't you know?" she asked him.

"Know what, girl?"

"About what she can do."

"She's Guild, Reeba, there's no end to the things they can do, but they don't usually put on a show."

"These aren't usual times, Dexter." Thea Leni sat back down in the chair.

"I thought the Guild were just, I don't know..." Reeba shrugged.

"Ladies of a certain age who sat around and talked?" interrupted Thea Leni.

"I suppose so." Reeba felt herself going a bit red. "How come...?"

"Because some things aren't written about in books, girl," said Pete, "and never will be."

"Enough chit-chat." Thea Leni clapped her hands sharply. "Has it all gone to plan out there?"

Pete nodded. "The four we got alive, and you had a little word with, have gone back across. Pity it wasn't more, but Turpin and his lot were a bit overenthusiastic and I think we were lucky they didn't kill every last one of 'em."

"You found *all* those men?" Reeba sat back, amazed. "How?"

"There were twenty-odd of them sneaking about, but hundreds of us looking – and they didn't know their secret wasn't a secret any more. Their problem is they think we're a chicken-brained rabble over here, but it's never a wise move to underestimate your enemy, a lesson you'd think the incident at the Savoy Quay would have taught them."

"But you let some of them go back!"

Pete nodded again. "Part of the plan, girl, all part of the plan. They went back with a story to tell, about mistakes made, fist fights engaged in, close shaves, comrades lost and eventual success; over the water those boys'll be heroes, I mean, look what they did..." Pete went over to the window and pulled aside the tightly drawn curtains.

The fact that there was daylight outside the darkened room made Reeba realize she had no idea what time, or even what day it was. Then she saw the smoke. She got up and rushed towards the window, Pete stopping her before she could get there.

"Is it safe, Leni?"

"Let her look."

Pete stood back and Reeba went to the window, staring through the dust-streaked, flyblown glass at the billowing clouds of greasy black smoke hanging low in the sky.

"I thought you said you'd caught them all – why didn't you stop them setting the fires?"

"They didn't do this, girl." Pete grinned. "We did!"

"We...?"

"They wanted smoke, we gave them smoke – which, contrary to popular belief, you *can* have without fire. If you know how..."

Everil Carne lowered his binoculars. He wanted to feel pleased that everything was going so well, that Nero was probably even now looking over the Isis at the smoke "rising from all across the rat-infested dung heap", just as he'd ordered. Except he had a disconcerting feeling in the pit of his stomach, a sourness in the back of his throat that no amount of water would wash away. Something wasn't quite right, but he had no idea what, and this uncertainty – something he'd forgotten it was possible to experience – was unnerving.

He suspected it might all be down to the completely unexpected defeat they had suffered at the hands of what he'd always assumed was a disorganized riff-raff. It might also be that he'd lost so many good men on this mission, far more than he'd expected. With an invasion force to muster, Mr. Carne turned his back on Dinium and these thoughts, his mind immediately taken up with the strategies and tactics necessary to put the next stage of the assault plans into action; looking up he found himself facing Darcus Cleave, a dozen or so of The Risen flanking each side of him.

"Darcus..." He forced a wide smile. "To what do I owe this pleasure?"

"My *dis*pleasure, Everil."

"At what?"

"At being kept in the dark. And at your subterfuge and deceit." Mr. Cleave's lip curled, the early morning sun catching the polished lenses of his spectacles. "You are playing a very dangerous game, the more so because you and Phaedra are not only plotting against Mr. Nero – the very embodiment of Setekh – but have done it all behind *my* back!"

"I don't know what you *think* you know, but there is no conspiracy, Darcus. And it was my decision not to tell you anything, to protect you..."

"Pro*tect* me?" Darcus practically spat the words out. "Have you never heard the old saying that ignorance of the law is no excuse, Mr. Carne? Well I think the UnderMaster might well claim that ignorance of a plot against him is also no excuse! First Ms. Webb, through carelessness or design, lets that girl escape, and then *you*, against what I understand was a direct order, fake an invasion... treasonable acts, both of them."

"Are you attempting to arrest me, is that why you've come here?"

"You are so much a man of science, Darcus..."

The UnderTaker all but jumped out of his shoes, the abrupt appearance of Ms. Webb from right behind him taking him so completely by surprise he was unable to speak.

"...your intelligence is blinkered, allowing you to understand only what you can see and what you can touch; you dismiss anything else as fancy and delusion. And your loyalty has made you blind to certain very obvious truths." Ms. Webb moved so that she was equidistant between the two men and their opposing viewpoints. "We are not being disloyal, merely realistic. Mr. Nero is...not himself...the nearer we get to Completion, the further he fades away from us, and the stronger the Lord Setekh's powers grow, the less stable they both become."

"But we have *always* done what has been asked of us, that is how we have achieved so much..." Darcus glanced over his shoulder, towards the pyramids. "We can't stop now, not with Completion in sight!"

"This is a dangerous time for us. What Nero demanded was impossible in the time." Ms. Webb looked from one man to the other. "At dawn tomorrow the Dark Soul Army will be following the trail that Everil has had blazed, so Nero will have his invasion...and the girl 'escaped' because I wanted her to. She has become my unsuspecting spy right in the heart of Dinium. This is not a conspiracy, Darcus, it's about survival."

"What do you mean?"

"She means that if we continue trying to follow our orders to the letter, we will perish. We used to be part of this, you, me and Phaedra, working *with* Nero, but as soon as

Completion has been achieved, Setekh won't need any of us. He will let us fall, like leaves in the autumn."

"What a paradox you are, Everil." Mr. Cleave raised one eyebrow. "A souldier with the heart of a poet."

Mr. Carne nodded to himself. "Better that, Darcus, than a souldier with no heart."

Mr. Cleave stiffened, not at all sure The Risen, whom he considered to be the pinnacle of his work, hadn't just been insulted.

Ms. Webb stalled any action he might have been about to take by holding her arms out, fingers splayed and pointing at him and Mr. Carne. "The three of us, working together as one, will have greater effect than if we work apart... remember that the whole is always greater than the sum of its parts," she said, then turned and pointed both hands at Mr. Cleave. "If you aren't with us, Darcus, you must be against us. Which is it to be?"

"I'll let you know, Phaedra." Mr. Cleave spun round and walked off, The Risen staying where they were until he snapped his fingers for them to follow him. "All in good time..."

"Well?" Mr. Carne said, watching as the UnderTaker disappeared from view.

"He is against us."

40 ARMIES ON THE MARCH

It was late, way past the witching hour, but Stretch, Ty and Marley were still out on the veranda; Sara Decima had Jazmin nestled against her, covered in a light blanket, and both were fast asleep on one of the benches. It had been a long day, but even though they all felt tired there was just so much to talk about, organize, argue over and ponder on.

They were an oddly mismatched group around the table: the Nikkei boy with a talent for organizing fights, and the scav who spoke the words of a god, both sitting with the worldly-wise owner of the Great Northern Caravanserai, a blind man who had found he could "see" with his mind's eye.

Together, they had realized, there was a chance they might be able to do what had been asked of them: attack Kaï-ro!

Stretch could hardly believe he was even thinking of doing such a thing, let alone actually planning it. But it was happening and not only did he have a part to play, without him all this would never have happened. The instant he'd discovered Horus, hidden deep inside Bloom's Mount, he had become the pivot on which the whole extraordinary idea turned. Whether he wanted it or not, he was now a person warriors would follow to their death.

It had definitely been a very long, very weird day indeed.

For Stretch, most of it had been spent merely as an observer. Since nightfall, when he'd stood up on the boxes and looked over the wall at the unforgettable sight on the other side, Horus had been in control, directing the course of events to make sure that, with the coming dawn, an army would begin marching on Kaï-ro.

Stretch had watched, mute and unable to control his own body, as Horus had ordered that the doors to Slip End should be opened and then "he" had walked out into the midst of the silent, waiting multitude. Pulled in from the wastelands, seemingly drawn by an irresistible force, these strange and frightening creatures – hellspawn, chaos-dwellers, bloodsuckers one and all – quietly created a wide and perfect circle for him to stand in. And while Stretch knew that with his jewelled hair, his diamonds and his gold he really did look awe-inspiring and regal, he still felt like a boy. A boy who was some way short of a man. A boy who did not in any way feel like a god.

But, he had to keep on reminding himself, no one was

looking at *him*. What they were seeing and who they were listening to was Horus, who was a god. And everyone knew that gods didn't die, that was the whole point of them. That was why they knew so much. That was why they had power. Power you could feel, power which drew you to it, even if you looked like a demon and had the instincts of a rabid dog. That's who the creatures were looking at. They didn't see the scav, they were looking at a god walking amongst them. And as Horus stood, arms upraised, turning round in the circle he was at the centre of, Stretch could feel that these creatures, just like the people inside the walls of Slip End, also had a need to believe in something.

Him...

"Stretch. *Stretch!*"

"What?" Stretch was jolted back to the here and now by a sharp poke in the ribs from Ty.

"You were miles away...I was asking you what it was like when those five, the kind of leaders, came out into the circle. How could you understand what they said?"

"They didn't *say* anything." Stretch shook his head. "It was odd, I could sort of *feel* what they were saying, inside me. And what Horus was saying back. I just understood."

"That is what they call mind-reading, boy." Marley relit the tall hookah sitting on the floor next to his chair. "Once, the stories say, we could all do it, like the way animals talk to each other, but we lost the ability when we learned to speak. I suppose them out there," he jerked a thumb, "must never've learned to do that."

"They have names, just like us," said Stretch.

"Do they?"

"They told Horus who they were."

"And who are they?"

"I only remember one name...the one in the middle, the one with a tail, who was almost like a cat standing up on two legs and had skin with dark spots and patches all over it. It sounded like he said his name was Mazzo."

"Only people have names, boy."

"They think they *are* people, Marley."

"People?" Marley spat on the floor. "Then why do they act like animals...why do they try to kill us?"

"Because we think they're monsters and *we've* always tried to kill *them*," Ty said. "They're not the same as us and we don't like that."

Stretch looked at Ty, a surprised frown on his face. "That's what Horus says..."

"Well it's true, isn't it...they scare me to my bones, but when I looked over that wall tonight I wondered what we must look like to them." Ty held up his arms, both heavily patterned with tattoos. "I mean, some of us aren't even *that* different."

Long after Sara had taken Jazmin with her into the house they'd finally fallen asleep on the veranda, slumped exhausted in their chairs. They'd all agreed that even though the deep-rooted hatred and fear both sides felt for each other might well fade with time, time was something they didn't have. What they'd failed to work out was how these two very different groups – the men inside Slip End, and what they started to call, for want of a better description, the Others outside the walls – would ever be able to work together as one. As an army should.

It was before dawn when Jazmin woke them up, and all three felt as if every joint needed oiling, every muscle massaging back into shape. She said she was sorry it was so early, but there were some messages and Auntie Skin said they needed to hear them.

Stretch stretched, yawned like his jaw was going to break and tried to rub the gritty feeling out of his eyes. **"They have gone,"** Horus announced. Stretch didn't speak, just flashed back the thought: Who? **"Our allies. They understood that there are many barriers to be torn down and made into bridges – a job that will have to wait – and they are on their way."** He had no doubt Horus was right, but decided to let the others find out in the ordinary way.

Following Jazmin, the three of them traipsed into the house and up to Auntie Skin's candlelit room, where they found the old lady wide awake and bright as a button, sitting in a chair and looking out of the window at the last of the night's stars.

"One of the few advantages to growing old is that, because you don't do very much you don't ever get very tired." Auntie Skin turned and smiled at them over her glasses. "Every cloud, as they say...but one of the many *dis*advantages is a memory like a sieve – why exactly are you all here?"

"The messages, Auntie," said Jazmin. "Remember?"

"Obviously not, child...what messages?"

"One was from the gates, and there was that bird from Dinium, Auntie."

"Of course! How silly of me! Right...yes..." Auntie Skin picked up a piece of paper from her lap and started to unfold it. "Firstly, it seems those remarkable, but quite terrifying creatures from the wastelands have gone. Simply disappeared as mysteriously as they came, apparently. And then we have the news from Dinium..." She peered at the letter in front of her, holding it up to catch the candlelight. "Thea Leni starts by saying I should tell you all that someone called Reeba is safe and well, which I hope means something to someone as I haven't a clue who she's talking about. And then she goes on to say that The Peeler has decided to attack Kaï-ro. I must say, he always was a bit of a hothead, even as a boy..."

There was an army to equip and move out, with no time to lose; there was food to be prepared and packed, horses to be shoed, gunpowder mixed, bullets of every size that needed manufacturing and blades that required sharpening! Stretch was about to follow Marley and Ty out of the room so they could get started on the gargantuan job ahead of them when Auntie Skin called him back.

"A moment of your time, dear, if you don't mind."

Stretch hesitated, Jazmin waiting for him with Bone at the door. "It's all right Jaz. I'll see you downstairs, I won't be long." He looked back at the old lady. "Yes?"

For a few minutes the room was quiet, neither of them saying anything, nothing moving except dust motes falling through shafts of early morning sun.

"Who are you?" Auntie Skin finally asked, a gentle curiosity in her voice.

"Now?"

Auntie Skin nodded.

"Now I'm the boy underneath."

"He comes and he goes, then?" It was Stretch's turn to nod. "Can you call him, I'd like a word."

"None of this is up to me...I can't tell him what to do."

"*Try.*"

Stretch took an involuntary step backwards, surprised by the sudden harshness in Auntie Skin's voice; he noticed a strange blue haze surrounding her hands at the same time that he felt the now-familiar push as Horus stepped forward.

"I sense an...*antagonism*."

"How very *sensitive* of you."

"You are angry, jealous, resentful, even vengeful...a dangerous mixture of emotions to find contained within such a frail body, yet so powerful a mind. You feel control, like grains of sand, running away through your fingers, and you do not like it."

"Would you?"

Stretch watched as Auntie Skin's face twisted into an ugly caricature of her normally sweet features.

"I have given my *life* to the Guild; the work we do and the knowledge we keep has been everything to me. *We* hold sway in the realms of the mystical and the divine, *we* have always known and controlled the truths of this world, and I intend to see it stays that way.

"Do you think you can appear out of the wastelands, claim godhead and the right to make war and miracles without *permission – our* permission? I was prepared to allow you a seat at the table because you appeared to have genuine power, but..."

"I do have power, but I don't need your permission to use it, and that goes against every rule in the Book of Rules you abide by."

"I will stop you! You are just a boy who has put on boots that are far, far too big for you..."

When Horus was in front Stretch was used to feeling detached from his body, aware that there was a distance between him and his skin and his bones, but as he stared at Auntie Skin through eyes he now shared with a god, he began to realize that the gap was growing. He was being pushed further and further away down into a blackness, and he knew, with a rising panic, that if she managed to force him back far enough there would be no way he could ever return.

Auntie Skin was trying to kill him...

By the time dawn finally broke every single person in the whole of Slip End was awake and hard at work. Smithies sweated at their forges non-stop, cooks, seamstresses and armourers all attempted to complete the work of days in a matter of hours. Later it would be said by some that miracles were performed that day.

At the centre of the hive of industry and production sat Marley. A man well used to marshalling large groups of individuals to work with a single aim, it was he who decided what needed doing and who should do it, while Ty took on the job of organizing single men into fighting units. Neither of them had ever tackled a job of such bewildering complexity before, but as they'd left Auntie Skin's room, they'd both felt as if Horus had spoken in their heads, telling them that anything was possible, if you had the will to do it.

And as they worked, so busy they were oblivious to the fact that Stretch hadn't come out with them, they had no idea how much their friend was going to have to believe those words were true...how hard he was going to have to fight to prove it.

41 THE FIRST BATTLE

Stretch was cold. Cold and more scared than he'd ever been.

In the first days after his father had been taken, the achingly lonely time he'd spent trying to scratch a living and hang on to what little was left of his life, he'd thought he'd experienced the depths of isolation and rejection.

He was wrong.

Here, inside himself, he was losing all connection with his own body. At least that was what it felt like. He could still see, but it was like peering down a long, darkening tunnel, the end of which was getting further and further away. He could still feel, but there was a numbness creeping up from his fingers and toes and as his contact with muscle, bone and nerve withered he knew that when it was complete he would be gone for ever. And not only did he not want to die, he didn't want to die on his own.

Where was Horus?

"He can't help you now, child."

Stretch heard the voice – Auntie Skin's voice – as a hoarse, thin whisper echoing in his head. What did she mean? Why couldn't a god fight an old lady who could hardly see and hear and had to be pushed round in a wheelchair?

"Because I am attacking you, not him," she hissed. "The physical you, which is nothing more than the marrow and the meat we all have to carry around so that we might call ourselves alive. Without that, he is nothing..."

The paralysis reached Stretch's knees and his legs cut out from under him and he fell, limp as a doll, onto Auntie Skin's threadbare carpet; as he landed he watched a small cloud of dust rise up from the ancient fibres and threads and wondered whether it was going to be the last thing he saw.

"I can't do this without you."

Stretch would have jumped with surprise, if he could. *Where have you been?* he screamed silently. *She's in my head too, and she's killing me!*

"She may look like a wizened old crone, but, as I have discovered to my cost, age has not dulled the steel of her mind...she is quick and she is clever and she managed to cut me off from you, and now I must try to reverse what she has done."

From lying on his side, face pressed into the worn, faded carpet, Stretch found himself twisted and hurled onto his back with a thud.

"It is always better to do battle with your enemy face-to-face. Fight back, and give me the means to win – anything is possible, if you have the will!"

He could see Auntie Skin staring down at him; she was gripping the arms of her chair so hard the skin on her knuckles was stretched taut and thin enough for him to be able to see the bones. With wild eyes, flared nostrils and her colourless lips pulled back in a cruel, ruthless snarl, she had hate drawn deep into her features. Stretch knew that at any other time he would have been terrified by this evil witch, but she wanted him dead. And he wasn't going to give in and let that happen.

He was *not* going to die!

He wasn't going to die because he wanted to see Bone and Ty and Jazmin again. He wanted to find out what had happened to Reeba...and more than anything in the whole world he wanted and needed to go across the Isis into Kaï-ro and find his father. He had promised himself he would, and outside this room an army was readying itself to do exactly that.

So there was no way he was going to let this wicked spell-caster win...

Jazmin sat on the front steps of the Guild house, Bone lying next to her, his head in her lap. The square in front of the house was so full of men, women and children rushing here, there and everywhere else that it reminded her of watching ants at work, only a lot noisier. With ants you could see that they were all in some chaotic way working together, but Slip End was so completely disorganized it looked like it had been taken over by mad people.

Marley and Ty were off either doing or talking about things she wasn't interested in. And Stretch hadn't come down from talking to Auntie Skin, which was odd. She'd said she only wanted a moment of his time.

"We heard her, dint we, Bone?" Bone's ears pricked up at the mention of his name. "So where's Stretch, eh...what's he up to?"

Bone sat up and looked back into the house.

"Good idea." Jazmin stood, patting the dog's head. "We'll go and get him."

It was cooler and quieter inside the house. In fact it sounded and felt like the place was empty, not an auntie or anyone else from the Guild in sight. Jazmin stood in the middle of the wide entrance hall and listened, her eyes wandering over the pictures on the wall – dark portraits of ladies in strange, unfamiliar clothes – the furniture, the ornaments, vases of dried flowers, and she wondered if that was why people built houses. They needed somewhere to put all the things they had, most of which they didn't appear to use very much, if at all.

Shrugging, Jazmin made for the stairs, which creaked and groaned as if they were in pain as she and Bone made their way up. The whole idea of something large and permanent where you lived was completely alien to her, having always, as far as she could remember, lived on the street; although she had to admit she did like the idea that houses gave you a pick of rooms to sit in, and allowed you to choose to be either inside or out. That was good.

It was quite dark on the landing at the top of the stairs; every window, while it was open to catch whatever breeze there was, had its shutters closed to keep out the sun. Jazmin went along to Auntie Skin's room and tried the door, knowing it was pointless to knock. The handle stuck fast and refused to move. She jiggled it up and down, then shook it.

There was no change.

"Stretch! You in there still?"

There was no answer.

Bone whined, scratching at the door, and Jazmin looked down at him. "Int there, boy." She hammered on the polished wood with her fist. "Don't look like it anyway. Must've gone out the back way...come on, let's see if we can find him..."

Somewhere in the furthest reaches of Stretch's understanding, some part of him was still aware that a world did exist outside the vicious battle of minds he was locked in. He was sure he'd heard Bone whining and Jaz calling out his name and he'd desperately wanted to call back; but, as well as being unable to utter a word he knew that he needed to focus his full attention on defeating Auntie Skin. If he didn't he'd never see either of his friends ever again.

When he'd found himself trapped inside Bloom's Mount, faced with the reality that he might die there, he'd found the wit and the sheer physical strength to drag and haul himself back out into the sunshine. Well now he had to do it again, only this time he'd have to use strength of a different kind to push his way back into the world.

As he tried to prepare himself he heard a voice, Horus's voice, say **"Fight fire with fire,"** and a kind of mist lifted in his head letting him see, with an almost dazzling clarity, what he had to do. For whatever reason, Auntie Skin hated him enough to want to kill him...hated him with a passion. Stretch realized that although he didn't know how to hate with such intensity, he knew what his passion was. Life. He wanted a future, a future in which he found his father, and he wasn't going to let her take that away from him.

Stretch made his eyes focus, locking them onto the old lady's. He imagined he was a beam of sunlight, collected and intensified by a mirror, blinding her with his intensity. And then he started to push back.

He could see, as he advanced down the tunnel he was looking out of, the expression of shock on Auntie Skin's face. It was followed very swiftly by an almost physical punch that sent him reeling backwards as she counter-attacked. But, for all her skills and arcane powers, there was one thing Auntie Skin lacked that Stretch had a deep, deep well of. Youth. His had been a short life of being knocked down and getting up again, and again, and again. Hers had been a long life that was well into its inevitable twilight, and hate is an acid emotion, wearing away and weakening the vessel which carries it.

Step by determined step, Stretch forced his way back into his own body, the numbness fading as he slowly regained control, one thought in his head: *anything was possible!* And then, as soon as he realized he could actually move, Horus slipped in front of him to take charge; part of him understood why, but he still couldn't help feeling irked at being sidelined, elbowed aside yet again. But this time he didn't fight it. This was a job he couldn't finish.

He found himself back up on two feet, looking down on Auntie Skin, who was slumped, pale and drained in her chair. She looked older, much older as she pushed herself away from him, fear in her eyes.

"What are you going to do?" she asked, her voice a tired, whispered croak.

"Win."

"But what are you going to do to me?"

"Let you go. I think it's time, don't you?"

Stretch wanted to close his eyes, but he couldn't; he had to watch as Auntie Skin nodded in agreement and then closed hers instead.

42 NOTHING IS FOR EVER

Mr. Nero, out beyond the limits of tiredness, had completely lost track of time. He hadn't slept in it seemed like days, but neither had he been truly awake. He now lived with a constant dull pain, as if a very blunt knife was being slowly pushed through his brain, cutting a small part of him adrift. Small, but significant. All that was left to him by the large, angry and extremely belligerent personality he was sharing the confined surroundings of his mind with.

Because, truth be told, Setekh was taking over.

It would not be long, Mr. Nero knew, before he didn't exist any more, and he also knew there was absolutely nothing he could do about it. But he didn't think of himself as dying, more like he was fading away, as the sun when the night came...except, for him, one day soon there wouldn't be a dawn when he could rise again.

Ever since he'd discovered the statue, just ten short years ago, he had become used to instilling a sense of fear in people; they had respected him even if they didn't like him. Him...they had revered *him*! But it was so different now.

Of his three most trusted associates only Darcus Cleave remained true, acting as if he was still the Nero Thompson of old, with even the canix seeming to sense that there was now a different person in charge. It felt like these vicious yet intuitive creatures – brought into existence by a combination of Setekh's knowledge and Darcus's skills – were now there to stop him from attempting anything rash, rather than guarding him from other people's rashness. How the world changed.

Phaedra and Everil obviously suspected the truth and were acting accordingly. Setekh didn't seem to have noticed, being so obsessed with the Completion, but Nero knew they were telling him one thing and doing another. Oh how the world had changed. Only a matter of days ago such behaviour would have been unthinkable! Only a few days ago, had he discovered it was happening, he would have had them swinging by their necks. Today he didn't care. And tomorrow, more than likely, he would care even less.

They were on horseback, riding over to the pyramids (he realized he'd begun to think of himself as two people), where men were slaving every hour of the day and night to satisfy Setekh's demands. It was early, the sun rising behind them and a low, dirty pall of heavy smoke creeping sluggishly into the sky to the north, across the Isis. The smoke he'd virtually screamed at Everil Carne that he wanted to see, when he had, such a short a time ago, still had some control. But deep in what was left of his soul Mr. Nero didn't believe he had been obeyed.

But again, did he really care?

Ahead were the three pyramids. Dark, sharp mountains cutting into the sky, they were a monumental undertaking which had consumed him like a disease for the last decade. Nothing else had mattered, no cost had been too great and every sacrifice completely necessary to achieve the Completion. The ultimate mystery. In all the weeks and years he'd spent with the Lord of Chaos he had never thought to ask what it was; what exactly would happen when it was achieved?

Although he, Nero, had personally drawn up all the major plans, toiling for long days and nights over the extraordinarily detailed schematics, diagrams and scale models, he'd still had no real idea why they were being built and what their true purpose was. At first he had assumed that because a god wanted them, the pyramids were intended to be the ultimate physical representation of his awesome power – *Look! Bear witness! Bow down before the supremacy of Setekh!*

But as work progressed it had become clear that this enormous project had as much, if not more, to do with the skies above as it had with the Earth below. It wasn't simply the immense size of the three buildings that had made the calculations incredibly complex, it was also where they were placed in relationship to each other – and, it turned out, to the stars in the heavens. But again, he didn't know why.

As the work had progressed, Setekh had made Nero delve further and further back into the very depths of the Before Times, and he was especially interested in star charts and maps; on this journey of discovery Nero had learned some astonishing things about the past. He'd already known, from pictures, that this was not how it had always been; he understood that those who had lived Before had somehow been responsible for many of the changes that had happened – they had caused the destruction of great cities, the death of entire habitats and civilizations, as well as bringing to life hellish creatures and nightmare diseases. Yet the more he found out about the past it seemed the less he truly understood about the present, or what the future might hold.

One of the things he had discovered was that humanity had not been guilty of bringing about the greatest of all the changes. At some point in the distant past there had been an event, one story he'd read had called it "an immense and literally earth-shattering cataclysm". Something vast and deadly had come hurtling out of the sky and hit the Earth a glancing blow. And the Earth had shifted. Changed its axis.

It explained a lot, like why a place such as Dinium, which the histories described as having a wet, cold climate, now baked in the desert sun. But it explained absolutely nothing about why a god, a power as old as Time, required these pyramids and demanded they be built exactly where and how he wanted them...

Nero was shaken out of his reverie when the horse came to an abrupt halt. They were at the top of a small hill, looking out across the plain at the construction site;

dropping the reins Setekh stood up in the stirrups, both arms outstretched, fingers splayed.

"**As it is above, and always has been,**" he bellowed, his voice raw and fiery, "**so shall it soon be below – *FOR EVER!***"

Everil Carne was alone in his tent at the Bethlehem command post, putting the final touches to the invasion plan he intended to set in motion just as soon as he had the latest report from Ms. Webb on what was happening over the river. No matter how much Darcus might dismiss and mock Phaedra and her strange, unearthly skills – which was odd as the man owed as much of a debt to alchemy and necromancy as he did to his beloved science – they did produce results.

"I am not happy."

Everil whirled round to find himself looking at Ms. Webb. "Phaedra." He smiled, knowing there was no point in asking how she'd got there. "What are you unhappy about?"

"I don't know, which makes it even worse."

"There's a problem in Dinium?"

"I told you, I don't know...I have the information you want, the places where they plan to launch their attacks from, everything you need, but..."

Everil turned back to the map laid out on the table in front of him. "Good, good, come and point them out to me."

"But I have this shadow, a suspicion that all is not quite right." Phaedra, the morning light dancing on the silver web on her scalp, walked round the table to stand opposite Everil. "Ever since someone over there slammed the soul window shut in my face I've had this sense that I'm being led, that I'm following breadcrumbs towards a trap, but I can't see how. I've sent one of my ravens back, and I would suggest you wait for his return before you do anything."

"Waiting isn't one of the choices open to me; in fact I only have one, and that is action."

"On our own heads be it; you are the warrior, Everil, I can merely see into the future."

"Shadows and suspicions do not create a clear picture; I need facts, not feelings."

"Words more suited to Mr. Cleave..."

Before Mr. Carne could reply the silhouetted figure of a souldier appeared at the tent's entrance. "A message, OverSeer General, from upriver."

Mr. Carne motioned the man inside the tent, took the folded piece of paper he held out and read it. He looked up, frowning.

"What is it?" Ms. Webb came round the map table.

"A report from the commander of the western border detachment. He thought I ought to know about a couple of outriders for a gang of slavers who'd made it back to the fort."

"Why?"

"They both died, but before one of them did he told the commander some story about an army coming in from the wastelands."

"An army...from the north?" Ms. Webb closed her eyes and held her hands out, palms facing upwards, as if she was trying to draw information from the air. "There are no people out there."

"He says the man told him it wasn't an army of people...

they were fiends and creatures. And they were travelling in broad daylight."

Ms. Webb opened her gold-rimmed eyes wide. "That's not possible, none of it!"

"You and I have heard an immortal speak, Phaedra...we live in a time when I believe *any*thing is possible."

"What are you going to do?"

Mr. Carne indicated that the souldier could now go. "I shall have to send men out to the borders. A brigade of Risen. If there really is something coming out of the wastelands, they would be my weapon of choice – any word at all from Mr. Cleave?"

"No word, but I am told that he has gone back into the Ministry and that the gates have been locked shut."

"If Darcus thinks he can simply turn his back he is sadly mistaken."

"Are you going to postpone the invasion?"

Mr. Carne shook his head. "We go as soon as I've briefed The Risen."

"Can you afford to lose so many men from this fight?"

"No...I shall have to replace them with troops from the eastern border and the pyramid garrison, pull out some men of the workforce as well."

"Mr. Nero...Setekh won't be pleased if you do that."

"Even a god can't have their way all the time, Phaedra."

43 THE TIME APPROACHES

Stretch had said nothing to anyone about Auntie Skin, had tried not to even think about it. He'd simply closed the door behind him when he'd left the room and decided, if he was asked, that he would say that the old lady was fine when he left her, that she'd told him she was tired and going to have a little rest. But no one had said anything. In the confusion and chaos of their departure from Slip End no one had mentioned her.

The image of the old lady cringing with fear as she stared up at him, then closing her eyes one last time, stayed with him, though. Was it actually murder if the person who died was trying to kill you in the first place? Stretch had no idea, and as thinking about it only served to confuse and disturb him, he concentrated on the job in hand.

Up on his horse, Stretch looked around him at the army. His army. The complete impossibility still made him want to burst out laughing...what was he doing at the head of an army? As ridiculous as the whole thing was, there was no denying that what he saw around him was real and that he wasn't dreaming. These people were following him. Or the god they believed he was.

Unlike the Great Northern Caravanserai, which could only move at the speed of the slowest member of the group, this phalanx of men and beasts had set a blistering, breakneck pace and made astonishing progress. He had no idea exactly how far ahead the Others were, but he felt sure they weren't going to be that far behind them.

They'd had to leave Marley with Sara Decima at Slip End, along with Bone, a parting which had torn Stretch apart. It had not been much easier with Jazmin. Stretch had wanted to leave her behind with Marley and Sara as well, but the girl had refused point-blank, making it clear she'd follow under her own steam if they didn't take her. She was now riding alongside Ty on a small black and white pony.

Marley's parting gift had been a map. He'd "seen" the route Horus had given to the spearhead of wasteland militia and Sara had sketched out what he'd told her. Stretch should make for a place close by the remains of an old castle. There, Marley had said, they'd find three islands in the river and it would be easy to cross to the other side. The plan, once across the water, was not to meet up with the Others but to carry on and attack Kaï-ro from the south, where they'd least be expecting it. The element of surprise would,

Stretch hoped, make up for the fact that the men had travelled so far and so fast to fight. Only time would tell.

Across his chest were two bandoliers, heavy with bullets, his loaded pistol was in the holster strapped to his right leg and Stretch had a short sword in a scabbard hanging down to his left. He was a boy...a boy riding into battle. There had to be a very good chance that he might die there, a bloody and painful death.

But he *might* find his father.

He could be captured and tortured.

But he might find his father!

As he thundered across the wasteland, Stretch had to keep that thought at the forefront of his mind because, although *he* was the one through whom the god-of-the-sky spoke to the world and *he* was the one people saw as hallowed, there were moments when he found himself doubting. Since his father had gone he'd got used to looking after himself and making his own decisions, surviving on his wits. Often he'd felt older than his years, now he felt like a child again with little or no choice about what was happening to him; although he wanted to believe in Horus, a small part of him whispered that he was just a voice in his head.

And why should his words make a difference? Why should Horus's passion change anything? Who was right and who was wrong in the only battle that counted, the often vain struggle to stay alive? These were thoughts that might drive you insane, if you let them; questions without answers, thoughts which led you down and down into the darkest places, with no guarantee you would ever find your way back again. If you let them.

"There are no guarantees."

Except, Stretch thought as he was pulled out of his musing, that I have someone listening to my every thought.

"Neither of us asked for this, yet we are both answering one another's needs. Faith is a delicate, fragile thing – mine in you, yours in me – which can be shattered at any time. You have to believe that we *must* win this battle, otherwise the dark to my light will dominate; I have to believe you are strong enough to trust me that it is possible. A lot to ask of one as young as you, but age brings with it no promise of strength or ability. And you have so far proved to have both."

Stretch urged his horse on, ignoring the hunger in his stomach and the pain in his heart; they would be stopping soon, for a very short rest, and he would be able to deal with his hunger. But the knowledge that this was all an intangible notion, that there was no proof – just words, only words – made him feel empty inside.

Could innocent people die just because he was desperate to try and find his father, or was Horus's "truth" worth risking everything for?

Only time would tell...

44 THE NEXT BATTLE

Bible Pete made sure Reeba was nowhere in the vicinity, opened the door and slipped into the room. The Peeler was already there, sitting at the table with Cheapside Mo. Pete nodded to them both as he went across to the window and drew the curtains on the pre-dawn sky. "Have either of you seen a raven out there? Thea Leni thinks there's one that's paying us too much attention."

"If I got worked up and spooked every time I saw a raven, brother, I'd never go outside." The Peeler carried on cleaning his fingernails with a silver toothpick. "A magpie, on the other hand, I would worry about."

"Can we get down to business?" Cheapside Mo rapped

the table with one of her heavy, gold rings. "You get a person up before the dawn chorus, at least have the decency not to waste their time with all this talk of birds. Especially magpies."

"To business, then." The Peeler began to work on his teeth with the silver pick. "Apart from having become overly suspicious of ravens, Dexter, is Leni happy that her ploy has worked?"

"She is, Asbel." Pete sat down at the table. "Reeba has 'overheard' all the conversations we wanted her to hear, so we must assume that whoever's listening knows what we want them to know – that we intend to cross at the Nightingale Line and launch a frontal attack on Bethlehem. Is everything else ready?"

"As it ever will be. We have all my men set to go, and as many others that Turpin Jakes has been able to persuade, pay or coerce into service. Which, Fates willing, should be enough." The Peeler shrugged. "Mo has called in all her favours, and more, which means we've the boats we need to get men over to the other side – we have a fleet, brother!"

"Any sign of them making a move our way yet?"

"None." The Peeler got up and went over to the crude map that had been drawn on the whitewashed wall of the room. "We've got most of our boats berthed out of sight here and here." He indicated a couple of tributaries that ran south into the Isis. "We've left enough in sight our side of the Nightingale Line so as not to arouse suspicions, but nothing of any real use. We're assuming they'll have troops waiting to repulse our 'attack' on Bethlehem, and as far as we can make out they've been massing their main forces down opposite the Bowfort Tower, and east, facing the temples."

"A classic pincer movement, Asbel, with Bloom's Mount and your place here as the targets." Pete changed glasses and examined the map carefully. "Not very imaginative of Mr. Carne, who I'd say had been reading the same books as me, if he could read. Pity it's not going to work."

"Don't count your chickens, Pete." Mo's beady, kohl-rimmed eyes glinted. "Let *them* be the ones blinded by arrogance, not us."

"They may have an army, Mo, with all those ranks and uniforms and discipline." As The Peeler drew arrows pointing north across the river from the Kaï-ro side the door opened. "But we have strategy and tactics..."

"And the Guild, Asbel." Thea Leni glided into the room, holding one large and very dead raven in the palm of her right hand. "Never forget us."

"Pawn to knight four." Reeba moved her chess piece on the board and sat back to observe the state of play. "Why did Thea Leni kill that bird?"

Pete didn't answer immediately, nearly making a move, then pulling his hand back at the last moment. "It was spying," he said, not looking up as he finally moved his bishop into a protective position.

"How could she tell?"

Pete shrugged as he frowned at the board. "Who knows...that last move of yours was a fake, wasn't it?"

"Maybe..." Reeba moved one of her knights. "What happens now?"

"I think you win this game in the next three moves."

"No! I mean out there," Reeba pointed out of the window

of the "safe" room, the only place where Ms. Phaedra Webb couldn't see or hear what was going on.

"Rather a lot, as it happens...I concede, by the way, no point in prolonging the agony any longer." Pete tipped his king over, gathered all the pieces together and moved the board out of the way. "Imagine..." he dipped his finger into his mug of beer and drew a wavy line on the surface of the table, "...that this is the Isis, and that these white pieces on your side are us, and these black ones are them."

"There's a lot more of them than there are of us."

"It's not always about how many people you've got, but what you do with them, and..." Pete arranged the black pieces in three places along the beer river, "...what *they* don't know is that we *do* have more people. A message came in by pigeon from Slip End: there are soldiers on the march. Mr. Everil Carne and his Dark Soul Army are going to be in for an even bigger surprise than I thought they were."

"Are Stretch and Ty and that little Jazmin with them?"

Pete nodded. "I don't quite know how he did it, but it's Stretch's army, apparently."

"*What?*"

"It was a very short message, and didn't go into too much detail."

Reeba looked at the chess pieces on the table, a worried expression on her face. "What's going to happen, Pete, how are we *ever* going to beat them?"

"Imagine you were a bird..."

Reeba and Pete both jumped at the sound of Thea Leni's voice.

"I wish you wouldn't do that appearing-out-of-nowhere

trick, Auntie L!" Pete thumped his chest with his fist. "Not good for the old ticker."

"And *I* wish you wouldn't call me 'Auntie L', thank you very much." Thea Leni walked behind Reeba and put her hands close to her dreadlocked hair, a faint blue haze drifting down from her fingers. "As I was saying, imagine you were a bird..."

45 A BIRD'S EYE VIEW

Reeba could practically see the wind. Soft, warm updraughts were keeping her floating as if she was a cloud, so high above the earth that she could see the horizon, not as a straight, flat line but bent like the gentle curve of a bow. She had had no idea that was what it really looked like, and wondered if Pete knew.

She glanced down, amazed at the astonishing clarity of what she could see below. The sun was rising and its light and warmth were flooding across the opposing cities facing each other across the Isis and she could make out every street, every building – the old in Dinium and the new in Kaï-ro – and every man, woman, child, dog, cat and rat.

At least that's what it felt like, hanging high up in the morning sky, floating high and wild like a...

No. Not *like* anything.

She was a bird, or at least she was seeing the world through the eyes of one. This extraordinary revelation made her twist and yaw, dipping and rising in a band of cold, singing air; or maybe it was just the wind, playing. Because, she realized, she didn't feel at all scared or frightened by the fact that she was flying, and into her mind came the lines of a poem she'd once found in some book of Pete's and memorized...

Black crow
black
against
storm child sky.
Rain bringer
floating
high and wild
where I can't go
with any kind of freedom.
Darkbird swooping
sleekly,
looks down
on all of me.
Quick crow,
get out of sight
before jealous man
shoots you
for
your
contempt.

Would someone try and shoot her? she wondered, as she swooped, sleekly, upriver and flew the cardinal points of the compass, from the west back round to the north. Watching. Following. Observing. Remembering everything she spied in crystal-sharp detail...

"Tell us what you saw, dear."

Reeba's eyes snapped open and she had to grab the sides of the chair to stop herself from falling off. She was back in the safe room, staring at Thea Leni. Not high up in the dawn sky. Not flying.

"How...?"

"Are you all right, Reeba?"

She turned to see Pete peering at her worriedly over one of his pairs of glasses. "I'm...I'm fine – what happened just then?"

"Just then? You've been...well whatever you've been doing, girl, you've been doing it for quite some time now."

"I was *flying*!" Reeba turned back to Thea Leni. "I was up in the sky, and I could go wherever I wanted to go and see everything, honestly, I could!"

"I know, dear."

"You do?"

"I do. Now please tell me what you saw. It's *very* important."

And so Reeba described the truly bird's-eye view she had had of the chess game about to be played – not on a table in the dilapidated remains of what had once been the palace of kings and queens – but by real people who, when "taken", would really die.

She told Pete and Thea Leni of the battle she'd seen, out to the west. She described the regimented forces advancing towards a confused horde of creatures who looked and acted like an enraged swarm of hornets. She told them that her curiosity got the better of her so, from the safety of her cloud-high position, she had dived down to see what was happening. And wished she hadn't.

"Those awful men, covered in scars, like the ones I'd seen in Kaï-ro," she said, her voice hushed and small. "And the other ones...they were things I haven't ever seen, even in a nightmare. Something terrible is going to happen out there..."

Reeba took a deep breath and went on to detail the activity around the pyramids, telling them about the Dark Soul troops she'd spotted stationed defensively around Bethlehem and of the ones with the boats, by the riverbanks opposite the temples on the border between the Cuven and the Lud territories. She gave them a rundown of the quiet evacuation of the young, the lame and the old as they made their way north into the relative safety of the Yards, and finally Reeba told them how she'd spotted surreptitious activity on the Dinium side.

"It looked like there were catapults," she said as she sat back in her chair, feeling quite tired from all the concentrating she'd had to do.

"That's because there were catapults." Pete rubbed his hands together. "We have what I suppose you might call a secret weapon."

"Let's hope it doesn't blow up in our faces, Dexter Tannicus." Thea Leni stood up and smoothed her dress down. "Just because you've read about something in an old book does *not* mean that this so-called Greek Fire of yours is going to work."

"Trust me." Pete stabbed the table with his finger. "I've done experiments...this works!"

"Is it that mixture you nearly set fire to the house with?" Reeba leaned forward. "That stuff even water wouldn't put out?"

"The very same, girl."

Reeba glanced up at Thea Leni. "It works all right."

"We shall see – I'm going to tell Asbel that everything is in order." Thea Leni swept out of the room, her right hand held up high. *"Let battle commence!"*

46 THE GAME BEGINS

Down by the Bowfort Tower, where the city walls met the river, Turpin Jakes let the first wave of souldiers almost finish disembarking before he did what The Peeler had told him to do and sent out a small group of his men to get within range; once there, they were to lay down some sporadic, fairly ineffectual fire, throw some rocks and make a lot of noise. From his vantage point on the roof of a nearby building, Turpin watched through his spyglass as the Dark Soul commander reacted to these events pretty much as The Peeler had predicted he would. His priority would be to get his men off the boats, the boss had said, but he would also want to deal with the annoyance. Swat the flies, as he no doubt saw it. But flies are a distraction.

As soon as the commander effectively split his force up by sending some of his men forward, Turpin gave the order for one of the catapults, hidden out of sight, to loose off the first of what Bible Pete had called his devices – two glass bottles, one full of a reddish-brown powder, the other with water, wrapped up together in paper and string – and if Turpin hadn't seen with his own eyes what happened when a couple of drops of water was mixed with a spoonful of the powder, he'd have thought Pete had been out in the sun for too long.

He watched as the small package sailed over the rooftops and arced down towards the ground, a little way off target, but not bad for an opening shot. Turpin saw the package land, saw the eruption of a ball of brilliant red and yellow flame and then, seconds later, heard the explosion. The ferocious intensity of the blast made him instinctively jerk backwards, and he could see by the souldiers reaction that it must have seemed to them as if a fireball had magically appeared out of nowhere. He gave the order for another one to be let go...

Led by Solomon, the ragtag group of men and boys standing around the catapult set up behind the Cuven temples heard the echoes of the explosion from the west and realized that it meant Bible Pete's bombs really did work. They waited, tense and nervous, for the signal from their own lookout that it was time for them to fire the first of their own stash, and then they saw the red kerchief waving from the rooftop. They knew, once they'd done their job of creating a fiery

Hell at the landing site, it would be the turn of others to move in and begin the real fighting...

High up on Bloom's Mount, the best vantage point in the whole of Dinium, The Peeler had had a temporary headquarters tent pitched. It was a location from which he could see much of what was happening, as well as be in a position to defend the heap – a place he knew that Mr. Carne and his Dark Soul Army were more than interested in – although he had no idea exactly why, unless they too had somehow found out there might be gold there. Whatever the reason, he was determined to do his best to stop them, even if it meant torching the ancient mountain of detritus and junk so no one could have what might be hidden beneath it. As The Peeler scanned the panorama in front of him, watching the two separate flotillas bringing troops across from Kaï-ro, over to his right he saw a violent red flower bloom into life on the banks of the Isis, the crack of the explosion following moments afterwards.

"This is it," he muttered to himself...

Down in the narrow, cramped streets of The Dile, Bible Pete had taken over an empty warehouse and put together a makeshift factory to mix up batches of the evil-smelling powder that caused such hellish devastation. The hard part had been working out what the formula for Greek Fire was, as the production process turned out to be reasonably simple, if you had the correct amount of quicklime, bones and charcoal. Right now what Pete needed was a *lot* of quicklime, bones and charcoal. The lime and the wood hadn't been such a problem, and if this battle was won no one, he reasoned, was going to bother very much that he'd had the bones removed from just about every one of the crypts in the nearby Città de'Morti; and if the battle was lost, well, there wasn't going to be anyone left around to care. As he licked his pencil and began to add up a column of figures he heard a loud, thudding bang, which sounded like it came from the west. The first of many, he thought to himself, crossing his fingers and touching wood as the men around him raised a cheer...

There was an eerie silence in The Peeler's tumbledown residence. Corridors were empty, doors closed and there was a feeling of abandonment that would have made Reeba feel melancholy if she hadn't been so angry at being left behind. There seemed to be just her, Thea Leni, the creepy dwarf, Venus, and some of the older servants left in the house, with armed men patrolling outside, guarding the place against attack. It was like being in an empty prison. The Peeler had told them it would be safer if they didn't leave the house, which had been more of an order than a suggestion.

Reeba didn't know where Thea Leni was and didn't really want to spend any time with Venus, whose two obsessions appeared to be juggling and eating, which he often did at the same time. She was on the ground floor, wandering through the labyrinth of passages, bored and poking her nose into whatever there was to see – which wasn't much – when she heard the first explosion. She stopped, realizing it meant that battle really had commenced. It was in the silence following the loud *whump!* that she heard a whimpering, grizzling noise coming from behind a nearby door.

Thinking it might possibly be an animal scared by everything that had been going on, she unlatched the door and opened it, revealing not a room, but a narrow cupboard. Inside, tied up and with a dirty rag stuffed in his mouth, was a grumpy looking, rather smelly man who cringed away from her, eyes screwed up against the light.

Reeba stood back, frowning at the unexpected sight of someone who wasn't hiding, but, rather, had been hidden. "Who are you?" she asked, then, realizing the man couldn't possibly reply with something stuffed in his mouth, she reached over and pulled the rag out. "Well?"

The man made noises like a cat with furballs, spat and then peered up at her. "Untie me."

Leaning slightly forward, Reeba scrutinized the man who, she thought, not only smelled but was rude as well. "I know who you are... You were following us on Bloom's Mount. Jazmin pointed you out to us. What're you doing here, in a *cupboard*?"

"I dunno what you're talking about." Samson Towd attempted to twist his mouth into something resembling a smile, and failed dismally. "You couldn't see your way clear to untying me, could you? Me hands and feet've gone numb as stone."

"Not until you tell me why you're locked up in this cupboard." Reeba folded her arms and stood looking down at Samson, tapping her foot. "There must be a reason someone put you in there, although I suppose it *could* be one of Venus's stupid games."

Samson shrugged. He had no fight left in him and just

wanted to crawl away somewhere and hide – a slightly bigger cupboard would do as long as he wasn't tied up. "Turpin Jakes did it before he went off."

"Why?"

"So I'd still be here when he came back."

"Well *obviously*." Reeba rolled her eyes. "But why is he interested in you?"

Someone had once told Samson that honesty was the best policy, which he'd considered completely ridiculous at the time, but the more he thought about it the more he wondered whether now might not be a good time to test the theory. "Because I've got to show him where it was you and the other two went into the heap – but if you let me go, I won't, I promise!"

"I should believe a toerag like you?"

"Come on..." Samson wheedled, trying to make himself sound reasonable and pleasant, even though he knew he didn't look either. "Do us a favour – I bet you don't like being stuffed away somewhere any more'n I do."

"What d'you mean?"

"I seen you, with that woman and Bible Pete."

"How? What did you see...?" Reeba spluttered.

"Why did they take off to that special room all the time...?" Samson shifted himself forward an inch or so. "And why does that woman never speak when she's with you? Always stands where you can't see her, doing sign language at Bible Pete instead of talking. Why is that?"

Reeba felt like she'd been punched in the stomach...what had he just said, *what* had this complete idiot just done?

Her mouth went as dry as chalk. She clamped her eyes shut and put her hands over her ears. She wished and hoped and wanted to believe *so badly* that she was asleep and what had happened was all a horrible, horrible dream and not a terrible mistake. Maybe it *hadn't* happened. Reeba half opened one eye and saw the man in the cupboard staring quizzically back up at her. It had happened. But maybe the witch woman wasn't still watching and listening.

Except what if she was?

Ms. Webb felt a coldness running down her spine, at the same time her cheeks were flushed red hot, as she fought to control the wildly different emotions – anger and fear, disbelief and certainty, helplessness and fury – that had been let loose by what she'd just witnessed. It took a few seconds, time measured in thundering heartbeats, but she finally brought her racing pulse back down to a more normal rate.

Her suspicions, heightened by the disappearance of her raven, had been correct. Something had not been right. Not right at all. But what did it mean?

Phaedra stood up, the night-black silk that she was wrapped in falling like dark water around her. It could only mean one thing: she'd been tricked. Every conversation the girl had "overheard" was a lie, everything she had "chanced" to see had been prepared, a piece of theatre. So all the information she'd given to Everil, and he had then used to plan his strategy, had been inaccurate and invented. And his men were marching into a trap.

Letting her connection with the crystal sphere die, Phaedra turned and strode towards the doorway; even though it was probably far too late, she had to let Everil know what had happened...

"Where have you left him, dear?"

Reeba glanced at Thea Leni, who'd found her wandering round the house, tears streaming down her cheeks and unravelling like a bad piece of knitting. "Downstairs, in the cupboard where I found him. I'm *so* sorry, I didn't mean to..."

"Spilled milk, dear, spilled milk – which I'm sure you well know there is absolutely no point in crying over." Thea Leni nodded to herself. "No point at all. When one makes a mess one must clear it up, though, so action must be taken."

"But what can *I* do, Thea?"

"We must go over to Kaï-ro, where you can help me find Ms. Webb."

"Kaï-ro? But aren't we supposed to stay here?"

Thea Leni smiled. "My dear girl, you'll never get *any*where in this life by doing *everything* you're told..."

47 MOVE AND COUNTERMOVE

Out to the west, on the unmarked borders of the wasteland, two forces were about to meet head-on.

Both were originally of human origin but neither were quite that now. The Risen had been crafted by Mr. Darcus Cleave's black knowledge, souldiers with no soul for whom true and final death was hard-won; the multitude of feral creatures rushing towards them had a much older lineage, but bad science was also at the heart of their mutant genesis in the Before Times.

While the Squadron Leaders massed the ranks of Dark Souldiers with a robotic efficiency, shouting orders which were obeyed instantly and to the letter, they watched the chaotic approach of their enemy with disdain. These seemed the most unworthy of opponents.

But while they might have looked like an ungovernable rabble there was a voice to which every single one of them listened: Mazzo. The name meant "Chosen" in the unspoken, telepathic language they all understood, and the leopard-like creature's word was law. He stood tall at over six feet, but when he ran it was on all fours with his tail held high, like the big cat he shared some of his ancestry with.

"*Surround,*" he silently ordered.

"*All around,*" came back the reply.

"*No quarter,*" he whispered. "*None at all.*"

"*None given...*"

Moving with such speed that they made difficult, often impossible targets, the Others were suddenly on top of their tightly drilled enemy, a fury of teeth and claws that came at them from all sides and never gave up.

There had never been combat like this.

Lifeblood fountained into the morning sky. Fur flew and skin was slashed and shredded. Howls of terror mixed with cries of rage. Risen fell. Others died. And there were no human eyes to witness such extraordinary sights. Men and beasts fighting like no animal ever had.

Mr. Carne, his binoculars practically glued to his eyes, watched with a growing horror and disbelief as the first wave of his men to land on the other side was engulfed in exploding balls of fire which seemed to have set even the water aflame. It was a nightmare vision, but he couldn't drag his eyes away as he tried to order his thoughts and work out what he should do.

The second wave of boats was already halfway across the river and the very first move had to be to redirect them, get the commander to land further upriver and launch his attack from there. Mr. Carne dropped the binoculars, letting them hang by their strap, and looked around for a runner so he could send a message with new orders to the semaphore tower. Instead he saw Mr. Nero, rigid with fury, rage making his muscles vibrate, standing glowering at him; he had a pistol in each hand, a pair of snarling canix flanking him.

"*SEND THEM BACK!*" Mr. Nero's face twisted into an ugly, grotesque mask as Setekh spat the words at the OverSeer, bringing up both guns and pointing them at him; the canix snarled, their jaws quivering. "**How *dare* you! You have the *audacity* to take men away from *my* work! *Nothing* is more important than the Completion!**"

"You ordered an invasion, My Lord." Mr. Carne gestured behind him. "And we are under attack ourselves...*I* need men to complete this task."

"**I do not care about *his* invasion...**" The canix both tensed.

Mr. Carne's gaze was fixed on Mr. Nero's face and he failed to notice the UnderMaster's fingers tightening on the triggers. But he saw both pistols buck in the man's hands as the recoil sent them jerking backwards. He heard the almost simultaneous detonations, saw the muzzle flashes, and caught the lethal whisper of the bullets as they whistled past him, a fraction of an inch away from either side of his head.

"**Send the men back, *NOW*!**" The two canix inched forwards.

"We shall see to it, my Lord Setekh...it shall happen."

Ms. Webb had appeared, a dark statue standing next to the person who Mr. Carne now understood no longer had much if any connection with the man who had once been Nero Thompson. In the midst of an atmosphere filled with bitterness and hostility she radiated a sense of stillness and calm, an elaborate mix of aromas – hints of sage, lavender, sandalwood and lime – infusing the air in the command post as she spread her hands out.

"Your wishes are our commands, Lord."

Mr. Carne took a deep, soothing breath of the delicately perfumed air, watching as the razor-edged tension slowly drained out of Mr. Nero's shell and the guns were lowered until they hung loosely, pointing at the ground. Only the two canix seemed to be immune to whatever spell Ms. Webb was casting as they remained on the verge of launching a deadly attack.

Every souldier knew, by the very nature of the job, that Death was a constant companion, but Mr. Carne was a warrior and felt he deserved a better, more fitting end than having his head blown off by a madman. He would forever be grateful to Ms. Webb for saving his life.

"They need you, My Lord." Ms. Webb, her eyes locked onto Mr. Nero's, glanced quickly and pointedly in the direction of the pyramids. "You have work to do, *important* work."

For a long moment it was as if Time had paused and was holding its breath as it waited to see what the reaction would be to Phaedra's words.

"**True...**" The ghost of Nero Thompson seemed to pass like a shadow across the face which now belonged to a god, the look of puzzlement gone as quickly as it had appeared, and everything returned to the way it had been moments before. Setekh turned on his heels and, grudgingly followed by the canix, left the command post.

"There's bad news, Everil," said Phaedra as she watched Setekh mount his horse and ride away.

"Worse than what we've just seen?" Everil hastily scribbled something on a piece of paper, snapping his fingers and waving at a runner. "Worse than what's happening over the river, or that we've had not a single report from The Risen in west?"

"Somehow they managed to turn my spy...they've been using her against us. All the 'information' has been false..."

Before Mr. Carne could reply one of his commanders came running up and gave a curt bow. "They've firebombed the other detachment as they disembarked at the temples, sir, and..."

"And what?"

"A force from the other side has landed at the Jamaica Banks, sir..."

The Peeler was old enough to know there was no such thing as a perfect plan and that, as was so often true, if anything could go wrong it more than likely would. While the reports coming back said that Turpin Jakes had routed the initial landing force, a second wave of Kaï-ro ships had managed to go upriver, landing out of range of his brother Dexter's firebombs, and those troops were now engaged in vicious street fighting as they tried to make their way towards Bloom's Mount.

That was bad enough, but the news from over by the temples was worse: the catapult had misfired, and the firebomb Solomon's crew had been attempting to launch had fallen back on them with devastating and terminal effect – there were no survivors, the entire stock of Pete's bombs had gone up in one huge explosion and an inferno was raging out of control down there. Looking on the bright side – and The Peeler was also old enough to know that it was always worth trying to do that – the fire had trapped the invaders, who were now caught between hungry flames and a river swarming with hungrier crocodiles.

But it wasn't the only thing that was making him nervous. Perched high up on the slopes of Bloom's Mount, he was only too aware that he was sitting on a highly explosive device. The heap might boast unprecedented views of the unfolding battle below – allowing him to witness the historic moment when his own invasion force had made a successful landing at the Jamaica Banks – but it was an unpredictable and highly unstable beast. The last thing Asbel Tannicus wanted was to win this war with Kaï-ro only to lose his life to one of the random methane flares which could erupt anywhere on the surface of this stinking, desolate place.

Not wishing to leave anything to chance, he'd had a small Lozzi idol brought up with them; it was a crude representation of the Measuring Man statue, which was his favourite totem. As he moved his binoculars back and forth over the city, trying to get a clearer idea of what was happening, he thought about lighting some candles to help ensure a long and prosperous life. But, given where he was, he realized that really might be tempting the Fates...

48 THE TIME COMES

Stretch recognized the feeling of being edged out, but this time, instead of wanting to fight back, he greeted it with a sense of relief. They were getting closer to the moment of truth, the moment when these two brothers would meet again after more time had passed than he was able to imagine. How it was possible for hate to last that long he didn't know, but then he'd never had a brother. And he wasn't a god.

As they galloped across the desert plains towards Kaï-ro, and the time for going into battle approached, Stretch knew the men around him would be looking for control and leadership, and another reason he was glad to be gently pushed aside was that he had no idea how to lead men into battle. He had done his job. From now until the ultimate battle was over, the rest was all down to Horus.

Stretch didn't mind that he was no longer needed. He wasn't exactly sure he knew what faith was, but, if it was anything like the feeling that you were doing the right thing, then he had faith in Horus. And even though he knew *he* could die (he supposed, if that happened, that Horus would live on) at least he would have died trying to do what he'd promised himself he would do: attempting to find his father.

He wanted to urge the horse to go faster, but it was an order he couldn't give any more. The frustration at having no control was hard to bear because if his father had survived – and more than anything else Stretch needed to believe that his father *was* alive – he wanted to try and find him. But there was a battle to be fought and won first. A battle to be survived before he could start the search for his father...

"The last time such things were made for us they were alabaster white and gleamed in the sun!"

Up ahead Stretch's attention was drawn to the dark, triangular silhouettes of the three enormous structures he could now see on the skyline.

"Now they are black, to match my brother's soul, and they must be destroyed..."

A sudden surge in speed brought Stretch back to the here and now and he saw that the spearhead of riders he was leading was approaching some kind of border post. Ty was up with them and Stretch really wanted to make some kind of contact before blood was spilled; this could be his one and only chance to say goodbye, but he couldn't look round as

Horus's gaze – the stare of a hunter – was fixed ahead. Jazmin had finally been persuaded that, because she was riding a pony, she wouldn't be able to keep up and should stay back with the hordes of foot soldiers who were bringing up the rear, so at least he knew she was relatively safe. And then the drumbeat of hoofs became thunder and they mowed down the Dark Soul Army guards as if they were grass...

They were now inside the southern boundaries of Kaï-ro and surging towards the pyramids, letting nothing stop them. Stretch wondered how many men they'd lost themselves, and tried hard not to imagine the sights that would greet Jazmin and the rest when they came sweeping in after them. He wondered about the other battle, maybe still raging somewhere not so far away, and he didn't envy anyone who had to fight that strange and awe-inspiring multitude of Others.

So this, Stretch thought to himself as they bore down on the huge, dark constructions now dominating the horizon, is how the end begins...

Out to the west the battle was over. For the Others, victory had been costly but swift; for the Risen, despite all their military prowess, weaponry and undoubted courage, it was to be their final conflict. There had been a frenzied hostility on both sides – centuries of unvoiced resentment pitted against a lifelong hatred of the enemy, any enemy – but in the end defeat had come down to numbers. The Dark Soul

Army had fought heroically to the last man, taking uncounted numbers of Others with them, until, soaked in blood and triumph, Mazzo had been able to stand high on a mound of ragged dead. Arms raised, claws out, he'd accepted the roared praise and approval of the exhausted survivors.

Like their new god had promised them, today was different.

Mr. Nero felt as if he was a guttering candle, with a flame so small, so weak it would take the merest breath to extinguish it for ever. But somehow a part of him was still aware, still alive. He wondered if that meant the Lord Setekh, for all his power and divinity, needed him in some way. Was the spark and flash of his spirit, no matter how insignificant, necessary to keep this body going? Would everything only stop if – when – he died? He had no choice but to wait and see.

What he did know was that the god he'd found, served, obeyed and believed in for all these years had turned on him. Once the great work – on which so much time and effort had been spent and so many lives lost – was nearly finished he had been discarded. Now the Completion was within his grasp Setekh had other priorities.

He should, Nero supposed, have noticed. He should also have taken notice of what the Board had said, but he had become so used to his every word being obeyed without question that listening to the opinions of others was something he'd lost the habit of doing.

As soon as he had ceased to be of any importance to

Setekh the god had ignored him and talked to no one but himself – as Nero had ignored the likes of Mr. Carne and Ms. Webb. But Nero could listen, and now that it was too late he thought he might have worked out what it was he had been responsible for bringing to life.

The Completion, which would occur when all three of the pyramids were finished, was somehow going to give Setekh access to the eternal and infinite power he had been seeking across the endless roads of Time, seemingly thwarted at every turn by Horus, his brother. He wanted to be supreme, to *finally* have the Throne of the World. To possess what he believed was, and always had been, his by right of birth.

Gods were born like stars, in the fires at the beating heart of the universe, to fulfil the everlasting and desperate need humanity always had for answers. Their names might change, they might be forgotten but they did not die, *could not die*, because there were always more questions. Always. All this Nero now understood. And these pyramids – earthly symbols of heavenly power and strength, pointing at the stars, where everything came from – were the Engines of Destruction that would be connected with the source. And once connected there could be no going back. Ever.

Setekh would have what he had always craved: absolute power.

Nero had also come to understand something else...that absolute power was not necessarily a good thing. With no checks and no balances, someone – man or god, good or bad – who had absolute power did not need principles, morality or compassion. What they needed was obedience. He, of all people, should know that.

The line between evil and virtue might look obvious and very definite, but, as he had found out, it really all depended on which side of that line you were standing. Nothing that Setekh had offered him – respect, status, a purpose – was fundamentally bad; nothing he'd done was wrong, if you looked at it from his point of view. He had built Kaï-ro, a city in a wilderness, he had...

A piercing, impassioned howl broke Nero's concentration.

"BROTHER!"

Across the southern plain, and coming towards the mounted Dark Soul squadrons on either side of him, Nero could see the dust cloud kicked up by what looked like a phalanx of horsemen in an arrowhead formation. He should have grasped what it could mean if the people of Dinium found a god of their own to believe in. Belief fostered hope, and hope allowed people to dream that life could be better...

"THIS TIME YOU *WILL* DIE!"

As he felt Setekh's outrage surge through him, like a wall of heat, Nero experienced a flash of insight. Whatever force drove life onwards was always in search of balance, fighting for an element of stability in a chaotic and random universe. Someone had to counterbalance the darkness of Setekh, and Nero had a feeling he was about to come face-to-face with whoever that was.

49 THE FINAL MOVES

They confronted each other for the first time in an eternity, their hostility and bad blood having outlasted uncounted civilizations. Stretch's horse faced east, Nero's west and, turned in their saddles, the man and the boy stared across the thirty yards of desert no-man's-land that now separated them. Unaware of anyone else out there in the punishing heat of the sun – two opposing armies, patiently waiting for the signal to unleash mayhem – the brothers watched through other's eyes.

"**I am the first and the older...***I AM THE ONE!*" Setekh's voice was raw with undisguised hatred. "**I am Lord of the northern sky, god of storm and cloud, rain and snow – I am** the dread fear, the shadow and the pain – *kneel before me!*"

Behind Setekh, sweeping up from the horizon like ink spilled in water, a darkness rose towards the sun. Heavily armed men swallowed hard, their horses suddenly nervous and skittery.

"**My right eye is the sun, my left the moon,**" Horus raised his arms, hands outstretched, "**and my wings are the heavens! I kneel before NO ONE!**"

Half the sky was now as black as pitch, a shroud torn by more and more bolts of lightning; rain fell in torrents, turning the ground to mud, and thunder shook the air.

"**I *will* have what is rightfully mine – the Completion will see to that!**"

"**And I am here to stop that *ever* happening...**"

These were the final moments of a battle which had begun so very far back in the past, when the world had been such a different place. And though it was a battle which could permanently change the future, it had nothing to do with the man and the boy. In the same way as a bottle isn't responsible for what is put in it, they were merely containers. If anyone on either side had any doubts of that, what they saw next wiped them away.

Both Nero and Stretch stood straight up in their stirrups; then Nero's body twisted and strained, giving the impression that something was being physically dragged out of him, while Stretch looked like he was gently offering a gift up to the sky.

As the two deities prepared to clash – an invisible dance, because Gods don't need flesh and blood to fight – their release into the ether was the signal for carnage and slaughter below...

This was battle.

There was the roar of guns and men.

The screams of pain, fear and bloodlust filling the air.

Steel meeting steel.

Blades and bullets slicing through flesh and bone.

Blood, warm and oh so red, flying.

Lives suddenly and brutally cut short.

Resistance angrily and systematically wiped out.

This was battle.

Short and very sharp.

The distant kick of adrenaline.

The shocked faces staring up at their last sky.

The cries of victory.

And on they went, because this was battle...

Stretch was aware that he was, for the first time in so long, alone in his head. At the same time he became fully conscious of what was happening around him, the extraordinary sights that he could only now properly take in – an elemental battle in the sky above, mirrored by a human storm on the ground. And in front of him: a man on a horse, staring back, looking as confused as he felt.

This man, he realized, must be the fabled Mr. Nero.

The chaos was astonishing, the noise deafening – cries, screams, the howling wind and the tumult of battle – but between him and Mr. Nero there seemed to be a tunnel of calm, and a recognition that they had both had similar, though very different experiences. An admission, too, that they were still enemies, still the figureheads leading opposing forces. The dark against the light. Where Stretch came from, the world had always been that simple, had always been about the black and white decisions. Like life and death, yours or mine, eat or starve.

He knew that Mr. Nero was having the exact same thoughts. He had to be. Only one of them could survive. And while he was sure Mr. Nero had been responsible for the deaths of thousands of people, Stretch had never killed anyone before (he didn't count Auntie Skin, whom he thought of as having made up her own mind to die). But this was about nothing less than staying alive, and as Stretch reached for the gun hanging at his side, cocking the hammer as he drew it from the holster, he saw his opponent do the same and knew it was either him, or Nero...

Up above, as mountainous hammerhead clouds fought against hurricane winds to dominate the sky and bring night to the day, the vicious struggle between the two brothers had reached a climax. There were no words any more, just Setekh's passionate rage manifesting itself in a spreading, black vortex that seemed to feed on the storm, pushing darkness on and on towards the southern skyline and certain victory. As hard as Horus tried to enfold his brother's intensity and force it back, the power of the light never seemed to be quite enough to douse his fanatical energy.

But it was exactly that energy which finally turned the tables.

With a blinding flash, out of the roiling clouds an enormous bolt of lightning cracked the sky, splitting into jagged forks that traced their way earthwards in search of something to hit. Three of these barbed fingers zigzagged down and found the three highest points in the plains south of the Isis. The pyramids.

The lightning struck as two pistol shots rang out one after the other...

50 WHEN THE LIGHTNING STRIKES

The Peeler stood high up on Bloom's Mount in the torrential rain, binoculars hanging limply in his right hand; he was soaked to the skin and transfixed by the panorama of destruction being played out on the other side of the river. The wind and the rain made it impossible to make any kind of offering to the small Lozzi shrine which, considering the fact that day had suddenly been turned to night, The Peeler thought he really ought to be doing.

The thunderous storm which was still battering Dinium was centred over Kaï-ro and in the unnatural darkness chasing across the heavens the blistering flashes of lightning only made him feel more uneasy. To add to his disquiet, since the skies had opened no one with any information had made it up to the command post so he had no idea what was going on and felt somewhat isolated on this unstable mountain of rubbish.

And then, rushing out of the deepest, blackest part of the sky came a bolt so huge it looked like the roots of the biggest tree in creation. Accompanied by a clap of thunder – loud enough to make The Peeler feel as if it had actually hit him in the chest – three strands of the violent filigree simultaneously hit the tops of the pyramids.

The explosion that followed seemed to happen in stages. Outlining the pyramids, white light danced crazily across their black surfaces; orange flowers unfolded and flourished at each of the highest points, turning into billowing gouts of flame, and then the sound – like a roar from the mouth of a beast – finally reached the bedraggled group huddled under sodden canvas at the summit of the heap. They watched, dumbstruck, as the power which had hit the pyramids was then launched back up into the skies in a blast of white, white fire.

"Someone up there does not like them over there," The Peeler muttered to himself, watching the fires rage. "I'd lay good money down that they've not been lighting the right candles..."

They had come in search of Ms. Phaedra Webb, against the direct orders of The Peeler and, Reeba was absolutely sure, the wishes of Bible Pete; he would not like what they were doing one little bit. She had been quite certain that Thea Leni wouldn't be able to get them across the river, but the woman had the strangest way of looking at people; as she talked to them they simply obeyed her every word. Which is why they were now in Kaï-ro and had two of The Peeler's men with them, armed to the teeth, one in front and one bringing up the rear.

"Prepare for the worst, dear," Thea Leni had said in the boat, "and you won't be surprised when it happens."

In Reeba's opinion the worst happened just as they were landing on the other side of the Nightingale Line. The northern sky turned an impenetrable black, and then the storm broke; within minutes conditions were so bad that you could hardly see your hand in front of your face. But if Thea Leni was at all surprised by these events, she didn't show it.

Following Thea Leni, not quite hanging onto the hem of her dress but staying very, very close, Reeba couldn't believe she was back on the other side in Kaï-ro, in the middle of a thunderstorm the like of which she had never seen before. It was as if the story in Pete's book was actually happening: the one where it had rained for forty days and forty nights and the god of that long-ago time had said he would wipe every living creature from the face of the earth.

Drenched to the skin, they were making their way across some open land when, up on a rise, Reeba saw a building she recognized: Phaedra Webb's house! She was about to point it out to Thea Leni when she saw the strange ink-black whirlwind twisting in the sky, and then a massive lightning blast struck all three of the pyramids. In the seconds that followed, when the pyramids exploded and it seemed to Reeba that the world must be going to end, a figure appeared at the gates of the house; tall and wrapped in silks, she turned her back to them to look over towards the firestorm.

Reeba grabbed Thea Leni's arm. "There she is!"

"Her?" A puzzled look crossed Thea Leni's face. "She has changed since we last saw each other." Thea Leni glanced at the two men. "Get her."

As she watched The Peeler's men lope up towards the solitary figure, catching her unawares, Reeba thought she could feel the torrential rain easing off and felt the sky might be beginning to clear. By the time she and Thea Leni had reached where Ms. Webb was being held at gunpoint, the darkness had retreated enough to let the sun through and steam was beginning to rise in smoke-like trails from the sodden ground.

"Leni." Ms Webb smiled as they approached, rivulets of water joining the delicate silver filigree which covered her scalp. "It has been some time."

"So it has, Tanith, so it has."

Reeba frowned. "But I'm sure she told me her name was Phaedra..."

"I'm sure she did, dear." Thea Leni smiled thinly and shook her head, gesturing to the men that they could lower their guns. "Phaedra is her *sister's* name; her identical *twin* sister. And I have a feeling even those she worked closest with here in Kaï-ro are probably unaware of that fact; true, Tanith?"

The woman just smiled like a cat.

"Phaedra Webb was a prodigy, a wonder child, and destined for great things in the Guild. But she and her sister disappeared when I caught them out playing this game, all those years ago; we only ever saw one of them as they were pretending to be a single person. This deceit allowed them to appear to do extraordinary things, to be in two places at exactly the same time, and that's what made me suspicious because, although she was good, that girl, no one in the Guild has ever been *that* good. Have we, Tanith?"

"If you say so, Leni."

"I most certainly do...where is Phaedra, by the way?"

"Right behind you, Leni." Reeba and Thea Leni turned to find a second Ms. Webb smiling at them. "Two places, at exactly the same time. You see, Leni, it can be done."

"But why didn't you tell me?" Reeba looked open-mouthed from one Ms. Webb to the other. "And how did you find out...*how* can you tell the difference?"

"We in the Guild keep our successes and especially our failures to ourselves." Thea Leni looked pointedly at the two women. "As you no doubt noticed, Reeba, they both have one blue and one green eye and people are always so fascinated by that it's all they ever see...that and the silver and the silk, the real gold on her lashes and the magic. All intended to dazzle and misdirect, of course, because what nobody actually notices is that they are mirror images of each other."

"No one except you, Leni,"

"The devil is in the detail, Phaedra. It really is worth remembering that." Thea Leni smiled to herself, her eyes like slits. "And now that the battle is over, what are we to do with you two?"

"Over?" Tanith moved round to join her sister, going behind her so that, for a moment, it appeared as if they were one person.

"You hardly need a crystal ball to see that, my dears." Thea Leni turned to look out across the plain at the devastated pyramids. "You played your part in all this, and as a consequence you really must pay."

"What with?" asked Phaedra.

"How much?" asked Tanith.

"Your lives?" Thea Leni raised one eyebrow, then waved her hand as the two guards cocked their weapons. "Maybe not, I have never been a believer in an eye for an eye. I think...banishment. Yes, total and absolute exile."

"Where?" asked Phaedra.

"There's always somewhere, dear." Thea Leni turned away.

"How?" asked Tanith.

"I don't care where *or* how. You must have money, go and find someone to take you across the water to Parigi. And stay there. For ever."

"And if we return, Leni, what then?" Phaedra reached out and took her sister's hand.

"I will know, Phaedra, then I will find you and you'll wish I hadn't. Take my word for it, both of you." Thea snapped her fingers. "Leave, now!"

Reeba watched, nonplussed, as the sisters beat a hasty but elegant retreat towards the river. "You're just letting them go?"

"No, my dear, I'm not letting them come back. Quite different." Thea Leni started walking towards the now abandoned house. "Come with me, Reeba, we have work to do!"

Not long after the darkness had finally faded from the sky, a raven swooped down out of the blue, circling lazily round the rough encampment pitched high up on Bloom's Mount before it landed on a rickety map table at which The Peeler was sitting with Bible Pete. The Peeler looked at the bird with undisguised suspicion and took out his pistol.

"Don't shoot the messenger, Asbel!" Pete pointed to a tiny canister attached to one of the bird's legs. "I wonder who that's from?"

"Feel free to have your hand pecked off trying to find out, Dexter."

The raven turned its shiny black head sideways and looked up at Pete, who leaned over and very carefully took off the small metal cylinder. Unscrewing the cap he removed a tightly folded piece of paper and smoothed it out; it was covered in spidery writing.

"Well?" The Peeler asked, watching the bird fly away. "Who's it from?"

"Let me see..." Pete changed his glasses, frowning as he glanced down the page. "It's from Leni; she's across the river, in Kaï-ro. With Reeba..."

"How in the name of Lozzi did they get there?"

"She doesn't say."

"What *does* she say, Dexter?" The Peeler snapped his fingers impatiently.

"'*Dear Asbel and Dexter...*'" Pete looked up, surprised. "How on earth did she know I was up here on the Mount with you?"

"She's *Guild*, brother, how else...now get on with it!"

Pete returned to the letter. "'*Reeba and I are on the other side, and we have managed to find a crystal and a number of feathered 'agents', who have been bringing us back reports. Reeba, I have to say, has a natural talent with the crystal.*'" Looking up,

Pete shrugged. "Something tells me I might be in need of a new assistant in the not too distant future..."

"The letter, brother...*read the letter!*"

"Right, right...where was I...yes, here we are: '*I am sure you would like to know what has been going on, as recent events have left everything in a state of some confusion. Firstly, you may well be surprised to find out that the Others, at what appears to be great, great cost to themselves, have defeated the force of Dark Souldiers sent out to stop them; they seem to be waiting at the boundary and I think someone should be sent out to make contact with them.*

"'*It is very clear to me that our futures are inextricably bound together; from now on they will be a part of our world, as we will be a part of theirs. Just because they don't look like us really shouldn't mean we hate them – although I do believe the likes of Marley Sheppard – who, by the way, reports say is on his way back from Slip End – might take some convincing of this fact.*

"'*The birds tell me that the Dark Soul Army is a spent force and on the run on both sides of the river; they have also brought word that, with the pyramids destroyed, the slave workers have rebelled. I can tell you, too, that Mr. Nero's associates, Mr. Cleave and Ms. Webb, have taken to their heels, while Mr. Carne died like the warrior he was, beside his men. Which only leaves the man himself.*

"'*From what we have been able to gather, Mr. Nero rode out to the southern plain to meet the first wave of the army raised at Slip End, and there was a battle. More accurately, I should say there was the most terrible bloodbath. Reeba is beside herself, and I am taking her down there now.*

"'*I think, Dexter, that you should come over here as soon as you can. She may well need you as there do not seem to be any survivors...'"* Pete's shoulders slumped. "Oh dear, oh dear, oh dear..."

"Is that all, brother?"

"Isn't it enough? Looks like the boy's died...I better get myself on a boat..." Pete glanced at the letter as he got up and sat down again. "Oh, there is a bit more..."

"Read it, read it!"

"'One last thing: we in the Guild have always been aware of the ancient and quite hostile force that Mr. Nero was playing with, and the recent and rather sudden appearance of an opposing influence. I'm sure you must have witnessed the quite unforgettable destruction of those three huge buildings; it is my feeling that what we saw was one of the presences being returned to the heavens. I can say that now I detect only one in our ether, and I'm pleased that it is benign and not malevolent. It would not surprise me if there was a new star in the sky tonight.'"

51 AFTERMATH

Jazmin reined her pony in and held tightly onto Bone, who was perched awkwardly in front of the pommel of her saddle. The exhausted dog had somehow managed to catch them up a few miles before they'd crossed the river and, footsore and weary, he hadn't put up a struggle when one of the men had dumped him on the pony like a piece of baggage.

But now he was rested and he wanted to get down. The dog knew, like she did, that something very bad had happened.

The weird, frightening storm they'd fought their way through had now cleared, the darkness completely washed out of the sky. No wind, not a cloud in sight, just the black silhouettes of vultures hanging in the air, and the pillar-straight columns of smoke rising up from what was left of the pyramids. Silent omens of death and destruction. Everyone had stopped on the edge of the rise that gently sloped towards the site of what could only have been the most frenzied of battles and, beyond, the now ruined pyramids; shock at what they saw stopped them from moving one step further.

A dreadful feeling of alarm gripped Jazmin like a cramp as she searched everywhere for any signs of life down amongst the tangled, ghastly shapes. Had the storm done this, or did men really fight until no one was left standing? And what about Ty? What about Stretch? Why hadn't that god of his protected them? What was the point of *being* a god if you couldn't stop people from dying?

Jazmin slumped forward, grief sitting like a huge weight on her shoulders, and her grip on Bone loosened. The moment it did he was off, leaping to the ground and running. With tears streaming down her face, Jazmin kicked the pony into a gallop and followed; she would not believe anything until she'd seen the evidence, no matter how painful, with her own eyes. Because how *could* the world give her friends, people who cared for her, only to take them away? It just wasn't right. It wasn't...

The pony veered wildly to the right and it took all of Jazmin's strength to pull it up to a halt. The smell of death and fear filled her nostrils and as soon as she'd jumped to the ground the terrorized animal bolted, intent on getting as far away as possible from this field of slaughter. She stood gazing at the aftermath of battle, suddenly aware of the blood; it was soaking into the ground, it was spattered on the scrub grass, it was everywhere she looked. And somewhere amongst the devastation were her friends. Bone's excited barking snapped Jazmin back into action and she ran over to where the dog was frantically trying to pull at some cloth.

"Please, please, please..." she babbled to herself as she kneeled down and tried to find out who it was Bone had found, not caring what she had to touch to do it. "Say it int Stretch...say it int..."

Jazmin stopped, frozen by the sight of the dragon tattoo.

She pushed away some rags to reveal the face, sightless Nikkei eyes staring up at the sky. Conflicting emotions washed through her. Relief that it wasn't Stretch fighting with the pain brought on by the realization that Ty was dead...

Jazmin slowly stood up knowing, just knowing that this was the worst of all possible signs, a hollow feeling spreading through her. She was going to be alone again. Looking up she saw that other people were hesitantly making their way down to search for their own friends and family and she crouched down by Bone.

"Find him," she whispered. "Please find him for me...I've gotta know..."

Jazmin stood still as she watched the dog. She wasn't aware of anything, not her own hunger and thirst, nor where she was or what she was looking at. And then Bone took off like an arrow, howling; running after him she stumbled to a halt in front of a fallen horse and rider.

And it was a black horse.

Jazmin's heart raced as she picked her way round to where Bone was standing, ears flat on his head, in front of the body curled up on the ground; she stared at the jewelled plaits and the heavily kohled eyes, the gold breastplate and the short sword at his side. Stretch looked just like he was asleep, a pistol still gripped in his right hand.

Sobbing and unable to move, Jazmin watched as Bone crept closer, whimpering as he nudged Stretch's face with his nose and licked his cheek. And then through tear-filled eyes she was sure she saw the boy move.

"Stretch?" Jazmin sank down next to Bone, trying unsuccessfully to wipe her tears away. "Stretch?"

"Jazmin...that you?" Bone leaped on Stretch as he tried to sit up, yipping, barking and not knowing what to do next he was so excited. "What happened?"

"You dint die, did you."

"No..." Stretch stood up unsteadily, searching the scene of total devastation until he found the horse and fallen rider he was looking for. He walked over and stared down at the man who had once been Nero Thompson, the man who, like him, had found a god; his face was turned away, eyes closed, and his fine silk shirt was stained with a massive gout of blood. "I didn't die but this man, Mr. Nero, did; it was like a duel between him and me, Jazmin, all in the middle of the most unbelievable storm and with a battle raging...except I felt as if it was just the two of us. And as I pulled the trigger my horse turned and reared up..." Stretch walked back over and looked at his mount's great head, "...he took the bullet meant for me, Jazmin. That's why I didn't die."

"Looks like everyone else did."

"You mean Ty...?"

Jazmin sniffed and nodded and the colour drained out of Stretch's face as the realization of where he was and what had happened sunk in. Ty was dead and he was standing, surrounded by the bodies of an army he had led into battle and the enemy they had fought into the ground. He felt the leaden burden of responsibility weighing him down and he waited for the voice in his head, the voice of the god who had led him on this path.

He needed to hear from Horus that what they'd done together was just. That all these people had died for a reason, and that it was the right reason. But all he heard was silence. Stretch felt a terrible sadness, a sadness tinged with an awful sense of guilt spread through him; he should be dancing with happiness because this was what he'd wanted more than anything else in the whole world, to ride into Kaï-ro and get his father back, but the cost had been so enormous. As he waited for some kind of reassurance he realized he was going to have to find whatever answers there were by himself.

"Alone..." he whispered.

"Still got me."

Stretch looked down to find Jazmin standing next to him. She reached up, slipped her hand into his and squeezed.

"Come on," he said.

"Where?"

"Let's go and look for my dad..."

"Seek, and you will find..."

ACKNOWLEDGEMENTS

Right at the very beginning, some years ago, this idea first came to life with the help and much-valued input of Annabella Serra and John Bolton. Further down the line I owe a debt of gratitude to Gill Brackenbury for introducing me to her friends and colleagues in Cairo – the very real and astonishing place from which my city borrows its spirit and some of its history; without the help and enthusiasm of Dominique Gygax, Randa Taher and Beth Noujaim this would have been a far tougher and much less interesting journey. And here I must mention my wife, Nadia, whose production skills got me to Egypt and back again with a head full of the stuff that stories are made of. Also, how could I forget the real Aunties, Rosie and Mags, as well as the Reading Boys, who kindly lent me their names. Finally, big, big thanks to Team Usborne!

A CONVERSATION WITH
GRAHAM MARKS

WHAT WAS YOUR INSPIRATION FOR *KAÏ-RO*?
This book is here because one summer lunch hour a few years ago I went to the British Museum for a wander around the Egyptian section. I worked a short walk away in Covent Garden but this wasn't a habit of mine and I really don't remember why I went there on that particular day. Happenstance.

In the cool and calm of one of the rooms I found myself standing next to a life-size stone statue of a dog and I stroked it as if it was a real dog, but also in much the same way as the man who had made it must have done so many times as he was carving the stone, three, maybe four thousand years before. My hand was where his had been, feeling exactly what he had felt, knowing how pleased he must have been with what he had done. A direct connection.

I walked back to the ad agency where I worked with my mind full of ideas about how the results of creating things can last for ever, about gods and belief and how little we've changed over the millennia. Within a couple of days the barest bones of what has become *Kaï-ro* were sketched out, although, funnily enough, the idea's first conception was actually as a computer game.

HOW DO YOU GO ABOUT RESEARCHING YOUR BOOKS?

That does depend on the book; for my previous book, *Snatched!*, because it's a historical novel, I had to rely on books – lots and lots of reading, which reminded me a bit of being back at school and cramming for exams, except a lot more fun and no actual exam to take. Although, come to think of it, waiting for your editor's opinion on what you've done is not unlike waiting for your results.

When it came to *Kaï-ro* I went on a major research trip to Egypt – to the real Cairo, where I got to go right inside one of the Great Pyramids and stand where a pharaoh was once buried. I've done quite a lot of travelling for my books and I like the thought that I've walked the roads taken by my characters, seen what they've seen and heard what they've heard. A story should try and satisfy all the senses.

WHERE DO YOUR CHARACTERS COME FROM?

That is one of the great mysteries. Some characters are there because you need them – where would you be without a hero, or a villain? – and some seem to be there, waiting for you. Jazmin was one of those who appeared out of the blue, fully formed and so full of life she just demanded to be written. Magic, really.

WHO OR WHAT INSPIRED YOU TO WRITE?

I have always, ever since I can remember, daydreamed, but I never wrote anything down until I began writing poetry in my late teens. I carried on doing it until my early twenties and I had a couple of books published, so I knew I was reasonably good, but it wasn't something I ever thought of doing as a job. My inspiration has always come from a combination of an overactive imagination and constantly wondering "What if...?", and now it is my job.

WHAT IS YOUR FAVOURITE BOOK?

My favourite kids' book is probably *The Prisoner of Zenda* by Anthony Hope, just the most wonderful adventure story that I only recently found out was first published in 1894! It whetted my appetite for books with great plots and terrific characters and that's what I love to read and hope I write.

WHAT IS YOUR FAVOURITE PLACE?

Probably my attic room, where I write; it's a place where ideas hatch, and there's nothing quite like watching a new idea make it into the world. I am also a big fan of cities, places that are so full of life and where I can quietly observe without being noticed.

WHAT AMBITIONS DO YOU STILL HAVE?

One of the things I try to remember, because I think it is true, is the rule that says "Never run out of ambitions, or you'll have nothing left to do", and one of the ambitions I still have to achieve is to have a film made out of one – or more! – of my books.

GRAHAM MARKS had his first book of poetry published while he was at art school, studying graphic design. After a successful career as an art director he decided it was time for a change and now works as a journalist and author. He has written everything from comic strips and film tie-ins to advertising copy and novels for children and young adults.

When he's not writing books, Graham is writing about them as the Children's Editor of *Publishing News*. He's married to fellow journalist and author Nadia Marks, and lives in London with his two sons and a cat called Boots.

Find out more about Graham Marks at
www.marksworks.co.uk

Also by Graham Marks

SNATCHED!

Shortlisted for the North East Children's Book Award

Daniel never knew his real parents – abandoned in a lion's cage as a baby, he was adopted into Hubble's travelling circus. When he suffers terrible visions of the future he desperately tries to change what he sees. But he cannot avoid being snatched away to London, where it seems he may have the chance to unlock the riddle of his past. Will he like the answers he finds?

Action-packed, filled with drama and excitement, *Snatched!* takes you on a helter-skelter journey – from the breathtaking theatrics of the circus ring to the very real perils lurking on the streets of Victorian London.

"Graham Marks' racy prose barely lets the reader draw breath. Snatched! *is as taut as a highwire and as much fun as a buggy full of clowns."*

Meg Rosoff

ISBN 9780746068403

£5.99

**FOR MORE
THRILLING AND COMPULSIVE READS
LOG ON TO
WWW.FICTION.USBORNE.COM**